An Uncommon Courtship

HAWTHORNE HOUSE

AN UNCOMMON COURTSHIP

KRISTI ANN HUNTER

BETHANYHOUSE
a division of Baker Publishing Group
Minneapolis, Minnesota

© 2017 by Kristi Ann Hunter

Published by Bethany House Publishers
11400 Hampshire Avenue South
Bloomington, Minnesota 55438
www.bethanyhouse.com

Bethany House Publishers is a division of
Baker Publishing Group, Grand Rapids, Michigan

Printed in the United States of America

Library of Congress Cataloging-in-Publication Data
Names: Hunter, Kristi Ann, author.
Title: An uncommon courtship / Kristi Ann Hunter.
Description: Minneapolis, Minnesota : Bethany House, a division of Baker
    Publishing Group, [2017] | Series: Hawthorne House
Identifiers: LCCN 2016034515| ISBN 9780764218262 (trade paper) | ISBN
    9780764230028 (cloth : acid-free paper)
Subjects: | GSAFD: Regency fiction | Love stories.
Classification: LCC PS3608.U5935 U53 2017 | DDC 813/.6—dc23
LC record available at https://lccn.loc.gov/2016034515

Scripture quotations are from the King James Version of the Bible.

Cover design by Kathleen Lynch/Black Kat Design and Paul Higdon
Cover photograph by Richard Jenkins, London, England

Author represented by Natasha Kern Literary Agency

17 18 19 20 21 22 23   7 6 5 4 3 2 1

To the Creator and Giver
of Perfect Love.

1 John 4:16

And to Jacob,
who may not be perfect,
but is perfect for me.

Prologue

Many a man has been inspired by a great father or a noble brother, and young six-year-old Lord Trent Hawthorne had been blessed with both. Standing by his father atop a hill that looked out over a large portion of their country estate, he didn't bother asking why he, a younger son, had been brought out to talk about the estate. Ever since he was three Father had included him in lessons, saying, "Life is unpredictable and you have to be ready. I hope you both live to see your grandchildren, but God may decide He'd rather have you as duke one day."

Trent didn't understand all that, but he liked spending time with his father and brother, so he didn't complain.

On the other side of the large man stood Trent's older brother, Griffith. Even at ten years old Griffith was showing signs that he would be as big as their father, if not taller. Trent stretched his back as straight as it would go, even lifted a bit onto his toes to see if he too could make his head reach Father's shoulder. The highest he could get was a little below the man's elbow.

"What do you think, boys?"

Trent gave off trying to stretch his spine and looked out over the land below. The vine-covered walls of an old stone keep rose from the hillside across the way, beneath a crumbling stone watchtower. The valley below boasted scraggly trees and patches of grass scattered amongst large puddles of water. More tufts of grass stuck up through the shallow water, giving it an eerie, dangerous look. Maybe they should dig out the field and make the puddles deeper so they could swim in them. But of course, there was already a perfectly good lake closer to the house.

Griffith tilted his head and looked up at their father. "Sheep."

Father squinted his eyes as he looked over the land, considering. "Sheep, you say?"

This was what Trent loved about his father. Most of the world would have been afraid to answer him. They'd have waited to see what he was thinking and then agreed with whatever it was. After all, the big man was a powerful duke. The only people in England more prestigious than he was had royal blood in their veins. But the truth was—at least when it came to his family— John, Duke of Riverton, was the most approachable man in the kingdom. Even if the idea involved throwing sheep into a boggy mess.

Trent had no idea whether sheep liked to swim. If they did, Griffith was smart to want to bring them here instead of having them dirty up the lake. It was probably a good thing he was the older son. Even though the title would never pass to Trent, he wanted to make his father glad that both sons were included in this discussion. He racked his little brain for anything he knew about sheep. "Won't the wool shrink if we let them swim in that? Nanny said that's why my coat shrank after I wore it into the lake last year."

Father beamed at his younger son and ruffled Trent's blond hair. Bright green eyes smiled down at him, making Trent feel six feet tall, even if he never would be. "I don't think it works that

8

way, son. It is a lot of water, though. Do you think the sheep like to swim, Griffith?"

Griffith looked from Trent back to his father with a hint of uneasiness that he quickly covered up. Griffith would be leaving for school soon, and their father had lately been pressing him more and more to start voicing his thoughts and opinions. He shifted his feet, almost tripping over the gangly legs of a tall ten-year-old. "I've been reading about the drainage ditches they're doing in Scotland. We could build some and turn most of the area into pasture for the sheep. Then plant crops in their current pasture."

Father bent down to be at eye level with Griffith. "Drainage ditches?"

Griffith's throat shuddered with his heavy swallow. "Yes, sir. We dig them out and put rocks in to keep the mud out. Then the water runs down to the river."

"Where did you read about these ditches?"

Trent tried to copy Father's impressed demeanor, but the wind kept pulling the hair from the short queue at the nape of his neck, sending a blond curtain into his eyes. It was hard to look composed, much less impressed, with hair blocking his face. He pushed the hair back with both hands to see Griffith gathering his words. Griffith always liked to think about what he was going to say. It took too much time as far as Trent was concerned.

After a deep breath, Griffith squared his shoulders and spoke without any of his earlier hesitancy. "When we visited Mr. Stroud several years ago, all he had were those peat bogs. But when he came to us last month he brought those excellent cabbages. I asked him what changed. He gave me a book about the new methods."

Father straightened back to his full height with a wide smile. His shoulders pressed back, and he put his fists on his hips. Trent poked at one of the jacket seams that looked a bit stretched by his father's proud stance. Had he worn his jacket into the lake too?

"As sure as I was blessed in birth, I've been blessed in progeny."

Father wrapped one strong arm around Griffith's shoulders and pulled him in tight. "God knew what He was doing when He gave you to me. Let the Lord guide you, boy, and you'll be a better duke than I ever was. In some ways, I think you already are."

They tromped back through the fields toward home, talking about drainage ditches and throwing stones.

Four days later, the duke died.

Chapter 1

HERTFORDSHIRE, ENGLAND, 1814

Lord Trent Hawthorne was convinced that breakfast was one of God's greatest gifts to humanity. What better way to celebrate the Lord's new mercies and fresh beginnings than rejoicing in the day's opportunities by eating a crispy rasher of bacon? Even after his father had passed, the morning meal had been a source of consolation for Trent, a reminder that God still had a reason for him to be in this world. Yes, for most of his life, Trent had awoken every day secure in the knowledge that nothing could ruin breakfast.

It took a wedding to prove him wrong.

Specifically, it took his wedding.

To a woman he barely knew.

Trent frowned at his plate, and the sweet roll plopped in the center of it frowned back. For the first time he could remember, the eggs looked unappealing, the bacon appeared dry and brittle, and the toast tasted like dust bound together by spoiled butter. He simply couldn't see a positive side to the way this day was beginning—and he'd been searching for the past three weeks.

Three weeks of listening to the banns read in church, bearing

11

the speculative glances and thinly veiled curiosity alone while his bride-to-be spent the weeks in Birmingham acquiring a new wardrobe, since clothes fit for an unmarried young lady apparently disintegrated into dusty rags when she finished reciting her marriage vows. He didn't remember such a thing happening to his sisters' clothing when they'd married last year, but Lady Crampton must have witnessed it at some point because she'd been adamant that her daughter be outfitted in an entirely new wardrobe.

Of course, she'd also been adamant that they not wait any longer than the required three weeks between the reading of the banns and the actual wedding, so Trent wasn't inclined to think her the most logical of decision-makers.

Not that he'd ever cared much for Lady Crampton. Or her daughter—at least not the daughter he'd known about. As he'd probably known at some point in his life but had rediscovered only three weeks ago, Lady Crampton had a second daughter. A second daughter with no debility or problem aside from the fact that she'd been born second—and that Lady Crampton was already focused solely on devoting her time to raising a spoiled, selfish, scheming, socially ambitious viper in her own image and hadn't found the time or inclination to raise a second one.

Of course, the countess was more than happy to claim that daughter today. She was marrying into the Duke of Riverton's family, after all, and what more could a mother want for her daughter? In Lady Crampton's case, she probably preferred that her daughter be marrying the duke himself instead of the duke's younger brother, but all in all it was still a rather nice match for a girl who knew all the best places in the district to gather mushrooms—including the depths of an old stone keep on a neighboring estate beneath a half-fallen roof and a partially collapsed floor.

Trent poked at his eggs before letting the fork clatter to the plate. "I'm going to rip those ruins down with my bare hands."

"Hardly necessary now that you've spent a whole day and night clearing the vines from one of the windows with a rock. An endeavor that did enough damage to your hands that I think you should reconsider using them on the stone wall."

Trent turned his head to glare at his older brother, seated next to him and having no issue with the meal whatsoever if the dents he was making in mounds of food on his plate were any indication. Griffith, Duke of Riverton, was a mountain of a man, but Trent had trained with the best pugilists in the country. He was pretty sure he could take his older brother down.

Griffith shrugged as he cut a perfect square of ham. "Well, you did. How are they doing, by the way?"

Trent flexed the appendages in question, pleased to note that the pain in both had subsided to a tolerable level. A few faint lines remained from the cuts he'd sustained while hacking away at a dense covering of thorny vines with nothing but a sharp stone for assistance. The knuckles he'd smashed in the near futile task could finally bend enough to curl into a fist. "My hands are fine, though I'm going to be much more conscientious about having a knife on me in the future."

A single golden eyebrow climbed Griffith's forehead. "You intend to make getting trapped in old ruins a regular occurrence? I suggest you make sure the next one isn't being occupied by a young lady. You can only propose once, you know."

Trent groaned and rubbed his hands over his face before letting his gaze crawl across the room in search of his new wife. Her slender form was rather easy to spot in a group of well-fed aristocrats—and was likely the reason she'd been able to walk back and forth across the floor that had crumbled beneath him. Once the floor had given way, the stair joist holes she'd used to climb down to the bottom of the ruins had become a useless ladder to nowhere, and they'd been trapped.

And not just for the night. Trapped for the rest of their lives by the bounds of propriety that demanded Trent salvage her threatened reputation by marrying her. Never mind the fact that no one knew they'd been there. Regardless of the fact that they'd managed to free themselves by breaking through the vines as the sun crested the horizon the next morning. As a gentleman, Trent could not leave her reputation to chance when he was the one who caused the problem in the first place. "Actually, you can propose as many times as you like. You can only be accepted once."

A spurt of laughter had Griffith lunging for his serviette as he tried to avoid choking while still keeping his bite of food in his mouth. He swallowed and dabbed at the corners of his lips. "Nice to see a bit of your humor coming back. For a while I thought you'd broken it along with your ankle."

"I didn't break my ankle." Though he should have, given the way he'd fallen through the rotten floor of the old stone keep. "The surgeon said it was simply a bad sprain. Made worse by the fact that I left my boot on all night and then proceeded to ride without removing it the next day."

Not that he'd had any choice. Escorting Lady Adelaide home from their adventure had been a necessity, as had discussing a wedding settlement with her father, the Earl of Crampton. Unfortunately the conversation had also included the sickening cloying of the socially ambitious Lady Crampton. That awkward meeting had also taken place over breakfast.

Griffith snagged the sweet roll from Trent's plate. "If you're only going to frown at this, I'm going to eat it. You might want to consider not looking so tortured, you know. People are starting to stare."

Trent grunted but adjusted his posture and tried to smooth his facial features. "They've been looking since I sat down. Why do you think they're avoiding this table?"

"Because they've all stopped by to congratulate you, and you've done nothing but nod in acknowledgment?"

Trent grunted again and shoved the rest of his plate in his brother's direction. A somewhat familiar-looking brown disk lay on the edge of Griffith's plate. "What is that?"

"Mushroom." Griffith grinned. "I think your new wife might be a bit of a wit. They're quite tasty. Would you like to try one now that it's been properly prepared?"

"No, thank you." Trent tried not to gag at the thought of eating the mushroom. During that interminable night, they'd had nothing to eat other than the flat, brown winter mushrooms Lady Adelaide had climbed down to collect. And while they were rather good even when raw, he wasn't sure he'd ever be able to eat a mushroom again without thinking about being trapped, sitting in the dirt of a partially crumbled stone castle, watching his life plans slowly fade with the setting sun.

Trent picked up his napkin and ran the edge through his fingers. "I've never paid much attention to etiquette at these things. When do you think I can leave?"

"You do intend to take Lady Adelaide with you, don't you?" A canyon of concern formed between Griffith's thick blond brows as they lowered over deep green eyes. It wasn't a look Trent saw very often, but it was the one that proved Griffith was going to make an excellent father someday.

"Of course." Trent balled up the square of fabric and tossed it onto the table. "It's no gentleman's trick to leave his wife in her father's house. Especially when it's inhabited by a woman like Lady Crampton. I'm still not thoroughly convinced Lady Adelaide was raised by that woman. She's far too sweet."

"And you've spent how much time in her company?"

Trent frowned. "A day and a night. But we spent those sitting in the dirt, and she didn't turn into a shrew. That has to count for something."

At least he hoped it did.

Lady Crampton and her elder daughter, Lady Helena, were two of the most irritating people Trent had ever met. And he'd met all of London's aristocracy and a good portion of the gentry. If the second daughter turned out to be cut from the same cloth, Trent's life was going to become difficult indeed. "I'm sure we've run into her at gatherings over the years, given that we live near the same village and all. The very fact that I don't remember her when I so clearly remember her mother must be a good sign."

"Looking at her now you wouldn't think she'd be so forgettable. She's rather unconventional."

Trent followed Griffith's gaze and had to acknowledge the truth in his comment. Lady Adelaide was rather unique in appearance, with thick hair so dark it was nearly black and enormous blue eyes that would have appeared even larger if she had been wearing her spectacles. Several locks of hair—too short to curl or smooth back into her coiffure—fell across her forehead. Without the black-framed spectacles, a few wisps of hair threatened to droop into her eyelashes. She'd accidentally burned the hair along her forehead while trying to use curling tongs one morning, and it was taking a long time to grow back.

That was one of the things he'd learned while sitting next to her in the dirt eating mushrooms. In the quiet darkness between short snatches of sleep and attempts to hack through the vines, they'd talked. It was the one thing that made Trent not completely terrified of this marriage. If they could find their way back to the way it had been before they'd admitted their fate, it was possible this marriage could at least be tolerable.

"I'm surprised Mother didn't make it back for this. You received a letter from her yesterday, didn't you? Did she say why she wasn't coming?" Griffith sliced through the sweet roll, releasing a waft of steam from the still-warm pastry that simultaneously made Trent's mouth water and his stomach roll over.

Although the queasiness in his stomach probably had more to do with the fact that the reason his mother hadn't made it to the wedding was because he hadn't told her. He'd tried. Sort of. He wanted to believe there was a way out of this situation, though, and putting it down on paper made it seem so permanent.

Rather like the parish register they'd signed a mere hour ago.

Trent cleared his throat and avoided Griffith's gaze. "Er, no. She didn't mention the wedding."

Griffith's eyes widened in surprise. "Really? I had no idea she disliked Lady Crampton that much."

"I am certain I once heard her say that one of the best things about getting remarried was that she didn't have to live next to the countess anymore."

The countess, Trent's new mother-in-law, didn't appear to be having any of the discomfort that the bride and groom were experiencing. She stood next to her daughter, smiling and talking, while Lady Adelaide's serene smile tightened and her unfocused eyes began to look panicked. Trent looked a little closer, trying to see if there was a problem or if the attention was simply getting to her. As she stumbled to the side it became clear the heel of her slipper had somehow gotten snagged in the hem of her dress and she was trying to free it without anyone noticing. She wasn't being very successful, if her mother's warning looks were anything to go by.

This was something Trent could save her from. If nothing else good came of this wedding, at least Trent would be removing Lady Adelaide from her mother's influence—and perhaps save London from one more vapid attention seeker.

"I'd like to make London tonight." He had a closer estate, a small one his brother had sold him for a pittance, but the bedchambers had been damaged in a recent storm and were still under repairs. Besides, going to London meant they had to leave right now, and even then it would be a hard ride.

"It's quite a large party, and you are the guest of honor." Griffith dabbed at his mouth with a serviette, but Trent was fairly certain it was with the intention of hiding a forming smile.

"You're enjoying this, aren't you." Griffith had always warned Trent that one of his schemes would one day blow up in his face, but this hadn't been a scheme. This had simply been him coming across a lone horse tied up by the ruins and investigating out of curiosity. Regardless, consequences like this were a bit much for even a brother to revel in.

"No. Though I have done a bit better job resigning myself to it in the past few weeks." Griffith set down his fork, and the smile fell from his face, leaving it solemn and thoughtful. "I'd take your place if I could. I considered it. Lord Crampton wouldn't have protested such a switch."

"As if I would have let you make such a ridiculous proposal." Trent closed his eyes and sighed at the idea of Griffith stomping his way into Moonacre Park with his younger brother dragging at his heels. It was a funny picture, and this situation could certainly use a bit of humor. "In all honesty, Lord Crampton would have fallen down and kissed your feet. After he shoved Lady Crampton out of the way, of course."

Griffith's answering smile was small and a bit sad, still tight with a look of regret as he shifted in his chair. Since boyhood Trent had marveled at his brother's size, wondering why God had chosen to make a man with such incredibly broad shoulders. Now it was obvious. Without them, Griffith wouldn't have been able to carry the abundance of responsibilities he'd claimed for himself. Responsibilities Trent had been unwilling to help with as he'd gotten older.

Watching his older brother rub his forefinger against his thumb like a world-weary old man instead of a young fellow of twenty-eight, it occurred to Trent that his own twenty-four years meant it was time for him to shoulder a bit of the manhood himself. As much as he wanted to avoid the consequences of his circumstances, he would never have been able to abide Griffith suffering in his place.

"God doesn't make mistakes." Trent's declaration cut through Griffith's guilt-ridden pondering.

"What?"

"God doesn't make mistakes. You told me that. When I was starting school and I said it was wrong that Father wasn't there with me." Trent swallowed hard at the memories. He hadn't cried over his father in years. Now was not the time to renew the old habit. "You said God doesn't make mistakes and He had something planned for our lives even though we didn't understand."

"Well, I . . ." Griffith eased back into his chair, looking once more like the sophisticated duke. "That's true."

"Then we trust Him in this. Yes, they'd love to have married a daughter off to the duke. But they got me instead." God willing, it was a title he'd never hold. "So I've married Lady Adelaide. And we're going to see what He has planned for that."

Griffith smiled. His proud, fatherly smile. The one that puffed up Trent's chest even as it broke his heart. "When did you become so wise?"

Trent grinned back, doing his best to look boyish, trying to bring Griffith back to being a still-young older brother. "Must have been when I was trying to be you."

Chapter 2

Lady Adelaide Bell—now Lady Adelaide Hawthorne, she supposed—had always thought the day her mother was finally proud of her would be a very happy day.

It wasn't.

She'd rather go back to the days of listening to her mother complain about how horribly average her second daughter was. As far as insults went, it wasn't such a bad one. Weren't most people in the world average? Wasn't that the very definition of the word? Honestly, being lumped in with the bulk of the populace wasn't such a bad thing. It meant you blended in better and were quickly forgotten.

Being forgotten was a mixed blessing, though. It was nice that the dressmaker, haberdasher, and various other local merchants forgot that her mother had at one point or another left her at each of their shops and she'd had to walk several miles back home. Of course, if her mother hadn't forgotten her in the first place, it wouldn't have been necessary to be thankful for the shopkeepers' lack of memory.

Today, though, Mother was determined to make up for all the years she'd ignored Adelaide. When Adelaide had woken this morning, her mother had been watching her from the foot of the bed, ready to impart wisdom upon wisdom on how to make the most of this day. Adelaide hadn't been out of her sight since. Thankfully, Mother had stopped speaking during the actual ceremony, but she'd been making up for lost time since they'd arrived at the wedding breakfast.

Adelaide smiled at Mrs. Guthrey. At least she thought it was Mrs. Guthrey. Without her spectacles—which her mother had insisted she not wear today—everything beyond the length of her arm was a complete blur. Not that it really mattered who was speaking to her. She'd done nothing but smile and nod all morning, unsure what to do with all of the attention being sent her way. Until three weeks ago most of these people wouldn't have even been able to remember her name. She doubted it'd been very far from their lips lately though. A hasty marriage to one of the favorite local bachelors tended to make for fine gossip, especially when the woman in question abruptly left town until the day before the wedding.

There was a break in the conversation, and she tried to nod and say her good-byes so she could move on to another group, but she had to free her slipper first. And she had to free it without being able to see what was actually caught. She was going to have to bend down to rectify the problem. And her mother was going to be mad.

She took two shuffling steps out of the conversation circle and knelt down to free her shoe. Sure enough, as soon as she rose, her mother was there, a smile on her lips but not in her eyes. "What are you doing?"

Adelaide blinked. Wasn't it obvious? She'd felt she was rather quick about the entire business, but it had taken her a moment or two to free her slipper. "My shoe—"

"Mrs. Guthrey was telling you how delightful she thought you'd find the Blossom Festival this year, and you simply dropped out of the conversation." The disappointed whisper in her ear was considerably more familiar than the praises her mother had been heaping on her since her engagement to the son of a duke.

"But you hate the Blossom Festival. You always say you wouldn't set foot in it even if they did give you an invitation."

Mother frowned, more a flattening of the lips than an actual turning down of the corners. She wouldn't want to cause wrinkles, after all. "That was before I understood what the event really was. Now that Mrs. Guthrey has expounded upon its virtues, I am anticipating her invitation with considerable excitement."

Adelaide resisted the urge to roll her eyes. She wished her brother, Bernard, had been in the vicinity so they could exchange knowing glances. The saddest part was that Mother actually believed the reason she'd disliked the Blossom Festival was because she didn't understand it and not the fact that she'd never received an invitation to the house party. Because that was what the "festival" really was—a prettily named house party to show off Mr. Guthrey's impressive collection of tropical plants residing in his conservatory. And now she was going to have to go so that her mother could go as well. "I'm sure it will be delightful."

With a small smile and a nod, the same combination she'd been doing for the past three weeks, Adelaide turned to walk across the room only to have her mother catch her arm.

"Where are you going?"

"Over there." Adelaide gestured toward a table in the general direction of away. She couldn't see what was on it, but there was a high probability it contained food. "I'm hungry."

She took another step, only to trip on her hem again and have to take two quick steps to keep from falling. The bottom seam must have come loose.

Lady Crampton sighed the beleaguered sigh of a countess doomed with incapable children before leaning down and snapping the loose thread Adelaide kept stepping on. "I've never known you to be so clumsy. This is the third time I've had to fix your clothing today."

And that was the truest indication of how much attention had been paid to Adelaide in the last few years, because her maid was constantly pointing out various things amiss with her clothing.

As the middle child of a very busy family, Adelaide had shifted back and forth between her parents and the governess, doing and being whatever she needed to in order to make everyone around her happy. And they always seemed happiest when they forgot she was there. She became the quiet daughter who smiled at the guests and then trotted up to the nursery or softly played the piano while everyone else visited or played cards. Adelaide played the piano as passably average as she did everything else.

Mother sighed. "I suppose we should at least be thankful that trains are no longer in fashion. They made all the gowns so elegant during Helena's first year in Town."

Adelaide tried not to wince at the mention of her beautiful, blond, spectacle-less elder sister. For as long as Adelaide could remember, Mother had been preparing Helena for a great future, molding her to be the most sought-after woman in the land. A future princess or at the very least a duchess. The fact that she'd ended up a mere viscountess still gave their mother fits of vapors. And now, somehow, Adelaide had stumbled into the position Mother had always wanted for Helena—well, nearly the position she'd wanted—and the expectations were heavy indeed. It was enough to make a girl long to be forgotten at the modiste again.

Not that she'd been forgotten recently. And she'd spent the better part of the last three weeks at three different modistes, selecting dresses, getting fitted, and hearing her mother badger the poor seamstresses into making the dresses in a ridiculously short amount of time. Didn't they know Adelaide was to marry the Duke of Riverton's brother? It had been awful, but at least they'd traveled to another town to do it. Adelaide was never setting foot in Birmingham again.

"And it wouldn't hurt you to smile. People are watching, you know. This is your wedding. Never again will you be able to command so much attention, and you're more interested in the food. No wonder you weren't able to catch the right brother."

Adelaide stopped trying to squint at the table to determine what type of food was laid out on it and turned wide eyes to her mother. "I wasn't trying to catch one at all. I was hunting mushrooms."

"And that, my dear, is the problem. How difficult would it have been to ask the duke to help you? You were on his property, after all." Mother brushed invisible dust from her skirt. "I was hoping you'd realized what a boon your unfettered access to his property was. Why else would I have left you down there all night?"

"Given how often I used to get mushrooms from the old keep, I could hardly ask him to . . . Wait. What do you mean you left us down there? There *was* a wagon!"

A stinging burn pricked Adelaide's eyes, and she blinked rapidly to keep the tears from forming. Once during that long afternoon they'd thought they heard someone driving by the old ruins so they'd shouted as loudly as they could. The lack of response led them to believe that they'd only heard their horses shifting around, moving from the patch of grass to the nearby creek. Only they hadn't been hearing things, and her mother had deliberately left her abandoned.

"Please do not call my visiting chaise a wagon. And yes, I was coming back from visiting Mrs. Pearson and I cut through Riverton lands. I thought you'd landed the duke, but I should have known not to get my hopes up that you would make such a lofty connection. Still, the younger son of a duke is a sight better than you were likely to attract during a summer in London."

Adelaide blinked while her mouth dropped open and snapped shut as if she were a fish. She wanted to say something, should say something, but what was there to say? The knowledge that they could have been saved or at least had a witness to their proper behavior changed everything and nothing at the same time. They were still married, would still have to be married, because if her mother had been planning to save her from the potential loss of reputation she'd have done so already . . . but what would Lord Trent do when he found out? Would he think they'd somehow planned the encounter, despite the fact that he'd climbed into the ruins out of his own curiosity?

"Pardon me, but may I claim my wife for a moment?"

The deep voice broke into Adelaide's thoughts, and she let out a squeak as she spun around to find her new husband less than a foot away.

"It's not my fault," she blurted.

"I'm aware of that." His lips curved into a crooked, dimpled smile. The brilliant green eyes didn't convey the same joy and charm of the smile, but she really couldn't blame him for that. She was certainly gaining more by this marriage than he was.

"Of course you can steal her away, my lord." Mother put on her most gracious smile and curtsied. "After all, you are family now."

His smile lost some of the little radiance it had, and his eyes flinched in a quickly disguised wince.

"Yes." He cleared his throat. "Thank you. My lady?" Lord Trent extended his arm in Adelaide's direction, and she took it numbly. Were they going to dance? Mother had hired a string quartet, but they were hardly playing anything lively at the moment. She clutched his arm tightly enough to feel the tensed muscles beneath. He might look like a relaxed gentleman, but the day was obviously wearing on his control. Not that she could blame him.

He led her up the short flight of stairs at the end of the room and paused in the open double doorway.

"Where are we going?" Adelaide whispered.

"To London," Lord Trent whispered back.

While she blinked repeatedly in an attempt to comprehend his statement, he turned them to the gathered crowd. "I want to thank you all for joining us today."

His voice carried over the room without sounding like he was shouting. One by one the conversations stopped until everyone faced the newly married couple. Even at this distance she could sense the expectation from some of the revelers, though she didn't know what they were hoping for. As far as scandals went, this one wasn't very interesting, and Lord Trent wasn't about to reveal what few details there were. Perhaps the crowd was hoping for something worth writing to their friends about. She found herself rather glad that she couldn't make out any faces at this distance.

Lord Trent smiled down at Adelaide. "My wife and I couldn't have asked for a better celebration, and I want you all to enjoy the hospitality of Lord and Lady Crampton for as long as you like."

Adelaide bit her lip to keep from laughing. Her mother had driven the servants to distraction preparing for a morning full of people, counting on all of them to have left by noon because her father refused to provide the funds to keep them happy longer than that.

"The time has come, however, for us to bid you farewell." Lord Trent's voice carried over the rush of gasps. "I've a new life in front of me, and I'm afraid staying here won't let me start it." He patted the hand Adelaide had wrapped around his arm.

The crowd melted in a unified sigh. Adelaide tried to smile because people were looking at her and it wouldn't do to look terrified as her new husband led her away, but she was. Oh, she was. His speech contained all the right words, and his demeanor would make even the most skeptical people question what they'd heard about this hasty marriage, but they couldn't see his eyes or feel the tension that ran through his body until his muscles quivered under her hand.

He escorted her from the room, and every step away from the gathering brought another measure of relaxation to the man at her side.

Neither of them said a word as he handed her into a waiting carriage and climbed in after her. The door closed, and he rested his head against the red velvet cushion, letting his eyes drift shut as his mouth flattened into a grim line.

Silence still reigned as they rolled down the drive. She pressed her head to the window and watched the already blurry house grow smaller and smaller until it disappeared behind a small rise in the drive.

She'd never loved that house. More than one afternoon had been spent with her nose in a book so she could escape to somewhere else, anywhere else. The sadness that crept in as they turned onto the main road surprised her. She might never have cared for Moon-acre Park, but it was all she knew. And it wasn't home anymore.

So what was?

Chapter 3

He was married.

It was difficult to move beyond the undeniable fact that the rest of his life would now include the woman sitting across from him.

From the time Trent was old enough to realize the freedom granted to second sons, he'd known that his eventual marriage would be one of the most significant decisions he ever made. Without giving it any conscious thought or particular care, an expectation had developed. He'd assumed it would be a happy occasion, filled with friends and family thankful for an excuse to gather together in the middle of the year. He'd anticipated loving his bride and sharing small smiles fraught with hidden meanings, like he'd seen his sisters exchange with their husbands.

Instead he had a wife who hadn't met his gaze once, not even during the ceremony. She'd spoken her vows to his cravat, so he hoped she wouldn't mind the fact that he didn't wear the same one every day.

It was his own joke, formed only in his head, but he couldn't resist the smile it inspired.

She didn't smile back, but that could have had something to do with the fact that her attention had drifted all the way down to his toes. Did that mean she would soon circle back around to the top and finally look him in the face?

"I hope you don't mind leaving a bit early. I thought we might be more comfortable in our own home."

"Our home?" Lady Adelaide blinked at him, or at least her gaze was directed in his general vicinity when her thick black lashes fluttered up and down over her crystal blue eyes.

The owlish blinks reminded him that her mother had insisted she not wear her spectacles during the wedding. He'd retrieved them from her maid, intending to give them to her at the breakfast, but she'd been pulled away as soon as they walked in the doors and he hadn't been near her since. Hopefully the lenses would make a nice peace offering now, a tiny gesture to set the tone he wanted for the marriage.

It was the one they were both stuck with, after all.

He pulled the spectacles from his pocket and extended them across the carriage. "Here. I obtained them from your maid earlier today."

"Thank you." She slid the frames onto her nose and looked him in the eye for the first time since that disastrous night in the old stone keep. "Isn't London a bit far to travel in one day?"

"I've arranged for fresh horses halfway along the route. If we push hard, we can make it." Trent shifted in his seat, wondering not for the first time if he'd made the right decision.

She nodded. "I'm sure we can. Perhaps one of the inns along the way will pack us a meal we can bring with us."

It was Trent's turn to blink. He'd expected a little bit of resistance, had even been reconsidering his options on places to stay the night. Now he couldn't help but wonder if her ready acceptance of his pushing to London meant she was in agreement with his thinking or that she expected him to be a harsh husband. Why hadn't it occurred to him before now that she might be just as wary of this marriage as he was? "I think we can take the time to eat properly."

"Oh. I'm sorry I misunderstood, Lord Trent." She blinked again and her gaze fell once more to his toes.

If this was an indication of how the rest of their lives was going to be, it was a sad sign indeed. With a sigh, Trent switched to her side of the carriage. Perhaps they could start over and find better footing before they made it to London.

Sitting shoulder to shoulder with her unsettled his insides, though. He couldn't recall ever sitting alone in the same carriage as a woman he wasn't related to, much less in the same seat. The sensation was far from unpleasant. He cleared his throat and reached for her hand. "I believe it would be proper for you to call me Trent, as my family does."

"If that is what you wish."

The silence pressed in as Trent waited for her to reciprocate the offer of a less formal name. When it didn't come he decided to press for it. "May I call you Adelaide?"

She turned and blinked those confused owlish eyes again. "Of course."

The carriage rolled easily along, but the conversation was mired in the deepest mud he had ever encountered. They'd found things to talk about when the sun had been high in the sky, beating down on them as they tried to find a way out through the vines. It was only as the moon had risen, and its silvery glow had sealed their fate, that the conversation had withered. Three weeks apart in anticipation of the wedding hadn't done anything to revitalize it.

The miles that had separated them while growing up seemed shorter than the distance between them in this carriage.

"I went down to the creek you mentioned. The one by the sheep fields that curves around and almost makes an island." When they'd talked about their favorite places to walk in the area, Adelaide had mentioned how she liked to go there and read because no one else ever disturbed the natural beauty.

"Did you take a book with you and sit in the gnarled tree?" She shifted her shoulders until she faced him more fully.

He grinned and turned his body to face hers as well. "I'm afraid I was a little too big for your reading nook. I had to sit on the ground and lean against it."

"Oh."

And the topic of the almost island was over as soon as it had begun. Adelaide turned back to the window, seemingly unperturbed by the lack of conversation and the high tension. It made Trent wonder what she was expecting of this union. If it wasn't interaction with him, what was it? Social connections? Managing the house?

Trent bit back a groan. His house. He'd been so focused on getting away from the prying eyes, so desperate to return to what was familiar, that he hadn't thought through all the ramifications of taking her home to London. "I should probably warn you."

She turned from the window, eyebrows lifted until they were completely lost behind the short hairs over her forehead. "About what?"

"Our home. In London." Trent smiled through the stabbing pain in his chest at using the word *our*. "It's a bit unconventional."

That was putting it lightly. He'd inherited half the staff when he moved in after Amelia, a family friend abandoned by her guardian in London, had moved into Hawthorne House as Griffith's ward. The staff had all but raised Amelia, which meant they acted more like family than servants. It had taken him a few weeks to adjust—and he'd known what he was walking into. How much worse would it be for Adelaide? He should probably try to ease into explaining the bizarre world she was about to walk into. Any woman who knew the extent of the strange way his household functioned would run in the other direction.

Not that Adelaide had that option anymore.

A small crease appeared above the center of her glasses as she tilted her head in thought. "You have been living in bachelor quarters, so I would assume things have been done a certain way. I can change that."

"No!" The word came out sharper than he'd intended, but Adelaide needed to know that she was not going to dismiss anyone from Trent's household staff. She could hire more if she wished, but he couldn't let go of the ones that were there. That would upset Amelia and all the other women in his family by extension.

"No?" More of that blinking. Did her eyes not get tired?

He rolled his shoulders and tried to look relaxed as he leaned against the cushioned seat back. "What I mean is that I'd prefer you not let anyone go who is currently employed. They do good work. It's just that the house is run a bit . . . differently."

"Oh." Her eyes widened in surprise. Long black lashes rimmed the large expanse of white with the clear blue lakes in the middle. The pupils were extremely small. That probably wasn't a good thing. "I'm sure I can adjust." She shifted farther into the corner of the seat. "Mother woke me quite early this morning. Do you mind if I take a nap?"

"Of course not." What else could he say? No, you may not fake sleep just to avoid an awkward conversation? With parents like hers—or rather a mother like hers, because Lord Crampton wasn't the worst sort of fellow—she had to have encountered more than her fair share of discord. Had she simply taken herself off to bed when things got difficult? Maybe that explained her constant state of mild dishevelment.

He watched his wife pretend to fall asleep. If he didn't keep calling her that, he was afraid he'd forget that he was married. Despite the uncomfortable morning, part of him wasn't convinced it had actually happened. Yet he'd stood before the priest and claimed her as his own, said the vows before God and man, and signed his name to the church register. What more did he need to do to convince himself the deed had been done? That he was now in possession of a wife?

He frowned. That probably wasn't the best way to think of her, even in the privacy of his own mind.

A light snore drifted across the carriage, surprising him enough to pull the beginnings of a smile from the corners of his lips. She'd either been truly tired or she was the most accomplished fake sleeper he'd ever encountered. Not that he'd encountered that many. There wasn't much call for pretending to sleep at social functions.

Trent settled into his own corner. He could have moved back across the carriage, but that was what couples did when they were courting. Even if he did not feel married, he needed to start acting like he was. Farce had become truth for Adelaide's sleep. Maybe the same thing could happen in their marriage.

Chapter 4

The race to London—for it could be called little else—left Adelaide confused, with a dull ache over her whole body and stabbing pain in the back of her head. In the last vestiges of sunlight, London was still busy as they pulled into the city, allowing Adelaide to marvel at the hugeness of it all.

She tried not to gawk as they rolled through, but it was fascinating to a girl who'd never seen anything larger than Birmingham. The columned façade of St. George's of Hanover Square jutted into the road, just as it did in the Ackerman prints. It was a wonder that Mother hadn't been willing to wait and have the wedding there.

It wasn't as if delaying would have given Lord Trent an opportunity to back out, would it? If that had been an option, Adelaide wished they'd taken it. She'd read enough books to know that loveless arranged marriages, where the parties barely knew each other, were quite plentiful throughout history, particularly amongst the aristocracy. But she was a modern woman, and being foisted off onto a man she barely knew felt wrong. Besides, there was no political gain, no great joining of estates or assets. Nothing but the societal requirement that Lord Trent's freedom be sacrificed on the altar of her reputation. At least women who had stumbled into truly compromising situations would know the man in question, would have chosen him in some way. All she knew about Lord Trent was he enjoyed reading novels.

And he had an affinity for punching things. The fact that he trained to be able to punch things better made her a little uneasy. She'd heard the stories before, whispers about the women who wore an extra shawl in the village marketplace even in the summer heat. She tore her gaze from the city scenery outside the window and took in the way his shoulders took up a large portion of the seat and stretched the seams of his well-tailored coat. A shawl might not be enough for Adelaide if he wasn't the man she hoped he was.

She snapped her head back around to face the window once more. The houses they now passed were beautiful and well-appointed, with large numbers of windows testifying to the wealth of the area. Was he taking her to Hawthorne House? That would explain his cautioning her about not having much say over the hiring of servants. She'd heard quite a bit about the splendor of the mansion on Grosvenor Square and looked forward to seeing it, but she hoped they weren't going to live with his family. "Where do you live?"

"*We* live in Mount Street."

The emphasis he placed on the word *we* brought a swift blush to Adelaide's cheeks.

"And here we are." Trent smiled as the carriage slowed.

Adelaide pressed her face to the window, anxious to see her new home in spite of the sudden trepidation that made her dinner shift uncomfortably in her stomach.

She'd heard enough about London to recognize that the homes in front of her were modest by aristocracy standards but were certainly better than many others in Town. Bay windows curved out from the light brown building, adding a sense of division to the attached houses. They were too small to house ballrooms, which suited her nicely. A small dinner party would be easy enough to handle, but were the drawing rooms in this house large enough to hold more sizeable gatherings?

"Do you host things?" She winced at the blurted question. Her tongue was really going to have to learn to phrase things better before letting them out.

"As a bachelor? I haven't hosted anything, aside from the occasional family meal."

He opened the door himself and jumped from the coach, leaving Adelaide to fret over whether or not that meant he expected her to arrange a lot of social gatherings now. Would a younger son have reason to host such things? She took the hand Trent extended back into the carriage and stepped down to the pavement, willing her shaky legs to hold her steady.

The door in front of them swung open to reveal a tall man with a large pointed nose and a shockingly bald head. Light from nearby candles actually reflected off of the man's scalp. Did he polish it?

"Welcome home, my lord."

"Good evening, Fenton. Is the household assembled?" Trent reached back for Adelaide's hand and pulled her arm through his before escorting her into the house. *Escorting* might be a misleading word to use. He nearly had to drag her into the house because her feet had somehow become disconnected from her brain and refused to walk next to him without inducement.

There was a household gathered beyond that door waiting to meet her. What if they didn't like her? What if they wouldn't listen to her? What if she didn't know what to say to them? There was no *what if* about that one. She hadn't the first idea what to say to them.

"Yes, my lord." The tall man swung his arm wide to indicate the line of servants along the hall wall. The hall wasn't large, but the staff wasn't either, leaving plenty of room for all of them to stare openly at the woman beside their master.

Had Lord Trent sent word? Did they know who she was?

"Everyone, I would like you to meet Lady Adelaide . . . my wife." Trent dropped her hand and stepped to the side, throwing his arm out with a flourish, as if he were presenting a prize mare at the market.

"Oh, how exciting!" A tall, thin woman with nearly nonexistent hips and tight grey curls framing her face stepped forward from the front of the line. The housekeeper, Adelaide assumed. She looked like a friendly woman. An overly friendly woman if the hug Adelaide found herself wrapped in was any indication.

The embrace was brief and the housekeeper soon stepped back to more fully address Trent. Her fists plopped on her hips, or rather the narrow section of her body where hips could normally be found. The woman looked like a tall, skinny column. "You didn't drive all the way from Hertfordshire today, did you?"

Trent ducked his head and shifted his feet like a little boy caught stealing biscuits from the kitchen. "Well, I . . ."

"Hmmph." The housekeeper sniffed at Trent before turning her smile back to Adelaide. "I'm Mrs. Harris, the housekeeper. Would you like tea in the drawing room? I'm afraid he told us only that someone important was coming, so I didn't air out the proper bedroom. It will take me a bit to set things to rights. Did you bring a maid?"

Why hadn't Adelaide considered her maid and her trunks? Their mad dash for London didn't seem to include an abundance of luggage. "I don't—"

Trent cleared his throat. "My apologies for the misinformation."

Adelaide blinked. He was apologizing to his housekeeper?

"Her maid and Finch will be arriving Monday or Tuesday with the remainder of our luggage. Lady Adelaide has a small trunk in the carriage. I was hoping Lydia could see to her needs for the next few days."

Would anyone notice if Adelaide simply sat on the floor? She hoped not because she was actually becoming dizzy. There was so much to take in. She assumed Finch was Trent's valet, which meant both of them were now here without their personal servants. Rushing to London was seeming more and more a bizarre decision with every passing moment.

"I'd be delighted."

Adelaide swung her gaze down the short line of servants until it landed on a blond moppet. Wild yellow corkscrews of hair jutted out from various places beneath her cap. At first glance, Adelaide thought the young woman was a child, but closer inspection revealed otherwise. Where Mrs. Harris was lacking any curves, this young lady had them aplenty. Including one in the front that gave her skirt a slight flare. Adelaide couldn't stop herself from going a bit slack-jawed. That maid was with child!

Trent slid her arm through his once more and leaned in until his lips brushed her ear. "Not a word. I'll explain later."

She was still shaking off the shivers his whispering breath had induced when the housekeeper shooed them toward a drawing room off the hall. "You two rest, and I'll see to the tea. There's no reason she can't meet the rest of them in the morning."

The staff scattered by some unspoken command, leaving Trent and Adelaide alone in the once elegant drawing room. She'd barely had time to take in the green-and-white-striped settee that had certainly seen better days when the butler entered. "Will you be requiring anything else, my lord?"

Trent smirked. "Besides refreshment and a proper bedroom for my wife?"

"Er, yes sir. I see your point. I suppose you'll need me to stand in for Finch as well."

"Indeed. It will give you a chance to tell me the latest news."

Adelaide looked from her husband to the bald butler. They were going to exchange gossip? She groped for the arm of the worn sofa and lowered herself onto the seat. She couldn't remember the last time anyone in her home—well, her old home—had conversed with a servant beyond what was essential to get a particular job accomplished. So far tonight she'd been hugged by the house-keeper, been assigned a pregnant lady's maid, and watched her husband set up a chat session with the butler. Unconventional was putting it mildly.

After the butler left the room, she looked up to find Trent observing her from beneath lowered lashes, almost as if he were waiting for her to pass judgment on her new home. His insecurity looked out of place on a face that had seemed confident and composed for as long as she could remember.

He rubbed his hand across the back of his neck and looked away from her before pacing to the window and back again. She might have worried about him wearing a track in the rug, but the floor covering already bore signs of more than one line of regular traffic. The room didn't look too out of fashion, but it had certainly been well used since it was decorated. It probably looked exactly as it had when he moved in. A bachelor wouldn't have much reason to redecorate the drawing room, after all.

She'd almost worked up the nerve to say something when a footman entered with a laden tea tray. He set the load on a tea table and left, closing the door quietly behind him.

Leaving her alone in a room with an unrelated man.

Yet another reminder that she'd gotten married that morning.

Was everything in her life destined to become unfamiliar because of that one event?

Porcelain clinked and she jerked her attention to the tea service only to find Trent taking care of the pouring duties. The teapot looked strange in a man's hands. "How do you take it?"

"The same way you do," Adelaide said quietly, cringing a bit as he dropped five lumps of sugar and a splash of milk into her cup. How did the man drink something that sweet?

She sipped at her tea before selecting a biscuit just to be polite. The biscuit was surprisingly bland, a perfect complement to the overly sweet tea. Someone knew the master of the house well. Afraid she was about to drop both, she set the teacup on the table and slid the half-eaten biscuit onto the saucer before folding her hands in her lap. Things were happening too fast for her to keep up so she latched on to the one thing she could demand an explanation for. "The maid. Explain."

Trent sat back with his own cup and a handful of biscuits. "She's married to my valet."

Adelaide was very glad she'd put her tea down or she would have certainly dropped it in shock. "I beg your pardon?"

"Lydia. She's married to Finch. It's worked out nicely so far. I only keep a couple of horses here so have need for only the one groom. Lydia and Finch live in the second groom's room above the stable. The baby's due sometime in summer, though, so they're going to take positions at my Hertfordshire estate after this Season. Well, he is. I doubt she'll be doing much of anything other than mothering for a while. They've talked of eventually opening an inn."

Trent stuffed his mouth with half a biscuit but still avoided her gaze.

"I see." Although she didn't. Who had a married valet and let the man live separate from the actual house? Didn't men need their valets close by? "Are there any other special cases I should know about?"

Trent shrugged. "Lydia, Fenton, and Mrs. Harris came with the house. Finch too, in a rather roundabout way. Oswyn, Digby, Mabel, and Eve have all joined the staff within the past two years. There was another scullery maid but she had trouble adjusting to Mrs. Harris's . . . uh, familiarity, so she went to work elsewhere. Everyone else seems to thrive on the environment."

"She hugged me." Adelaide couldn't help the flat tone of her voice. She couldn't remember the last time her parents had hugged her, much less a servant.

"I know. She usually eats dinner with me. Fenton too. We've also been known to share a glass of port in the evenings." Trent blushed and looked into his teacup.

Adelaide didn't know what to say. Or think. Or do. She'd spent every spare moment the last three weeks poring over any home management book she could find, lamenting the fact that she'd never really learned how to run a household. Helena's lessons had always come first, and there never seemed to be any time left to teach Adelaide anything. Not that any knowledge she might have gained would be useful here.

While it was nice to know life wasn't going to be like the dry and discouraging situations mentioned in the book she'd pulled from her father's study, she wished she wasn't quite so lost as to what to expect. The constant surprises weren't helping the pain in her head any. "Well. I'm sure everything will settle in nicely."

Trent smiled at her. A wide, genuine smile that made her breath catch. Did he often go around smiling at women like that? If so, she was sure to run into more than one lady who had been hoping for her position.

A brisk knock preceded Mrs. Harris popping her head into the drawing room. "My lady, your room is prepared. Feel free to finish your tea. Lydia's waiting for you when you're ready."

Ah yes, the pregnant lady's maid. It boggled the mind, really, and gave her a better understanding of the social rule that servants never married. It was awkward knowing the person waiting on you was in a delicate condition.

More important, though, the fact that her room was ready meant that her bed was ready. She peeked at Trent through her lashes. A bed that her husband had the right to visit. After tonight there could be children. She had never even danced with the man, much less kissed him, and they could be having children together.

It was enough to make her want to order another pot of tea.

Chapter 5

There was a surprisingly large amount of tea in the cup Adelaide slid onto the table, considering the fact that she'd tilted the cup to her lips nine times. Trent knew. He'd been counting.

She smoothed her skirts and cleared her throat. "I suppose I'll go up to my room."

Trent nodded, but Adelaide didn't move from her perch on the edge of the settee. He looked up from his teacup and frowned. Was her glove inside out? He was sure it hadn't been that way during the wedding.

Adelaide shifted on the settee and wrapped her arms around her middle as if she were trying to shrink into the very fabric of the furniture.

What was wrong? Trent's gaze flew over the tea service. It wasn't the most elaborate spread, but given that they'd been traveling all day it seemed adequate. On days when Trent had been boxing or riding all afternoon Mrs. Harris brought out cold meat and bread with the evening tea. Perhaps traveling was more strenuous for a woman than it was for him. "Are you still hungry? I can have something more substantial sent up from the kitchens."

"What? Oh, no. It's not that. I . . . well, I don't know where my room is."

Her voice was so quiet he almost couldn't hear what she said, and then he wished he hadn't because her words made him feel like the veriest dolt. Of course she didn't know where her room was. She'd barely seen more than the front hall.

He cleared his throat and set his teacup back on the tray. "It's not that late, yet. Would you like a tour of the—"

"Yes, please."

Trent chuckled at how fast she'd jumped at his offer. It reminded him of the day he'd taken up residence in the house two years prior. He'd spent the entire first day wandering room to room, trying to adjust to the fact that it was all his now. Granted some of the furniture was shabby and very little of the decor was in the current fashions, but it was his, and that had made him feel like a proper adult for the first time. He'd even set up a study. Not that he did much more than answer correspondence in it, but still, he had one.

He rose, surprised to find his hands were a bit sweaty at the prospect of showing his new bride around the house. What if she didn't like it? Perhaps he should have spent the last three weeks in London fixing up the house. No, she'd probably want to decorate everything herself anyway. His mother always did. Not to mention there wasn't much he'd have been able to do sitting on a sofa with his ankle propped up.

"Obviously, this is the drawing room." He swung his arm in a wide arc, indicating the room they were occupying. As her head swiveled to take in the faded green silk wall coverings, he tried to surreptitiously wipe his hands on his trousers before offering her his arm.

"It's very . . . green."

Trent laughed. "It's at least a decade past needing redecorating. You can take care of that, if you wish. I've never had much use for the room before, so I've left it as it was when I acquired the house."

"It's a very nice place for a bachelor." She stood and slid her hand into his elbow.

"I know. Griffith inherited it, and since he didn't need two homes in London, he gave this one to me." There was more to the story than that, of course, but it all seemed like a bit much to get into with Adelaide right now, so he left it alone.

His wife blinked up at him. "That was very . . . nice . . . of him."

Wasn't that the kind of things families did for each other? In his experience it was, but the older he got the more he realized that his family might not fit in with the aristocratic norm. Or any norm for that matter. "Yes, it was."

He cleared his throat, wondering how to explain his family to Adelaide or if he even needed to. She'd discover it on her own soon enough. His mother and sisters would shower her with more affection than she could handle. Once he got around to telling them he'd gotten married. "The dining room is through here."

On and on the tour went. It wasn't an especially large house, but many of the upper rooms had been closed up for several years. "I'm not sure what this set of rooms is supposed to be, but you can turn it into whatever you wish."

Adelaide, who had been smiling softly through most of the tour, suddenly dropped her gaze to the floor and turned bright red. "I believe it's the nursery."

Trent looked around. This couldn't be the nursery. It was too stark. Not a single thing about the room looked like a child had ever lived in it. "We'll have to do some extensive renovations up here, then. I remember the Hawthorne nursery as a bright and cheerful place. I'll want the same for my children." He darted a quick look at the woman who was now destined to bear those children. "I mean, our children."

"Perhaps we could find my room now?"

The small, quiet voice was back. She'd almost begun to joke with him as the tour progressed, and one awkward conversation had her pulling back into herself. Trent didn't know how to handle that, having grown up around women who were more than willing to make their presence and their opinions known. Of course, they'd done so in the most polite and ladylike way possible. His mother would have had it no other way.

His mother would also not have him staring stupidly at his wife after she'd made a request.

"Of course. Your room." He took her down a flight of steps and escorted her into the small parlor shared by their bedrooms.

"My room is through there." Trent pointed to his door. "Yours is here."

"Thank you." She paused at the door to her room. "Is there, I mean, I . . . good night, er, for now . . . that is . . . I . . ."

Before Trent could make sense of the jumbled words spilling from her mouth, she'd jerked the door open and slipped inside, shutting it just as quickly.

———

Even if Gentleman Jack himself beat him to a bloody pulp, Trent still wouldn't admit it out loud . . . but he'd been looking forward to marriage for a long time. He leaned back in the leather wingback in his study and crossed his extended legs at the booted ankles, wondering how things had gotten so messed up and what on earth he was supposed to do to put them right again. True, he'd never sat around with other men at the club chatting about what he hoped his future wife would be like, but he'd spent more than one evening in the same position he was in now, imagining her. Not necessarily of her appearance—he'd never been infatuated with one woman enough to picture her in the role—but of their life together.

Never did those imaginings begin with his wife being a stranger from a family he could barely tolerate. They had never included the uncertainty of whether he would ever learn to like his wife, much less love her. His wildest scenarios had never included him wondering if people would think it anything other than a love match, or if anyone would have the gall to ask him how he felt about the pairing.

And they had certainly never included him sitting restlessly in his study on his wedding night.

He shifted his shoulders against the dark leather, trying to find a more comfortable position in the massive Chippendale wingback. His best thinking was usually done in his father's old bergère chair, but he hadn't lasted five minutes in that chair before retreating to this one. His father's chair, situated as it was in Trent's bedchamber, was entirely too close to the problem to allow for proper consideration of the issue. A mere six steps from the door connecting his room directly to Adelaide's. He'd counted, twice, before bursting through the door to the sitting room and retreating to his study.

This was the real reason he'd wanted to get to London tonight. Here, in his own home, with servants he trusted and surroundings he was comfortable with, he could acknowledge something he'd been worrying about since the engagement had been officially announced. Upstairs, in a room that hadn't been used since he took up residence, slept a woman. Well, he assumed she slept. He didn't really know because she was up there and he was down here. It had been more than two hours since she'd closed her bedroom door. He really hoped she wasn't still waiting on him.

Unlike a lot of the boys he'd gone to school with and the men he encountered at his athletic clubs, Trent hadn't yet participated in the physical side of romantic relations. Griffith had always frowned at the boys swaggering into the room with smug smiles on their faces, getting congratulatory elbow nudges and knowing laughs. His opinion had been that he had no right to expect something of his wife that he didn't expect of himself, and if waiting weren't a feasible thing for a man to do, the Bible would never have indicated they should. Trent thought those rather profound and true statements, so he waited. It hadn't always been easy, but he'd waited.

And now he was married.

He had the wife upstairs to prove it. Well, legally anyway.

But he didn't feel married, and that was the thing that had driven him downstairs when his normal place of pondering was in direct view of the door connecting his room to hers. After years of building walls around his natural urges and convincing himself to ignore conversations that exhibited the difference of popular opinion, he'd finally gotten his body to align with his mind on the subject. But now they were in a state of disagreement again. His mind knew there was a wife upstairs, one who'd been raised to see marriage as a duty. She wouldn't understand why he was down here swirling a glass of untouched brandy instead of knocking on her door in his dressing gown.

Part of him didn't understand it either.

But the fact remained that he'd convinced himself to wait until he was married, to have his wife be the only woman he ever touched. And he'd always pictured that wife as someone he chose, someone he loved, someone he was eager to start a family and build a life with. Instead he was married to Adelaide Bell, and he didn't love her. He didn't even know her aside from the fact that she wore spectacles and didn't like carrots.

He'd always thought he'd know his wife a bit better than that.

What if she wasn't asleep? Should he send word? What would he even say? There wasn't a way to word such a message that wasn't cold, insulting, or both. He'd been counting on her to quietly fall asleep while waiting for him in the bed.

That would save all of the awkwardness for the morning breakfast table.

Trent frowned. Was this marriage going to ruin every breakfast for the rest of his life?

Nothing could be done about tomorrow's breakfast, but something had to be done to salvage the rest of them.

Tomorrow they would do whatever married people did—well, whatever they did during the day. He'd been fairly young when his father died, so his remembrances of his mother and father together were dim and colored by the mind of a child. Adelaide's parents, however, were still alive. And while it irked him to model anything in his life after something Lady Crampton did, the truth was that she and Lord Crampton seemed to rub along well enough. Adelaide would know what married people did. He could simply follow her lead.

Once they acted like a married couple, he'd feel like part of a married couple, and then the idea of knocking on the connecting door wouldn't make him feel so guilty. The whole process shouldn't take more than a few days, a couple of weeks at the most.

Trent lifted the glass to his lips but never tipped it to drink. There was only one problem with his plan of action. How in the world was he going to explain it to Adelaide?

Chapter 6

She debated pleading a headache. Didn't some women require a day of rest after traveling? She could become one of those women. Or maybe she could become one of those women who took their breakfast on a tray in their room. As the lady of the house it was her prerogative to do so, if she wished. She was really ready to do anything that meant she didn't have to finish dressing and face the man she'd married.

Never had she been so embarrassed. What must he think of her? Once she'd entered her room last night, the events of the day had finally caught up with her and she'd become extraordinarily tired. Lydia had been very competent, if a little rough with the hairbrush, and within twenty minutes Adelaide had been tucked into bed wearing the new negligee her mother had insisted she purchase.

Even now Adelaide's face flamed as she considered the flimsy garment now draped across the back of a chair. She'd hated being measured for the thing, disliked even more the conversation with her mother insisting she get it. Never had she dreamed that her maid—her temporary, increasing maid—would be the only one to see it.

What had he thought when he came to her room and found her sleeping with the blankets pulled all the way to her chin? She must have appeared the most unwilling wife in England. The poor man had already been trapped into marriage to her. And now he would think she was a . . . a . . . Adelaide didn't actually know what to call such a woman, but she was certain a man would know the right word. And now she was one.

There was no choice but to go down to breakfast and somehow tell him that she was open to his visiting her room. She considered leaving the connecting door between their rooms open, but that might embarrass the maid. Of course, her current maid was married so the regular rules of decorum might not apply in this case. Still, she couldn't impose upon Trent's privacy like that.

"I pressed this lovely blue gown last night. Will it do for the morning? I'll see to the rest of your garments while you eat." Lydia bustled out of the dressing room showing only the slightest waddle in her walk. Being with child certainly didn't slow the girl down as she herded Adelaide into the dressing room and whipped the gown over her head almost before she could blink. Within moments Adelaide found herself sitting on the stool in front of the dressing table with Lydia undoing the loose plait she'd created the night before.

Her mother had always admonished her to never talk to the servants about anything other than their duties, but Adelaide had a feeling that wasn't the way things were done in this house. She was going to have to learn some new rules if she wanted to meet her husband's expectations. "Do you know . . . Has my husband risen yet?"

"Oh yes, my lady." Lydia ran a comb through Adelaide's hair, drawing forth a wince. A good night's rest hadn't made the maid any gentler when it came to hair ministrations. "He's gone riding in Hyde Park, though I expect he'll be home any time now. He never misses breakfast."

Adelaide started forming a mental list of all the things she knew about her husband. There wasn't much to work with yet.

- *Enjoys morning rides*
- *Likes breakfast*
- *Writes with his right hand but fences better with his left*

That last thing was one of the few pieces of information she remembered from their conversation on That Night, as she'd taken to thinking of their time in the stone prison that had started this whole business. Despite the fact that she knew for certain there had been no way out of those ruins, the whole story felt a bit pathetic. Trapped into marriage by a mound of vines and stones. And one opportunistic mother.

"Does he ride every morning?" Adelaide fiddled with a pile of hairpins on the dressing table in front of her, trying to ignore the gouges Lydia was making in her scalp. Honestly, Rebecca couldn't get there fast enough.

"Yes, my lady."

Perfect. She'd have Father send her mount to London and she could ride with her husband in the mornings. If he wanted her to. Oh, bother. Figuring out what Trent expected husbands and wives to do together was going to be quite difficult.

Or maybe not. Breakfast was already going to be unpleasant enough with the whole conversation about nighttime visits. She might as well throw in a discussion about other marital duties while she was at it. Maybe that would make the whole thing less unpleasant. It certainly couldn't make it any worse.

⌒

Half an hour later Adelaide was frustrated as well as embarrassed.

The problem with conversations is that someone had to speak in order to start them. A cordial "Good morning" from one person followed by an equally polite "Good morning" from the other person didn't create much of a verbal foundation. Obviously he

51

wasn't willing to ask the other frequent morning question of "Did you sleep well?" and she didn't really blame him. She wasn't willing to ask it either.

The sideboard of the breakfast room was piled with platters of food. Eggs, toast, bacon, and a large assortment of pastries made her mouth water. He gestured for her to go ahead of him to fix her plate. As she took more than she would probably be able to eat, she tried desperately to find something to say. Anything that didn't sound as if she was mocking him with the previous night's events.

When she turned from the sideboard, her mind was absorbed with another problem. Where was she supposed to sit? The small breakfast table was round, so she didn't know where the foot was. Normally she'd choose the seat with the best view out the window, but what if he did that as well? Not that it was a very spectacular view, as it mostly overlooked the kitchen yard and small stable, but it did let in a bit of sunlight.

A footman relieved her of the decision by sliding a chair out and bowing her into it. Adelaide gratefully settled in, almost missing the servant's inquiry as to whether she would like tea, coffee, or chocolate to drink.

"Oh, coffee!" Adelaide couldn't contain her excitement. She'd had coffee at her aunt's house and adored the drink. Her mother considered it too plebeian for an aristocratic household, so Adelaide never got to drink it at home. The fact that as a married woman she would now get to start every day with the hot, bitter beverage made her happy enough to try to start a conversation with her husband.

Unfortunately, her glee also took over her thought processes because the next words out of her mouth were "Did you sleep well?"

Adelaide froze with her cup of steaming coffee still an inch above the saucer. The very thing she'd wanted to avoid was now floating between them, waiting to choke them like the infamous London haze.

What were the chances that he would notice if she excused herself now and didn't show her face again for a while? A month or two ought to be long enough for the fierce heat in her cheeks to subside. She lifted her lashes enough to peek at him. His green gaze was aimed directly at her, proof he would notice if she attempted to slink away. The only saving grace was that he, too, was in possession of a rather alarmingly red face. He ran a hand through his hair, sending his blond locks tumbling over his forehead, but that did nothing to hide the two spots of color riding his cheekbones.

If they were both embarrassed by the reference, they should be able to move on to a new topic of discussion without the other one complaining about it.

As soon as one of them found something else to say.

"I have a horse." Adelaide nearly followed her bumbling spill of words with a groan at how desperately abrupt they sounded, but she managed to restrain the sound by stuffing her mouth so full she nearly choked on her eggs.

"Ah," Trent stammered before taking a delaying sip of tea. "As do I. Were you intending on having your horse sent to Town? We could send her to one of the estates if you'd rather."

Adelaide gulped down her half-chewed mouthful. "Will we visit the Hertfordshire estate soon? You mentioned repairs?"

Trent nodded. "The bedchamber wing suffered considerable damage during a recent storm or I'd have taken you there last night. The journey wouldn't have been as grueling."

Both of them blushed again. If this kept up they would be able to save a bundle of money on heating the house. Even now she was giving serious consideration to throwing some coffee onto the small fire that had been built to ward off the early morning chill. It was a bit ridiculous to blame her current discomfort on the flames burning so low in the grate they could really only be described as smoldering, but it made her feel better to do so.

Adelaide determined it was best to finish eating in silence. It seemed safer that way. Surely tomorrow things would be less awkward since the delay, for lack of a better word, wouldn't be between them anymore.

Would it?

What if her falling asleep wasn't the reason he hadn't visited her room? What if he had no intentions of truly making her his wife? He was a second son. He had no real need for heirs. He could ignore her, ship her off to one of his estates, and continue living life as he pleased. It had never occurred to her before now that she might not even get children out of this forced marriage.

Her toast stuck in her throat. Not even a large gulp of her quickly cooling coffee could wash it down.

Trent cleared his throat and stood. Adelaide looked up at him, not trusting her legs to hold her as she convinced herself this new fear was ridiculous and unfounded. Traveling was exhausting. Surely they weren't the only couple to wait a night.

"I usually go over to Grosvenor Chapel for Sunday services. I'm afraid I haven't rented my own pew yet. I can look into obtaining one at St. George if you'd rather not use the family pew at the Chapel."

Adelaide had completely forgotten that today was Sunday. They would attend church together. She would enter on his arm and sit in his pew. Their marriage would be efficiently announced by such an event without her having to suffer through personal introductions and less than subtle questions and skeptical looks at her midsection. "The family pew sounds wonderful."

"Can you be ready in half an hour? Most of the servants attend St. George, so I take the curricle over to Hawthorne House and then walk to Grosvenor Chapel."

"That sounds splendid." It did, actually. By the name it sounded like a smaller, cozier place to attend worship. Perhaps even similar to the village church at home. She'd spent a lot of time in that church, visiting with the rector and his wife when Mother would accidentally leave her behind on Sunday mornings, particularly once her brother, Bernard, was born. An even number made such a more elegant picture walking down the lane, after all. The rector had an affinity for jacks, and he and Adelaide would play the game while discussing the sermon.

She doubted that she would be playing jacks at any point today, but the distraction of attending services and actually having something to do caused the shaking of her legs to cease. She was fairly certain she could walk now, and she needed to if she was to have any hope of being ready to leave in a mere half an hour.

"May I escort you back upstairs?" Trent gave a half bow, unstyled hair flopping against his forehead once more, making her want to reach out and brush the strands back into place even though they wouldn't stay there.

She slid her hand into his arm with a smile of agreement. As she thrilled at the warmth she felt holding a man's arm with an ungloved hand, it suddenly became real to her. She was married. This man was her husband.

And for the first time in three weeks, she thought maybe that was a going to be a good thing.

He could have waited a week. They'd only been married yesterday. Most people wouldn't expect to see them out and about for several days, if not several weeks. The complete disconnection from everything he was familiar with left him craving a return to his normal routine. Though with Adelaide perched next to him in the curricle, the routine felt nothing like it used to. Her blue skirts draped against the dark brown of his trousers, a stark contrast that he'd never looked down and seen before.

Taking women for rides in his curricle wasn't something he did. Unless they were related, he confined his social encounters to more public venues. When he decided to court a woman it was going to be special, as exciting for him as it was for her.

At least, that had been the plan.

But now he was riding with his wife, and though he'd expected the worst after they'd bumbled through the morning's breakfast, there was something thrilling about looking over and seeing the morning sun glinting off her bonnet, highlighting the chin ribbon that had come untied and blown away from her face to tangle in the feathers on the side of the bonnet.

He smiled. A beautiful woman was riding down the street with him, and he was bemoaning the fact that the relationship was already a guaranteed success? At least guaranteed to reach matrimony. What would he do if he were courting Adelaide? If he'd gone to her house and picked her up like other gentlemen did when they went courting?

"Have you a favorite color?"

She blinked at him. "Color?"

"Yes. Color. Blue, green, brown. That sort of thing."

"Oh." She faced forward again, scrunching her nose until small wrinkles formed between her eyes. "I like blue. At least, I tend to buy a lot of blue dresses. I get to choose bolder blues now, which was a delightful change when Mother took me to the modiste a few weeks ago."

This was hardly the first time a woman of his acquaintance had brought up fashion in his presence. He'd even been known to carry his weight in a conversation or two on the subject. But it felt different talking about her dresses. Perhaps because he would now be buying them. "Did you get everything you needed? I don't expect you were able to outfit yourself for an entire Season in a mere three weeks."

"Oh, well, not for a normal Season, no, but as a married woman I'm sure what I have will be sufficient."

They fell into silence for the rest of the short ride. Where was the glib tongue that had gotten him invited to every society function in the vicinity since he was fifteen years old? He was the fellow who had talked his way around every bad mark in school, convinced the Earl of Egleshurst's heir to set up a desk and work on his Latin conjugations in the middle of the Eton athletic field, and very nearly came close to actually convincing one of the patronesses to let him into Almack's at five minutes past eleven.

With all of that experience he should be able to find *something* to talk to his wife about.

They left the curricle with the grooms at Hawthorne House and walked the short distance to Grosvenor Chapel, stumbling their way through a stilted discussion on tree leaves. Even that topic deserted them as they climbed the chapel steps.

How many times had he walked through these doors without thought for who else had passed through before him? For the most part he saw these people at various other events he attended. And while many of them viewed church as another place to see and be seen, his family had always been more interested in the service itself, part of the reason they elected to attend Grosvenor Chapel instead of St. George's.

Today, however, Trent was aware of every person they were escorted past. As the Duke of Riverton, Griffith had rented a pew at the very front of the sanctuary, and Trent and Adelaide had to walk past everyone to get there.

And everyone was very interested.

The door of the box pew clicked shut, putting a period on the statement that Adelaide was now a member of the Hawthorne family.

Hundreds of whispers created a low murmur right up until the first strains of organ music echoed through the chapel. As a boy, Trent had always prayed for a short and succinct sermon. Today he found himself hoping the message droned on. Not that he was interested in it—he had barely heard a word, highly distracted by the small shifts Adelaide made every few minutes.

She wasn't the first spouse to have sat in this box. Both of his sisters' husbands had sat here a time or two. Colin and Georgina still used the box when they were in London, though Ryland and Miranda now rented the one across the aisle. Adelaide was, however, the first of Trent's spouses to sit here. The only spouse. Because if this awkwardness was what other marriages were like, he had to call into question the sanity of the men he'd heard about who took more than one wife.

All too soon the service concluded, and Trent faced the difficult decision of when to leave the pew. Behind them, feet shuffled along the worn floorboards and pew boxes opened and shut in their own form of familiar benediction. It was the sounds of people, and people meant questions. He should have waited a week. Next week Griffith was supposed to be in town. With the duke at his side, no one would have dared approach him. Griffith was simply too intimidating. Never before had Trent considered his innate personable friendliness to be a disadvantage.

"Shall we get this over and done then?" Trent asked the fretting, dark-haired, unconventional beauty by his side.

She blinked up at him. He was becoming addicted to those blinks, crazy as it sounded. Her eyes were mesmerizing, capturing his attention even without the help of the slow blinks or the enhancement of her spectacles that made them appear even larger.

Trent cleared his throat. "There will be introductions, I'm sure. Are you prepared for them?"

Adelaide nodded. "Oh, yes. I'm rather good with names, I think."

"Once more into the breach, then." Trent reached across her to release them from the pew enclosure.

Her soft giggle caressed his ear as he pulled his arm back.

An answering grin slid across his face. He was glad she found his reference to *Henry V* amusing, even if Shakespeare would probably scoff at Trent's comparison of running the gauntlet of church members to a near-hopeless war invasion.

If the wide-eyed looks sent in their direction were any indication, news of their nuptials had yet to spread through London. He had half expected Lady Crampton to do everything shy of take out a column in the newspaper to let all of the aristocracy know she'd married off her second daughter to the son of a duke. Everyone he introduced Adelaide to seemed thoroughly shocked, as if they'd tried to convince themselves she was a visiting cousin or some such thing, even though all of the Hawthornes' cousins were considerably fairer in coloring. One young lady even seemed to be fighting to hold back tears.

That one seemed to bother Adelaide as they broke free of the throng and made their way back to Hawthorne House.

"Did you know her well?" The hand at his elbow tightened momentarily before the fingers smoothed along his forearm once more.

"Who?"

"Miss Elizabeth. The one who cried when you introduced me. Were you courting her?"

Trent stopped and turned to face her on the street. "I was not nor have I ever courted anyone. I go to gatherings because I have to. Occasionally I even want to. I dance. I smile. But I do not court. I'm certain she was upset about something else."

"Hmm." Adelaide glanced him up and down and then looked back over her shoulder at the church.

"Regardless," Trent said as they resumed walking. "I'm married to you."

"Yes. I suppose you are."

And with that, any hope they'd had for maintaining a pleasant conversation on the way home disappeared.

Chapter 7

Trent's customary morning stretch was hindered by the sofa arm above his head and the upholstered back pushing against his right shoulder. With a groan, he rolled himself to the side and swung his legs up until he could lower his knees to the floor and stretch his arms out along the couch. A night of sitting up in a chair followed by a few hours of tossing and turning on a narrow sofa had left his muscles screaming in agony.

He rolled his head back and forth, hoping a good stretch would alleviate some of the tension and the headache that had come with it.

It didn't.

Marriage certainly wasn't doing him any favors yet, though he didn't know why it really should. He'd done it because he had to, because there'd been no other way around it. It'd been a gentlemanly duty, like dancing with wallflowers and holding the door open. Yes, this duty had more far-reaching consequences than doffing his hat in deference to a passing lady, but did it really have to change his entire life? He hadn't been courting a woman before, hadn't even been interested in one, so in a large way, nothing had changed.

He could continue on as he had been and it would almost be like the marriage had never happened in the first place.

One mighty push propelled him up from the sofa, ripping a groan from his chest as all the kinks rolled through his body in protest. He'd be good as new after a few hours of his customary morning exercise though.

The house was still quiet as he slipped up the stairs to his room, making a point not to look at the door across the upstairs parlor. More often than not, Trent readied himself for his morning ride, so he could easily avoid looking too closely at why he didn't want to ring for Fenton to come fill in for his valet. Though thinking about the fact that he didn't have to think about it diminished the benefit.

Digby's eyes widened and cut to the clock on the wall to note the early hour, but he didn't say anything as he readied Trent's horse. The sun was barely forcing its way through the clouds and smog when Trent trotted off in the direction of Hyde Park. A good run down the bridle path would set his mind back on track, and he could set about putting his life back the way he'd had it. So now there was a wife at home. That didn't really have to change anything.

The horse danced sideways as a leaf blew across the path. Apparently even Bartholomew wasn't buying that lie. Trent patted him on the neck and gave him the signal to stretch his legs into a near gallop. The wind blew Trent's hair off his face and cut through the seams of his coat, bringing with it the sharp chill of morning and the feeling of being alive.

A few other men were spaced along the path, some running their horses as he was, while others rode at a more leisurely pace. Seeing a black gelding with foam drying on his haunches as his rider walked him back toward the main road reminded Trent that he couldn't take out his need to escape on his horse. An easy pull on the reins slowed the horse to a jog. A good move for the health of the horse, but one that left him accessible to any other riders who were feeling a bit chatty. A rare occurrence this early in the morning, but when the news was interesting enough, people would ignore an inconvenience.

"Ho there, Hawthorne!" A gorgeous brown horse pranced over and fell into step beside Trent's. "There's talk that you had a wife sitting next to you at church yesterday."

Trent glanced at Mr. Bancroft over his shoulder and made himself grin. "Well, I'd hardly make her sit in the free seats."

Bancroft chuckled. "Made my own wife cry into her tea, you know. She'd had hopes for our Hannah. Didn't think you'd marry for years."

That made two of them, not that Trent had ever thought such things about Bancroft's daughter. He wasn't even sure he'd ever met Hannah, was fairly certain she wasn't yet sixteen. Still, it wouldn't do to insult the other man's wife. Or his own wife for that matter. "What can I say? I fell into the match when I wasn't looking."

"Ah, yes, love will get you like that. Happened that way with my own wife. Yes, sir, we're the lucky ones, you and I. The good Lord saw fit to bless us in spite of ourselves." Bancroft patted his horse on the neck. "Ulysses is getting restless. See you around, Hawthorne."

Trent could do no more than lift a hand before Bancroft's horse had taken off down the path.

One of the lucky ones. Trent didn't feel lucky. He felt the exact opposite. The conflict between reality and people's assumptions crawled under his cravat and shot an itch down his back, effectively ruining what freedom he'd found in the morning's rough gallop.

He turned the plodding horse toward home, resisting the urge to restrain the beast when his pace picked up the closer they got to the small stable.

The uncomfortable irritation had spread across his entire back by the time he walked in the house for breakfast. It wasn't helped any by the fierce scowl on Mrs. Harris's face when she met him at the door.

"I took a tray up this morning."

Trent rubbed a hand along the back of his neck. "I'm sorry to put you out. I always take breakfast down here after my ride though."

She crossed her arms over her chest, the dark frown on her round face looking out of place on his normally doting housekeeper. "I didn't make it for you."

"Oh, yes, Adelaide. Good." Trent pulled off his riding gloves. "Just so we're all clear here, why, exactly, is that a problem?"

"Because the sofa in your study wasn't made for sleeping." She sniffed. "I've half a mind to serve you gruel this morning."

And he'd half a mind to get a new housekeeper. Not that he'd tell her that. Or follow through on the threat if he ever did get up the nerve to say it aloud. The other half of his mind knew that he was quite stuck with the woman until she chose to retire, unless he wanted to suffer the wrath of at least half of his family. "I'd really rather you didn't. If I had to start the day without your cinnamon butter and perfectly turned bacon I'd never manage to get anything accomplished. If I'm to function at all I can't be pining away for your inspiring breakfasts."

One side of her mouth ticked up. "Go on with you, then. Upstairs to freshen up. I'll tell Fenton you've returned."

Crisis averted and breakfast salvaged, Trent made his way upstairs, treading carefully, so as not to announce his return to the entire house. Talking his way past Mrs. Harris was one thing. Talking his way past his wife, whom he'd abandoned . . . again . . . was another thing entirely. He was more likely to stammer and blush his way into oblivion.

He ate breakfast with an eye on the door, fearing that despite having had a tray sent upstairs she intended to make an appearance downstairs as well. But she never showed, and he was left sitting in front of an empty plate, staring at the walls and wondering where he could go in his house that he could be assured of not running into her.

The pickings were slim, so he made the next logical choice. He left the house.

⁓

Another breakfast tray, another harsh reminder that yet another day and night had gone by without any significant interaction with her husband. Adelaide frowned at her coddled eggs. Forget significant. She would have been happy with something as simple as "Good morning" or even a nod of acknowledgment. That, however, would require they be in the same room, and aside from a brief discussion about where to store her trunks, she hadn't seen him since her maid and clothing arrived from Hertfordshire.

She plucked the rose off the tray and spun it in her fingers. Mrs. Harris always added the flower—probably her attempt to make them both forget the reason she'd taken to having a tray sent up. After lifting the flower to her nose for a brief sniff, she slid it into the vase on the writing table she'd taken to eating at. Four roses. One for each day she'd avoided her husband in the morning. Monday's rose was starting to brown on the petal edges, yet another sign of how much time had passed since she'd spoken with Lord Trent.

Beneath the roses was a small pile of folded papers, the only type of communication she'd had with her husband in days. He sent a message every afternoon, delivered by Fenton, each more inane than the last. On the first day it had been a reminder that he'd instructed Oswyn, the footman, to make himself available should she wish to go anywhere, something that was already part of the man's job.

The following days had been even more ridiculous, telling her things such as where he'd left the newspapers if she wanted to read them and reminding her to tell Mrs. Harris what her favorite foods were. As if Mrs. Harris wouldn't track her down to find out that information on her own. Adelaide spent a great deal more time with the housekeeper than her husband, a fact that wouldn't have bothered her overmuch if she'd been spending any time with her husband at all.

The corner of her toast fell against her eggs and she nudged one side of the browned bread until it poked a hole in the pile of eggs. How many times had she wished for breakfast on a tray while growing up? It meant she wouldn't have to sit at the breakfast table, listening to everyone else plan a thrilling day while she contemplated which tree she was going to sit beneath while reading. Unless, of course, her mother needed her for something such as dancing lessons. That was the real reason Adelaide had always made an appearance at breakfast. If Helena's lessons required a partner, Adelaide was required to be present.

But now Adelaide was married, and she wasn't required to be anywhere.

Adelaide blinked, straightening her spine as the implications rushed through her. She didn't have to be anywhere, do anything, or help anyone if she didn't want to. While there might not be children in her future—a possibility she hoped to one day to rectify—there could at least be life in her future, and she was going to take control of it.

Rebecca, her lady's maid, gave a startled shriek when Adelaide all but pounced on her as she entered the room with a freshly pressed gown over her arm. After taking a deep, calming breath, the maid went about preparing Adelaide for the day in quiet efficiency, as any normal servant would do.

Except this morning she was humming.

Ever since Rebecca had arrived late Monday afternoon—along with the rest of Adelaide's trunks and Finch, Trent's valet and Lydia's husband—Adelaide had been fighting the urge to question Rebecca, speak to her, indulge in conversations she'd never dreamed of having with a servant before. After three days of Lydia's constant prattle and scalp abrasions, Adelaide expected to nearly wallow in Rebecca's more demure behavior. Instead she chafed against it, though her scalp found considerable solace in it.

The humming was the final push, though. Adelaide looked out the window, but the low grey clouds appeared to be ushering in the most dismal day they'd had since coming to London. It wasn't a beautiful day that inspired the maid's apparent good mood.

"Are you having a good morning, Rebecca?"

The maid smiled and moved toward the small dressing room at the back of Adelaide's bedchambers.

Adelaide followed with narrowed eyes. The dressing room was small, forming more of a large closet, so Adelaide had been getting ready out in the main room. Why was Rebecca changing things this morning?

"Of course I am, my lady. Why do you ask?"

Could she possibly not know that she was practically singing as she worked? "The humming."

"Oh, yes." Her gaze darted down to the left before swinging back around to Adelaide's. An overly bright smile curved the maid's lips. "Do you like it? We thought it might brighten up the morning."

A perfunctory agreement had been poised on Adelaide's lips— after all, what did she care if the maid hummed while she worked— but the phrasing of Rebecca's answer gave her pause. "We?"

"Er, myself, Mrs. Harris, and Lydia. And Finch, of course." Rebecca began tugging at Adelaide's nightclothes. "It's a bit strange, really. Of course there's always talk in the servants' quarters, but this is well beyond the usual gossip. They actually want to help you, and . . . Oh dear. I'm saying the wrong things, aren't I? I told them I wasn't going to be any good at this. I haven't the slightest idea how to be so familiar."

Adelaide's eyes were wide. She thought her mouth might even be hanging open.

Rebecca slid the dress over Adelaide's head and walked behind her to work the fastenings. "Don't worry, Lady Adelaide. As of this moment I'll go back to being quiet, like a proper servant. We'll both be more comfortable that way."

Adelaide said nothing as silence fell in the room. Near silence, anyway. A bump and rustle echoed through the door connecting her room to her husband's, causing her to snap her head around in that direction. "Is he in there?"

Rebecca looked down, seeming to busy herself with Adelaide's slippers. "Yes, m'lady. Finch said he was running a bit behind his normal schedule this morning so you might hear when he came up to dress for the day. Mrs. Harris and Lydia said I should hum so you wouldn't notice."

The staff at this house was beyond Adelaide's understanding. Still, her earlier resolve remained—to do something with her day other than stare at the walls of her bedchamber or tiptoe around the house as if afraid she'd run into anyone, even though she was supposedly the mistress of the house. She hadn't the first notion of where she could possibly go beyond the house, so that left the house itself to serve as the focus for her industriousness.

And she intended to start with the drawing room.

After she finished her coffee. That should give her husband enough time to finish dressing and go to wherever it was he spent each day.

⁓

Trent adjusted the sleeve on his jacket and turned to Finch so he could put the finishing touches on Trent's cravat.

"Will that be all, my lord?" Finch turned to gather Trent's discarded riding clothes, once again avoiding looking Trent in the eye.

"You're mad at me too, are you?" Trent shoved his hand through the hair Finch had just finished styling. "Mrs. Harris stands in the front hall and glares at me any time I leave the house or come home. Fenton hasn't shared a single piece of gossip since Tuesday. And now you're acting like the world's most exemplary valet. I could only imagine what sorts of things your wife is saying about me."

Finch cleared his throat. "They're not very complimentary, my lord."

Trent grunted and dropped into his father's bergère chair.

"Will you be leaving for the club now, my lord?"

"No." Even that pleasure had been stolen from him. Trent couldn't go anywhere anymore without someone wanting to talk to him about his wife. With new people arriving back in London every day, it was remaining the fresh and favorite topic of conversation. He hadn't even been able to pick up a foil at his fencing club yesterday, given the number of congratulations and condolences he'd received as soon as he'd stepped in the door. "I'm staying home today."

Finch's entire body seemed to lighten. His shoulders popped back, and a smile stretched across his face. "That's fabulous, my lord."

Trent closed his eyes and sighed. The valet obviously thought Trent intended to do something with his wife. He didn't. There were weeks' worth of correspondence piled up in his study that he had yet to get to, despite the fact that he'd spent every night this week sleeping in that room. But he didn't tell Finch that. It wouldn't hurt for one of them to hold on to his dreams for a little longer.

Chapter 8

As the most public room, and quite possibly the shabbiest, the drawing room was in desperate need of an overhaul. The only problem was that desire and intent did not guarantee ability. Adelaide didn't have the first notion regarding what to do to redecorate a room. Change the drapes, certainly. That couldn't be too difficult. They were merely fabric hanging from rods.

Adelaide pulled back the heavy green brocade to look up at the fixture to see if it would need replacing as well. From what she could see, the rod and hooks were fairly simple in design. Something more elaborate would have been nice, but the existing ones were sufficient.

A movement on the other side of the windowpane caught Adelaide's eye, and she found herself staring into the faces of two women. One was young, likely around Adelaide's own age. Her eyes widened as she took in Adelaide's presence in the window. When the young woman wrapped her hand around the elbow of the older woman, gesturing toward Adelaide with her free hand, Adelaide's instincts took over and she jerked away from the window.

Unfortunately she still held the curtain she'd been inspecting.

Her foot landed on the fabric, sending it sliding across the floor and Adelaide tumbling backward onto her bottom.

With the curtain on her head—rod, hooks, and all.

So much for not replacing the curtain fixtures.

Had the clumsy accident caused enough noise to bring one of the servants running? She rather hoped not, as she wanted to stay down on the floor until the two women outside had been given more than enough time to finish gawking and move along.

No hurried steps echoed through the house, indicating that at least one thing was going in her favor today. After waiting a few more minutes, she extricated herself from the old brocade and left the entire mess in a pile behind the settee.

If the drawing room hadn't topped her list of rooms to redecorate before, it certainly did now.

Trent requested that his breakfast tray be delivered to his study the next morning. He'd even given instructions for Oswyn, arguably the most deferential of the staff, to deliver the tray. As familiar as they were, his staff had never gone against a direct request before, so when the knock came he had every confidence that Oswyn was on the other side of the door.

And he was, tray in hand and frown in place. And ranging behind him in a half circle of disparagement stood the rest of his staff. His goal had been to avoid their disapproving frowns, but he clearly was doomed to disappointment. Only Adelaide's lady's maid seemed to be missing. Even Digby had come in from the stables for the confrontation.

With a groan Trent ripped the tray from Oswyn's hands and kicked the door closed in their faces.

He'd taken care of his correspondence the day before, so after finishing his breakfast he settled into the wingback chair with a book. He considered stretching out on the sofa, but the sofa was getting enough of his attention lately.

The last thing he expected as he turned another page without really knowing what he'd read was for Mrs. Harris to burst into the study unannounced.

She stomped across the room to collect his breakfast tray but didn't pick it up from the desk where he'd left it. "I've never taken you for a coward, my lord. I'm not sure that I cotton to working for such a man."

The book fell from Trent's stunned fingers and lay open, forgotten in his lap, page lost.

"She's such a lovely young lady." Mrs. Harris picked up the tray. "An utter pleasure to work with."

Trent frowned. A pleasure to work with? Doing what? As near as he could tell, Adelaide never left her room. Not that he'd know because he so rarely left his study, but he knew what his house had looked like before, and it didn't look a bit different now. Even the food was the same, so she wasn't having much effect on the menus either.

"Having a woman in the house again is so nice. Not since Amelia was here have I had reason to pull out the fine china."

A laugh, born of equal parts despair and humor, threatened to bust through Trent's lips. The only difference between the fine china and the plates Trent had been served on before he got married was that the fine china had four matching place settings. On the rare occasion that he'd had the family over, he'd borrowed dishes from Hawthorne House.

Mrs. Harris walked toward the door but turned back before leaving the room. "Hiding in here, reading a book. When's the last time you read in the middle of the day, my lord? You think about that and what you're hiding from. I think you'll agree with my assessment of your recreant tendencies."

Trent coughed. "Recreant?"

"I read it in one of Lady Adelaide's books. She said it meant to give in to a trial. More than applies in this case, if you ask me."

And then she was gone, leaving Trent to stare at his unread book and wonder if she was right.

After wrecking the drawing room, Adelaide had retreated back to her solitude, finding comfort, as she always had, in books, both novel and academic. By Sunday morning, she had abandoned her plans to cry off going to church, because she simply couldn't stand to be in the house any longer. She was waiting in the front hall, pressed and coiffed and ready to go when he came trotting down the stairs. He paused in the middle of the staircase when he caught sight of her by the door but did no more than nod and say a quiet "Good" before ushering her out the door to the curricle.

Church was little better than it had been the first week. They arrived just before the beginning of the service, and Trent ushered her out before most of the other people had a chance to open their pew doors.

Back home they'd stood awkwardly in the hall, facing each other but staring at points on either side. Adelaide chose a strange still-life painting to inspect, noting that all the fruit in the bowl appeared to have faces. Her humiliation was being witnessed by a painting of sentient fruit. She'd truly reached the bottom of her ladder.

Perhaps that sensation of having nowhere to go but up was what gave her a spurt of gumption when the sun rose Monday morning. So what if she'd pulled the curtains from the wall in the drawing room? It was simply another sign that they needed to be replaced. Eventually someone—her mother, if no one else—was going to come for a visit, and she would have to use the drawing room. It might as well look presentable.

All she had to do was pick new curtains and she would be off to a great start.

Reality splashed a bucket of cold water on her plans for the day, however. She could practically hear the shopkeepers laughing at her trying to buy things under Trent's name with no proof that she was at all connected to him. Church-fueled rumors weren't likely to be enough to make them part with their goods. And she had no idea how much money she had to spend. That would require talking to her husband, which would mean spending actual time together in the same room—something he didn't seem inclined to do.

Perhaps she should send a note through Fenton? Perhaps ask to have an appointment in his schedule? Did he even have a schedule? Her father did. It was managed by the secretary who came by the house twice a week to assist her father in correspondence and other paper-related things. Being a second son, would Trent have need for such a thing?

With her hands on her hips, Adelaide stood in the middle of the front hall, unwilling to give up yet another week to melancholy. Where else could she stake a claim in the house? The door to the servants' domain caught her eye. As the lady of the house, she should know the kitchen—shouldn't she? What sort of food stocks did they have?

Simply walking through the door to the lower floor made her giddy. There weren't many servants in the house, but at least half of them were likely working belowstairs at the moment, and Adelaide was going to go spend some time with them. She might not have any interaction her husband, but she could certainly embrace her bizarre new household.

After Mrs. Harris's admonishment, Trent had moved back to his desk. As days passed, he'd gone over every account book, every estate report, until his eyes had nearly crossed. His poor sleep habits had caught up with him, and he found himself nodding off at the desk more than once. And finally, he'd exhausted even the remotest account-related work. For a man who had always taken as little interest as possible in the business of his estate, Trent was finding an awful lot of reasons to hide away.

Desperate for something that could be deemed productive

while still keeping him in the study, Trent yanked open the bottom drawer of the cabinet behind his desk. A pile of papers and a discarded cravat were on top, but he shoved them aside to pull out the farm management book he'd stashed there a few months prior. When he'd come across the book he had flipped through it, thinking it would be something interesting to pass along to his brother. But soon he found himself actually reading it. He'd been fascinated by the discussion of how to grow pineapples in less-than-tropical weather. He even caught himself pondering ways to make the process better as he rode his horse through Hyde Park in the morning.

That was when he buried the book. The thoughts and ambitions running through his head scared him. They were thoughts of a responsible, take-charge man, not a carefree, athletics-obsessed boy. And he wasn't ready to be a man, appearances to the contrary. Just because he had his own house and now his own wife didn't mean he wanted to show God how capable he could be in other areas of his life.

If he wanted to remain in his study, though, this book was all that was left. All of his correspondence was up to date, even those he'd originally had no intention of answering. He'd had Fenton deliver any and all invitations to Adelaide, but she had yet to tell him which events they were to attend. Granted there weren't that many to choose from so early in the Season, and the attending crowds would be small—which made it harder to avoid speculative questions—so he wasn't really bothered by their lack of activity. No one else would think a thing of it either, since the few people who were already in Town wouldn't expect a newly married couple to spend all of their evenings out and about. They probably didn't even expect them to stay in Town.

He should have taken her on a trip.

But then he wouldn't have an entire town house in which to avoid her.

He should ask her to sort through the invitations and accept one or two, to give them something to do.

But that would mean seeking her out. And the mere thought of doing such a thing caused his cravat to feel too tight. Mrs. Harris was right. He was a coward.

Since he already was one, it wouldn't hurt to bear the title one more day. Holding on to the topic would give them something to actually discuss, should they find themselves in the same room. If he sought her out he wouldn't have anything to fall back on when they accidentally encountered each other again.

Apparently he was pathetic as well as a coward.

He plopped the farming book onto his desk, and it fell open to the page he'd marked with a tattered scrap of parchment. Trent grabbed a clean sheet of paper and a pencil and began sketching out his idea for growing the pineapples in tiers, thereby saving more of the heat. Though it was rather disgusting to think about, he'd need a steady supply of horse deposits if he wanted to actually implement this process. Trust the Dutch to figure out that the stuff would generate enough heat to keep a glass enclosure tropically warm.

Adelaide's dowry estate was in Suffolk, very near to Newmarket, with its abundance of horse farms and racetracks. Getting a steady supply of the necessary product would actually be feasible.

Not that he had any intention of actually implementing any of this. It was simply something to do while his wife . . . He laid the pencil on the table and sat back in his chair, brows lowered in thought. What was his wife doing? Some of the people she knew from the country had to be arriving in Town. Was she going to visit them? Letting them know of her changed status by leaving cards around the city?

He jerked upright, bumping his hand against the pencil and sending it rolling across the desk and clattering to the floor.

Cards. He'd forgotten to have new cards made up for her. She couldn't visit anyone without them. And if she couldn't visit anyone, she couldn't leave the house, which meant Trent could bump into her at any moment.

Clearly his wife needed calling cards. Today, if at all possible.

Pleased to have a mission, Trent threw the book back into the drawer and slammed it shut with his booted foot.

He nearly ran down the stairs to the front hall. "Fenton! My hat and coat, please."

His hand twitched with impatience, beating his thumb against his thigh as he waited for the butler to bring the requested items. When had the man gotten so slow? Granted he was on the older side, but he'd always seemed quite spry, despite his lack of hair. It had taken Trent six months to convince the man to stop wearing the ghastly powdered wig and just embrace the natural look. It shocked a few people, of course, but it wasn't anywhere near as bad as his brother-in-law Ryland's butler. Those wishing to visit the Duke and Duchess of Marshington had to get past a hulking man with no neck and a rather prominent scar on his face. In comparison, a bald butler was nearly normal.

Mrs. Harris came bustling into the hall with Trent's coat thrown over her arm. Fenton was on her heels with the hat, his lips pressed into a thin line of displeasure. Sometimes Trent wondered if his butler and housekeeper weren't a married couple as well. They certainly acted like one at times.

"And where do you think you're going?" Mrs. Harris crossed her arms over her chest, effectively holding Trent's coat captive.

Trent grinned, knowing he had an answer the woman would approve of. "To get my wife calling cards. She needs to be able to tell the world of her new status, doesn't she?"

The motherly housekeeper looked torn as she held out the garment. "I suppose. Maybe being able to get out and about will lift her spirits."

The triumph he'd felt at getting his busybody of a housekeeper to relinquish the coat dimmed. "She is unwell?"

Mrs. Harris shrugged. "Don't know what else you expect when you haul a woman into an unknown house and leave her to her own devices. Poor Lydia's taken to working in the kitchen because she feels so terrible. Her ladyship cries whenever Lydia enters the room. Makes it awfully hard for a maid to do her work that way."

"Lydia shouldn't be working anymore, anyway," Trent grumbled. Weren't pregnant women supposed to be delicate?

It bothered him, though, that Adelaide was so unhappy. During their night in the ruins she'd told him that she spent most of her time reading and going for walks unless one parent or another wished her to do something else. Trent's library wasn't large, but it was respectable. And if her maid wasn't willing to go out he had other maids and a footman who could escort her wherever she wanted to walk in London. He thought she'd be happy.

Apparently not.

Hardly more than a week into his marriage, and he'd already broken his wife.

"Calling cards." His voice was thin, like a man taking his last gasping breath before drowning. "She needs calling cards so she can get out more. That's all."

Mrs. Harris frowned. "It's a start."

Trent grabbed his hat from Fenton and restrained himself from running out the front door as if he were a convict escaping from prison.

Chapter 9

He took a hack to the print shop, where the helpful man told him he could have a batch of cards delivered tomorrow and send a larger box within a week. Unwilling to return home so soon, he convinced the man to do a small batch right away and have them delivered to Trent's club. That he was willing to pay for such an extravagance was a true sign of his desperation.

It was as good an excuse as any to spend the remainder of the day within the walls of Boodle's. Perhaps now that he was actually doing something for his marriage, no matter how small, he wouldn't feel so pinned down by the questions and stares. Besides, it had been over a week. Surely it was old news by now. He certainly hoped so, anyway. He couldn't figure out what to say to his wife, much less what to say about her.

Trent wasn't sure what all the fuss was about anyway. Yes, the marriage was a surprise, but it had taken place in the country during the late winter. There was no reason for anyone in London to think it had been anything less than planned. Unexpected, yes, but not scandalous. Unless, of course, someone from Hertfordshire had decided it was interesting enough news to write their cousin about.

Trent sank into one of the tufted leather club chairs, a book open on his lap that he hoped would be a deterrent to those looking for a casual chat—even if he wasn't reading it. All he wanted was to breathe. And to not be married. But since the second wish wasn't about to come true unless God decided to dabble in time travel, the first one was increasingly difficult.

It was obvious that he'd failed at the one thing he thought this marriage would accomplish. While it was entirely possible Adelaide cringed every time her manipulative overbearing mother entered the room, he was fairly certain no one at Moonacre Park could cause her to cry with their mere existence. So why Lydia? The girl wasn't always the sharpest mind in the room, but she was very sweet and incredibly loyal. She would never have said or done anything to Adelaide, at least not on purpose. One never knew when a person had hidden issues waiting to be stumbled upon by an unsuspecting person, though. That was why Trent was careful to keep his social interactions as light as possible. He had close friends, but they were carefully selected.

"How is married life treating you?"

Trent looked up to find someone who decidedly didn't make the list of close friends. Mr. Givendale would be one of those who would ignore the unspoken signal of the book.

"Splendid," Trent lied. "I happen to be waiting here for a delivery to take back to surprise my wife."

Givendale smirked and adjusted the sleeve of his almost too closely tailored blue coat. "Why not have it sent to the house so you wouldn't have to leave your new bride?"

Trent turned the page in his book, making a point of looking at the pages. "I didn't want to risk her coming across the delivery without me. I wish to give it to her myself."

"I hear she's quite striking. You'd think someone that memorable would have been recognized by someone, but no one knows who she is." As rude as he was loud, the obnoxious man settled into the chair to Trent's left.

"She's my wife." Trent tried actually reading the book to see if the movement of his eyes would convince the other man to leave. It wasn't that Trent wasn't willing to talk to anybody today, he just didn't particularly want to talk to Givendale. Perhaps he could abandon the book and make his way into the billiard room. If Givendale followed, Trent could accidentally skewer him with a cue stick.

"Is she a lady?"

"Of course she is. She's married to me." Trent snapped his book shut in a rare show of irritation and rose. "I'm going to get a drink."

Givendale raised his light brown eyebrows toward the edge of his carefully waved and waxed dark blond hair, looking at the porter who had just passed them and could easily have gotten Trent's drink. But the man didn't say anything and he didn't rise, so Trent left him there to go in search of a drink he really didn't want.

Was this what life was going to be? A series of doing things he didn't want to do in order to keep himself from thinking about the fact that he didn't know how to do what he needed to do?

He got a glass of port and joined a casual game of whist. The conversation was general with no mention of his home or his wife. It was exactly what he'd thought he wanted, yet he found himself having to make a conscious effort to go through the proper motions. Obviously he wanted to be elsewhere—he just didn't know where that was.

Mixed feelings shot through him when the package finally arrived with the setting sun. Part of him was eager to get home and see if Adelaide liked the gift, but the rest of him still wanted to avoid his wife. Some delusional part of him believed if he pretended she wasn't there, he would wake up and discover he was still a bachelor.

He took out one of the calling cards. *Lady Trent Hawthorne* strode across the stiff card in black script. It was there. Undeniable. Real.

It was time for him to grow up and make the best of it, become a man in at least a few aspects of the word. Life wasn't going to change, and he really missed enjoying his breakfast. He would like his wife to feel as if she could leave her room for breakfast. Not that he blamed her for not coming down anymore. As he had yet to appear at her bedroom door at night, it stood to reason she wouldn't want to see him in the morning.

With renewed if shaky resolve, Trent stabbed his arms into his greatcoat and strode home, unwilling to wait around for a hack to be called. Energy spilled through him, lengthening his stride until he was nearly running toward home, though he had no idea what to do when he got there.

The thought pulled him to a stop at the corner of Berkeley Street and Bruton Place. Intention was all well and good, but what was he actually going to do?

A wagon rolled down the street next to him, rattling over the cobbles and jarring him from his introspection. He continued strolling home, though with less power than before. God had put him into this situation, so Trent was just going to have to trust that God was going to tell him what to do next.

~

Adelaide's afternoon in the kitchens had gone better than she'd expected. The staff had welcomed her with smiles and pulled a chair up to the worn worktable for her. She'd stayed to visit with them after eating the snack they put in front of her, even helping Mrs. Harris knead bread. The time had been very educational. Aside from learning the proper way to punch a pile of dough, she learned that Digby, the groom, had started his working life as a chimney sweep before moving to the considerably cleaner and less hazardous job of mucking stalls. She also learned that Lydia and Finch had grown up near each other before going into domestic service. They'd occasionally bumped into each other when they visited with their mothers and that was how their romance was born. It was all very sweet, but she still couldn't bring herself to look at Lydia's extended front. The idea that her maid was going to have a child and Adelaide wasn't was depressing.

Adelaide even learned more about her own maid, having had no idea that Rebecca had an affinity for licorice candy. It was an insignificant detail, but it made her feel connected to the weird little group that had formed a strange sort of family in the servants' quarters of the town house.

She would probably have to look into hiring a cook soon, and it would be an added difficulty finding one that would work well with the existing staff. Mrs. Harris had been overseeing the meal preparation for Trent since he moved in, a simple enough task when the man frequently ate dinner at his club or one social engagement or another. But they were married now and more meals would be taken at home, and eventually they might even have guests. Assuming she ever saw her husband again, of course. She wasn't about to invite anyone over so they could see that she'd been exiled in her own home.

As the afternoon wore into evening, she waited expectantly for Fenton to relay the day's message from Lord Trent.

Today, however, there had been no message for her. Nor had Mrs. Harris received word that he was planning to dine elsewhere, which meant that he would likely be coming home for dinner. Determined not to miss him, Adelaide plopped herself in the dining room to await her husband.

The servants hadn't let her wait alone.

She'd started out playing Patience since it could be played on her own, spreading the cards out along the table so that it didn't feel quite so empty. Before long Mabel, the parlormaid, asked to join her, followed by Oswyn, the footman, and they'd started a simple game of Maw, using the silver utensils from the sideboard as markers. After the first round, Fenton joined in, and before long most of the staff were seated around the dining room table. It was somewhat amusing to see a pile of gleaming flatware in the middle of the table. And since none of it represented real money, they were making the most ridiculous wagers and taking outlandish risks with their card play. She hadn't had so much fun in weeks. Maybe even years.

"Hullo?" a voice called from the main hall.

Adelaide jerked at the sound of her husband's voice and darted a look at Fenton. The butler was in the dining room playing cards instead of manning his post, and it was her fault. Trent had said she wasn't allowed to fire any of them, but that didn't mean that he couldn't.

"We're in here, my lord!" Fenton called, never taking his eyes from his cards while he decided which one to play.

Trent entered the room and didn't even blink at the scene he found. "Ah, Silver Maw. Who's winning?"

Adelaide blinked. They'd done this before? No wonder Oswyn had been so quick to suggest they pull out the silver.

Fenton glanced up. "My lady is rather good at this, my lord. You'll definitely want to partner with her at your mother's card party in a few weeks."

Adelaide blinked again. She was going to a card party? But she'd already exhausted her entire repertoire of card games.

"Mother's having a card party? I didn't even know they'd arrived in Town." Trent shrugged his coat off and draped it over the back of a dining chair before settling into the seat next to her. He placed his arm along the back of her chair, leaned in to look at her cards, and grinned at the rest of the players. "I'm afraid all of you are doomed."

Adelaide looked at her cards. They were rubbish. She had nothing worth playing and expected to lose every trick.

Fenton narrowed his eyes in Trent's direction before looking at Adelaide, obviously trying to discern her hand from Trent's statement. "Your mother has not yet arrived, but she sent word to her staff in Town to prepare for a gathering and that invitations have been delivered to the most essential guests."

Essential guests? Adelaide had never been considered essential anywhere. Convenient, yes, but never essential. The idea caused panic to curl her toes in her slippers. That was easily ignored, though, as her brain was entirely taken up by the confusing man who was her husband. Fortunately her cards were nothing of note, and as long as she made sure to follow suit, no one would notice that she wasn't applying anything anyone could remotely call a strategy to her playing choices.

What was Trent thinking? He'd ignored her for days, essentially acting as if he didn't have a wife, and now he wanted to watch her play a simple game of cards? Looking over her shoulder as if this were a leisurely family evening?

Her fingers curled tighter around the cards, and the worn edges bit into her palm. She leaned away from the warmth emanating from Trent's body and sucked slow, steady breaths between her teeth. She'd been ignored a lot growing up, and more often than not she'd found comfort in assuring herself that as long as she was being ignored she at least wasn't disappointing anyone. Her parents had hoped for a boy when anticipating her birth, so she'd never really blamed them for not having much use for her.

This man was her husband, though. He didn't have a single viable reason for ignoring her until her presence was convenient, yet that appeared to be his intention.

She slid her card carefully onto the table so as not to display the desire to chuck the whole hand—along with the mass of silver in the middle of the table—at her husband's head.

The hand finished and the servants rose to return the silver to the cabinet, moving back to their jobs as if they'd often taken this kind of interlude. Maybe they did. They seemed to know their place in the house, know what they were to do, where they were to go. She never thought she'd be even the slightest bit jealous of anything a maid had, but there was no denying that she was jealous of the servants' comfort and security.

"I got you something." Trent pulled a small package from his pocket and set it on the table in front of her.

Her heart pounded as the muscles in her middle relaxed. What did it mean? Was it an apology gift? Was he regretting the distance of the past week? Perhaps she'd been too hard on him in her mind. This wasn't the marriage he'd grown up expecting, after all. Unlike her. She'd always expected her marriage would be little more than a business arrangement. Such a thing would be convenient for her father, after all. She hadn't even been all that surprised when her mother had played an underhanded part in the situation.

The string tying the package closed slid away easily and she was soon staring at a small stack of stiff cream-colored cards.

Lady Trent Hawthorne.

It was the correct form of formal address, she knew. It was what everyone expected. It was what she'd expected. It didn't make any sense to resent the fact that the new calling cards he'd gotten her looked more his than hers. Not only did she not have a husband in anything beyond a legal sense, but now she didn't even have her own name.

Adelaide was no more.

The anger that had simmered in her chest since his arrival spewed forth in a volcano of hurt and frustration she'd never experienced before and certainly never come close to unleashing before. He dared to bring her this. After leaving her to wander the rooms of this house for days with only his staff for company, he expected her to be delighted over the fact that she now got to use his name.

Delight was not what she felt.

"They're lovely." Adelaide pushed the stack of cards back at him. "When you have a wife, I'm sure she'll be happy to use them."

Chapter 10

He didn't leave the dining room for hours. Eventually he rose from his seat and paced to the window and back. He leaned on the back of the abandoned chair, the wall, the sideboard—anything in the room that was capable of holding his weight—but always, always his eyes strayed back to the stack of cards still sitting on the table. The servants were worried about him, finding any and every excuse to walk past the open dining room door. Even Mrs. Harris refused to take the opportunity to admonish his choices.

And his choices were definitely at fault here.

With the sun long gone and the single candle Fenton had left him threatening to gutter out, Trent finally left the room to meander toward the leather chair he'd already spent too much time in. He didn't know what to do. Though they'd been little more than strangers before, somehow they had managed to grow even further apart. He was still adjusting to the fact that this marriage was real, that nothing was going to come and magically take it away—that this was his life now, and he couldn't go back.

He'd finally accepted the truth, but how was he going to convince Adelaide of that fact? Would anything he did now be seen as genuine effort instead of simply a reaction to her cutting outburst?

As he passed through the hall on the way to the stairs, a collection of calling cards on the silver platter by the door caught his eye. When he had been a bachelor, people rarely felt the need to drop their cards by to let him know that they'd arrived back in Town. Word of his marriage must be spreading for people to start the formal observance with him now. That or they were hoping to be among the first to receive a visit from his wife.

His wife who hadn't been able to do any calling of her own because he'd been so busy trying to pretend she didn't need to.

And now that she was trying to pretend the same thing, he realized just how badly he'd handled the entire situation.

Longing for a distraction, and perhaps even a miracle, he flipped through the cards to see who had stopped by.

One familiar name caught his eye and made him groan and laugh at the same time. His Grace, the Duke of Riverton. With a handwritten note along the bottom that said he wanted to let Trent know he was back in town but didn't want to disturb the newly married bliss.

If only he knew.

The fact that Griffith was now only a brief walk instead of a grueling daylong ride away started an itch under Trent's skin. For as long as he could remember, when Trent hadn't known what to do he'd asked Griffith. Trent knew his brother wasn't God and that, despite his steadfast personality and rock-solid presence, the man had made a mistake or two in his life, but his advice was rarely wrong. Griffith had a way of cutting to the heart of the matter, simplifying an issue until a person knew exactly what he needed to do.

If ever an issue needed simplifying, it was this one. In a matter of days Trent had made one complicated mess of his life and marriage, and it needed to get sorted out. Tonight, if possible.

His hat still hung where he'd placed it on the hooks by the front door when entering. Someone, likely Fenton, had retrieved Trent's greatcoat from the dining room and hung it beside his hat. A tall clock stood next to the hooks, the hands pointing to an hour somewhere between ridiculously late and insanely early, depending upon one's perspective. Waiting until true morning wouldn't hurt anything, but the restlessness and desperation that had driven him to pace the confines of the dining room for hours were now pushing him out the door. He'd reached the edges of Grosvenor Square before he even knew he'd made up his mind to go.

The imposing yet familiar front of Hawthorne House was unsurprisingly dark when Trent bounded his way up the steps. His knock was still answered promptly, though by a footman instead of Gibson, the butler—further proof that Trent had lost his grip on what was considered polite and appropriate at this hour.

"My lord?" The footman stepped back to allow Trent to enter, but he looked poised to run around waking the house for what he probably assumed was an emergency.

"My brother is back in Town, is he not?" Trent shucked his hat and coat and handed them to the anxious footman, whose name he couldn't quite remember. Odd that he knew everyone on his own staff but not here. It really wasn't home for him anymore.

"Yes, my lord, but I'm afraid he's already retired for the evening. Shall I wake him for you?"

Trent rolled his shoulders, trying to ease the desperate tension. "Don't bother. I believe I'll stay here for the night. Please leave a message for Cook that there will be another for breakfast." When only one Hawthorne was in residence, the staff didn't lay out a spread on the sideboard, instead fixing a plentiful plate of the family member's favorites. Trent had been beyond lucky to have avoided the notice of footpads on the way over here. He wasn't chancing a walk back to his own house tonight. And since he had high hopes of finding the solution to his problem within the next hour, he wanted breakfast in the morning.

A good breakfast to welcome the promise of a new day.

"Very good, sir. Can I get you anything?" The footman looked confused. Griffith liked to have someone manning the door at all hours of the night in case urgent news arrived, but whatever footman drew the duty rarely had to do more than polish a few extra pieces of silver.

"No. I can see to myself." Trent ran up the stairs before the servant could respond. He walked right past the door to his old room and down the passage to his brother's. The elegance and grandeur of the corridor caught his attention like it never had before. Growing up this had simply been home. The gilded frames, spotlessly polished wall sconces, and gleaming floors were things to walk past, not be admired at length.

But Trent now stopped in front of a tall vase on a narrow table. The artful arrangement of flowers and branches nearly reached the ceiling. Why hadn't he put such beautiful things in his own home? Trent had made an effort in a few rooms because his mother and sisters had insisted, but by and large he'd left the place in its semi-neglected state of genteel poverty. Hawthorne House might not feel like home anymore, but he wasn't all that certain his place in Mount Street felt like home either. If he'd been waiting until he found the person to share his future before he made his home, where did that leave him? Sitting on threadbare sofas until he settled things with Adelaide? Sipping from mismatched teacups for the rest of his life because she would never forgive him for ignoring her the week after they were married?

Trent pushed open the door at the end of the corridor. He needed to talk to Griffith, and it wasn't going to wait the seven hours until proper morning visits commenced.

A large lump lay under the simple blue bed coverings. It looked like a mountain in the middle of the room. A light snore reached Trent's ears, proving that Griffith had more than gone to his room for the night. He'd actually gone to bed.

The kind thing to do would be to slip quietly back out of the room and let the man sleep. Fortunately, loving brothers didn't always have to be kind to each other.

Trent took two quick steps and launched himself into the air, landing on the mattress and sending the slumbering mountain bouncing across the bed while the bindings holding the mattress up creaked in protest.

Snuffles and snorts accompanied muttered half words as Griffith grappled with sudden wakefulness. Trent turned on his side and propped his head in his hand, taking care to plaster an enormous grin on his face.

Griffith pushed the covers down and ran his large hands over his face, blinking in the dim light coming through the not-quite-closed curtains. His voice was rough and thick, and it took two attempts to get a single word out. "Trent?"

"Last time I looked in a mirror, yes."

The deliberate blinks Griffith used to focus himself and complete the waking-up process reminded Trent of Adelaide's blinks. Those infernal, distracting blinks that did strange things to his insides that he was going to have to live with for the rest of his life. He flopped down onto his back and covered his own face with his hands.

Griffith's groan as he sat up in the bed sounded like rocks tumbling over each other. "What are you doing in my bed?"

Trent uncovered his face and turned to look at his brother. "I need to talk to you."

"And it couldn't wait until morning?"

"I'm afraid not." Trent sat up as well until he was shoulder to shoulder with his brother, a man who'd stepped in to fill the role of father, though he couldn't even grow whiskers at the time. "I've created a bit of a tragedy, Griffith."

Griffith's face lost all signs of sleepiness as he snapped his head around to frown in Trent's direction. "Are you well? Mother? Georgina? Miranda?"

"No, no, nothing like that. I'm well." Trent raised his hands to calm Griffith's sudden worry. "Last I heard our family is all healthy as well."

A grunt that bordered on a sigh was Griffith's only response as he turned to drop his feet over the side of the bed. "Well, if we are going to have a conversation, let's have it elsewhere. I find having you in my bed rather awkward."

Trent bounced up from the mattress. "Agreed. Would you like me to wait in the upstairs parlor?"

Griffith shrugged into his dressing gown and shook his head. "The study. I prefer to surround myself with manliness when I converse in my dressing gown."

"You do this frequently?" Trent's eyes widened. He knew he hadn't kept up with all the demands on his brother after their father died, but did dukes truly have many middle-of-the-night conversations in their dressing gowns?

"No," Griffith muttered, "but I have decided that manly surroundings will be a rule for any future occasions."

Trent grinned—a real grin born of a spark of good humor. Coming to Griffith had been the right thing to do. "Very well. I shall meet you in the study."

Griffith's study was almost as familiar to Trent as his own. More so, in some ways. Griffith had inherited the room at ten years old. Since then the brothers had spent many a day sitting in the old leather chairs, mulling over the important things in life like frogs and puddings while pretending to be adults. Then they'd actually become adults and the mullings over life had gotten more serious.

Theological debates aside, though, Trent didn't think they'd ever discussed something as personal as this.

Griffith tightened the sash on his dressing gown as he entered the study and collapsed into a chair. With one hand he rubbed the last of the sleep from his green eyes and with the other pushed his dark blond hair back off his forehead. "Talk."

The urge to pace was tough to quell, but Trent made himself sit in the matching chair and face his failure like a man. "I've ruined my marriage."

"I couldn't have even traveled to Scotland and back in the amount of time you've been married. What on earth happened?"

"Well, if you had taken the mail coach and turned right back at the border you could probably have gone to Scotland and back. It would be close." Trent plucked at a piece of grass that had gotten stuck to his trouser leg when he cut across Grosvenor Square.

"Trent."

There was no sigh, no rolling of the eyes, nothing to mark Griffith's frustration over Trent's delay. The simple utterance of his name was all it took to convey the sentiment that had become something of a mantra for their family. Their mother had said it first after quietly telling them their father had died, his heart simply stopping while he slept. Griffith had repeated it before getting in their uncle's carriage to hie off to Eton. He'd said it again when Trent took the same ride to join him. It had been Trent's turn to remind Griffith the first time he took his seat in the House of Lords. The admonishment had always been the same—that they would face reality with God at their side and England beneath their feet and do what they could to make the world better.

Right now Trent didn't find it very comforting. He dug his fingers into the arms of the chair, watching the skin around his fingernails whiten as he pressed the wooden trim. "I don't know what I did. I think it's more what I didn't do."

"Which is?" Griffith rubbed his forefinger up and down along the edge of his thumb, the only sign that Trent's slow answers were perturbing his older brother.

"Nothing. I've done nothing." Trent gave in to the desire to pace and strolled over to the desk and picked up a large, round paperweight. The black marble ball was cold and heavy, grounding Trent in the moment. "I've ignored her."

Griffith cleared his throat. "Completely?"

"Yes." Trent rolled the ball from hand to hand and leaned one hip against the desk. "I didn't want to believe I was married. Still don't, for that matter."

One thick blond eyebrow climbed, and Trent knew he was about to be handed the Word of God in such a way that he was going to feel ridiculous for not having turned to it himself. "'The lip of truth shall be established for ever: but a lying tongue is but for a moment.'"

Griffith had always liked the book of Proverbs. Trent placed the weight back on the desk, knowing the time for lying was over, even if he'd only been lying to himself. "Well, when you put it like that."

Trent crossed back to the chairs. He placed his forearms on the back of the old upholstered wingback and stared into the cold fireplace. "I suppose my moment caught up with me today, then. The thing is, this isn't what I thought my marriage would be. I always pictured myself taking my time, courting my wife through the Season, maybe even longer."

Griffith sighed and leaned his head against the back of the chair. "What's stopping you?"

Trent really should have let Griffith sleep, because apparently his mind was addled by the middle-of-the-night interruption despite his ability to quote Scripture. "I've already got a wife, Griffith."

The raising of a single eyebrow called Trent's intelligence into question and made him want to plop down in the chair and sulk. The words that followed knocked the breath from his lungs. "I guess you can take your time courting her, then, can't you."

Chapter 11

Adelaide wallowed deeper into the mattress and tucked the covers in around her shoulders, determined to stay abed until morning. She had no idea what time it was, and the drapes had been pulled tightly together, blocking out any attempts the rising sun might be making to light the room. It had to be morning, though. She'd been staring at the ceiling so long that time must have passed.

Still, she was going to stay in bed until Rebecca arrived. The maid had been wide-eyed but silent during Adelaide's nightly routine, not saying a word about the fact that the numerous negligees Adelaide had continued to wear in an effort to pretend her marriage was normal had been replaced by the oldest, softest cotton night rail Adelaide owned. The comfortable sleeping gown should have made it easier to stay in bed, but instead it only served as a reminder of the pique she'd been in the night before.

She'd begun to regret her outspoken behavior before Rebecca had even left the room. Regretting the words didn't mean she knew what to do, however. She'd had plenty of time to consider her options, though, since she wasn't about to seek him out in the dark, quiet house. She would wait until breakfast, when they were seated in a nearly public room, to make things right.

Her fingers curled around the edge of the coverlet, and she

moved it aside to stare across the room at the dark shadow that was the door connecting her room with his. Was he sleeping? Watching his windows for the sun's permission to rise, as she was? Had he sat up last night, waiting for her to come apologize? He had to know she'd never seek him out in his bedroom. If she'd been willing to do such a thing she'd have done it days ago. Then they might not have had last night's incident at all.

A light sleep finally overtook her tired brain, but Rebecca's quiet early morning movements had her flying from the bed like a freed raven. She dressed quickly but sat still long enough for Rebecca to take extra care with her hair.

Adelaide's mother had never let anyone, including her husband, see her at anything less than her best. Adelaide had never taken quite so much pride in her appearance—mostly because it never lasted past the door of her dressing room—but it couldn't hurt to show a bit more consideration for her position as the wife of a duke's son.

Rebecca tried to curl the short hairs falling over Adelaide's forehead and brushing the edges of her eyebrows, but the short hairs only sprang into a strange band of loops around her face. She considered leaving her spectacles off but decided tripping down the stairs wouldn't make an advantageous impression, so she left them on as she hurried from the room.

She hadn't been down to breakfast since their first morning in the house. Hopefully he would see her presence this morning as a sort of peace offering.

The first sight to greet her was a trunk.

Her feet stumbled to a halt three steps from the hall floor, eyes glued to the traveling trunk. The rather large traveling trunk.

She took the last three steps slowly, swallowing hard at the evidence before her. A rather large traveling trunk that she recognized as belonging to her husband.

A slight burn preceded the pool of wetness across her lower

eyelid. She blinked it away, sinking her teeth into her lower lip in hopes that the sharp bite would grant her some composure. Until yesterday he'd been willing to ignore her from underneath the same roof. If she'd ever needed more proof that life was easier if you just let everyone else have their way, this was it. A single moment of standing up for herself and she was doomed to be a married widow. Or would she be a married spinster? Surely they had a term for women whose husbands deserted them after hardly more than a week, and Adelaide was sure to learn it, even if she only heard it whispered behind nearby fans.

In her hurry to get to the breakfast room and try to rectify the situation, she tripped over her own feet and caught herself on a nearby table, knocking over a candle that had been guttered out but still contained a pool of melted wax in the top. Wax that now graced the hem of Adelaide's morning dress. With a sigh, Adelaide righted the candle and continued at a more sedate pace to the breakfast room. At least the wax was a translucent white. No one was likely to notice, particularly once she was seated and the smudged hemline was safely hidden beneath the table.

He was standing at the window, much as he had been their first morning in London. In some ways it seemed like years had passed in hardly more than a week, and at other times it felt like mere hours. Despite his presence, there were no place settings waiting on the table, no food on the sideboard. Only him, standing at the window, outlined by the early morning light, and looking as handsome and athletic as a young woman could ever hope her husband to be.

Adelaide would have traded all of that handsomeness for a bit of direction on what type of marriage they were to have. Or rather a different direction than the trunk in the hall seemed to be pointing them.

His head turned toward her as his body stayed angled toward the window. A thick lock of hair fell across his forehead as his green eyes met hers and he smiled.

The dimples appeared in his cheeks as his lips curled and displayed straight, white teeth. She swallowed hard. Perhaps she wouldn't trade all of the handsomeness.

Mrs. Harris bustled in with a frown before Trent could say anything. A grimace crossed Trent's face before he turned back toward the window.

Adelaide turned questioning eyes back to the housekeeper. "Good morning?"

The housekeeper plopped her hands on her narrow hips and sniffed. "If it is, it won't be on account of Lord Trent. Thinking like a man today, he is."

Adelaide blinked. "Well, I should hope so."

Trent's laughter burst across the room, effectively cutting off any tirade Mrs. Harris had been planning. A small, indulgent tilt of the housekeeper's lips was followed by a shrug. "I suppose that's true. We can't expect anything else of them, can we? He probably even had another man agree that this preposterous idea was a good one. Will you be taking breakfast down here then, my lady? Would you like me to fix you something particular?"

Adelaide hated not knowing what was going on. Had she been in a normal house, with servants who at least pretended to mind their own business, she wouldn't have any notion that her husband had cooked up a potentially preposterous scheme. But now she did. And she had no idea how long she would have to wait until learning what it was. Her gaze tripped from the housekeeper to her husband and back again. "I'm not very particular. Whatever Lord Trent is having will suit me."

"Well, I wouldn't know what he's having, seeing as he felt the need to have breakfast elsewhere this morning." She sniffed in Trent's direction before turning a smile back to Adelaide. "I'll fix you my specialty." Mrs. Harris strode toward the door with purpose.

Leaving Adelaide alone with her husband. A husband who had

apparently eaten breakfast elsewhere this morning. She wasn't sure what to do with that information.

Trent stepped forward and pulled out a chair for Adelaide, even as he frowned at the door Mrs. Harris had walked through. "There's no law against a man eating two breakfasts," he grumbled.

A giggle threatened to climb up Adelaide's throat, but it was squashed by the reminder that she still didn't know where the man had eaten that morning.

Adelaide cleared her throat and waited as Oswyn set a cup of coffee down in front of her. Once he'd left the room, she turned to her husband, who had settled in the seat to her left. "Where . . . That is, er, um . . ." She swallowed and blinked at her coffee. "You've already had breakfast?"

Trent nodded, taking a sip of the tea the footman had brought him. "At Hawthorne House. I stayed there after talking to Griffith last night."

Tension Adelaide hadn't fully realized she'd been holding seeped away. It was perfectly acceptable to have breakfast with his brother, if a bit odd. It had been rather late when Adelaide left him in the dining room last night, and he'd given no indication that he had any intention of leaving the house again.

Adelaide ran a finger on the curve of her coffee cup handle. "Was it business?"

"No. Our discussion was of a considerably more personal nature."

"Oh."

Had she really wished to spend more time with her husband? If this morning was any indication, they were better off apart. Yet they'd had such a nice time in the ruins before they were, well, ruined. And the ride to church their first morning in London had been awkward but pleasant. For the most part, anyway. Why couldn't they get back to that?

Trent cleared his throat. "The thing is, Adelaide, I've decided to eat breakfast there for a while."

That explained the traveling trunk in the front hall. Adelaide took a gulp of coffee, wishing her food had arrived so she'd have something more substantial to focus on. "I see."

"You've never had a Season, Adelaide."

And now she wouldn't even have a marriage. Not a real one. She nodded, not knowing what to say. She'd spoken her mind last night and he'd moved out. What would he do if she said anything this morning?

He cleared his throat again, and Adelaide tilted her head so she could watch him fidget with his coat sleeves out of the corner of her eye. "Well, I'd like to give you that."

Her head jerked up so fast that her spectacles tumbled off her nose. Trent's arm jerked forward to catch them before they could clatter to the table. Gentle hands slid them back onto her face, smoothing the loose tendrils of hair away from the earpieces. Adelaide's heart thundered in her chest, the blood making a crackling noise in her ears as too many thoughts crossed her mind, the implications of his statement making no sense to her. "You want me to have a Season?"

⁓

Trent wanted, desperately, to examine the swirls in his teacup. Or perhaps the play of light across the back wall of the breakfast room. Truthfully he wanted to look anywhere besides Adelaide's face, but he had been enough of a coward in this relationship already and he forced his gaze to remain on hers, where he could watch the rapidly changing emotions as she took in his declaration.

He couldn't blame her for any of them, even though she was too composed for him to decipher the flickers of emotion with any sort of confidence.

Oswyn delivered a plate piled high with Mrs. Harris's best breakfast offerings. The dark frown as he looked back and forth between them let Trent know what the servants thought of his plan.

He'd tried to keep it quiet this morning, but in a household such as his, no one was going to let Finch pack Trent's trunk without learning exactly where the master of the house was intending to go.

Not that Trent felt much like the master of anything right now, much less his own household.

Adelaide looked down at her plate, blinking as if she couldn't imagine where the food would have come from. Eventually she picked up a fork and poked at a piece of ham. "Are we talking about a proper Season?"

"Yes. No. Well, after a fashion." Trent rubbed a hand along the back of his neck. Somehow his decision that seemed so brilliant at dawn now felt weak and foolish as he tried to find the words to explain his plan. "You'll still be married to me."

She glanced up at him without lifting her face. "Comforting."

The dry comment had Trent choking on a chuckle. Now wasn't the time to laugh, but it was nice to know that there was some wit buried inside his quiet wife, though he'd had little doubt of that after her cutting remark the evening before.

Part of him wanted to tell her she was safe, that she was free to unleash the woman he saw glimpses of when she was caught off guard by the unexpected. What if the hidden woman was like her mother, though? He'd take sullen solitude over living with a power-hungry she-wolf any day.

He cleared his throat and gave in to the desire to look down into his tea, afraid she would look up and see disdain on his face and think it was meant for her instead of her family—if she was indeed different than the other women in her family. Pain stabbed behind his ears as he clenched his jaw together. No matter her parentage, they were married and he needed to accept that. "What I mean is that I'd like to get to know you."

She cut the ham with slow, steady swipes of her knife. "And you feel the best way to do that is to move out of the house?"

A burning sensation touched his ears, and he struggled against the urge to shift his hair so that it covered the tips, which were likely reddening. His heart beat faster, as if he were in the boxing ring instead of his breakfast room. Her breakfast room? If he was moving out, even temporarily, should he think of the things in the house as hers instead of his?

He shook his head and leaned forward to brace his forearms on the tables, clasping his hands loosely together, hoping he looked sincere and earnest instead of desperate. "I would like to court you."

She froze, the precise square of ham dangling from her fork halfway between the plate and her lips. Her head lifted and she blinked at him. Blinks that were as slow and steady as her knife had been moments before. Blinks that seemed to cut through his simple statement to the fear beneath. Fear that this plan wouldn't work. Because if it didn't, he was out of ideas.

"If that is how you wish to do it." She gave a slight nod and turned back to her breakfast.

Trent stared at her, watching her eat until his eyes began to burn. That was it? That was all she was going to say? What did she think of the idea? Had she already given up hope that they could have a good marriage? Had she ever had that hope in the first place?

"How—" He snapped his teeth shut. If he asked her how she felt about it, he would look insecure. And he didn't want to. As much as he wanted to fall in love with his wife, he needed her to fall in love with him as well. Part of him was more concerned about her feelings than his. If she loved him, she'd care more about the marriage than their social standing and she wouldn't push him to try to be more than the happy-go-lucky man everyone thought him to be.

Whereas if he loved her more than she loved him, what would that drive him to do? Take a greater interest in his estates? Apply himself to improving their standing? Would he do things that were better suited to a duke than a second son? Would he prove himself capable and put Griffith in danger?

Not that there was much danger of Trent being a better duke than his brother, given that God had chosen Griffith to take over the dukedom at the tender age of ten, but Trent knew God saw things men did not, and if He saw greater potential in Trent, what would happen to Griffith?

No, it was more important that Adelaide become at least infatuated quickly, before Trent became too emotionally invested and hatched more foolish plans in order to win her heart.

She was watching him. How long had she been watching him? Had she said anything?

"I'm sorry. Did you say something?" Trent winced. Ignoring her at the breakfast table was not a good beginning to their courtship.

Her face remained stoic. "I said if you aren't sure of the *how*, you could borrow my deportment book. It was Helena's, but mother gave it to me when Helena married. Left it on my bed one night, actually."

"Your deportment book?"

She shrugged and looked down at her plate. "The instructions would be from the female's perspective obviously, but it would stand to reason that you could deduce the male side of the interactions from the descriptions."

They wrote books telling women how to be courted? "I'll remember your offer. Thank you."

The words came out stilted, but what else could he say? One side of her mouth tilted up a bit and he felt considerably less regret over the awkward exchange. Much better to leave her with a smile, even a minuscule one, than a perplexed frown.

"I'll pick you up this afternoon to go riding then, shall I?" Trent could make this romantic. He would sweep her off her feet and give her the experiences and attention she would have gotten if she'd had a Season. Should have gotten many years before now, given the standing of her family.

She nodded but didn't look up from her plate. "If you wish."

Trent stood and adjusted his coat sleeves, wishing there was something he could do now, but courtship rules didn't include breakfast for very obvious reasons. "Yes. Well, then. I'll just . . . be off. I suppose."

The walk through the house felt strange. He hadn't thought the shabby rooms felt like home before, but now he was second-guessing his decision to move his residence, even temporarily. Mrs. Harris was standing by his trunk, frowning.

Her disapproval strengthened his weakening resolve. "I'll be back this afternoon."

"See that you are."

"You will support me in this, Mrs. Harris."

Her eyes widened, and one hand went to her throat before falling to her side. Her posture straightened and she looked more like a servant than he'd ever seen her. "Yes, my lord."

Trent had never felt the need or desire to exert his position in this house, and the fact that he'd done so now surprised him. He'd taken comfort in his unconventional servants, knowing that any man who ran his house thusly wasn't fit to be a duke.

He didn't want to lose that comfort now, so he stepped forward and wrapped the thin housekeeper in a hug, leaving her open-mouthed in shock as he fled out the door. His plan was going to work. It had to.

Chapter 12

Six hours later, Trent was practically shaking as he stared at his front door. He hadn't been this nervous on his wedding day. Somehow that hadn't felt quite as life changing as this moment standing before his own front door.

Trent smoothed his cravat and glanced back at the curricle he'd had Griffith's grooms polish to a high gleam. The horses were brushed until every hair shone in the sun. Even the harness buckles twinkled in the afternoon light. This courtship was a guaranteed success—he was already married to the woman, after all—but right now it didn't feel like a sure thing.

The normal goal of a courtship was to win the lady's hand in marriage, but Trent needed to win her heart and, in some weird way, try to give away his own. Neither of those things was a foregone conclusion. All of the ways this endeavor could fail suddenly punched their way into his mind. She'd seemed to be in agreement when he left this morning, even if it was a resigned sort of agreement. What would he do if she rejected him? Move back into the house? By living at Hawthorne House he hoped to give this courtship as authentic a feel as possible, but did that leave too much room for failure?

He knocked on the door.

It swung open to reveal Fenton looking as unsure as Trent felt. Was that because Adelaide had some sudden hesitation or because Trent was visiting his own house?

"Er, please come in, my lord. My lady has bid you await her in the drawing room as she's not quite ready yet." Fenton opened the door wide and gestured Trent in with a sweep of his hand.

Relief sagged Trent's shoulders as he crossed the threshold. She was coming. That was good.

He walked into the drawing room as if he owned the place—which he did, but that wasn't how he'd intended to play this game. Not that it mattered unless Adelaide was in the room.

"Can I get you anything, my lord?" Fenton asked from the doorway.

Trent declined without much thought. His focus was on the pile of fabric that looked like his drapes and the warped metal rod that had once held them on the wall. What had happened? When had it happened? He'd been avoiding his wife with such diligence that he hadn't stepped foot in this room all week. He'd heard that some women went into frenzies when they were upset, hitting people, throwing things, destroying furniture. Had she done this in a fit of pique? If so, why start in the front rooms, where any visitor would see the damage right off? He had to admit that the room was better off for the loss of the old and faded drapes, but there had to have been a simpler way to remove them.

The click of the door latch opening distracted him from the window dressings, and he whirled around to see Adelaide standing in the door, her hair swept up into a simple knot on her head, those thick locks still hanging over her forehead, curling against the tops of her spectacles and framing her eyes. Trent knew it was highly out of fashion, but he rather hoped she kept the look. It suited her. Her dress was light blue with darker blue embroidery across the bodice. The skirt was sheer over a dark blue underskirt. Her eyes looked wide behind their lenses, brightened by the matching blue of her unbuttoned spencer.

Trent tried to speak, but his mouth had gone dry. Why hadn't he asked Fenton for some tea? He could certainly use it now. It took a bit of work, but eventually his tongue freed itself and he blurted out, "You're lovely."

The inelegance of the compliment made him wince, but the light blush that ran up her neck to her cheeks proved she found nothing wrong with his delivery. Maybe the lack of charm had leant it a note of sincerity. Still, he was going to endeavor to show a bit more sophistication.

"Would you care to go for a ride?"

Her brows drew together, and she blinked at him. "Isn't that the purpose of this . . . visit? Are you visiting?"

"Yes, I rather thought I was. I mean, I suppose I could court you from the next room over, but that loses a bit of the intent, I would think." Trent shifted his weight and adjusted his hold on his hat. Last night he'd thought his plan brilliant. This morning he'd still been convinced of its cleverness. Now, faced with the actual execution of his plan, it looked like the plot of a mad man. He'd be lucky if she didn't try to have him committed.

"I know you said you've never courted anyone, but is this how it's truly done? I've never heard of such a thing. We're already married. Doesn't that defeat the purpose?" Adelaide settled her bonnet on her head, knocking her spectacles slightly askew. She fixed them, but not before the earpiece pulled a lock of hair out of her bun and left it curling against her shoulder.

The errant curl made him smile and returned to him a modicum of confidence. "I . . . well, frankly I've never heard of such a thing either, but it seemed the thing to do since we missed it the first time around."

Dear God, please let her find the entire concept the slightest bit romantic or at least appealing. He couldn't live with Griffith forever, and he really wanted to return home as the husband and leader of the house. Even if it meant he had to actually take charge of something. He hated to think of having to slink back in simply because his plan had failed.

"I see." Adelaide seemed to consider his words for a while, and then a slow smile spread across her face.

That smile hit Trent in the gut, stealing his ability to speak all over again—along with his ability to breathe. Her smile was wide, her teeth just peeking out from between slightly parted lips, one of the front ones just the slightest bit crooked. And for the first time he was grateful she was his wife. He would never have considered courting someone related to Lady Crampton on his own, but God had allowed the decision to be taken out of his hands, and now this gorgeous creature before him was going to be his for the rest of his life. And if he could make that smile appear more often, it'd be a sign that he was succeeding in his ultimate goal of having a happy wife.

It was a good goal to have in life. One worthy of a husband who hadn't another care in the world other than seeing to the well-being of his family. He offered her his arm. "Shall we go for a ride, then?"

Adelaide slid her small hand into the crook of his elbow. "Yes, I believe we shall."

⁓

Adelaide felt a little absurd as Trent handed her up into the shiny yellow curricle. In all the time spent in the same house they hadn't even managed a good-morning greeting, and now they were going to spend upwards of an hour within the confines of a small vehicle. What were they going to say to each other?

She'd been in his curricle before, on their two trips to church. Her focus, then, had been on her husband and all the people she was soon to meet. Those worries had distracted her from the strangeness of riding in something so high and open. Before coming to London she'd never ridden in anything other than a coach or a landau, safely tucked away with cushioned seats and closed doors. Now she could reach out and touch the wheel while they rolled down the street if she were so inclined.

Not that she could imagine a single scenario in which she'd feel the need to deliberately stick her hand on a moving wheel. The fact that she could, though, made her a little nervous, and she took a moment to make sure her dress was securely tucked underneath her leg. It was the best she could do, though it didn't make her trust the safety of the shiny yellow wheel. With her luck she'd somehow catch her bonnet ribbon in the spokes.

The vehicle dipped and swayed as Trent climbed in on the other side. Adelaide clenched her fingers together to keep from grabbing the side and launching herself out to the pavement.

"Are you comfortable? There's a lap blanket under the seat, if you'd like it." Trent picked up the reins and smoothly directed the horses down the road behind a high-perched phaeton.

Adelaide was suddenly thankful for Trent's more sedate curricle. The wheels on the phaeton were nearly as tall as her head while seated in the curricle. And then to be seated on top of that would be unthinkable.

"No, this is pleasant." And it was. Once the curricle was moving it wasn't so scary. Trent kept the horses at a slow trot, enough to create a soft breeze but not so much to make her uncomfortable.

At least not physically.

The painful silence was another thing altogether, though. The steady clop of the horse hooves was worse than a ticking clock, counting off the moments until one of them broke the silence. The longer it lasted, the more desperate she was to say something but the more profound she felt it needed to be. Breaking such a long silence with a mundane comment on the weather would only draw attention to the fact that they had nothing to talk about.

"Have you ever eaten a tomato?" Trent's words pulled Adelaide's attention from the various buildings they were passing.

She blinked at him. Did the man start every conversation with food? That night in the ruins they'd discussed their least favorite dishes. He declared favorite dishes too common a conversation choice. On the way to London their only conversation of any significant length had debated the merits of the different meat pies and pastries they'd gotten from an inn along the way. Once again he was turning to food to start a conversation.

He glanced at her with a small smile. "Ryland sent Griffith a few, and I had one with breakfast this morning. Mrs. Harris refuses to touch the things, but I'll bring one over if you'd like to try it."

Adelaide ducked her head to hide her silent laughter. She'd read once that the way to an Englishman's heart was through his stomach, but she'd never seen evidence to support that notion before. Her father was certainly more interested in the land that grew the food than the food itself, whereas Trent seemed nearly obsessed with it. At least he seemed obsessed with anything eaten before noon. He'd yet to discuss a single brace of roasted pheasant or bowl of turtle soup. "Why haven't you hired a cook?"

The shifting of his shoulders could have been a shrug or an adjustment of his coat, but there was no question that the rush of red appearing over his cravat was the beginnings of a blush. "Mrs. Harris has been cooking in that house for years. She suits my needs well enough. I brought in a chef to help with a small dinner party I had last year."

Given what little Adelaide knew of the protective housekeeper, another cook in her kitchen might not have gone over well. "How did that go?"

Trent grinned. "He quit before the end of the soup."

They fell into silence, and Adelaide went back to watching London slide by. She recognized some things from her sister's frequent descriptions, but it was soon obvious that Helena had left out many of the more interesting aspects of London architecture. If it didn't have to do with social interactions, it hadn't been worth discussing. A wide, tree-lined dirt path angled off the road in front of them, and Adelaide's heart beat faster, though she wasn't sure if it was trying to hurry the horses along or run in the other direction. This was Rotten Row. Even if she hadn't seen a drawing in a magazine last year she'd have known it from her mother and Helena's excited discussions of who they'd seen and talked to while riding along the popular path.

Tension broke into the easy silence. Even though London wasn't packed for the Season yet, there were still enough of the *ton* in town that the path was scattered with carriages and riders. People were going to see her. They were going to see that while she and Trent were riding together, they weren't having much to do with each other. It was bad enough that the outing didn't feel like one between a husband and wife. She didn't need everyone else knowing it too.

She turned her head and opened her mouth, but nothing came out. She had nothing to say. They could talk about food again. Now that she thought about it, it was a fairly genius contingency topic. After all, everyone ate. "They had tomatoes at the fair last year, but Mother wouldn't let me eat one. She said they were poisonous."

Trent tilted his head to the side, appearing deep in thought. His hair slid out of its slicked-back style to flop boyishly against his temple. As his wife she should feel free to reach up and brush the lock of hair back into place. But there were quite a few things she should feel free to do as his wife that she hadn't been able to do yet.

He turned his face back toward her with a self-assured grin that made her fidget in her seat. "If they are, they're rather slow acting. I had my first one at least ten months ago and haven't felt an adverse effect yet." He pursed his lips together, looking to the sky for answers to the deep questions he appeared to be pondering. "Although I did have a nasty head cold this winter. Do you think I could blame that on the tomatoes?"

Her smile arrived before she realized it was coming. "I'm afraid not. While some scientists believe that the stomach essentially ferments what we eat, I don't think anyone believes the process takes months. We eat too often for that."

Trent's laughter drew the attention of what few people weren't already looking their way. "Do I even want to know why you know about the fermenting theory of digestion?"

Unfortunately her bonnet did not have a very wide brim on the sides, leaving nothing to hide the blush she was very afraid was encroaching. She knew better than to share her collection of strange facts with anyone other than her brother. He found them fascinating, while her mother despaired of the amount of intellectual reading Adelaide had to do to collect them. Her father simply shook his head, knowing he'd started her off on the bizarre hobby and regretting it ever since. Now Trent would know her mind was full of useless information instead of social niceties.

"I must have read it somewhere," she mumbled.

His eyebrows rose as he settled back in the curricle seat, angling himself into the corner and holding the reins in one hand. "So I would assume. My only question is why?"

Adelaide sighed and let her eyelids fall closed over her burning cheeks. "My father despaired of the number of novels I was reading. He admonished me to choose something from the library that would feed my intellect instead of rotting it away." She swallowed before continuing. What if he thought less of her for trying to outwit her own father? "It took me two days of looking through every title in the library before I found something that would suit my purposes. I read *Observations on Digestion* and proceeded to share everything I learned with him. He looked at his food strangely for a month. I'm still not sure why he owned a copy."

Laughter escaped Trent's chest again, though this time it was more like a low chuckle. "I assume you've been able to read whatever you wish since?"

"Yes. Though I found myself picking up many of the other educational books I'd come across during my search. Some of the information out there is fascinating."

"What else did you learn?"

She watched him for a moment, searching his words and face for any sense of condescension or derision. There was none. He looked at ease, comfortable, even interested in what she had to say. She liked him this way. It made her want to join him, to be as comfortable as he was with this courtship idea. Her shoulder brushed against his as she made herself stop clinging to the edge of the curricle. "The French are measuring things in meters now."

"We'll have to get you some more current books to study." Trent guided the curricle around a horse and rider that had stopped against the fence. "They stopped doing that two years ago."

Adelaide couldn't stop her own lips from curving into an answering smile. The moment was intimate. They were a *we*, sharing and planning for the future as if they were forging ahead together. Yet when this ride was over he'd be leaving her behind, alone in the house with the servants. Who knew what they thought of this entire situation?

Well, she probably would know by the time she went to bed tonight. Mrs. Harris wasn't exactly known for keeping her opinions to herself.

A couple drove by on the other side of Rotten Row, not even hiding their curiosity as they stared into Trent's curricle. She hadn't thought much about the implications of Trent's claim that he'd never courted a woman before. Had he never even taken one for a drive? The curiosity aimed in their direction indicated that this was a very unexpected sighting. A sudden thought stole the glimmer of pleasure that had been blooming inside her middle during their brief conversation. What if there had been another young lady—one he'd taken riding on a regular basis—and that was why people were staring. Despite his claims otherwise, had she stolen him away from the love of his life? It would certainly explain his distance over the past week.

"Have you been into our library yet? I don't think we've any books detailing the functions of the human body, but there is a volume somewhere with a chapter on the molting patterns of tropical birds."

She didn't miss his use of *our*. That flicker of hope ignited once more, that awkward sense of unity that didn't sit well with their current situation. While part of her still worried about who she might have taken him from, she liked the idea of them being a unit. Being able to use *our*.

"I did peruse the library a few days ago. You—we—have several books I hadn't heard of before. I took both volumes of *Don Quixote* up to my room. It's an incredibly long book."

A look of pain flashed across Trent's face. It was so sudden she looked to see if he'd pinched his hand in the reins or somehow bumped his leg against the edge of the wheel, though he'd have had to dangle his leg over the side to accomplish that. "You've probably finished it by now," he said in a low voice. "Did you like it? I've never managed to get through it myself. It was one of Father's favorites so I borrowed the volumes from the Hawthorne House library and forgot to return them."

How nice it must be to be so comfortable with not caring for something a parent was fond of. The fact that he was at odds with his father's opinion gave her more courage to share her own. "I'm not sure what to think of it. Some parts of it are entertaining, but at times it seems to belittle the man. I would not want to be written about in such a way."

He tilted his head, as if she'd made a point he had not thought of before but that merited consideration. "Our library isn't that large, but the one at Hawthorne House is quite extensive. You can borrow anything you'd like from there. Griffith keeps his particular favorites on a set of shelves in his study, so you don't have to worry about borrowing something he'll need or want later. Of course, if there's something in his private collection that you wish to read, I can make arrangements for that as well."

Adelaide blinked and stared straight ahead at the horses' heads swaying slightly back and forth. She was going to be able to casually borrow books from the Duke of Riverton whenever she wished, had access to his house, even. Her mother was going to be incredibly jealous. "I would like that."

They fell into silence once more, but this time it wasn't uncomfortable. It was actually pleasant to ride alongside him and watch the scenery go by. She looked around and realized this was her first time in Hyde Park and she'd spent every moment thus far looking at the curricle or the backside of a horse. She was missing all of the beauty around her. "This is lovely."

A masculine arm crossed in front of her vision, distracting her from the scenery. "Over there is the Serpentine. We'll have to come here on foot one day so you can get a better look at it. It isn't a bad walk from the house if the weather is nice."

"Do people swim in it?" The only body of water she'd seen like that was the lake in Hertfordshire, where her father had taught her brother to swim. After much cajoling from her, he'd taught Adelaide as well, though only after she'd sworn to never tell her mother he'd let her out of the house in her brother's clothes.

Trent smiled again. She could easily get addicted to those smiles. "Not intentionally. More than one person has taken an accidental swim or been dropped in by their friends after a night of over-zealous drinking."

They continued down the path with Trent pointing out different features of Hyde Park or occasionally another member of the *ton* making their way down the fashionable riding path. Adelaide couldn't remember a more pleasant outing. Not once did she find herself wishing she could reach for the book she'd tucked into her reticule. The weight of it rested in her lap, all but ignored as she found herself responding more and more freely to Trent's comments.

As they approached the exit to the park, she couldn't help but hope that the rosy glow of the curricle ride would follow them home. For surely he meant to return home now that they were speaking pleasantly again. It didn't fit with the plan he'd outlined this morning, but if they were getting along, was there any reason to stay at Hawthorne House? Unless he meant to quietly make the move permanent. What if this ride was only for show? To make everyone think they had a happy marriage when he still wanted nothing to do with her? The Hawthorne family marriages were rather notorious for being happy ones. Was he afraid to break the pattern?

The traffic on the path thickened, and the horses had to slow to a plodding walk. Trent reached one hand across the bench to wrap his gloved fingers around her own. The touch was brief, and then he squeezed her hand and returned his grip to the reins.

No one could have seen that. It wasn't meant for anyone but her. She straightened her shoulders and didn't bother to hide the smile on her face. In fact, it wouldn't surprise her if she was still smiling when she went to bed that evening. The attentions of a man such as Trent were heady indeed.

Her smile suffered a blow much sooner than she anticipated however, for another carriage passed them as they crept toward the exit. Inside it was her mother.

Chapter 13

And this was the fly in the ointment of his potentially, hopefully, one-day-to-be-happy marriage. That he would have to spend the rest of his life knowing that the most socially aggressive and annoying woman he knew could show up in his life at any time.

He was too much of a gentleman to allow his aggravation to show as he smiled politely and nodded his head in Lady Crampton's direction.

She wasn't satisfied with a simple acknowledgment, though. "What unexpected fortune to see my daughter and new son! Such a shame we're traveling in opposite ways. We must catch up at the Ferrington ball tonight. I am quite looking forward to it!"

Her voice carried across the park until there wasn't a soul in sight that didn't know of the countess's plans.

It was enough to make Trent want to schedule a very prominent appearance somewhere else. Anywhere else. Even if it meant making a scene at Vauxhall Gardens to make sure everyone knew they'd gone somewhere other than where Lady Crampton expected them to.

Unfortunately it wasn't up to him. The mere sight of her mother seemed to crumble all of the confidence and camaraderie he'd been building with Adelaide for the past hour. Her shoulders fell into a slight slump as she nodded her head slowly. "Of course, Mother. I'm looking forward to the ball as well."

Adelaide's voice didn't carry nearly as far, but it wouldn't matter if no one else had heard her but him. They were now committed to the ball. Trent didn't even know if they'd received an invitation, though it was highly likely that they had. There weren't many events that Trent didn't receive an invitation to, and the one time he'd gone somewhere without one he hadn't been turned away. Of course, he wasn't an eligible bachelor anymore.

The ride back to the house was even more painful than the ride to the park had been. He had half a mind to turn around and go through the park again to try to reclaim the feeling of fragile connection. Neither of them needed or wanted the speculation a thing like that would cause, though. Trent was all too aware of the unconventionality of his plan and that it was probably in his best interest to let everyone else think the marriage was progressing normally.

Assuming anyone else had a clue what normal entailed. If they did, he'd like to know about it.

Still, they were probably better off if no one knew he was currently living in Hawthorne House. He bit back a groan as the wheels clacked over the cobblestone street. This was getting much more complicated than he had anticipated.

The house came into view, inspiring relief and dread. The ride was certainly uncomfortable and he'd be glad to get back to familiar ground, but he hated that their first outing was ending on such a note. He wove desperately through his memory as he helped Adelaide from the carriage, trying to think of some interesting fact he could share since minutiae seemed to be the most common ground they could meet on. As Adelaide steadied her footing on the pavement, he noticed the sleeve of her spencer jacket was tucked into her short glove. How had she managed such a thing while sitting in the curricle?

He found it adorable. With a gentle touch he slid one finger between the glove and the sleeve, moving it in a circle around her wrist to dislodge the garment. He didn't let go of her hand, even when the sleeve hung free once more. It was like a game he got to play every time he saw her, looking for the hidden flaw in her appearance. It was never the same thing twice. It filled him with a sudden urge to pull her close and kiss her.

The urge stunned him even as it shot an arrow of heat down his spine.

He wanted to kiss his wife.

It wasn't a bizarre concept, of course. Men did it every day. But he hadn't done it every day. Hadn't done it all. He hadn't even wanted to, which was part of the problem in the first place. But he wanted to kiss the woman who had ridden through Hyde Park with him, not the shy creature asking his boots if he planned on attending the ball with her that evening.

As if he would leave his wife to attend her first social gathering in London alone. It would be like feeding a lamb to the wolves. "Of course I shall escort you." They should probably dine together. But the thought of sitting in their dining room, just the two of them, while Mrs. Harris frowned in the doorway wasn't the least bit appealing. "Would you like to go to dinner beforehand? There are some lovely restaurants in London."

"Of course." She swallowed visibly and blinked up at him. "Wherever you wish to go. I've seen so little of London that I'll not be particular."

And just that quickly Trent felt like a brute once more. How long had his wife been in London and she'd seen little more than the Great North Road and Rotten Row.

⌒

There was a lot to love about social gatherings, but Trent had never quite caught on to the appeal of balls. No one really got to know anyone there, and the constant dancing was rather exhausting. Of course he wasn't a bachelor anymore. He didn't have to feel duty bound to take to the dance floor every time he saw a young lady look longingly at the swirling couples. He would, however, get to swirl his wife onto the dance floor. Anticipating that moment as he'd helped her down from the curricle when they returned from their afternoon ride, he couldn't help but pray that she knew how to waltz.

He would really like to waltz with his wife.

For the first time in years he also wouldn't have an unmarried female to look after. He'd married off both sisters last year, leaving him free to enjoy Society without any chaperone duties.

If it weren't for the promise of Lady Crampton's presence he might actually get excited about the coming evening, despite the crushing crowd and pandering that always accompanied the bad punch and subtle maneuvering for partners.

Griffith was attending the same ball, so Trent rode with his brother over to the town home to pick up Adelaide.

It was a bit strange to stand in the front hall beside his brother like visitors. Fortunately, Griffith was taking it all in stride, acting like any other gentleman arriving to pick up a lady for an event, though where he'd gotten the practice Trent couldn't begin to guess. While Trent had been careful to never connect himself too closely to any one female, Griffith had perfected the art of keeping all of Society at a distance.

The town house was too narrow for a grand stairway, and instead had a straight staircase cutting down through an opening in the ceiling. Trent watched the break in the ceiling above him, waiting for his wife, praying that this night would go well. Everything that could go wrong went through his head. His mother and sisters weren't in town yet, so he had no guarantee that any of the other women in attendance tonight would welcome Adelaide. He wouldn't put it past her own mother to give her the cut direct if the woman thought it would boost her popularity.

All the worries and concerns fled his mind at the first appearance of deep blue velvet. Slowly the rest of the dress appeared, a silky white gown with a blue velvet overdress that fit Adelaide perfectly. One more slow, steady step and she was fully revealed. Her dark hair pulled into an intricate arrangement of curls with the short strands still falling over her forehead to skim the top of her eyebrows. Her spectacles didn't detract from the image at all, instead seeming to magnify the blue of her eyes, highlighted even more by the blue velvet hugging her shoulders.

Perhaps Trent should have waited in the drawing room instead. At least then he'd have somewhere to sit if his legs followed through on their threat to give way underneath him.

She hadn't had time to mess up her outfit yet, so she looked flawless. The belt of the vest-style velvet ensured that the gown would be flattering from every angle. Trent had a feeling he'd be seeing each of those angles, because there was no way he was taking his eyes off of her for the entirety of the evening. One gloved hand reached up to sweep the short hairs to the side, though a lock or two immediately fell back into place. Trent liked it, liked the softness it brought that the most perfectly formed curls could not. Perhaps he could pay Rebecca to burn them again after they grew out a bit more.

Gold embroidery danced along the open edges of the blue velvet, and a large gold medallion kept the exposed white bodice from being plain against the decorative vest. A scalloped lace trimmed the neckline of the bodice, keeping the low cut from being immodest.

"I do believe worse things have happened to you than having that woman as your wife," Griffith whispered.

Trent couldn't answer. His mouth had gone dry. For the first time since his forced betrothal, Trent thought he just might have gotten very lucky in this arrangement. If they could manage to make every moment half as magical as this one, they'd have a marriage to be envious of. Griffith's large hand planted against Trent's back and gave him a light push, knocking Trent out of his trance so that he could cross the floor and offer Adelaide his arm.

"You are beautiful." His gaze became snared in hers as he offered the compliment in an almost reverent fashion. Her eyes seemed to widen until they were all he could see, glistening pools of fear and excitement surrounded by the black frames of her spectacles. How had he forgotten that this wasn't just her first ball of the Season? It was her first ball ever.

Horrid mother or no, he was going to make sure this night was the best she'd ever had.

Trent didn't realize that they'd been standing in the hall simply staring at each other until Griffith cleared his throat. "I can send the carriage back for you if you aren't ready to depart yet."

"We're ready." He reached up to brush a stray hair from her cheek, grinning at the light blush that stained her cheeks in response. "Aren't we?"

She nodded and reached for the wrap and reticule waiting by the front door. The reticule was enormous. He knew Georgina always carried a slightly larger than average reticule in order to have spare slippers and a small sewing repair kit with her at all times, but even hers wasn't as large as Adelaide's. Nor was it as heavy, if the way it pulled down Adelaide's wrist was any indication.

"Do you have everything you need?" It was the closest he was going to be able to come to asking her what was in the bag. One day though, he promised himself, one day he'd be in a position to know because he'd see her pack it. He'd never dare ask a woman he wasn't related to what was in her reticule, so he couldn't ask Adelaide. Not if he were going to commit to actually courting her as he should. He had to treat her as if they weren't married. Two days ago he'd have thought that the easiest thing in the world. Now he wasn't so sure.

Chapter 14

On her fifth birthday Adelaide got a pony. Her baby brother wasn't old enough to ride the estate with their father yet, but she was, and he took her out riding to every corner of land he owned. She'd felt so important on that pony, one step below the queen herself. For the rest of her life she'd wished she could feel that way again.

Tonight she did.

Entering the ballroom on Trent's arm and hearing the bailiff cry out "Lord and Lady Trent Hawthorne" had given her an even bigger thrill. She'd felt as if she could rule this ballroom, that there was no one in the crush who could touch her. She knew the feeling wouldn't last, not with her mother and dozens of other women like her in attendance, but for the moment none of those women meant a thing because Trent had walked her straight onto the dance floor as the first notes of a waltz drifted through the room.

She thought she'd be nervous about her first dance. How many times had she thought about making her first bow in a London ballroom? She'd begun to think her mother never intended to give her a chance, and she certainly hadn't expected to do it as her dance partner's wife.

Never in all her imaginings had so many eyes been trained her direction, though. But it didn't seem to matter. The rustle of silk and satin that filled the floor around them faded into the background as Adelaide felt the heavy weight of Trent's arm curl around her waist. Her gaze fixed on his cravat, the strong jawline above it edging into her field of vision.

It felt different, dancing with Trent. Bernard was still a young boy—his dancing skills reflected as such—and the few times she'd taken lessons with Helena, Adelaide had been placed into the man's position. There was something comforting about Trent's steady guidance across the floor. It felt like a promise of support as she faced the women of London for the first time. It was fanciful thinking, of course, because he was likely to disappear once this first set had completed. For the moment, though, she would allow herself to believe it and enjoy the blissful sensation of dancing, trusting Trent not to twirl them into any of the other dancers.

The dance set ended before she was ready. Not that she would ever be ready. Leaving the dance floor meant facing the elite of London from an approachable place. A church pew and a moving curricle were rather protected locations, but at a ball, she was utterly exposed. Helena had told her what a cruel lot they were, lying to each other until no one knew what truth was anymore. Having spent enough time sorting Helena's lies from her truths led Adelaide to believe the other women weren't the entire problem. Still, it didn't take much to believe that aristocratic women were a difficult bunch to impress. Her mother certainly was. They couldn't all be like that though, could they?

Trent escorted her to the side of the floor, stumbling to a halt at the edge of the dancing area. He glanced around and then back down at her before pulling her into the edge of the gathering people. After looking around once more, he slid her hand from his elbow and ran one hand across the back of his neck. What could possibly be wrong? Was he trying to find a way to tell her he was going to wherever the men went when they didn't want to dance? She didn't mind, honestly. It wasn't as if she expected him to remain in her company all evening. Her mother was going to be there, after all, even if Adelaide wasn't quite ready to see her.

And that, of course, was part of his issue. If Trent had truly been courting Adelaide he'd have taken her to her mother at the conclusion of the dance, but her mother was nowhere to be seen. A rather mixed blessing at that moment, but one that left them with an awkward situation. What did they do now? Did they simply part ways and go about their own business for the rest of the evening? Stand together until they came across someone they both wanted to talk to? Would he introduce her around until she knew enough people for him to leave her to her own devices?

The awkwardness shifted into a burning sensation that ran from her middle to her chest as other attendees took the question of what to do next out of their hands. People swarmed to their side and Trent began introducing them as quickly as politeness would allow. Adelaide smiled and nodded at all of them, keeping her gaze firmly on everyone's chin so they would hopefully miss the heat crawling up her neck and the aching tension creeping across her shoulders. The introductions began blending together, and she knew she'd never remember everyone's name.

No one seemed to care, though. In fact, the conversations were easier than she would have dreamed if she'd ever dreamed of conversing with this many people in a single night. Years of practice at saying whatever her mother and father expected her to say gave her a natural ability to allow the other person to lead the conversation. Sometimes she had no idea what or whom they were talking about, but her noncommittal answers seemed to please most people, and they moved on from the encounter with a satisfied nod or even a smile.

And thus went the next hour of her evening. It wasn't unpleasant. If she hadn't felt like such a charlatan she might have even enjoyed it. But every time Trent appeared at her side with a cup of lemonade or simply to share in the conversation, women around her would enthuse over her luck and fortune. While some seemed envious of her new position, most simply wanted to gossip on her newly married life. When she wasn't forthcoming enough, they began to speculate. She let them. She wasn't about to share the truth of her situation or how the marriage came about. It was reasonable for people to assume they'd had a quiet romance in the country, so she felt no need to contradict them.

In her experience, people would believe whatever they wished to anyway.

"Married life seems to suit you well, Adelaide." Mother approached and hooked her arm with Adelaide's during a rare lull in the attentions.

Adelaide murmured something between a yes and a groan because she wasn't really sure how to answer that statement. Nothing good ever came from being the solitary focus of her mother's attention. It inevitably ended with Mother lamenting the fact that Adelaide wasn't Helena and Adelaide wishing her parents' second child hadn't been born to wear skirts.

Mother pulled Adelaide along as they started a slow walk along the edge of the ballroom. "Now that you've settled in so well, you should have Helena around for dinner. With her husband, of course. Did you know that Lord Edgewick has been trying to get an introduction into Alverly's fencing club?"

Adelaide let her sigh puff her cheeks out before silently sliding out between her teeth. Even now it was about what Helena needed, what leant her the most social advantage. Perhaps Adelaide should be thanking God for her unconventional marriage instead of sending questioning glances to the sky. Who knew how Mother would have tried to manipulate Adelaide's potential suitors if she'd come for her Season as planned.

"He's been trying for a sponsorship to White's, you know," the countess continued. "But Boodle's would be nearly as good. His current club has no influential connections to speak of."

Adelaide sighed, knowing she had to crush her mother's dreams before they grew to unfathomable proportions. "I'm afraid I won't be able to help him with those."

Mother laughed.

Adelaide winced. Had her mother's laugh always been so grating and false? Or was this something she saved for London because she thought it made her look more sophisticated?

"Dear Adelaide, you've only to mention it to your husband a time or two. It's obvious he dotes on you. I knew he would. The family is notoriously obnoxious about their marriages."

Perhaps because they notoriously married for love, which Trent had not been able to do. No wonder he didn't want to live under the same roof as her. "I'm afraid you're mistaken, Mother. Lord Trent feels nothing but obligation for me. We aren't even living in the same house anymore."

Mother froze, the flattering, false smile dropping from her face. "What?"

Adelaide shifted her weight from foot to foot. She should not have brought this up in public, despite the fact that it felt like an enormous relief to finally admit the problem to someone. Her voice dropped to a whisper in the attempt to keep her secret. "He's staying at Hawthorne House."

"Useless," her mother hissed.

"I beg your pardon?" Adelaide's eyebrows drew together as she leaned forward to better hear her mother's quiet words.

"You. You are useless. All you had to do was keep him happy and then you could have helped Helena rise to her rightful place in society." Mother dropped her arm from Adelaide's elbow and smoothed her skirts. "I should have known this wouldn't work out when you merely managed to catch the younger son. The duke would have been so much better. I blame myself. I should have looked over the wall to make sure it was the duke, not simply assumed you'd gotten it right."

Adelaide blinked at her mother, trying to bring the words into focus, but it didn't work. Mother had never been complimentary, but *useless* was a good bit harsher than her normal declarations. "I . . . didn't . . . I mean . . . what?"

Mother looked around the room and pasted her smile back on her face. "We can fix this. Come along."

Adelaide trailed after her mother, trying not to trip over the hem of her gown. "What are we doing?"

"Jealousy, my dear. It's time you learned how to use it. A smile here, a little flirting there. Nothing grabs a man's attention faster." Mother's sharp blue eyes cut through the crowd. What was she looking for? Who was she looking for?

The implications of her mother's plan finally formulated in Adelaide's confused brain. Obviously her mother had gone mad, because the last thing Adelaide wanted to do was flirt with a man who wasn't her husband. There were so many reasons to avoid doing such a thing—not the least of which was the fact that Adelaide hadn't the foggiest notion how to flirt. If she did she'd have certainly been using her skills on Trent and not some other man of her mother's choosing. "Mother, this won't work."

Mother rolled her eyes. "Of course it will, darling. How do you think I got that new diamond necklace last year? A solid month of dancing with the Viscount of Strenwhite at every possible function. Believe me. This is the fastest way into a man's attentions."

A month didn't seem very fast, but what did Adelaide know about marriage? Perhaps a month was a veritable blink in marital relations.

And then the introductions began. Adelaide had already been afraid of forgetting the women she'd met tonight, but now she was being inundated with men as well. Most of the gentlemen were polite, even as they sent puzzled looks her way when her mother tried to rather obviously manipulate them into asking her daughter to dance. Did married women dance at these gatherings?

Adelaide had rather thought the dancing was mostly for the unmarried young ladies—a classification she was feeling an increasingly urgent need to remind her mother she did not possess any longer.

Her mother finally achieved her goal, and as Adelaide danced with a man named Mr. Givendale, she tried to come to grips with this new look at her mother. She'd always known there wasn't an abundance of affection between her parents, but she'd assumed that was the fault of both parties. What if it wasn't? What if her father had simply grown tired of her mother's scheming and trickery? Her need to constantly push for more? It didn't make any sense, really. The woman was a countess. She outranked over three quarters of the ladies in the room, and still she worried, still it wasn't enough. Of course, Helena was only a viscountess and hadn't been invited to tonight's ball. And it was always about Helena.

"Are you enjoying living in Town?" Mr. Givendale asked.

Adelaide tried to bring her thoughts back to the dance at hand. No matter how uncomfortable she was with her mother's maneuverings, there was no cause to be rude to a man who had asked her to dance. The dancing was something she'd been particularly looking forward to before she'd gotten married.

"Town is lovely," Adelaide answered. And it was. The beauty of London, despite the smog and crowdedness, was about the only positive thing she could say about her current living arrangements.

"You make it lovelier."

A flush burned up Adelaide's neck to her ears as she turned to follow the dance pattern. She might not know how to flirt but it seemed at least some of the gentlemen could more than make up for her lack of competency. What was she supposed to say to that? Should she say anything? Nearly half a minute had passed before they were shoulder to shoulder once more.

"Have you been to the opera yet? I've a box there you're welcome to use any time." He paused as another couple passed between them. "Your husband too, of course."

Adelaide didn't have to feign her sudden difficulty breathing. As much as she craved the oxygen she was suddenly deprived of, she was more than grateful for the excuse to leave the dance floor. "I beg your pardon, Mr. Givendale, but I don't think I'm feeling quite up to finishing the set."

"Of course."

He pulled them from the formation and escorted her to the side of the dance floor, where she immediately dropped his arm and kept walking. With every step she took her chest seemed to loosen until she could finally breathe properly again. Was this what Trent had wanted for her? He'd said he wanted to give her the experience of the Season she'd missed out on, but it didn't seem right to include any other men in that experience. Now she just had to convince her mother of that.

"Whatever did you do that for?"

Mother appeared at Adelaide's elbow, but Adelaide didn't stop. She kept going, even as her mother began yet another tirade on Adelaide's inability to see a plan through properly. As they rounded a large pillar at the side of the ballroom, Adelaide collided with an older man coming from the other direction.

"Oh, pardon me!" Adelaide took a quick step back, almost tripping over the velvet train of her ball gown. The dress was gorgeous, but maneuvering in it was proving exceptionally difficult. Trent had shown her how to hold the trailing skirt when she was dancing, and as long as she moved forward while walking she did all right, but backward was a tricky endeavor. The older man reached for her hand, giving her support until she was steady on her feet.

"All right, then?"

She nodded. "Yes, thank you."

The man was obviously important. Some men just held themselves with power. Given that his clothing was also very fine, she assumed him to be an important personage indeed. She waited for her mother to introduce them.

A glance to her side showed that her mother had disappeared. She twisted her head, looking for the dark orange of her dress, but the vicinity was full of pastels and whites with the occasional deep purple or blue.

She turned back to the old man and gave him a small smile before moving to walk past him. Without an introduction she could do no more, but she was burning to know who he was. Whoever he was, her mother wanted nothing to do with him. Which might make him one of her favorite people in London.

Lady Crampton wasn't to be avoided for long, however. Once Adelaide was out of sight of the old man, her mother reappeared at her elbow seemingly out of nowhere.

She turned her head to see if the old man was still visible, but he'd gone on his way and was nowhere to be found. Trent's brother, however, also occupied the fringes of the crowd on this side of the ballroom, and he stepped forward with a frown of concern that made Adelaide worry that her panic was starting to show on her face. The entire evening had been a series of questions that left her second-guessing her every move.

"Would you care to dance?" The duke took Adelaide's hand and bowed over their connected fingers.

"Of . . . of course."

Adelaide had a feeling the man didn't really want to dance. If the speculative glances in his direction were any indication, he didn't do it all that frequently. She soon understood why. Even though he showed a greater than average amount of grace, he took up a considerably larger than average amount of space on the dance floor, leaving him bumping shoulders with the other people in the quadrille formation.

"What am I to call you?" Adelaide asked as they linked elbows and circled another couple.

"The family calls me Griffith. You are welcome to do the same. Or Riverton, if that is more comfortable for you." He angled his shoulder to avoid another couple.

Adelaide noticed they were garnering more than a few whispers and stares as they went through the dance.

"They are trying to verify with each other that you are indeed Trent's new wife," Griffith murmured in her ear.

Adelaide looked up at him to see if he too was noticing the many people paying attention to him, but his gaze seemed to rest solely on her. It was unnerving. His eyes were nearly identical to Trent's in color, and his features were similar enough to declare them related at a glance, but Griffith's gaze held solidity, a strength that Trent's lacked. The marked power of duke versus the comfort of the second son had never been so evident to her, and she found herself thankful that Trent had come to the ruins that day instead of Griffith.

"How do they know?" she whispered back.

"I'm dancing with you." Griffith took her arm and led her down the line, having to fold nearly in half to go under the raised arms of the other couples.

"Do you usually avoid dancing, then?" Adelaide asked as they came to the end of the line and added their arms to the tunnel of dancers.

"I avoid anything that requires singling out a specific female. The speculation is too great. I only dance with family. I always seem to have a cousin or two in London for the Season."

Adelaide blinked. What a lonely existence. How would Griffith ever find a wife if he didn't participate in one of the hallmarks of aristocratic courtship? Not everyone could expect a floor to give way and make the decision for them.

Nervous laughter lodged in her throat, but thankfully the dance separated them for a moment to allow her to regain control before needing to speak again.

As the set continued, Adelaide tried to subtly steer the conversation to his brother, though she had a feeling he knew exactly what she was doing and she wasn't gaining any knowledge he didn't specifically want her to have—which wasn't anything Trent hadn't already told her. When the dance set ended, Griffith escorted her to Trent's side on the opposite side of the room from her mother.

Wondering if she was actually free of her mother for a while, Adelaide looked around as Trent talked with a man she'd met earlier but whose name she had forgotten . . . and her gaze connected with her mother's, and she actually wasn't frowning for once. Perhaps the reminder that Adelaide was now solidly connected to a duke had softened her disapproval. She was, however, headed in Adelaide's direction. Adelaide's shoulders sagged.

Then her mother's eyes cut to the left and she changed direction, veering off to the door leading to the women's retiring room.

Adelaide glanced over, wondering what had caused her mother's change of mind. The old man from earlier stood a few feet away, drinking a glass of lemonade and talking to a younger man who was most definitely related to him, given the shape of the nose and chin.

She waited for a break in Trent's conversation before leaning in. "Who is that man?"

Trent followed her gaze. "The Duke of Spindlewood. Why? Would you like an introduction?"

"Yes." Adelaide wound her arm into his. "I believe I would."

Chapter 15

Sweat ran down Trent's face, stinging his eyes and threatening to impede his vision, a dangerous thing when a man was in the ring with Gentleman Jack himself. He feinted left and threw another punch that was easily blocked by the seasoned boxer who immediately threw a punch of his own. Trent managed to block it, though without the finesse of the other man.

Finally the prizefighter stepped back, declaring they'd had enough. "You're a bit heavy on your feet today, Lord Trent."

Trent grunted as he climbed out of the ring and joined the mass of men milling about the exclusive boxing club.

"Feeling a bit off today, Hawthorne?" Lord Worthorp slapped Trent on the back and handed him a linen towel to mop off the sweat. "Not surprising, considering you haven't been in for weeks. I think even I'd be willing to have a go at you after that long of an absence."

Trent had no idea what to say to the man, so he buried his face in the towel. Bringing up his marriage would only lead to questions or worse, comments and jokes he had to pretend to go along with even though he hadn't a clue what they were talking about. He had no idea what it was like to have his wife change his regular menu or throw the servants into chaos. He could only hope another man would inform Lord Worthorp and they could find their teasing hilarious and leave him to shrug in silence.

As he'd hoped, another man, whose voice he didn't recognize, decided to join in the good-natured ribbing. From the sounds of shuffling feet, the conversation was drawing the attention of more than one other man.

"Haven't you heard, Worthorp? The infamous Lord Trent is no longer on the market."

Worthorp laughed and slapped Trent on the back, forcing him to pull the towel from his face or look like an idiot. "I had no idea you were married."

"Neither does Hawthorne." Mr. Givendale pinched a bit of snuff from his tin before grinning like a man who was betting on a race he knew was rigged.

Trent did his best to look like Griffith at his haughtiest and didn't grant Givendale an answer.

Worthorp looked from Givendale to Trent and back again. Obviously debating the merits of friendship versus good gossip. "What do you mean?"

Trent bit back a sigh. This was London. Good gossip always won.

Givendale leaned against the wall. "Lord Trent here is residing over on Grosvenor Square these days. I doubt he's even seen his wife since he left her in Mount Street yesterday afternoon."

How could Givendale know Trent had returned to Hawthorne House after taking Adelaide riding yesterday? He'd had the servants take his curricle around back and then he'd ridden his horse over to Hawthorne House.

Worthorp looked at Trent with surprise. "No—you're not."

"I had business with Griffith last night, and we didn't finish until late. It made sense to stay at the house last night. Contrary to what Givendale seems to think, it is not a change of residence."

The other man in the group, whom Trent still didn't recognize even after seeing his face, clapped a strong hand on Trent's shoulder. "Good. I'd never believe it if you couldn't talk your way around your wife. You've always been able to charm the ladies."

Trent winced at the suggestive look in the man's eyes that implied Trent had done much more than pull a smile from a nervous wallflower or two. How was a man supposed to correct an image like that? There was no evidence, no reason for anyone to make such a claim, when he hadn't ever done so much as pull a lady into an alcove to steal a kiss. He supposed he should just let people think what they were going to think. He and God knew the truth, and one day soon Adelaide would as well. Those were the only people who mattered. Weren't they?

"Have you met the lady yet, Stapleton? She's quite charming herself." Givendale lowered his face to look at his snuff box before tilting his eyes back in Trent's direction.

Trent shrugged out of his sweat-soaked linen shirt and dropped a clean one over his head, trying not to look concerned. Givendale had never been one of Trent's favorite people, but they'd never had a row. So why did the man seem determined to bedevil Trent at every opportunity? And why was he so interested in Trent's marriage? Whatever the reason, it was time to put a stop to it.

The boyish grin Trent plastered onto his face might have been a bit overdone, and it certainly felt silly, but then again wouldn't a man who was happily married be likely to grin in just such a way? "She is rather charming, isn't she? Why else do you think I married her before any of you lot got the chance to meet her? There's not another one like her in all of England, boys. You'll have to settle for who's left."

Stapleton snorted. "Another Hawthorne beset by love. It's like a curse with your family."

Yet one more stone on the monument to Trent's unsuitability to ever take over as head of the family. He'd be grateful if it didn't come with a life sentence to a woman he didn't love.

"Have you looked into the horses racing about this year?" Givendale asked. "I've been thinking about investing in a stable. Rumor is you've just acquired one along with your wife. We should discuss it sometime."

Had he? He knew her dowry included an estate in Suffolk, but he'd thought it just that, an estate. Did it have horses on it? Was this something he should know? "Of course. Any time."

With a final nod to the group of men, Trent left the building, doing his best to avoid the knowing smile still on Givendale's face—and the niggling idea that holding his wife's hand was quite a bit different than holding her heart.

Two days later Trent was still mulling over the thought as he leaned against the billiard table in Hawthorne House, idly rolling the balls across the smooth green surface with no real rhyme or reason. How long did a courtship take? What did people even do when they were courting? The clacking of the balls against the bumpers and each other was somewhat satisfying, but it didn't answer any of his questions.

He knew couples went riding together, and they'd done that every day for the past four days. Rotten Row was becoming more and more crowded as London's aristocratic population settled in for the Season. People barely glanced at them now as they rode along, Trent pointing out the same sites over and over again because he didn't have anything else to say. Neither of his sisters had taken conventional routes to marriage, but they'd had some suitors before finding their husbands. Trent had just never paid much attention to what they did.

Flowers were obvious, and he'd taken a large bouquet of them to the house when he took her riding the day after the ball. Sweets were often mentioned by the women in his family as well, so he'd asked Griffith's chef to create one of his famous sugar confections. That too had drawn a serene smile and a thank-you from Adelaide, though Mrs. Harris had sniffed and frowned even as she gave the elaborate creation an intent examination. He hadn't taken any gift yesterday and yet he'd still been granted the same greeting, the same smile, the same everything. He wasn't accomplishing anything other than becoming adept at maneuvering his curricle in a crowd, and he'd already been a rather better driver than most of London.

There were couples that announced their engagements mere days after meeting each other. Shouldn't Trent at least feel like he was making ground? It wasn't as if he had to convince Adelaide to marry him. He simply had to convince himself they were actually married. Why was that so difficult?

He'd driven his curricle over to Hawthorne House last night, hoping that it looked less suspicious than him simply riding his horse. The grooms were shining the vehicle, readying it for his afternoon ride, but he considered borrowing Griffith's carriage, since the sky looked a bit heavy. How desperate was he if he took her riding in a closed carriage that he couldn't even drive himself? Where was his famed charm and creativity that he could think of nothing else to do with his wife besides ride down an old dirt lane in the middle of a park?

The smirk that had been on Givendale's face two days ago sliced through Trent's memory, firming his resolve to do something special to court his wife today. He would not let a day go by that they didn't do something together in an effort to create some sort of affection or at least connection between them. He would take the carriage and they could go for a walk if the weather held out. That was at least a bit different than going for a drive. If it rained, though, they would have to visit in the drawing room. With nothing to look at but each other and the curtainless window.

He still hadn't asked about that window covering, though he probably should. Surely she was planning on replacing it soon.

Didn't all women yearn to redecorate? Claim a space as their own? Maybe Adelaide was having as much trouble accepting the situation as he was.

He wouldn't know unless he talked to her about it.

And if the conversation went nowhere? If they ended up staring at each other with nothing to say? Trent rolled a billiard ball around with his flattened hand. There was a fine chess set in his study. Surely the precious progress they'd made, little though it may be, could withstand a bit of intellectual competition on a chessboard. It wouldn't be at all strange to play a friendly game of chess without an inkling of conversation.

He gave the ivory ball a particularly hard shove, sending it ricocheting across the table, scattering the balls until the entire table appeared to be in motion.

They could do dinner. He had taken her riding and now he would take her to dinner. At least then they could blame any lack of communication on being too polite to speak with their mouths full.

Her mother had arrived.

To be honest, Adelaide was rather surprised it had taken the woman four days to make an appearance—assuming she'd taken the ride on Rotten Row the day she'd returned to London. She might have been in Town upwards of a week.

And now she was in Adelaide's drawing room.

The one without a curtain on the window.

The one that had borne up well under more than two decades of use but was still showing the age of the decor.

The one that Trent picked her up in every day so they could ride through the park like near strangers.

Adelaide supposed she should be grateful for those rides. They were certainly the highlight of her day, as she spent most of the remaining hours wandering the rooms trying to avoid the staff while she worked her way through the books in Trent's—no, their—small library. Still, she'd thought he'd have moved home by now. She'd been peaceful and serene. Nothing like the irate woman that had sent him packing in the first place. There was nothing else she could do to convince him that she would be a proper, meek wife. The small smile and soft words had always been enough to appease her mother.

The mother who was even now sitting in the drawing room. Alone.

Probably making a list of all the ways Helena would have handled this situation better.

Mrs. Harris was waiting at the bottom of the stairs. "Tea, my lady?"

Adelaide nodded, wanting to smack herself for not thinking to request a tray. She had never liked the stuff, but everyone else seemed to consider it a social necessity.

Taking one last deep breath, Adelaide pushed the door open and entered the room.

"I don't know how you expect to make the most of your new position if you don't take advantage of everyone's current curiosity. You've been seen in the park so often that hardly anyone talks about you in the shops anymore."

Adelaide stumbled to a stop three feet into the room and blinked at her mother. "Good afternoon, Mother. I've ordered tea."

Mother huffed out a breath and lowered herself to the sofa. "Of course you've ordered tea. I've taught you to always do so even if the guest claims not to want it."

Confusion drew Adelaide's eyebrows together. When had her mother taught her anything about tea? Perhaps she assumed that teaching Helena was as good as teaching both of them, but Adelaide had never been allowed to sit in on the lessons unless they needed another person. Still, it wasn't worth bringing up now. There was nothing to be gained from it, since Adelaide didn't think she'd need to know much more than how to keep her skirt out of the carriage wheel and not embarrass herself in a ballroom. Both of those she could manage nicely. "Of course, Mother."

"Have you been by to see Helena yet? She got into Town three days ago."

Adelaide had left a card, the only calling card she'd actually left anyone, but at that time Helena hadn't yet arrived. "No, she wasn't there when I went by. I didn't know she'd returned to Town."

Fenton entered with the tea tray, setting it lightly on the low table before bowing his way out of the room. Mother picked up the teapot before Adelaide could say anything. It was impossible to tell if the slight had been deliberate, but Adelaide let it pass. Even if it were, what did it matter if her mother thought she had the upper hand? It was simple enough to smile and nod and then ignore her wishes.

Adelaide didn't really care for pouring tea anyway. She accepted the cup of tea with a splash of milk, noticing that the delicate white tea service trimmed in gold was more elegant than the service she saw when Trent had tea delivered. The fact that she hadn't known they had two complete tea services bothered her.

"I saw her the day before yesterday. She's doing well but is anxious to establish herself a bit more. They're sure to have children soon, and she's worried she'll lose some of her status during her confinement."

Adelaide tilted her head as she watched her mother sip tea, wondering if the older woman even realized the implications of what she'd just said. Helena had barely had a chance to shake the country dust from her hems before Mother had gone to visit. And yet this was her first time coming to Mount Street.

"I'm sure Helena will have a fine Season."

"Of course she will." Mother set her teacup down. "With your new connections it shouldn't be difficult to secure her a few more coveted invitations."

Adelaide seriously doubted that she had more pull than her mother. Mother was a countess, after all. Adelaide was just married. "My position is merely circumstantial. Trent isn't due to inherit a title."

"Hmm, yes, not unless something happens to his brother. The duke is still unmarried, so your husband would be the next in line should something unfortunate occur."

"Mother!" Adelaide fumbled her cup to the table, cold shivers making small bumps rise from the skin of her arm. "That's a horrible thing to say."

Mother sighed, lowering her chin to spear Adelaide with a chiding glare. "Really, Adelaide, accidents happen. The duke wouldn't be the first man to die conveniently."

Memories of the large man dancing with her, welcoming her to the family, contrasted with the callousness of her mother's statements, making Adelaide shudder. "Perhaps we could discuss something else?"

Mother sighed. "Very well. But you would do well to take advantage of people's curiosity. Right now you're a novelty. You could get invited anywhere and easily request that Helena and I come with you. Everyone would understand your desire for a friendly face."

Adelaide rather thought everyone would expect her husband to be the only comforting presence she needed, but she knew better than to say anything. Smile and nod. Smile and nod. Most of the time Mother would forget what she'd asked of Adelaide in the first place.

Dear God, don't let this time be the exception.

Chapter 16

Trent dropped to the pavement and sent an anxious look at the sky. They weren't going to be able to go for a walk. The weather was entirely too unpredictable to risk taking Adelaide out in it. Still, he didn't want to forgo his visit. He was trying to shove weeks if not months of courting into as short a time as possible. He couldn't afford to miss a day because of the threat of rain. This was England, after all. He'd never get anywhere if he limited himself to blue skies and sunshine.

Having to do something other than go for a drive, however, made him sweat. For all of his reputed charm and grace, he didn't have much practice in one-on-one situations with females. Particularly ones who weren't his sisters.

Perhaps he should treat Adelaide like he did one of his sisters.

No. No. He shook his head fiercely to shake free any vestiges of that thought. Adelaide was most certainly not his sister, and he didn't even need to consider trying to see her as such. It was much too disturbing.

The door opened behind him, and he turned to ask Fenton if he thought the weather would hold long enough for him to take Adelaide to Gunter's for ices.

It wasn't Fenton in the doorway, though.

It was Lady Crampton and her maid.

Trent cleared his throat and shifted his weight. "Good afternoon."

Lady Crampton looked from him to the carriage and back again.

Trent could only imagine the thoughts that would be running through her head. It must look strange, him standing by the road in front of his house with a carriage that wasn't his own. Had Adelaide told her mother about their circumstances? What they were attempting? He rather hoped not. He hadn't told his own mother. Of course, he still hadn't gotten around to telling his own mother that he'd gotten married either. She was going to be beyond cross with him, but he couldn't figure out what to say. He started the letter three times a day and always ended up chucking the thing in the fire. She was going to have questions. And he didn't want to answer them, was afraid he wouldn't know how to answer them. She was sure to be arriving in Town soon, and it wasn't going to be pretty when she learned his unintentional secret.

Very well, his intentional secret. He was going to have to take total responsibility for keeping it from her, but at least then he'd know why she was disappointed in him. That was far better than having her be disappointed and him be left wondering why. And after going against the norm and raising her family to marry for love, she was certain to be disappointed in Trent's situation.

He bit his cheek to stave off the urge to defend the carriage on the street. It was much better if he pretended there was nothing curious about the situation.

"What are you doing?"

Of course, pretending was so much easier if the other party went along with it.

Trent went with the simplest answer. "Taking Adelaide to dinner."

Her eyebrows lifted. "At half past three in the afternoon?"

Hair flopped against his forehead as he tilted his head to the side and tried for a boyish grin. He hated playing the idiot, but sometimes it was the easiest way out of a conversation. "Is it that early? I must have gotten anxious."

"To eat dinner." She adjusted her spencer jacket.

He shrugged. "I'd be eating dinner anyway. It's the company I'm looking forward to."

A frown pulled the countess's lips into a wrinkled pink slash across her face. "One would assume you could have the company regardless of whether or not you were eating."

Maintaining his smile and relaxed posture grew difficult. Perhaps he'd bought into this courtship ruse a bit too much and he'd forgotten that the rest of London assumed he was still living under the same roof as his wife. And while it shouldn't matter if Lady Crampton knew the truth or not, Trent didn't feel it was in his best interests to let her know. Especially with some people already suspecting. "There's something satisfying about letting the rest of London know how lucky I am."

And while Lady Crampton made noncommittal noises, Trent looked over her shoulder to find the luck in question standing in the doorway.

Adelaide brushed the hair off her forehead and attempted a smile, though the corners of her mouth pulled down and her lips poked out the way they do when a person clenches their jaw. Her gaze kept flitting from him to her mother and then around the entire area, taking in the number of people witnessing the strange meeting in front of a house he supposedly lived in.

Nothing about this tableau looked like a man returning home. It looked like exactly what it was—a man coming to visit a woman.

Trent bit back a sigh as he wished Lady Crampton a good afternoon and pushed past her into the house. He had a feeling life had just gotten a bit more complicated.

Even though the visit had gone horribly, Adelaide wished her mother had stayed. As uncomfortable and embarrassing as the ensuing conversation would have been, it had to be better than the awkwardness now covering the dilapidated drawing room. She'd just choked down tea with her mother so she wasn't about to suggest Fenton bring another loaded tray, but without the sights of London to focus on, she and Trent were left without a common distraction.

The fact that they apparently needed a common distraction was possibly proof that Trent's courtship plan wasn't having the effect that he'd planned. Assuming he planned for them to actually become closer—perhaps even find love—during this time. He'd said that was his objective, but then again he'd also moved out of the house, thereby limiting the amount of time they spent in each other's presence.

Adelaide didn't know what to think anymore.

Trent shifted, causing the settee to creak. His eyes widened as he cast a worried glance toward the thin, curved legs. He rolled his shoulders and sat up a bit straighter. "Did you have a pleasant visit with your mother?"

Did anyone have pleasant interactions with the countess? Well, perhaps Helena did. The two saw the world in much the same way, after all. "My sister has returned to Town."

"Oh. Do let me know if you'd like to visit her one afternoon. I can easily adjust our ride." He coughed and looked at the holes in the plaster where the curtain rod had once hung. "Assuming you wish to continue our rides, of course."

"Oh yes," Adelaide rushed to assure him.

Silence fell once more. Should she suggest he take some time to catch up on things in his study? Didn't men need to spend time on their business things every day? Her father always spent the majority of his time in his study. And Trent had been essentially blocked from his for several days. But if she suggested that, would it start a pattern? Would he keep coming by only to seclude himself in his study?

He cleared his throat.

She sniffed.

He shifted in his seat, causing another ominous creak to cut through the room.

But none of those sounds could lift the weight of silence caused by two people in a room who didn't know what to say to each other. If the furniture bore the weight of the silent expectation as heavily as she did, Trent had reason to be concerned about the stability of his seat.

"You can't hum while holding your nose."

Trent startled, his mouth dropping open slightly as if he, too, had been about to break the silence. Adelaide wished he had. Whatever he'd been about to say couldn't be as inane as her blurting out a random fact she'd come across in a book one day.

"Seriously?" he asked.

And before she could find a way to extricate herself from his embarrassing scrutiny, he lifted one hand and pinched his nose while pressing his lips together. No noise emerged until he released his nose and opened his lips to let a gush of air out. "Fascinating."

She blinked at him. Fascinating? While it was true he'd seemed to enjoy her bits of trivia on their rides, she'd never pulled out something so obscure before.

He leaned forward, bracing one elbow on his knee. "Did you know that you cannot lick your own elbow?"

Adelaide looked down at her arm. "Why on earth would anyone want to do that?"

Trent shrugged. His eyes crinkled slightly at the corners and a small smile tilted his lips. "Who knows? But I won two pence from Griffith once by telling him he couldn't accomplish it."

"How old were you?" The words tumbled out along with Adelaide's laughter.

"Six. I'd just lost one pence to Henry Durham because he'd challenged me to the same thing."

Adelaide's laughter eased into a quiet smile. "I once dared my sister to climb onto the gardener's tool shed to get our kite so we wouldn't get in trouble."

"And . . . ?" Trent's even, white teeth split his face in anticipation of a good story, making Adelaide realize this hadn't been the best continuation of the topic.

"She told my mother I'd gotten it snagged up there deliberately and tried to make her bribe one of the stableboys to retrieve it."

One hand clamped over Trent's mouth as he tried not to laugh but it sputtered out anyway. "How old were you?"

Heat crept up Adelaide's neck. "Fifteen."

A loud crack of thunder cut through their shared laughter. Trent rose and crossed to the window, sighing as the rain began to pelt the glass panels.

Adelaide stood beside him, watching the rain. Did this mean he would leave? His time in the drawing room had been as long as most men stayed to visit with ladies when they were courting. At least, as far as she understood it. Right now she would have been more than happy to forfeit half her knowledge of various trivia for the chance to have witnessed one of Helena's Seasons. Any insight would be better than the darkness she now found herself in.

"I had planned on taking you to the Clarendon to dine tonight."

Adelaide blinked. He wasn't going home? They'd spent a mere hour in each other's company while they rode the last several days and now he wanted to spend the entire evening with her? In the confines of a dining arrangement? That seemed like considerable progress to her. "Is the food good there?"

Trent nodded. "French. I had been hoping the rain would hold off long enough for us to enjoy the outing."

Did that mean that now that the skies had opened up they weren't going? If that was what he wanted, why had he mentioned it to her in the first place? Unless that wasn't what he wanted. "We could dine here."

Her voice had been so quiet, she wasn't sure he'd heard her. Wasn't even sure the words had gone anywhere outside her head, until he turned his face from the window and smiled at her. The smile was tight and his eyes looked a bit wide and fearful, but her suggestion was rather terrifying. They were going to spend an evening together. Alone. Without a single distraction or activity to refocus their attention on.

He stared at her, holding her gaze with his own until her eyes started to dry out, and she blinked to break the connection.

"You would do that?" he asked. "Forgo an evening at the Clarendon to stay here?"

She blinked at him, partly to relieve the burn from her eyes but also hoping she could somehow find the question he was really asking, because it felt like his words were weighted. By agreeing to this change in plans, was she setting them in an entirely new direction? If she was, she could only hope it was a good one, because she found herself nodding and leaving the room to see to the arrangements.

They were deviating from the courtship plan, veering into waters no courting couple would dare to go. If it failed, their fledgling relationship would take a while to recover, but if it succeeded . . . Adelaide floated off to find Mrs. Harris, dreams of a real marriage filling her head and raising her hopes.

Dinner was simple, with Mrs. Harris being torn between grumbling about the late notice and rejoicing over the fact that they were dining together at home. Where no one could see them. It hadn't stopped Adelaide from dressing for dinner, though, and Trent's breath had been stolen all over again as he waited for her at the bottom of the stairs.

Just as she had when he picked her up for the ball, she'd stolen his wits for a few moments, and for the briefest time he'd been

148

inclined to whisk her out onto the Town despite the rain. To show her off in her finery and splendidness.

But he didn't. They'd chosen to stay in for the night, and he marveled at the decision too much to take it away from her.

Sliced roast in their own dining room was of no benefit to Adelaide's social status. There was no gain from it outside of their own personal connection. It was hard to imagine the daughter of Lady Crampton being willing to eat a simple, private meal when they could have been prominently seated at one of the best restaurants in London.

But when she tossed a grape at him, daring him to catch it with his mouth, he had no choice but to believe it was true. She was untainted by the desperate measures of the *ton* debutantes, never having had to weigh a friend's happiness against her own future well-being, never having had to betray herself or someone else in order to gain social standing. While he didn't fully understand her view on life, he was willing to admit it wasn't as tarnished as he had feared.

She was a different person in the privacy of their dining room. Different than she'd been on their rides, and certainly different than she'd been at the ball, where she'd tried to fade into the background. She hadn't been successful, of course, with her unique eyes, gorgeous dress, and well-trimmed figure, but he'd seen her try.

While Mrs. Harris fixed dinner, they'd played chess. During dinner, she entertained him by retelling the story from one of the novels she'd read lately, complete with commentary on the foolishness of the hero and heroine. She never volunteered her opinions, but he soon found all he had to do was ask and she would tell him what she thought. For a woman so inclined to keep her opinions to herself, she had formed surprisingly decisive ones.

The rain tapered off while they ate, and eventually Trent could put it off no longer. The evening had been splendid, more than he had hoped for. But he was still committed to his plan. After all, wasn't tonight an indication that it was working?

She walked with him to the darkened front hall, saying nothing, both of them barely breathing as Fenton saw to having Trent's coach brought around front. Her hands felt small in his, and he clasped them lightly. In the dim light of a single lantern, he could make out the glint of gold in her necklace. The chain had gotten twisted during the evening and now the brilliant dangling sapphire was trapped near her collarbone, pointing somewhere beyond her shoulder, the clasp twisted against it.

Somehow the flaw made her even lovelier than she'd been when she'd stolen his breath earlier in the evening.

"I enjoyed dinner." He kept his voice low, afraid that anything above the gravelly near whisper would break the peaceful bubble they seemed encased in.

"As did I." She must have felt the same as he did, that the glow around them was delicate and needed to be cared for. Her words escaped on a breathy sigh, quiet and deep with meaning.

He wanted more. She'd been so much more than he'd expected today. He hated that he'd wasted the past weeks, setting their marriage off on the wrong foot because he feared she would be too much like her shrewish mother. It was clear now that Adelaide was nothing like Lady Crampton, and Trent couldn't wait to start them back on the path they should have been on before he messed everything up.

Slowly he released his grip on her hands and trailed his fingers up her arms, past the edge of the gloves that draped away from her elbows after the busyness of the evening. Past the puffed blue sleeves of her dress, and over the embroidery dancing across her shoulders. Finally he slid his hands up her neck until they softly framed her face. Fingers that spent most of their time gripping a foil or curled tightly into a fist now trembled in an effort to cradle her head gently. One thumb traced the side of her jaw as he looked into her eyes, wondering, hoping, praying she wanted him to kiss her as badly as he wanted to.

Her lips parted on a gentle sigh, and he lowered his head to touch his lips to hers.

It was a mere brush of flesh on flesh. Intellectually he knew this, knew that this meeting of skin couldn't be all that physiologically different than the holding of hands, but it felt like so much more. It felt like that moment of beauty when the morning sun hits the glass just right, showering the room with tiny crystals of light.

He brushed his lips against hers again, unwilling, unable, to leave it at a single touch. It felt like the special, stolen moments as a child when he curled up in front of the Yule log on Christmas Eve and fell asleep on the settee, waking in the morning to find his mother had simply draped a blanket over him and left him there so he could enjoy the magic.

Finally he pressed his lips harder against hers, taking her sigh as his own and sliding his hands deeper into her hair until he fully supported her head.

It felt like home.

He didn't know how long they stood there, trading breath and sharing space. When he finally lifted his head, her wide eyes blinked up at him slowly, glazed and unfocused, the large, dark centers threatening to take over the blue he was always tempted to drown in. He could stay here tonight, he knew. The barriers keeping him from knocking on her bedchamber door had been obliterated the moment his hand had grazed the bare skin of her arm. And if the way her tongue darted out to catch his taste from her lips was any indication, she would open the door when he knocked.

But he wanted more.

What had seemed like a desperate and almost ridiculous notion a few days ago was now the battle plan that was going to get him what he wanted more than anything in his life.

Because he didn't simply want his wife anymore.

Now he wanted Adelaide.

Chapter 17

By morning Adelaide was beginning to understand why she'd never completely understood how God worked. Given that He had made the bewildering, maddening, incomprehensible species that was man from His own image, it stood to reason that the Creator would be a complicated mass of logic never meant to be understood by the female mind. That, or the fall of man in the Garden of Eden had taken them even further off the path than she'd ever realized. Because the fact was, despite a night of tossing and turning and deep contemplation, Adelaide was no closer to understanding her husband than she'd been the day before. And while she was considerably more hopeful this morning—she had that kiss to think about, after all—she was still confused by the fact that she was going to eat breakfast on her own.

She rose with the sun, tired of lying in a bed that wasn't granting her any sleep. Again. Rebecca hadn't come to the room yet, but Adelaide didn't feel like ringing for her. There was something peaceful about wandering her room in solitude until she ended up by the window, amazed at the view of the city while it was still sleeping.

A few clouds drifted across the sky, making shadows dance down the back alley and across the buildings. Occasionally an industrious ray of early sunshine broke through and highlighted a window or lamppost.

The growling of her stomach reminded her that she hadn't eaten much dinner the night before, too focused on keeping the conversation flowing with Trent. As if it were only awaiting the acknowledgment, her stomach cramped in hunger, making her dread having to wait for Rebecca to come and spend the appropriate amount of time preparing her to go downstairs.

Letting the drape she'd been clutching slip through her fingers, she realized she didn't have to wait. This was her home, and it was past time she start living like it.

It didn't take long to go through her dressing room and find her older dresses. She wasn't sure they'd be there, since her mother had seen to her packing, but at least three of her favorites were tucked away in the corner. Back home—or in the country, rather, since she needed to remember that this was now her home—she'd grown accustomed to dressing herself in the morning, only requiring her maid for the more elaborate afternoon and evening clothes.

Her braid from the night before wasn't as destroyed as she'd expected, given the amount of tossing and turning she'd done through the night. She coiled it into a knot on her head, securing it with more pins than Rebecca would have required, but no one would know that but her.

A glance in the mirror above her dressing table showed that she was woefully out of fashion, but that didn't matter. She wasn't going to see anyone but the servants this morning. Her husband wouldn't arrive until afternoon, and no one was going to come calling this early. Except maybe her mother. She hadn't been happy with Adelaide's lack of agreement in helping Helena and her husband, so she might return for another go at it.

The thought of her mother stopping by again made Adelaide reconsider leaving the room in her comfortable, worn gown. While it was highly doubtful that the woman had even woken yet, and she wouldn't dare step out of the house without the full attention of her lady's maid, her mother was also very adept at catching Adelaide at her absolute worst.

But this was her home, and if she wanted to walk around in near rags she should be able to.

Adelaide's moment of disgruntlement faded into delight. She had a butler. Her own butler. She could ban her mother from entering her home until a more appropriate visiting hour or even a more convenient day. What a freeing realization.

She threw open the door, sending a *whoosh* of air to ruffle her skirt. As she skipped down the corridor, the frayed hem of her old morning dress flipped about her ankles in a manner that she could never have gotten away with in front of anyone. Helena had written Adelaide three times since getting married, but never once had she mentioned how wonderful it was to be in control of one's own home. Adelaide completely understood the point of dowager houses now. If Trent were the duke, she would definitely be grateful that his mother had remarried and lived elsewhere. The more she thought about it, the more grateful she was that Trent wasn't the duke. A duchess probably didn't have the luxury of running about in old clothes and banning people from the door.

Adelaide's feet hit the floor in the main hall, reveling in the freedom of being able to go downstairs in nothing but her dressing gown, if she was so inclined. That would draw the notice of the servants, of course, but Adelaide had a feeling her staff wasn't prone to gossiping about their employers the way other servants did.

With a twirl through the hall and another bout of skipping, Adelaide danced her way to the breakfast room before her joyful scamper came to a stumbling halt in the doorway. Nothing was laid out in the breakfast room yet. Despite the realization that this was her house and she could do whatever she wished, she was still at the mercy of what she told the servants to do. They couldn't be expected to know that she was going to rise hours earlier than normal today.

She could, however, go down to the kitchens and get something herself, because they were, after all, her kitchens.

A giggle escaped, and she felt like a child venturing into places she'd never dared go before, despite the fact that she'd been down to the kitchens already. It had felt like Mrs. Harris's space then. But now, now it was Adelaide's. Though she wasn't quite brave enough to say as much to Mrs. Harris yet. Maybe she'd ask the housekeeper for cooking lessons.

She paused at the top of the stairs heading down into the servants' domain, thinking this must be what Evelina felt like in Fanny Burney's novel before she took those first steps into Society. Once Adelaide crossed that threshold, life would never be the same. There would be no area of her house that she hadn't claimed. It would be well and truly hers.

Her foot looked small as she extended it onto the first step. The rough planked wood, worn smooth in the middle, was unlike any set of steps she'd descended before. Somehow the frayed hem lying against her leg made it seem right though. The worn dress matched the worn steps. She'd clearly dressed appropriately for this morning.

Easing down the steps, she relished each moment of this freedom, this declaration of ownership. What would she find when she reached the kitchens? Mrs. Harris rolling out more of that splendid cinnamon biscuit dough? Fenton, Lydia, and the others taking their breakfast? What happened in the kitchens before the rest of the house awoke?

Her mind danced with all the options of what she might find belowstairs. By the time she reached the opening to the kitchens at the bottom of the stairs she was half expecting to find them feeding a tame monkey or spinning each other in an impromptu dance. No matter how fanciful her imagination, however, she'd have never guessed that there would be another lady present amongst the servants.

Yet there she was, seated at the worktable, cutting out biscuits with an apron thrown over her pink-and-brown morning gown. Her dress was certainly not from a previous Season. In fact, Adelaide remembered seeing that exact dress in an Ackermann's Repository last month, though not in pink, of course. She didn't know anyone who bought morning dresses in pink.

She also didn't know anyone who visited someone else's kitchens without being announced to the people who actually lived in the house, so that probably said something about the type of lady that bought pink morning dresses. Assuming, of course, that the woman at the worktable was indeed a lady. She certainly had money and taste, but why would she be up at dawn and in Adelaide's kitchen? She appeared very comfortable. As if she'd been there many times before.

Air got trapped in her chest and she had to force it through a throat that was suddenly thick with a heavy heartbeat. A woman. A refined and elegant woman was comfortable in Trent's kitchen. Why? What was his relation to her? She wasn't a sister. The brown hair coiled into a neat bun and framed with perfect curls was enough to declare her a nonmember of the Hawthorne family. But what if she'd thought she would become one? Trent had said he wasn't courting a lady, and Adelaide believed him, but that didn't mean feelings hadn't existed for another woman. What if this was her? What if she'd returned to Town and hadn't yet heard that Trent had gotten married? Worse yet, what if she didn't care?

Between the tight, shallow breathing, the slow thudding heartbeats, and the massive race of questions, Adelaide was beginning to lose her steadiness. The room was out of focus, and her legs were threatening to give way at any moment. No one had noticed her yet, so it would be a simple matter to slip back up the stairs and pretend she didn't know of this woman's existence. She'd pretended not to notice all kinds of things growing up. Namely anything her mother and sister did. It couldn't be that much harder

156

to ignore a strange woman who may or may not be connected to her husband.

With one hand on the plain wooden newel post at the base of the stairs, Adelaide stepped backward, thinking that if she could just keep her eye on everyone, she'd be able to will them into not looking at her.

She'd forgotten about the buckets of water that had been set near the stairs, ready to be hauled up to prepare the house for the day. They'd been conveniently placed for Oswyn to take them upstairs. Which also made them inconvenient for a quick escape by a woman who wasn't looking at them. Adelaide knocked the bucket sideways, her grip on the newel post making her swing around and land on the stairs instead of splashing into the river of water now gushing across the kitchen floor. If that wasn't enough to attract everyone's attention, the bucket rolled into a collection of brooms, sending them crashing down on Adelaide's head.

It was safe to assume that everyone was now aware of her presence.

Several concerned voices called out as a rush of feet clattered over the stone floor of the kitchen. "My lady!" There were several gasps and another crash or two as they slipped in the spilled water. Adelaide squeezed her eyes shut before admitting the brooms weren't going to hide her existence and she might as well pull herself up from the stair tread jabbing her in the back. As she hauled herself upright, she mumbled a quiet prayer for strength and perhaps a shred of regained dignity. There was no evading it now. She was going to have to be polite to her husband's . . . someone.

Mrs. Harris reached her first, grasping Adelaide's arm tightly until it was clear she wasn't going to do something horrible like topple into the oven or knock down the bread rack.

Easing one eye open at a time, Adelaide took in the concerned circle of servants, the lady in pink right in the middle of them and not even trying to hide. There was no sense in putting it off. The hope Adelaide had woken with was shattered right along with a bowl the scullery maid, Eve, had dropped when she slipped in the newly installed kitchen brook.

Adelaide looked straight at the kitchen inhabitant she didn't employ. The nerve and resolve straightening her back were foreign but not entirely unwelcome. "Who are you?"

It took a moment for the lady in pink to realize Adelaide was talking to her, and then a blush stole across her cheeks. Now that everyone was standing, Adelaide could see that the other woman was incredibly tiny, with dark brown eyes that matched the perfect curls framing her fine-featured face. There was a delicate grace in the way she moved, even when she'd made her way across the slippery kitchen floor. She probably didn't trip over buckets or accidentally turn her gloves inside out.

Mrs. Harris wiped her hands on her apron. "Oh dear, Lord Trent must have forgotten to mention Miss Amelia's visits. She's only just arrived in Town, you know."

No, she didn't know. The last shred of hope that this woman wasn't connected to Trent froze into a lump of ice that dropped into the pit of Adelaide's stomach and radiated cold down her legs until she thought her knees might give way. Again.

"Yes, he must have forgotten." Even though they'd talked for hours last night, and he'd had more than one opportunity to mention this Miss Amelia.

With an exasperated glance at the housekeeper, the woman in pink pushed through to the front of the group. "I'm afraid I didn't realize that Trent had gotten married until Mrs. Harris told me a few moments ago. Had I known, I would never have presumed to visit without speaking with you first. I'm Lady Raebourne."

Adelaide blinked. She was fairly certain her mouth was hanging open. As all her emotions shifted into a massive, undefinable pile, her brain struggled to comprehend this new information. This tiny, smiling woman was Lady Raebourne? This was the harridan her mother and sister claimed had ruined Helena's chance at an advantageous marriage? For the past two years Adelaide's ears had been filled with so many vile diatribes against this woman that Adelaide had expected Lady Raebourne to be nothing short of an utter virago. Instead she looked rather like a woodland fairy.

Adelaide curtsied. "H-how do you do?"

Lady Raebourne's smile was wide and caused her eyes to crinkle at the corners. "I am well. I hope you don't mind if I come visit the kitchens. Trent told me to come whenever I wished as long as I didn't venture upstairs without someone warning him first. Since I was coming to visit the servants, that wasn't a problem."

Placing her feet carefully on the slick stones, Lady Raebourne made her way back to the worktable. Slowly everyone else followed suit, returning to the jobs they'd been doing before Adelaide's inelegant arrival.

"No, no, I don't mind." Adelaide stumbled over to a stool. There was a marchioness cutting out biscuits in her kitchen. She was wearing an apron and everything. Why was a marchioness visiting Adelaide's servants? What sort of person did something like that?

"Good." Lady Raebourne began placing rows of dough on the pan. "I can't believe Trent got married and didn't tell us. Where did you meet?"

"In Hertfordshire." Adelaide took a deep breath and plunged on. Despite Lord Raebourne's country seat being in Hertfordshire and, in fact, bordering Lord Crampton's estate, Adelaide's family had nothing to do with him. Or rather the women didn't. Her father still went over to visit, and on a couple occasions Adelaide had seen the marquis as he was leaving her father's study, but given Mother and Helena's animosity toward the man's wife, they never saw the family socially. "I'm Lord Crampton's daughter."

Lady Raebourne's brows scrunched together while she tried to place Adelaide. It wasn't a surprise when she failed. No one ever remembered Adelaide.

"I didn't know Lady Helena had a sister." The confusion cleared from her face, replaced once again by the sweet, welcoming smile. "I'm pleased to meet you."

She handed the filled pan to Mrs. Harris and took off the apron. "Why don't we go upstairs and get to know one another?"

Adelaide pressed a hand over her stomach, afraid it was going to loudly protest the prolonged wait for food. "Well, I came down to ask about breakfast."

Mrs. Harris herded the two women toward the stairs. "I'll have Oswyn bring some up to you. Go on now. Coffee and chocolate will be following you up to the breakfast room."

"Thank you, Mrs. Harris." Lady Raebourne kissed the old housekeeper's cheek before climbing the stairs without a bit of the hesitation Adelaide had felt on her way down. Her familiarity with the house disturbed Adelaide, who had only yesterday tracked down where they kept the flint in the drawing room.

They settled into the breakfast room, the promised beverages sending fragrant steam up from their cups, Adelaide's bitter while Lady Raebourne's was sweet. Adelaide truly hoped there wasn't anything symbolic in that. Lady Raebourne's marriage had been a love match by all accounts so Adelaide was no longer worried about the woman's connection to Trent, but that didn't stop her from thinking about all the other things that could go wrong given the bad feelings between the lady and Adelaide's family.

"I grew up in this house." Lady Raebourne looked fondly around the shabby breakfast room. "Mrs. Harris and Fenton practically raised me."

"Here?" Adelaide choked on her coffee. She remembered the story, or at least Helena's version of it, where the eligible Marquis of Raebourne had fallen in love with the Duke of Riverton's newly acquired ward. She just hadn't realized that prior to the duke's patronage Lady Raebourne had been left in the care of servants. It made the story much more romantic than Helena's rantings made it sound.

Lady Raebourne nodded. "For ten years. Then everything changed quite suddenly."

Adelaide couldn't even begin to imagine how different being married to a marquis would be than living in a home with only the servants for company. It must have been like family if Lady Raebourne still visited. More like a family than Adelaide's. It had taken her mother nearly a week to visit her, and here Lady Raebourne was visiting the housekeeper who had raised her after being in Town a mere day.

"You're welcome any time. I didn't mean to cut your visit short." Adelaide fiddled with the handle of her cup before lifting it to take a long drink of coffee. She'd nearly finished the cup but didn't think it would be enough to help her gain any equilibrium. There'd been too many ups and downs already this morning.

"Thank you, but I'll try to arrange a more regular schedule now. When it was only Trent here it didn't matter much, as he left the running of the house to Mrs. Harris." Lady Raebourne took a delicate sip of her chocolate. "Will Trent be joining us soon?"

Heat flushed across Adelaide's chest and up her neck. She hadn't wanted anyone to find out that Trent wasn't living with her, yet there was no hiding the fact that he wasn't home from Lady Raebourne. "He's not here."

"Has he gone riding already, then? Would you like to wait and eat when he returns?"

Adelaide forced herself to look unworried, though she wasn't quite sure what that entailed. A choked laugh and a flip of her hand would have to do. "Oh, no. We don't need to wait on him. It could be hours before he returns."

Oswyn entered and set a plate piled high with all of her favorite breakfast foods in front of Adelaide. A similar plate was set in front of Lady Raebourne. As they ate, they talked.

It was surprisingly easy to talk to Lady Raebourne. They discussed the village of Riverton, comparing thoughts on which of the two teahouses served better cakes. The topic of books came up and they chatted about their favorites until both women were contemplating the crumbs on their plates. Finally the conversation rolled around to social engagements.

"Have you been out anywhere yet? Anthony and I only arrived into Town yesterday morning and wanted to take the day to settle in, but I would be happy to suggest a few things. You simply must see the opera. I've heard the new one is fabulous. What else have you put on your agenda?" Lady Raebourne leaned back in her seat, abandoning the proper ladylike posture she'd held while she was eating. She closed her eyes and inhaled the steam off the cup of chocolate that had just been poured.

Adelaide fiddled with her discarded serviette, poking at its corners until it stood up like a tent on the table. "I don't know. We haven't really discussed it. Trent told me I should go through the invitations and let him know what I wanted to attend, but I don't know where he left them."

Lady Raebourne tilted her head to the side. "Fenton usually piles them on the desk in Trent's study. I've come over with Miranda a time or two to sort through them for him. He neglects them terribly, sometimes shoving them in the bottom drawer of his cabinet and ignoring them completely. For so long he was at the whims of his sisters since he had to escort them. I think he just goes to whatever event he hears people talking about at one of his clubs. I'm surprised Miranda hasn't been by to coordinate your schedules yet. She arrived in Town two days ago."

Adelaide said nothing. What could she say? She'd seen nothing of Trent's family, other than his brother. She was beginning to think the reputed closeness of the Hawthorne family was a very elaborate ruse to fool society.

The other woman suddenly sat up, sloshing the light brown drink over the edge of her cup. "Oh my! Miranda doesn't know, does she? I would have expected her to write me if she knew, but I can't imagine Trent not telling her he got married."

"I . . . well, that is, it was all very sudden and . . . I'm not sure." Adelaide blinked nervous tears away, hoping the spectacles hid the telltale sheen, not magnified it. She had tried not to let it bother her that Trent hadn't seemed very anxious for her to meet his family as his wife instead of the neighbor, not even ensuring his mother attended the wedding. It was as if he were trying to pretend the marriage had never even happened. But his sisters were sure to be coming to London with their spouses for the Season and his mother usually returned with her second husband, the Earl of Blackstone, as well, so Trent couldn't expect to hide Adelaide forever. Especially not now that he'd introduced her to a good portion of the *ton* at the ball and with their subsequent rides in the park.

Lady Raebourne clapped her hands together. "Oh, this is going to be fabulous. You must send me word on what engagements you plan to attend next. I'll make sure to be there in a show of support. The rest of the family should be in Town within the week. I'll have everyone over for dinner if Lady Blackstone doesn't take care of that first."

Chapter 18

No matter how old a man got, there was something decidedly uncomfortable about being in trouble with his mother. And if the thin line of tightly pressed lips as she stared at Trent across the expanse of Griffith's study was any indication, Lady Blackstone was decidedly not happy with her son.

"You got married."

Trent ran a hand through his hair. He should have written sooner. He'd finally drafted a letter last night and sent it off to the post this morning, but that wasn't likely to appease the woman in front of him. "Yes, Mother, I did."

"And you knew about it." Mother turned her icy blue eyes to the Duke of Riverton, staring him down the way only a mother could—for no one else would dare to glare at such a powerful man that way.

"Yes, Mother, I did." Griffith didn't squirm under their mother's scrutiny and his voice was calm and steady, but he rubbed his forefinger against his thumb.

Trent cleared his throat and shifted in the chair beside Griffith's desk. They'd been talking about the upcoming horse races when their mother had arrived, storming through the house without waiting to be announced. One of these days she was going to regret that habit. This was now a bachelor's residence, after all. "And how did you find out? The letter couldn't possibly have reached you yet. I sent it to the country."

One of Griffith's eyebrows shot up in inquiry at Trent's claim that he'd sent a letter. It was an affectation Trent found annoying and arrogant. Mostly because he'd never been able to do it.

Their mother could, though. She held a similar expression of skepticism, proving that not all of Griffith's imperious habits had come from their father. "You wrote?"

"Yes." Trent swallowed hard enough to make his ears crackle. Hopefully it wasn't as obvious to the rest of the room's inhabitants.

"Your pen seems to be a bit tardy, as I had to hear about it from my lady's maid, who heard it from the housekeeper next door, who learned about it from reading the scandal sheets after her mistress discarded them." Mother folded her hands in her lap and gave Trent the look that always had him squirming as a child. It was still effective on the twenty-four-year-old man. "I have many questions, but the first of which is why you are here instead of home with your wife."

Trent tapped his fingers on the arm of the chair. "How did you know to come here?"

She sniffed and folded her hands tightly in her lap. Trent thought she might prefer them about his neck at the moment. "I didn't. I was coming to ask Griffith if he knew more about your situation. I've already been by to see Miranda and Georgina. Both of them were as surprised as I was. Surely your wife wondered why I wasn't at the wedding. I didn't want to walk into your home without knowing what else I should expect. I'm rather glad I took the precaution."

"Oh." What else could he say? He could claim to simply be visiting Griffith, but that lie wouldn't hold up long. The family was a stalwart fortress when it came to keeping their business out of the public eye, but within the walls of family, keeping a secret was a difficult endeavor. A glance at Griffith proved he wasn't going to be of any help, as he'd opened one of his ledgers and appeared intent on ignoring the entire conversation.

"Why. Are. You. Not. At. Home?"

He had been hoping she would move on to another line of questioning, but it had been a fairly weak hope. His mother wasn't very distractible. He looked at her, wondering how to phrase the situation in a way that would cause him the least amount of trouble. Age had added a few lines to her face, but her hair was still mostly blond and her posture still perfect.

Not that the former Duchess of Riverton and current Countess of Blackstone would have it any other way. For as long as Trent could remember, his mother had been the definition of a well-bred lady. She would never have gone about town with her glove inside out or even a crooked hem. Adelaide couldn't seem to help it, which Trent found endearing, and it brought a smile to his face even as he worried about what his mother would think of her.

"I'm courting her," he finally mumbled.

"I beg your pardon?" Mother's reticule slipped from her hand and rolled down her lap before landing on the floor with a light *plop*.

He swallowed again and resisted the urge to adjust his cravat, feeling a bit irritated at himself. A grown man shouldn't feel like he needed to cower when he explained himself to his mother. Of course, he so rarely had to explain himself to his mother. Whatever trouble he'd gotten into at school had been handled with a self-deprecating grin and a well-timed joke. By the time he'd outgrown that, Griffith had come into his own, and more often than not people deferred problems to Trent's brother instead of his mother. He could only hope this situation felt as strange to her as it did to him and she wouldn't be willing to drag it out much longer.

"I am courting my wife." With some effort, Trent straightened his shoulders and looked his mother in the eye. It wasn't as if he should be ashamed of his plan. It was a good plan.

"That is a terrible plan." She frowned before picking her reticule up and slamming it into her lap.

No, it wasn't. "She's never had a Season, Mother. Lady Crampton robbed her of her chance, and I'm restoring it the only way I know how."

Trent and his mother stared each other down. The only sound in the room was the occasional scrape of Griffith's quill against his ledger. Trent had sat in this room more than once while Griffith worked in his ledgers, and the duke was writing considerably slower than normal. He wasn't going to wade into the conversation, but he was apparently not above watching with fascination as it played out.

Mother blinked first, but it was a short-lived victory for Trent. "While you will get no argument from me that Lady Crampton is a poor example of motherly devotion, it is not your job to fix it. Do you think you can keep your living conditions secret? What do you think will happen when everyone finds out you are not living with your wife?"

Trent hadn't thought much about it. He'd instinctively been discreet, but he'd never had to think much about gossip and scandal rags. His life was far and away less interesting than those of other young aristocrats. While he'd taken care to never show too much affection toward any particular woman, he hadn't had to watch much else. His well-known skills in the pugilist ring kept him out of other non-exercise-related confrontations.

His mother was right—people might start talking—but the past week had proven that his idea had merit. He and Adelaide were forming a relationship, and all of London thought them adorable. "It's been working quite well for the past week. Much better than the week before, if I'm being honest."

Narrowed blue eyes conveyed the mistake in Trent's statement. "How long have you been married?"

The scritching of the quill ceased. Even the clock on the mantel seemed to fall into silence. That or it simply couldn't be heard over the blood rushing through Trent's head. He couldn't resist the urge to adjust his cravat this time. "About two weeks."

"Two weeks. And the banns were properly read, I assume?"

Trent cleared his throat. "Yes, Mother."

"Five weeks. Five weeks and you've only recently seen fit to write to me?" She pushed up from her seat and swept toward the door of the room. "Here is what will happen. While I'm certainly not through talking to the pair of you about how this possibly came about, I'm not going to let another day go by without welcoming your wife to the family. We will be there for tea. See to it that she is aware and your staff prepared."

Trent stumbled to his feet, knocking his knee against a table and making a lamp jump. "We?"

"But of course. You don't think Georgina and Miranda are going to wait to meet her, do you?"

"But you've already met her. All of you. Surely you all know her better than I do."

Mother smiled, that indulgent smile only women seem to be able to perfect—the one that told Trent he obviously didn't understand and that he was rather pitiful and adorable at the same time. He hated that smile. "My dear son, I'm not coming to your house to have tea with a neighbor. I'm going to meet my new daughter."

⌒

Bravado can only carry a woman so far before reality intrudes with crushing abruptness. In this case, it came in the form of a door. More specifically, it came in the form of the room on the other side of the door.

Adelaide had seen Lady Raebourne off with a smile a few moments ago, but she wasn't really sure how she felt about the tiny woman who knew more about the workings of Adelaide's home than Adelaide did. That jumble of feelings could be sorted out later. Of considerably more pressing concern was what to do about her social calendar.

If she were going to build a life in London, she needed to go out. Meet people. See and be seen. It stood to reason that the sooner people got used to seeing her around the sooner they'd stop whispering behind their fans every time she walked by. Besides, she was tired of cowering in the house.

She could ask Fenton about the invitations Trent had said he'd put aside for her, but that felt like something she should know or should have learned from her husband. Asking the servant meant admitting that she and Trent weren't communicating. Not that there was any real reason to hide it from the servants. Still, she couldn't bring herself to admit it out loud. Especially not when Lady Raebourne knew more about where her husband kept his correspondence than she did.

Which was why she was standing at the door of his study, facing the realization that this wasn't really her house at all. She could ban her mother from the premises—and in a fit of power-declaring pique had done so by giving Fenton instructions to keep the woman away for the entire day—but at the end of the day the house was Trent's. He could truly go anywhere he wished, while there were rooms that were nearly impossible for her to enter.

His study, for instance.

But if that was where the invitations were, then that was where she needed to be, and it was his own fault that she was going to have to invade his territory to get them. If he'd been home like he should have been, this wouldn't be happening.

She built up a large well of irritation at the situation and used it to open the door and propel her way into the room. Once over the threshold, it didn't seem so scary. It was a masculine room—one of the few in the house that seemed to have had some attention recently—but it wasn't overly imposing. Trent probably had no need to appear imposing, unlike her father, who had actually set his desk up on a dais so he could always look down on his visitors.

The desk surface was clear, which meant she would need to go digging in the drawers as Lady Raebourne mentioned. Adelaide's heart threatened to beat its way through her stomach and down to her toes. It was one thing to enter his room, but quite another to go through his drawers.

As fascinating as she was finding the strange little group of people living under her roof, though, they all still had jobs to do and trying to have social interactions with a person holding a cleaning rag left her feeling a bit lazy. Useless. In the end it was the thought of spending another week with nothing to look at but the house and no one to speak to but the servants that had her yanking open drawers and looking for cream and white squares of parchment.

Instead she found drawings.

In a drawer behind the desk sat sketch after sketch of a greenhouse. It was laid out differently than any other greenhouse she'd ever seen. It didn't appear to be for growing flowers, though. It looked as if Trent was planning to grow crops inside the greenhouse. Actually, just one crop. She adjusted her glasses and squinted at the words scrawled across the top of the page.

Pineapple growth plan, adjustments to Dutch method, version 5.

Trent was planning to grow pineapples? A pineapple was something that grew? She'd read about carvings of them but had never seen a picture. With spikes all around the body and huge leaves sprouting off the top, the pineapple looked nothing like any apple she'd ever seen. How did one go about eating something so . . . prickly?

"My lady?" Fenton's voice drifted down the upper corridor.

Adelaide squeaked and dropped the drawings back into the drawer, slamming it shut with her foot and scampering around to the front of the desk. "What is it, Fenton?"

Fenton's eyebrows rose as he stood in the open door to the study.

Wrinkles formed, making him look like a pug dog she'd seen one of her mother's friends carry around. "What are you doing in here, my lady?"

The curse of Trent's unusual household. Where else would a servant question the intentions of the lady of the house? Adelaide considered lying and saying that Trent had asked her to get something, but the potential mess such a lie could cause wasn't worth it, so she opted for the truth. "Lady Raebourne mentioned that this was where you usually placed the invitations. I wanted to go through them."

The pug wrinkles dropped into a wide smile. "I've been placing those on your desk now, my lady."

Her desk? She had a desk? Why didn't she know she had a desk? And where in the world was it? Unfortunately none of these were questions she could ask the butler. It was embarrassing for a lady not to know where her own desk was. There weren't that many rooms in the house. She'd be able to find it on her own. "Thank you, Fenton. I'll just go look at those now then."

She stepped forward, but Fenton didn't shift away from the doorway. "I beg your pardon, but Lord Trent is looking for you. He said his mother is coming for tea."

Chapter 19

Her drawing room was full of blond heads. Three of them to be precise, each more elegantly coiffed than the last. And the women attached to the heads were equally elegant. Peering at the women through the crack in the partially closed door, Adelaide took a moment to compose herself.

Would she ever not feel like an intruder wandering around someone else's home without permission? Her early morning burst of confidence and optimism had lost a good bit of its strength. Even Lady Raebourne knew more about Adelaide's husband and house than Adelaide did, proving that Adelaide was certainly not the most important lady in Trent's life.

And now her shabby drawing room, complete with broken curtain rod, was occupied by the other three women in Trent's life. She'd met all of them at one point or another, though they may not remember it. If the gossip columns were to be believed, few people in London had even realized Lord and Lady Crampton had two daughters. Being overlooked by her mother and the second choice of her father had never bothered her before, possibly because it was all she'd ever known, but she was beginning to wonder what was so wrong with her that they'd all but hidden her existence from the world.

There was no hiding anymore, though. Three of the most popular women in London were in her drawing room, and they'd come for the sole purpose of seeing her.

At least she'd had warning and was now wearing her nicest afternoon dress. Trent had offered to stay, but she'd foolishly insisted he leave. How would it look if she wasn't even willing to sit down with her mother-in-law for tea without her husband at her side?

Lady Blackstone was going to expect her son to have married a composed, elegant young woman. And while no one was going to confuse Adelaide with the more gregarious ladies, she could probably manage to appear a bit more put together than normal for the sake of a good impression.

With one last deep breath and a quick smoothing of her skirts, she pushed her way into the drawing room.

Three heads turned. Three faces smiled.

No words emerged from Adelaide's mouth.

"It is nice to see you again, Lady Adelaide." The cultured voice cut through the air, almost drawing a wince from Adelaide. The power had been claimed by the eldest lady in the room, though she didn't appear nearly as old as she had to be, given that all four of her children had reached adulthood already.

The countess's presence nearly knocked aside Adelaide's plans for composure and poise, but she gave a regal nod. "Lady Blackstone. It has been a while."

Lady Blackstone was sitting neatly on a settee next to the most gorgeous woman Adelaide had ever seen. It had been some years since she'd seen Lady Georgina, but it was obvious why Helena had been so determined to marry before the young woman made her debut bow in Society. That Lady Georgina had married a businessman so far beneath her on the social ladder was a testament to how much love matches meant to the Hawthorne family.

The welcoming, humor-touched smile on the beautiful young woman's face did nothing to quell the clenching of Adelaide's heart even as she refused to let herself fret, at least not outwardly. She and Trent weren't a love match. They weren't even a marriage of convenience. They were the product of bad luck and a conniving, status-hungry woman.

"Would any of you care for tea?" Adelaide asked as she looked toward the third lady in the room.

The Duchess of Marshington, the older of Trent's sisters, stood by the window. She didn't fidget or move about but she still projected a nervous energy, as if she were too agitated to sit until she absolutely had to. It had to be her eyes. For while Her Grace's posture remained perfect and calm, her eyes immediately flitted in Adelaide's direction and assessed her in one long, sweeping gaze before tightening at the corners. "Tea would be lovely."

Grateful for any excuse to step from the room, Adelaide turned back to the door to give instructions to the waiting footman. She shouldn't have been surprised to see Fenton already making his way through the house with a loaded tea service. Of course the servants would know what Trent's family members liked and see to it as soon as they arrived. Like Lady Raebourne, the three ladies in the drawing room probably knew more about the house than Adelaide did.

At least the prompt arrival of tea would give her something to do with her hands.

She just hoped they didn't shake. Nothing gave away nerves like a clattering teacup.

With Fenton on her heels, she walked back into the room. "Here we are."

Another several minutes were spent arranging the tea service and pouring tea. Lady Blackstone waited until her daughters had been served to request hers with a light splash of milk. Adelaide handed the cup to Lady Blackstone before giving her tea the same treatment.

"I hear you married my son." Lady Blackstone's voice wasn't

cold, but Adelaide didn't think the woman was particularly happy about the statement she'd just made either.

"Mother, kindly remember that Lady Adelaide is your daughter by marriage, not birth. There's no need to lecture her." The Duchess of Marshington dropped back in the chair to Adelaide's right, saluting Adelaide with her teacup before bringing it to her smiling lips. "Welcome to the family."

"Miranda, a lady never slumps in a chair, particularly not in public." Lady Blackstone frowned at her oldest daughter, but it looked like nothing more than habit, her eyes conveying loving indulgence.

Her Grace sighed but righted her posture. The smile on her face tilted a bit higher on one side, making it look impish. "I'm not in public. You know, I outrank you now. If I wanted to I could make slumping in drawing room chairs the *de rigueur* thing to do. Particularly if I got Georgina to join me."

"I'll thank you to leave me out of this." Lady Georgina cut her hand through the air. "Besides I don't know how you can abide sitting like that. It makes it very uncomfortable to drink your tea."

"She knows." Lady Blackstone lifted an eyebrow in the duchess's direction even as a smile teased the corner of her mouth. "And regardless of your rank, I am your mother. And since, as you reminded me, we are not in public, it means that at this moment, I outrank you."

Adelaide swung her gaze back and forth among the ladies, marveling at the banter. She couldn't imagine having such a conversation with her own mother and sister. Was this what all families were like, or was it Trent's family that was different than normal? Her eyes were threatening to dry out with her wide-eyed staring, so she blinked a few times and took a sip of tea, hoping the women would continue to talk amongst themselves until they decided they'd stayed the proper amount of time.

She was not to be so lucky.

The duchess grinned at her mother before turning the wide smile in Adelaide's direction. "You may call me Miranda. There are too many dukes and duchesses in the room when the family gets together to go around Your Grace-ing everyone. Besides, it makes Georgina feel left out."

"Hmm, yes, quite. That's why I've started going by Mrs. McCrae in more informal situations. I crave the ranking."

Adelaide wanted to shift in her seat as all three women turned in her direction, but she forced herself to remain still—with the proper ladylike posture, of course—and asked Georgina, "What should I call you?"

"Georgina will suffice when it is family. I do still go by Lady Georgina in London, though. It makes things a bit easier for Colin if people remember he married the daughter of a duke."

Miranda snorted. "It makes things easier for Colin when people remember how much money he helps them acquire."

Lady Blackstone set her cup in the saucer and sighed. "Miranda, a lady never discusses money with anyone except her husband. And even that should be avoided whenever possible."

Adelaide was fairly sure she could slip out of the room and none of the three ladies would miss her.

Georgina looked from her mother to her older sister. "Kindly remember we came to visit Lady Adelaide, not discuss your on-going difference of opinion on proper behavior for a lady." Her green eyes speared into Adelaide, proving she could be as lethal as her mother if she decided Adelaide wasn't good for Trent.

Not that there was anything they could do about it. The marriage had already occurred. The worst that could happen now was Adelaide being banished to the country and Trent continuing on as if she didn't exist. He wouldn't be able to marry again, but he'd at least have his home back.

"So we are." Lady Blackstone slid her cup onto the table and folded her hands in her lap. "I apologize for not visiting sooner.

I'm afraid I didn't learn of your marriage until yesterday. I know I haven't been to Riverton much since my marriage, but I wasn't aware that you and Trent were even acquainted."

"We aren't," Adelaide stammered before she had a chance to think it through. That probably wasn't the best thing to have said. Trent had told them the circumstances, hadn't he? He could hardly hide his presence in Griffith's house from his family. Still, she tried to lessen the shock her words seemed to have brought to the other ladies' faces. "Or rather we weren't. It's a bit complicated."

"I see," Lady Blackstone—who had not invited Adelaide to call her anything else—said quietly. Adelaide was rather afraid that she did.

Three pair of eyes stared her down. Despite the fact that Lady Blackstone was the scariest woman in the room at the moment, Adelaide chose to meet her light blue gaze. The other two were a green much too similar to Trent's for her comfort.

Moments passed. Adelaide's heart couldn't decide if it wanted to beat uncontrollably or stop altogether.

Despite the earlier banter, the daughters seemed to be waiting on some signal from their mother. Adelaide didn't know what she could do to satisfy the countess beyond what she'd already done, so she simply sat there and focused all of her energy on not breaking eye contact, though she probably blinked a few more times than was absolutely necessary.

Finally, Lady Blackstone spoke. "I don't know what happened, and at this moment it bares little significance, as the deed is done. But regardless of the situation my son's happiness is of great importance to me. So I have one question, if you don't mind my asking it."

Adelaide swallowed and nodded. There was truly no other possible response.

"Do you love my son?"

"I barely know him, my lady," Adelaide whispered, stunned at the truth that popped out of her mouth. She spoke again before she could really think about it. "But I'd like to. It seems like it would be a nice thing to love one's husband."

The answer seemed to satisfy the countess because she nodded and broke their connection. "I'm positively thrilled that Lady Yensworth has decided not to do a particular theme for her ball this year. Last year's masquerade was tedious."

Miranda groaned while Georgina tried not to cough into her teacup. She took a hasty swallow before looking up. "Yes. Quite tedious."

"Are you and Trent attending the ball?" Miranda slid her cup to the table and folded her hands in her lap.

Adelaide blinked. "I . . . that is . . ."

"Of course she is going." Lady Blackstone rose to her feet and extracted a paper from her reticule. "Since Trent is determined to give you the Season you never had, I've taken the liberty of making a list of events you shouldn't miss over the next few weeks." She handed the paper to Adelaide.

"Thank you." And Adelaide was thankful. Without guidance, determining their social engagements had been daunting at best, but more often than not the task terrified her. It wasn't lost on her that Lady Blackstone was providing more assistance and care than her own mother. Did Trent know how fortunate he was?

Lady Blackstone's lips curled into a smile a bit broader than the polite smile she'd been wearing earlier. "Now for the fun part. We must get you ready."

Georgina clapped her hands together with glee. "I love spending other people's money."

Miranda frowned. "Do I have to go? I hate shopping."

Lady Blackstone lifted an eyebrow again. "We are showing solidarity for your new sister. As the Duchess of Marshington you will participate."

"Shopping?" Adelaide's knees shook as she rose to her feet. "I don't think that's necessary, Lady Blackstone. I haven't discussed pin money or anything with Trent yet."

"I know how many bills my son can manage. Just because a lady never talks of money doesn't mean she shouldn't know a thing or two about it." Lady Blackstone swept across the room toward the door. "And do call me Caroline."

Chapter 20

"I assured your lovely wife that you would not be upset at her missing your ride this afternoon. While I'll endeavor not to interfere in your plans in the future, I'm afraid it was unavoidable today."

Trent stared wide-eyed at the mother who only that morning had informed him that his courtship plan was nonsense. "Of course I don't mind. But, er, what were you doing?"

"Spending a great deal of your money, which you should have seen to already. Also, I was making sure no harm would come from your ridiculous plot. You may thank me later."

She handed Trent a piece of paper. "These are the events I recommend you attend if you want to give her a complete social experience as quickly as possible. I assume once you've done that you'll move back home and stop this nonsense?"

Trent took the paper with numb fingers as he nodded.

"Good." Mother folded her hands in front of her. "Until that happens I suggest you spend as much time at your clubs as possible. People must see you out and about, not gathering dust here in your brother's home. You will send Adelaide a note each morning, detailing where you expect to be so that she will not be caught off guard by any visitors looking for you."

Trent hadn't thought about that, though his experience with

Givendale at the boxing ring had made him a bit concerned. Trust his mother to come up with a solution before he'd even realized the full problem. Because it was better than being shamed by his mother's accusatory glare, Trent looked at the list of events. Nearly every day had something, and some days even listed two events. They were going to be a very busy couple, which he had no problem with. A bit of excitement unfurled within him at the thought, proof that his courtship plan was working. "It's not nonsense."

Mother sighed. "It is. But somehow you've convinced her it's romantic. Miranda seems to agree with her."

Trent knew there was a reason he liked Miranda. Less than a year apart in age, the two of them had always been especially close growing up. He knew he should have expected her to see what he was trying to do. Still, something about the way his mother was talking about the entire thing made him uneasy. "What do you mean you were making sure no harm would come from my plan?"

Mother tilted her head and sighed, making Trent feel like a foolish child instead of a grown man. "You have left your wife, a woman unknown to most of London, alone. She has no established friends, no history. My son, you are the brother of a duke. A duke with a reputation for actually caring what happens to his family. Do you honestly think no one will try to use her to get to you and by extension, Griffith?"

Apparently there was very good reason for Trent to feel like a foolish child. Had he missed this sort of subtle political manipulation before or had he been left alone, seen as the careless younger brother not yet worth the effort? Funny how marriage suddenly matured a man in the eyes of society. "I hadn't thought of that." He swallowed. "I'll move home."

"While I would obviously think that wise, it goes against the course of action you have chosen. Your situation is ridiculous enough without your adding bitterness or some other such notion to the mix. You've nothing to worry about. We have set up a visiting rotation. As her new family we will be able to chaperone Adelaide without raising suspicion among anyone. And as much as I've never understood the familiarity you have with your staff, in this case it is a boon, because they will look out for any mischief as well. Whenever you go out, you will escort her home and send the carriage away. After thirty minutes you will come out the back, where Griffith's driver will be waiting in a simple hack. There's no need for all of London to know about this foolishness."

If Trent had ever wondered how his mother managed to raise a duke after the death of his father, all of his questions would now have been answered. In less than twelve hours his mother had concocted and put into motion a plan that was more thought out than his simple idea had ever been. She'd looked at every angle and effectively planned against potential pitfalls. No wonder his father had always looked at her with such awe on his face.

Trent smiled and leaned forward to kiss his mother on the cheek in a show of affection he hadn't given her since he'd been a boy. A hint of pink brushed her cheeks.

She cleared her throat and clasped her hands together at her waist. "Now. We've a few minutes yet before I need to return home and ready myself for the evening. I hadn't planned on going out much this Season but that has obviously changed for the foreseeable future. We will be out in full force to show support for your new wife. Speculation about the marriage is already rampant, and that foolish woman Lady Crampton is only fueling it. I've always thought that woman would throw her own daughter to the wolves if it achieved greater popularity." Mother pressed her lips together in irritation. There weren't many people who bothered his mother enough for her to show it, and even then she only released the emotion in private, but Lady Crampton had always been one of them. The two women had known each other since their own London Seasons, and more than once Trent had wondered if something had happened then to cause the lingering animosity.

182

Unfortunately, Mother's irritation was now redirected at him. "In these remaining moments, you are going to sit down and explain to me exactly how you ended up in this situation. And you"— she pointed to somewhere over Trent's shoulder—"are going to tell me why you didn't stop it."

Trent turned to see Griffith coming down the stairs with a stack of papers in his hands. He'd obviously been headed toward his study and looked confused by his mother's interruption. Though he couldn't possibly have known what was going on, the confusion soon cleared from his face. "My study, then?"

"No. The drawing room. The white one with all the spindly furniture you both despise. I have a feeling I am not going to like this conversation, and so you are not going to like it either." Mother sniffed and turned toward the formal drawing room off the main hall.

Trent groaned and followed. He was convinced there wasn't a man alive who didn't hate this room, though none of them had ever complained when they came to visit Miranda or Georgina. Done almost entirely in white, it made a man feel like an awkward, bumbling schoolboy. It had been decorated for his sisters to receive callers in during their Seasons, and both of the brothers were convinced it had been intentionally designed to make men feel ill at ease in order to give their sisters every possible advantage.

Now it was their mother holding the advantage. The brothers walked to the drawing room like men headed for the gallows.

The glaring white of the room was broken only by the occasional accent of gold. From the gold-veined white marble fireplace to the thin gold stripes on the white settee and the lightly gilded frames that dotted the white silk-covered walls, there wasn't an inch that would forgive the slightest bit of dirt on a man's clothing or boots. The room was famous across London, and Trent guessed that many a man had made sure to come calling straight from his rooms so as not to be the one to mar the white perfection.

Mother preceded them into the room, but instead of sitting to the side on the gold-striped settee she'd occupied through her daughters' Seasons, she settled into a white-on-white-brocade armchair, gesturing for the two men to share the sofa across from her.

Trent eyed the thin curving legs before easing onto the seat. Griffith plopped his massive frame down with more force than normal, his feet actually lifting from the floor as his back landed against the back of the seat. Trent wished he'd had the foresight to join him. If they'd broken the sofa, their mother couldn't make them sit on it, might not have even wanted to stay in the same room as the splintered furniture.

But the spindly legs held, and there was nothing left to do but face their mother and smile.

She didn't smile back.

"I was staying at Riverton," Trent began.

"Because he didn't want to stay at his own house while the construction was going on." Griffith settled farther into his corner of the sofa, trying to look as confident as a large man on a delicate piece of furniture could.

Trent glared at his older brother. "The entire bedchamber wing was in shambles. I'd have been sleeping on the drawing room sofa."

"But you wouldn't be married."

Trent couldn't think of a single remark cutting enough to be a proper response to that low blow.

"Boys." The quiet word brought them both to a halt the way it always had. Trent and Griffith never came to actual blows, but when the matter was personal, they could verbally spar with the best of them. It didn't happen often, but when it did the only one with the nerve to come between them was their mother.

Trent turned back to face her. "I was cutting across the west fields by the ruins—the small keep built into the hill beside the old watchtower—and I heard singing and saw a lone horse. I climbed in to investigate."

Mother closed her eyes and sighed. "The mushrooms."

Trent looked at Griffith, who appeared as surprised as he was. "How did you know?"

"She walked out there with me ages ago and asked if she could collect them. It must be nearly ten years ago now. She walked across that old wooden floor, confident as you please, and then climbed down the holes from the old stair supports. But she was a child then. Surely she wasn't still scampering up and down the wall as a grown woman."

Mother had always kept strict rules for her girls on what lady-like behavior consisted of. Trent couldn't imagine her ever letting Miranda or Georgina climb into ruins to collect mushrooms, even when they were children.

Trent shifted in his seat, wondering if he should feel embarrassed on Adelaide's behalf. "Er . . . yes. She was."

"But that floor could give way any day now."

Griffith coughed. "Not anymore."

Trent frowned at Griffith. "And you wouldn't have allowed curiosity to trump your good sense for a few moments? I'll have you know—"

"Boys." Mother cleared her throat. "I surmise you were the reason the floor finally fell?"

Trent nodded his head. "And it took all night to cut through the vines and find another way out."

He left off the story there, deciding it was best to keep to as many cold facts as possible. No one else needed to know how scared he'd been or how the miserable pain in his ankle and hands had prevented him from finding a moment's sleep. It wasn't necessary to share the despair he'd felt when the moon broke through the clouds, sealing his gentlemanly fate.

"And then he proposed," Griffith muttered.

"You proposed?" Mother asked with clear surprise. She hadn't been surprised by the rest of it, knowing that something outrageous had to have happened to force Trent's unexpected nuptials. But his unforced proposal seemed to knock her off guard.

Trent really didn't understand why that was the part of the story that seemed to shock everyone instead of the ridiculousness of falling through an obviously rotten floor.

"Yes, I proposed. It seemed the thing to do since we were spending the night together—alone." How could he explain to them how despondent he'd felt when Adelaide's ruination became a done thing? When her reputation was lost to the stars and lack of proper chaperone? Within miles of their respective homes, they'd been condemned by circumstances. He knew at that moment he would never get the chance to propose to anyone else. And it had bothered him. Looking back, part of him had wanted to feel like he wasn't just a victim in the whole mess.

He'd pulled up one of the early blooming violets and twined it into a circle before offering it to Adelaide and asking her to marry him. It was a moment that had been just for the two of them. A moment they'd claimed before the world condemned them. That way, when they finally climbed out of that stone prison, they would be able to declare their fate instead of having it declared for them.

But he didn't know how to explain that to his mother.

So he didn't.

Mother's brow creased. "And in all that time, no one came looking for her? No one came by? I can't believe no one knew she was going out there."

"There was a wagon of some sort, or we thought we heard one. We shouted as loud as we could but no one answered." Trent rubbed his hand along the back of his neck. "Her mother knew she was headed to the ruins, but Adelaide said it wouldn't be the first time the countess had forgotten about her."

Griffith shifted in his seat. "And you believe her?"

Trent and Mother both frowned at Griffith, but it was Mother who finally spoke. "Why shouldn't he? You've met Lady Crampton."

Trent wanted to jump to his wife's defense, but he couldn't. Griffith had always been able to see the bigger picture, to know what was going on beyond the portrait's frame. What was he seeing now?

"Consider for a moment if you did actually hear a wagon. How often does one of us ride through there alone? What if she wasn't simply down there for mushrooms? It's an incredibly risky gamble and highly unlikely to pay off, but did it really cost them anything? I can't put it past Lady Crampton to leave her daughter there as potential bait and then come back to help her out of the ruins later. Only this time she kept driving because she'd actually been successful."

They all sat in silence for a moment until Mother broke it with a rough laugh. "That's rather farfetched. Even for one of those Minerva Press novels."

But Trent couldn't completely shake the idea. They'd been so certain they heard someone drive by. And if someone had, Trent knew they'd heard the shouting. Trent had been able to hear Adelaide's singing clearly as he approached.

Not that it mattered. Trap or not, he was married, and no amount of plot discovery now would change that fact. "The deed is done. This is the last time we speak of how it came about. Adelaide is now my wife, and there's nothing I can do about it." He bit his tongue before he could spout the rest of his bitter thoughts. Things like telling the rest of them to go on and enjoy their love-filled marriages, or chance at a love-filled marriage in Griffith's case. For whatever reason, God had chosen this trial for Trent to bear, and it didn't matter how much he'd wanted to court a woman and fall in love, this was his life and that was all there was to it.

He didn't say any of those things because he didn't know how. There wasn't a way to phrase them that didn't sound pitiful and pathetic. And he already felt plenty of that for being forced into marriage in the first place.

He stood and looked at his brother and then his mother. "If you'll excuse me, I need to go dress for whatever event you've arranged for me tonight."

"A card party at Lady Lyndley's," Mother said quietly.

"Very good, then. An evening of whist awaits. I will see you all there." Trent left the room without looking back and tried very hard not to think about the discussion they'd just had. Because if he didn't think about it, it wouldn't hurt.

Chapter 21

Rebecca finished dressing Adelaide's hair, *tsk*ing over the strands that insisted on nearly falling into her eyes but refused to lie in a reasonable-length curl. Tonight she'd tried pinning them straight back off Adelaide's forehead. It looked a bit odd to Adelaide, who'd gotten used to not seeing her forehead, but it was considerably closer to the modern hairstyles.

As the lady's maid hooked a simple gold chain around Adelaide's neck so that the small stone cross dangled just above the edge of her dress, Adelaide looked at the maid in the mirror. "Are you settling in well enough, Rebecca?"

"Er, yes, my lady. I believe I am." The maid looked a bit startled by the question. Understandable given the fact that such a question would never have entered their conversation before coming to live in this house. What a difference a few weeks could make.

What a difference a day could make, for that matter. This morning, she'd arisen alone and confused by her husband's departure, but now she felt as if she had friends, or at least the beginnings of what could become friendships, and she was actually excited for her husband to arrive. It was sweet of him, really, to try to give her what she'd lost. Miranda had pointed out that all he was doing was giving their marriage the foundation that most normal

189

marriages got, although they had the added benefit of being allowed to wander off by themselves if they wished.

Adelaide had flushed bright red at that comment, as it brought forth the memory of his sweet, gentle kiss the night before as well as inspiring the hope that he might give her another one tonight.

"I believe that should hold, my lady."

Which was the maid's way of saying she'd done her best to put together an ensemble that could withstand Adelaide's unique way of, well, living. She never knew how she managed to get so disheveled, but it never seemed to fail. Rebecca had been working for her since Adelaide's eighteenth birthday, and in those three years the maid had never once admitted defeat, constantly trying to find new ways to ensure Adelaide remained presentable.

"Thank you, Rebecca." Adelaide rose from the dressing table bench and then stopped. What was she supposed to do now? Georgina had made her promise not to be waiting in the drawing room when Trent arrived, assuring her that descending down the staircase provided the most impactful entrance a woman could make. "I'll wait here. Have someone come get me when my husband arrives."

"Very well, my lady." The momentary twist of Rebecca's lips let Adelaide know the maid thought this entire scenario was a bit silly, but she didn't say a word as she left the room.

And now Adelaide had nothing to do but wait. She paced the room, wondering how long it would be, wishing she could go downstairs even though the only difference would be that her pacing had an audience. She'd promised Georgina, though, and since the younger lady had been the talk of the Town during her Season, she probably knew what she was talking about.

It was difficult, though, as the view from her room did not include the front of the house, and so she couldn't see when Trent arrived. The anticipation was threatening to make her start sweating, something she did not want to do in the bright blue evening gown. If she wanted to preserve her sanity she was going to have to change rooms. The house was very narrow, meaning only one room on each floor faced the road. That left Trent's study, Trent's bedchamber, or the nursery.

Her eyes strayed to the door leading to Trent's bedroom. Of all the rooms she could go to, it was the most logical. Whoever came for her would be coming to this floor and she'd be able to hear them, and who did she think she was fooling? Ever since she saw the study she'd been looking for an excuse to enter Trent's bedchamber. If any room in the house could tell her more about her husband it would be that one, wouldn't it?

Before she could talk herself out of it, she threw open the connecting door and barreled through it, stumbling into a room that mirrored hers in layout, but boasted much more masculine decor, with clean lines and the most beautiful bed she'd ever seen. The wooden headboard reached to the ceiling before curving out and forming a half-tester wooden canopy over the top portion of the bed. The vertical portion of the headboard boasted an elaborate carving of a hunting party. It was an exquisite piece of art, so detailed she expected to feel the wind that whipped through the horses' manes or hear the cacophonous bark of the dogs mingling with the melody of the horns. The base of the bed was simpler, squared off below the mattress and covered with elaborate carved vines and flowers.

The bedding was a rich swirl of blue cut velvet, the darker blue giving way to the light blue base. It looked so inviting she couldn't resist running her hand along the edge of the fabric.

What kind of man chose a bed like this? For it was obvious he'd chosen it. Nothing else in the house was like this. She stood in the middle of the room, turning circles on the golden-edged Persian rug that took up most of the floor space in the room. Unlike the house she'd grown up in, the room wasn't crammed with as many expensive things as possible. Every item in the room was splendid and placed in a way that proved it had been chosen with care. Each piece was there because Trent liked it, wanted to see it when he awoke each day. The art on the walls wasn't chosen because it was expensive, though a glance at the signatures proved the paintings hadn't been chosen for economical reasons.

A collection of antique swords hung from one wall, with an oversized bergère wingback chair underneath them. The chair was old and well-worn. More worn than Trent alone could have made it. Next to the elegant chair sat an old military drum instead of a matching side table. A Bible lay on the drum along with a pocket watch and a pair of emerald-jeweled shirt-cuff studs.

Somehow it was the jeweled studs that made her realize what she was doing.

Trent had gone so far as to move out of the house in an attempt to give their marriage a semblance of normalcy and she was repaying him by invading his most personal of spaces.

She rushed back to her own room, pulling the door closed with a quiet click. In comparison to the handpicked beauty behind her, the room in front of her looked cold and uninviting. It looked like an Ackermann print, with coordinating furniture and bed linens. A beautiful room, but containing not a lick of the charm and warmth of Trent's room.

They were going to have to find time to discuss a redecorating budget. Any man who put that much thought into his bedchamber deserved an equally thought-out house.

In the meantime she'd give him what she could. She resumed her pacing, this time with a book in hand. Something in this extensive tome on bridge building had to be interesting enough to share.

⌒

Trent covered Adelaide's hand and gave it a gentle squeeze as they walked into the drawing room, where a scattering of tables and chairs held groups of men and women and piles of fish-shaped tokens. The shuffling of cards meshed with the murmur of voices, broken by an occasional laugh and accompanied by a young woman softly playing on the pianoforte in the corner.

In return she hugged his elbow tighter, bringing her body closer to his side. He liked her there. Niggling doubts from Griffith's theory had plagued Trent all afternoon, but now, looking at Adelaide's wide-eyed wonder at everything that surrounded her, he felt absolute confidence that she was as much a victim of coincidental fate as he had been.

Wide doors stood open on all sides of the drawing room, inviting the guests to wander through the library, another smaller drawing room, and the dining room. Trent led Adelaide on a casual stroll through the rooms. "Let's see who's here, shall we, before we settle down to a game?"

Adelaide nodded. "I've no strong desire to play, my lord. If you've a group you wish to make a game with, I'm happy to sit by and watch as those young ladies are doing."

She leaned her head to the side to indicate a table with four gentlemen deep in play. Two young ladies sat at the table watching the card play and occasionally joining in the conversation. It looked supremely boring to Trent. "Nonsense. I'd much rather you enjoy the game."

"I'm not very good." She reached up and adjusted her spectacles. In the carriage, she'd confessed to having considered leaving them at home, but worried she wouldn't be able to see the cards clearly if she did that. Trent had made a mental note to have an extra pair made and keep them in the coach in case she ever followed through on the foolish notion. He would rather she be able to see than conform to some silly inclination of fashion that required women deprive themselves in order to look a certain way. Even Georgina had briefly worn spectacles at the end of last Season, and the world hadn't ended. Fashions were entirely nebulous anyway, changing on the whim of who even knew.

He, for one, was supremely grateful that heavily boned corsets had gone the way of the powdered wig. Some of the ladies had worn the contraptions to a masquerade ball last year, and he'd felt as if he were dancing with a chair. He dearly hoped that whoever was in charge of naming the next fashionable affectation wouldn't return to those monstrosities.

As they moved through the rooms, it was clear his mother hadn't been jesting about sending support for Adelaide in force. Family friends who normally only attended smaller, more intimate gatherings stopped them to exchange pleasantries and offer congratulations. By the time they made it to the dining room he was fighting to keep his grin at an acceptable size. Their poor hostess had likely been overrun with considerably more attendees than she'd anticipated after his mother finished convincing people to accept the invitation or even talk their way into the party without one.

In the dining room, however, he lost the fight for decorum and laughed out loud. Standing disgruntled in the corner was Miranda's husband. Since their marriage, the Duke of Marshington only went out socially when his wife forced him to. After spending a decade as a spy for the English Crown, he found the constraints of social gatherings exhausting. Yet here he was.

Trent had never felt so blessed. He didn't know why God had plunked him down in the middle of such a family, but he was ever so grateful for it.

He smiled down at his wife, who didn't seem to be sharing his enjoyment of the surrounding cohorts. If anything, she looked overwhelmed. She'd already met Miranda, though, so perhaps a moment in discussion with her husband would calm Adelaide's nerves. He patted the hand trying to press permanent wrinkles into his coat sleeve. "Come. Meet Miranda's husband. I'm sure she talked about him while you were shopping today. She's annoyingly obsessed with the man."

Trent led the way, but for the first time all evening Adelaide pulled against his arm. He turned to her with an inquiring look.

"Is that him? In the corner?" She blinked her eyes twice. "He looks mean."

"He only does that so no one will come talk to him."

"An excellent idea. Let's accommodate him."

"He's not actually going to do anything. Not here, anyway." Trent grinned, remembering the time Ryland had snuck into Trent's house and rearranged everything in his study in exchange for Trent's trapping him into spending an evening discussing the merits of the latest opera. There was still a log book Trent hadn't found.

"No, really. I think I've a mind to indulge his preference." Adelaide stopped walking entirely, forcing Trent to stop as well unless he wanted to bodily drag her across the floor.

"We'll simply greet Miranda, then, shall we?" Not that he was going to pass up an opportunity to try to haul Ryland into a conversation. It was so rare for Miranda to force him out to large parties that Trent couldn't resist having a little fun whenever it happened.

Miranda was talking to Amelia, which meant Anthony, Marquis of Raebourne, was around here somewhere as well. The gossip papers would certainly have something to say about the attendees of this party tomorrow.

As Trent rounded the refreshment table, he noticed that three large curls were about to escape Adelaide's coiffure. He gave them a gentle tug, freeing them the rest of the way and draping them over her shoulder. Fortunately he'd left his gloves with his coat and he could feel the soft slide of the dark strands across his fingers, the weight and length making them feel so different from his own hair.

She looked at the black tresses lying in stunning contrast to the bright blue of her gown before blinking up at him.

"I like it," Trent said with a small shrug of one shoulder. "You're beautiful. I don't know if I remembered to tell you that earlier. I think I forgot to speak at all."

A soft pink touched her cheeks, and she looked a little flustered by his statement. He'd meant every word he'd said, but he'd wanted her that slightest bit distracted as well so she wouldn't notice when he pulled her to Ryland's corner.

"Your Grace, may I present my wife? Lady Adelaide, the Duke of Marshington."

Her momentary glare was more welcome than she would have believed. Over the years Trent had learned that women only showed their ire to people they felt safe with, close to. If Adelaide was willing to glare at him, even for a moment, it meant they were getting to know each other, that she cared about him and felt she could trust him. Of course, he'd just betrayed that trust a little bit, but not enough to damage it.

He hoped.

Ryland pushed off from the wall and executed a perfect bow, causing Adelaide to rush into her curtsy. This was a notorious and powerful duke after all. Probably someone she'd never expected to meet even though she was the daughter of an earl. "Your Grace."

"Please call me Marshington, or Ryland as the rest of the family does, or Duke in public, if you prefer." The scowl lifted from Ryland's face, proving it was a habitual affectation more than true irritation. "And may I offer felicitations on the union?"

His grey eyes swept toward Trent, making him wish he hadn't insisted on coming over here after all. With his connections, Ryland probably knew more about the marriage circumstances than Trent did. "Thank you."

The three of them fell silent, all trying to figure out how to get around the unspoken topic Ryland had just dropped into the circle. How was it that they had graciously accepted numerous congratulations already tonight, but the way Ryland said it made it obvious he knew the marriage had not been planned? And there was nothing Trent could say. He certainly couldn't address the unspoken question, and he knew he couldn't broach another topic without receiving smug looks from Ryland for the rest of the evening.

In the end it was Ryland who came to the rescue, though Trent had no doubt it was more for Adelaide's sake than for his. "Have you played a game yet this evening?"

Trent shifted his shoulders so that his coat would settle more comfortably across them as he relaxed. There was no doubt Ryland would eventually pin him down and make him share the story, but at least it wouldn't be tonight. "No. We were making the rounds before sitting down to a table."

"Well, then, shall we play? It's why my wife chooses card parties. I grumble less because there's actually something to do." Ryland, nearly as tall as Griffith but not quite as broad, cut through the small gathering of people next to them to collect his wife. Miranda left her conversation with a smile, and the four of them made their way into the drawing room to find an empty table.

"Shall we take on our men, Adelaide?" Miranda asked as she took one of the seats at a table set up near the front-facing windows. The noise of the horses and carriage drivers could be heard from the other side of the window, but it wasn't loud enough to make conversation difficult.

Trent was more than happy to partner with Ryland since it meant Adelaide sat to his left instead of across the table. He already missed the weight of her hand on his arm and shifted his leg under the table until his knee rested against hers. That light contact seemed to settle something in his chest, something that was beginning to accept that he and this woman were united.

Ryland shuffled the deck of cards while Trent distributed the pile of fish.

"Shall we play for dinner?" the duke asked.

Adelaide blinked at him, the candlelight from a nearby candelabra reflecting off her spectacles and framing her eyes in light. "Dinner?"

Trent shook himself from his fanciful thoughts and looked at the cards he'd been dealt. "Yes. Whoever loses has to have the entire family over for dinner. It's not the actual hosting that's an issue—it's the fact that the winner usually spends the evening taunting the loser."

"But if I'm partnering with Miranda, who will host the dinner when we lose?"

Miranda coughed. "I have no intention of losing."

Adelaide fingered the cards she had yet to pick up from the table. "I'm afraid I'm not very good."

Trent thought of everything Adelaide had missed out on in life. He couldn't recall ever seeing her at gatherings, even as children. Her sister Helena had always been there, decked out in bows and curls and other frippery that a child should never be subjected to. In later years he recalled seeing her brother, Bernard, though he was quite a bit younger than Trent and they'd never spent any time together. But he'd never seen Adelaide.

Adelaide, who hadn't been brought to London for a Season even after her oldest sister was married off.

Trent tapped his cards into a stack and leaned toward his wife. "Adelaide, do you know how to play whist?"

Her eyes darted around the table, her gaze flitting from person to person but never landing on anyone long enough for her vision to actually focus. "I've read about it."

Without a word, Ryland and Miranda began laying their cards face up on the table, sorting them by suit and rank. Trent helped Adelaide lay hers out before doing the same with his own.

They played three hands with the cards down, Miranda calmly explaining the rules and basic strategies that went along with the game. By the fourth hand, Adelaide felt confident enough to try it on her own.

Trent smiled almost as wide as she did when she took her first trick, even though she'd thrown a low trump on top of one of his kings.

"Well done, Adelaide." Miranda smiled and gathered up the cards. "We really should circulate a bit more. No one is seeing you together in this corner."

Ryland grunted. "Is that why we had to come tonight? Then let's plop them on top of the table and be done with it."

Trent sat back in his chair, still pressing his knee to Adelaide's. When his leg had followed hers the first few times she'd shifted, she'd finally relented and stopped moving it. "I thought the point of these outings was for Adelaide and me to get to know each other."

Ryland sighed. "How is it I understand Society better than you do?"

"Because I haven't spent the past ten years dissecting it for weaknesses," Trent grumbled. He'd never had to think about the consequences of his actions that deeply. Until a few months ago, he'd only had to consider the immediate ramifications of a deed upon himself. His reputation was nearly untouchable because he never did anything to endanger it, but he didn't think about it like that. He tried to do what was right and then moved on with his life.

The fact that everyone else seemed to know how to see life beyond that made him feel like a child.

Miranda frowned with indulgence at her husband and then turned her annoyance to her brother. "Courtship is as much about declaring yourselves a couple to everyone else as it is about getting to know each other. It's possibly even more important in your case, as . . . well, the men who like to get to know unhappily married women aren't very principled."

Adelaide's face lost all signs of victory. "I don't have to play whist with someone else now, do I?"

Trent shook his head and covered her hand with his. "No. There's enough people standing about that we can move around without much notice." He stopped and turned to his sister and her husband. "We can do that, can't we?"

Ryland bent his head in a poor attempt to hide his ensuing laughter. Miranda jerked and Ryland's laughter only got worse, a clear indication she'd attempted to kick him beneath the table.

"Of course you can. Only take care not to stay in one room too long. People might start to notice you aren't playing."

With four rooms to wander through, that shouldn't be too difficult. Trent rose and offered Adelaide his arm again. They worked their way from conversation to conversation until Adelaide asked for a moment to collect herself. They stepped to the side of the library, sipping at glasses of punch and discussing some of the books on the nearby shelf. Actually, it was more like Adelaide discussed them and Trent tried to come up with questions to keep her talking. Was there anything the woman hadn't read?

The crowd around them began to thin, but Trent didn't think about what it meant beyond the fact that he could hear Adelaide better.

It took Amelia's husband, Anthony, tapping him on the shoulder to break him free of the conversation.

"Were you planning on spending the night? I'm sure it wouldn't put out Lady Lyndley too much to make up a guest room for you." The marquis leaned against the library shelves and crossed his ankles. "Although this is a splendid library as well. She might just let you stay in here all night."

Amelia didn't say anything as she stepped forward to place a hand lightly on Adelaide's shoulder. "I'm going to come by tomorrow, if that's all right. Caroline arranged for several pattern books to be brought by so you could be making plans for the drawing room. I thought I'd take a look at them as well, since I'm thinking of redoing our upstairs parlor."

One dark brow lifted over one of Anthony's blue eyes. If Trent needed any more convincing that he would make a horrible titled aristocrat, the fact that he couldn't do the arrogant single brow thing solidified it.

Anthony cleared his throat. "We're redecorating the parlor?"

"Yes. We are." Amelia looked over her shoulder, and the marquis and marchioness stared at each other for a long moment, communicating in the way that only people completely connected to each other could do.

Jealousy churned in Trent's gut. That was what he wanted, what he'd always wanted in a marriage. And while he was coming to respect and even enjoy his growing relationship with Adelaide, he didn't know if it would ever become what he saw in the couple before him or what his sisters had found. He'd spent the past hour listening to Adelaide talk about educational books, something he'd avoided as much as possible. He didn't want to be any better at numbers than he had to be, and philosophy made his head spin. He enjoyed certain scientific texts, but he always felt guilty for reading them. Fiction hadn't been something emphasized as he was growing up, but he'd turned to it in order to stay away from the more learned texts. After hearing about Adelaide's favorite titles he was willing to consider the practice for its own merit.

At the very least it would give them something in common, because what else did they have? That they took their tea the same way? It was hardly the kind of connection that built the unspoken communication before him.

Finally Anthony shook his head and gave Trent a bland look. "We're redecorating the parlor. I hope you enjoy it."

Trent gave Anthony a quizzical look. "Why would I—"

"Our parlor windows face the same way your drawing room does," Amelia broke in. "So the lighting will be the same. And it's ever so much more fun discussing decor with someone else instead of debating with yourself over everything."

Adelaide looked as if she didn't know what to say, but she agreed to have Amelia come to the house.

Trent didn't know if he liked his mother being so high-handed about the decorating, but he did feel better knowing that Amelia would be there if anyone else decided to come calling.

Chapter 22

A low grunt ripped from Trent's chest as he felt the pressure of Anthony's blunted foil tip press against his shoulder.

Again.

The marquis laughed as he pulled off his protective mask and grinned at Trent. "Either I've gotten exceptionally better at this in the last few months or you're a bit distracted."

Another, deeper laugh came from the door to the terrace. "I believe even I could beat him today."

Trent glared at his brother from behind the shield of protective mesh. "I'm sure Anthony would let you borrow his sword."

"And have to trust you to avoid taking advantage of my lack of protective clothing? I think not."

How much would it take to bribe Griffith's valet into shaving off that irritating eyebrow? Just the image of Griffith walking around with only one eyebrow drew a grin to Trent's face. He pulled the mask from his head, feeling the flop of sweat-soaked hair against his forehead. "Scared?"

Griffith scoffed in big-brotherly disbelief. "Smart."

Trent stacked his gear on the table on the terrace and began pulling the protective arm and chest pads from his body. "Weren't you planning on fencing this morning when you invited Anthony over?"

Anthony inspected the tip of his foil before jabbing it in the duke's direction. "You did tell me to bring my gear."

"Foresight on my part, I'm sure. I wanted the two of you to be able to entertain yourselves should I be delayed for our meeting."

Trent narrowed his eyes at his older brother. Had he noticed that Trent had been avoiding his fencing club? Every time he went he ran into Mr. Givendale or Sir Durbin, who couldn't seem to stop themselves from making snide comments about the state of Trent's marriage. Blunted tip or not he was ready to run the both of them through with his foil. It didn't help matters any that Givendale had dropped his card by the house yesterday. Trent had wanted to give Adelaide a Season, but he wasn't about to let her entertain other gentleman callers.

"Did your wife mention if anything unusual happened while she was visiting Adelaide yesterday?" Trent's attempt at nonchalance didn't fool either of the other men.

"As a matter of fact, yes." Anthony began peeling off his own protective shirt. "Your housekeeper sat down to tea with them, and the entire household took luncheon together in your dining room."

Trent frowned. "I said unusual, not odd. That happens all the time when Amelia comes to my house."

"Something that is considerably more acceptable for her to do now that it is no longer a bachelor residence."

The men fell silent as a footman carried out a tray of lemonade and biscuits to the terrace. Trent wasn't particularly hungry, but he wasn't about to turn down the lemonade.

Griffith contemplated one of the biscuits while he waited for the servant to depart. "You know, it's still a bachelor residence. Just one of the female variety."

"She's not unmarried." Trent gripped his glass tighter.

His brother shrugged. "Might as well be."

Anthony stepped between the brothers but couldn't contain

his laughter. "Griffith, I'm going to have to step in for Trent here. Until you've treaded the waters of love yourself, you should avoid throwing stones at those who are." He glanced at Trent. "Even if they are drowning."

"I hope Amelia redoes your entire house in shades of puce," Trent grumbled.

"She won't." Anthony crossed his arms over his chest, the picture of male confidence. "She's never liked that color much."

Did Adelaide like the color puce? Did anyone? Was Trent going to return home to discover his drawing room covered in drab linen? These were the moments Trent hated the most when it became so glaringly obvious how little he had connected with his wife. "What is Amelia's favorite color?"

Anthony thought for a moment. "Pink? I think? Although she used a good bit of yellow when she redecorated her bedchambers." Then he shrugged and bit into a biscuit.

Trent tried to look casual as he fell into a nearby chair. Anthony and Amelia were as in love as anyone Trent had ever seen. They'd braved the displeasure of Society to be together, and while there were many who still whispered about them behind their fans, everyone enjoyed a good love story. But Anthony wasn't sure of his wife's favorite color?

The other men sat in chairs around the table as well.

Trent wished he had a better relationship with Anthony at that moment. In the four years they'd known each other they'd become friends, but friends of the athletic variety—fencing often with both foils and words, but never going much deeper than that. He and Griffith were closer . . . but he was unmarried. Right then, more than anything, Trent would have liked to feel comfortable enough to ask, if love wasn't knowing and appreciating all the little things about a person, what was it?

After three days it became very obvious what the ladies Hawthorne, or formerly Hawthorne, were doing. Each day a different one came up with an excuse to spend the bulk of the afternoon in Adelaide's drawing room. They would stay until Trent arrived to take her for a ride, which he did at the end of each afternoon. After Trent brought her back, she'd prepare herself for the evening's activities and then await his return.

It was helpful to have someone else there when the visitors started coming. Adelaide was going to have to decide which days she was going to be at home because the constant flow of callers was making her feel frantic. What did all of these people want from her anyway?

Today Miranda was sitting with her, and if Adelaide hadn't already figured out what the Hawthornes were doing, Miranda's arrival would have tipped her off. She didn't have an excuse to be there. She'd simply come.

Miranda had come armed with several decks of cards and even a container of dice, determined to teach Adelaide all the latest games so she wouldn't feel out of place at her next gathering. Between visitors, they went through the rules of faro, basset, and a new game called skat that Miranda had learned from some visiting German dignitaries.

After one particularly long conversation with a caller, they had tea brought to the drawing room before returning to their practice game of piquet. Adelaide had just finished dropping three lumps of sugar into Miranda's tea and an equal number into her own when Fenton announced that she had another visitor.

Adelaide was thankful she'd been practicing her smile all morning, because it threatened to droop when he announced the visitor was her mother.

They'd seen each other at two of the places Trent had taken her that week, but their encounters had been blessedly brief. She spent enough time fretting over the progress of Trent's strange courtship, and she didn't need her mother's constant advice on how to hurry it along. She'd yet to hear anything that didn't sound more detrimental than helpful. Small wonder her father tended to stay in the card room all night.

Miranda took a large swallow of tea. "Show her in, Fenton, but if she's still here in twenty minutes have Mrs. Harris invent an emergency."

Adelaide blinked. Why hadn't she thought of such a thing? Mother would catch on if it happened every time, but for days when she really didn't want to see someone, the method was genius.

"As you wish, Your Grace." Fenton bowed and left to collect Adelaide's mother.

Adelaide and Miranda moved the tea service away from the card table and over to the grouping of seats upholstered in the outdated green-and-white stripe. Adelaide had finally decided the room really needed new furniture and had chosen not to reupholster the pieces that were here. Determining what furniture she wanted was delaying the entire process, though.

Miranda sat herself next to Adelaide on the sofa, not leaving room for a third person to join them. Mother would have to sit in one of the chairs facing the settee.

Mother's lip curled as she came into the room and took in the faded wall coverings and drapery-less window. Adelaide had finally had the pile of curtains removed, but she hadn't yet replaced them. Choosing room decor was turning out to be much more difficult than she'd thought it would be, though that was possibly because she was trying to make every room as special for Trent as his bedroom was, and that was difficult when she was only just now getting to know the man.

"Haven't you done anything with this place yet, Adelaide? The duke has plenty of money, you know."

Did her mother not realize that Miranda was in the room? Did she care? Adelaide was torn between simply letting her mother prattle on like she normally did, or exerting herself and her wishes the way Miranda did. Since she couldn't let the reference to the duke pass with Miranda in the room, she tried to find a response that fell somewhere in between. "I didn't marry the duke, Mother. I married Lord Trent."

"Yes, yes, but he's the duke's brother, so I'm sure you could get him to give you enough to redo this room. Probably even enough to move to a nicer location." Mother sat on the chair and gave a pointed look at the tea service before looking at Adelaide. It was the first time she'd actually looked her daughter's way since entering the room, which might explain why she hadn't noticed the presence of another person. Miranda had been sitting unusually still for the entire exchange.

Mother had the tact to look a bit embarrassed. "Your Grace, my deepest apologies. I should not have spoken so boldly."

Adelaide poured her mother a cup of tea with a liberal amount of milk and passed it across the low tea table, trying not to cringe as she waited for Miranda to berate Lady Crampton with the bluntness Adelaide was coming to expect from the duchess. It never came.

"Perhaps not," Miranda said calmly, "but I shall overlook it. The room is in rather desperate need of refreshing. It was in need of it when Lady Raebourne lived here as well, though she didn't have access to any funds at the time. Now she does, of course, since she married the marquis, but the house had already passed on to Trent by then. Rest assured we have no intention of letting anyone in the family retain such shabby accommodations. We've been trying to trap Trent into agreeing to redecorate it since he moved in, but you know bachelors. They can be so elusive about such things."

Miranda gave a smile that projected camaraderie before lifting her teacup to her lips.

Adelaide looked down into her own cup. So that's how it was

done, then. In a single minute Miranda had put Adelaide's mother in a very uncomfortable position without saying anything overtly rude or cutting. In fact the words themselves were congenial and even friendly. Yet her mother's tight face proved she hadn't missed the underlying meaning. The reminder that a nobody like Amelia had stolen the marquis away from Helena, that everyone in the family knew Adelaide and Trent had been forced to marry, and even that they knew Lady Crampton intended to use the marriage for her own gain. There had even been the subtle hint that Adelaide was part of their family now and they had every intention of protecting her. All of that without stepping a foot from the parameters of cordial, ladylike behavior.

Adelaide gaped at Miranda in a bit of awe, thankful now that she'd been given Miranda's blunt observations instead of being subjected to this polite warfare.

Still, whether awed or not, she'd rather not have her new relations battle her old relations in her drawing room. "Mother, have you settled in? What are your plans for the Season?"

"What are my plans? Honestly, Adelaide, what else does a woman plan for during the Season?" Mother frowned into her tea and set the half-full cup on the table. "You must convince your husband to let you purchase a better quality of tea, Adelaide. This is terrible."

Given that Adelaide hated all versions of tea, she hadn't noticed whether or not this one was particularly worse than the others. She nodded though, the same as she'd done all her life, already making plans to ask Mother's London housekeeper what type of tea Mother took so that she could keep some on hand. If Trent liked their current tea, Adelaide wasn't about to change it, but she would make sure her mother didn't complain about it next time.

Miranda sighed and smiled into her own cup with a sort of reverence for the tea within. "My deepest apologies. I brought over my own special blend. I'm afraid I've become rather accustomed to it, and Adelaide was indulging me. We didn't know you'd be joining us."

It was enough to make Adelaide smile. Almost enough to make her laugh. Until that moment Miranda had been disturbingly honest, so she did have to wonder if Miranda had actually brought over her own tea. "I'll be sure I have different tea next time, Mother."

"Yes, well, I'm sure this is one I could become accustomed to. It's just an unusual blend."

The trio fell into silence. Mother was obviously expecting Miranda to leave soon, assuming the duchess was here on a normal call. They exchanged pleasantries about the weather and complaints about the pollution. Mother must have decided she was tired of being there because she finally came to the point of her visit. "I do hope you are planning to attend the Sutherland ball tomorrow night."

"As a matter of fact, I am. Will you be there as well?" The idea of being pulled around another ball by her mother made her want to come down with a sudden debilitating headache.

Mother shifted in her seat, looking extremely uncomfortable as she perched on the edge of the chair, as if she were afraid the worn upholstery might contaminate her new gown. "Of course I will. Your father is even going to be there."

It would be nice to see her father again. Adelaide hadn't seen him since the wedding, though she had received a letter from him telling her when they could be expected to arrive in London.

Mother turned to Miranda. "Will you be in attendance, Your Grace?"

"Oh, yes, we never miss the Sutherland ball."

Adelaide's eyebrows drew together. The duke and duchess had been married a mere year. How could they have anything they never missed yet?

"Yes, well, I'm sure we'll all see each other, then. If you have time, Adelaide, do see if you could mention your brother-in-law to your husband. He's having a difficult time locating a sponsor for Boodle's. Good afternoon." Her mother gifted Miranda only with a curtsy before taking her leave, apparently unwilling to completely snub a duchess.

Silence fell until the thud of the front door echoed into the drawing room.

"Sweet mercy, how did you not turn into a shrew?" Miranda plunked the teacup she'd been sipping at down onto the table. She'd been working on the same cup the entire visit, taking a small drink after every sentence she spoke.

Adelaide gathered up the rest of the tea things so that the tray could be returned to the kitchen. "I never saw much of her growing up. She was too focused on Helena. It was always her turn to go first since she was the oldest."

"Did she think you were just going to stay a baby until she had time to raise you? Well, I wouldn't normally say this, but I think you're better off for the negligence." Miranda frowned at the tea. "But she is right about the tea. I can't believe you're still drinking it."

Adelaide stood to ring for Fenton to come get the tray. "You didn't like the tea either?"

"No. It's a wretched blend. That's why I brought it over to Trent. He drinks anything. Half the time he lets it sit and get cold. I thought he'd have used it up by now. Didn't you notice it was awful?"

"I assumed Trent liked it." Adelaide frowned down at the tea. Had they been serving this same blend to everyone for the past few days? Why hadn't anyone else said something?

Miranda stuck out her tongue and made a strange coughing noise. "He wouldn't know good tea if it hit him in the face. We'll go by my favorite tea house tomorrow, and you can give the rest of this away."

"But isn't tea expensive? There can't be that much of it left to use up."

"Trent still hasn't talked about household budgets with you, has he. You can buy some new tea. But to make you feel better, we'll tell Mrs. Harris to keep serving Trent this horrid stuff."

It didn't sit right with Adelaide to deliberately tell the housekeeper to serve Trent disgusting tea, but it didn't seem right to get rid of it either. She supposed she could forgo her coffee for a while until the rest of this tea was used. How much of it could they possibly have?

Masculine voices drifted into the drawing room from the front hall, drawing the attention of both Adelaide and Miranda. One belonged to Fenton, but Adelaide couldn't place the other one.

Miranda frowned. "That's not Trent."

Adelaide crept to the door, but she couldn't see anything. Curiosity was making her shake, though, or perhaps it was Miranda's bold nosiness that was motivating her. All afternoon Adelaide had been doing her best to keep up with Miranda's energy and enthusiasm. Regardless of the initial spark of motivation, Adelaide was devoured by curiosity to know who had come by the house.

Her house.

In which she was free to walk through the front hall, if she so wished.

"Miranda, would you care to see what I'm thinking of doing in the bedchamber?" Adelaide gestured Miranda toward the drawing room door.

The duchess sauntered forward with a grin. "You mean the bedchamber we would have to climb the stairs in the front hall to go see?"

Adelaide's mouth curved into an answering smile. "The very one."

"I'd be delighted."

The two women strolled into the front hall to see Fenton in discussion with a handsome young man who seemed very disappointed until he saw them over Fenton's shoulder. "Your Grace, my lady."

Miranda looked as if she might be ill, but she made the introductions anyway. "Lady Adelaide, this is Mr. Givendale. Mr. Givendale, Lady Trent Hawthorne."

Adelaide wondered at Miranda's use of the more formal name, but she stepped forward to greet the man with a smile anyway. "Yes, we've met. Good afternoon, Mr. Givendale. Is there a problem?"

"Not at all, my lady." Fenton took a side step toward the door. "The gentleman was seeking an audience with Lord Trent, who I'm afraid is unavailable."

The man held up a calling card with Trent's name printed on it and a date and time scrawled underneath the name. Adelaide glanced at the clock. The current date and time. "Were you to meet him here?"

Mr. Givendale nodded, his dark blond waves barely moving with the motion. "Yes, I am certain. It was a rather pressing business discussion about his estate in Suffolk. Are you sure he's unavailable?"

"Quite." Adelaide felt badly for the man to have made the point of coming to an appointment that the other party hadn't seen fit to be in residence for. That alone was enough to make her irritated with her husband. The fact that he was doing business with the estate she'd brought him and yet was still unable to bring himself to live under the same roof simply firmed up the feeling.

Whenever gentlemen left her father's study disappointed with the results of the meeting, her mother had consoled them with tea saying it was bad for a family's reputation for anyone to leave the house unhappy. Knowing the currently brewed tea blend was bad almost made her send the man on his way regardless, but if her mother was right it would mar her already fragile public opinion. "I'm afraid we've just finished taking tea, but there is probably some left if you wish to have some before you leave."

"You're too kind, my lady. I do so hate to impose, but the dust is quite dreadful today."

He was already moving toward the drawing room Miranda and

Adelaide had just left. The ladies returned to the drawing room with him to partake of yet another awkward cup of tea. To his credit he didn't stay long, but the conversation flowed with incredible ease, even with Miranda's unusual silence.

Adelaide couldn't help wishing that—despite the banal nature of her conversation with Mr. Givendale—she and Trent could sit and talk in the same easy manner. While she and her husband generally talked of things other than the weather and the beauty of some of the local architecture, it always seemed to take them a while to get going. Perhaps they should start with the same inane conversation Mr. Givendale had.

As the man took his leave, Miranda stood, crossing her arms over her chest and tapping her foot until the closing of the front door echoed through the house once more.

"Do be careful with that man, Adelaide."

Adelaide paused in the act of cleaning up the tea tray for a second time. "Why? Mother always said not to let anyone leave your house unhappy because it was bad for your reputation."

Miranda scoffed. "Well, my mother says ladies should always be on guard for a scheming man, and this, my new dear sister"—Miranda held up the calling card Mr. Givendale had left behind—"is not Trent's handwriting."

Chapter 23

Adelaide couldn't keep the smug little grin off her face as she hopped into the curricle with the barest amount of assistance from Trent. Thanks to their nearly daily rides, she was growing quite comfortable with the vehicle. She was even considering asking him to teach her how to drive it.

Not that she'd have anywhere to drive to while they lived in the city. But perhaps later, when there were children—and she was beginning to believe that one day there would be children—they would spend more time in the country. Then she could drive herself places, perhaps even get her own wagon, like her mother used.

But for now, she was satisfied with the fact that she no longer gripped the seat in abject terror or spent the whole ride worrying about falling out or catching her skirt in the wheel.

She didn't even blink at the curricle's rocking and swaying when Trent climbed in the other side.

As the wheels began to roll, though, the comfortable familiarity disappeared. Every day they'd gone to Hyde Park, rolling down Rotten Row to see and be seen. Adelaide knew every inch of the road to the legendary pathway, and this most certainly wasn't it. "Where are we going?"

Trent grinned like a little boy, cheeks creasing into deep dimples as his nose crinkled in obvious glee. "Somewhere new. I truly can't believe we haven't done this yet. I can only blame my nervousness over the entire courting situation."

Adelaide blinked at him, forgetting all about watching for clues as to their new destination in favor of examining her husband for signs that their relationship was changing. Never before had he said anything so personal, so closely connected to something relating to feelings. "You've been nervous?"

His eyes were wide as they glanced her way before returning to the traffic. "Haven't you been?"

"Well, of course, but I didn't think you were. I assumed this marriage was a mere inconvenience that you were trying to decide what to do with."

One hand twisted to take both reins, freeing his other hand to run through his hair and across the back of his neck. "I suppose it was, at first. I can't deny that I wished more than once that it would simply go away."

"That I would go away." Adelaide dropped her gaze to her lap, where her fingers were tightly laced together.

They were silent for a while as Trent maneuvered the horses under a cluster of trees in one of the open Mayfair squares. He hopped down and walked around the curricle but didn't help her down. Instead he stood, arms braced on either side of the opening on her side of the carriage. She'd never seen his green eyes so dark and serious, his mouth relaxed but straight without an inkling of either smile or frown. "I thought I did, for a while. Want you to go away, that is. But I'm truly coming to believe that God doesn't make mistakes and He had something planned for our lives even though we didn't understand"—his wide grin returned—"and so I'm going to treat you to something no other woman has ever had."

Resisting the answering joyful grin that tugged at her lips was impossible, so she gave in to it, throwing herself into whatever experience he was so excited to share with her.

A man in plain, black clothing stepped over to the curricle. "Good afternoon, my lord."

"Ah, yes." Trent rubbed his hands together and bounced on his toes. "Two Hawthorne Special Concoctions, if you please."

The man nodded and then turned to dart through the traffic and into a shop on the corner of the square. From his drawings, she recognized an elaborate pineapple on the shop sign, and that made her wonder if their outing had anything to do with Trent's pineapple-growing aspirations, but then another plainly clothed man darted through the traffic, this time with a pink confection in one hand and a yellow one in the other. He took them to another couple in another carriage positioned much like Adelaide and Trent's curricle was.

"We're at Gunter's!" Adelaide clasped her hands to her chest and met Trent's excited gaze with her own. She'd heard of the famous confectioner, popular not only for his cakes but for his delicious ices. "I've never been here."

Trent laughed. "I know. I can't believe I haven't brought you here before now."

Adelaide looked at him with narrowed eyes, waiting to speak until a particularly loud wagon and a large, noisy carriage passed on the street behind them. "But what, exactly, is a Hawthorne Special Concoction?"

"The only way to eat an ice at Gunter's, my lady." He leaned one shoulder against the curricle, rocking the vehicle slightly as he crossed one ankle over the other and folded his arms over his chest. "James Gunter himself worked it up for me after I spent half an hour trying to decide upon a flavor one day."

"And what did you do to deserve such special attention?" Adelaide was a bit awed that Trent had received such personalized service that he could order the confection by simply giving his name. Everyone in the aristocracy came to Gunter's and there were plenty of people more important and powerful than Trent.

He gave a one-shouldered shrug. "I pay my bill on time."

Adelaide was still laughing when their waiter ran back across the street with two of the most ridiculous-looking desserts she'd ever seen. Shaped like a pineapple, each ice was a mottled collection of at least a dozen different colors, each pineapple segment bearing a different shade. Coming out of the top was a delicate, lacy biscuit.

She held the dish in one hand and a spoon in the other without the faintest idea how to start eating such a concoction. "What is this?"

"Fifteen flavors of ambrosia and a sprinkled sugar biscuit." He scraped a spoon across the top of the ice and slid the bite into his mouth with a sigh of contentment.

Adelaide stabbed her spoon into her own frozen treat, drawing a groan from her companion.

"No, no, don't do it that way." He thrust his dish toward her. "Here. Hold this."

She stuck her spoon in her mouth and let it dangle inelegantly from her lips so that her second hand could be free to balance his ice as well as hers. The utensil was nearly a lost cause at least three times as Adelaide couldn't stop laughing at Trent racing around the curricle to climb back up into the seat.

He took his ice back from her, his fingers feeling even warmer than usual against her chilled hand.

"This is a delicate combination of flavors and you must eat it a certain way to obtain as much enjoyment from them as possible."

"You've put a lot of thought into this."

He leaned toward her until his nose was a mere three inches from her own. Adelaide blinked, trying to bring him into focus as her spectacles caused him to blur in such close proximity. His breath was already sweetened by the few bites of dessert he'd eaten, and it washed over her like a comforting autumn wind. "I take my frivolity very seriously."

She saluted him with her spoon. "Then, as your wife, I consider it my duty to give proper consideration to it as well."

"Quite right." His gaze dropped from the spoon to her lips and then back to his own confection. "Pay attention then, wife, and learn the only proper way to enjoy the best that Gunter's has to offer."

Trent was certain that one day he'd be able to look at his wife all dressed up for an evening out and not lose his breath. One day his heart wouldn't forget its job for a moment and would maintain a steady rhythm in her presence. One day. But today was not that day. Especially not after sharing his treasured ice combination with her that afternoon. She'd applied herself with gusto, diligently copying every movement he made with his spoon until he began making some up. He'd discovered that, while swooping up a dollop of lemon and chocolate in the same bite was positively blissful, the lemon and the rose should never be mixed.

She'd coughed through that combination with a smile on her face, though, and once she'd regained her composure, waited patiently with spoon poised for his next instruction. The memory of her anticipatory grin had him smiling even now. At that moment she'd been the most riveting woman he'd ever seen, and he was baffled as to why. Why she'd pulled at him so much then—and even more so as he stood in the hall watching the top of the stairs.

It wasn't that she was exceptionally beautiful, though he supposed he saw her as such now. If he had seen her for the first time in a crowded ballroom, he would certainly have noticed her unusual looks, but she wouldn't have called to him like she did now. There was something about the knowledge that she was his, that he had the permission of God and man to look at her with appreciation, to hold her in his arms and kiss her each evening when he brought her home.

The fact that he was the only person who ever saw her this way

218

left him feeling protective, special. By the time they reached their destination, a slipper would be smudged or a jewel knocked askew. He hadn't quite figured out how she managed it when she always came down the stairs looking like utter perfection, but it never lasted beyond the carriage. He wondered sometimes if she even knew when she became disheveled. It didn't stop her from doing anything.

As was becoming common, he saw the hem of her dress first as she descended the stairs. Gold satin slippers peeped out from beneath the white-and-gold gown. This one, too, was cut like a belted vest, with pearls lining the white dress beneath as well as the gold satin overdress and belt. The rest of her emerged as she slowly descended the steps, giving Trent time to admire her grace and form. Even when he moved back into the house, he was going to make a habit of waiting for her in the front hall. Watching her come down the steps was turning into one of his favorite moments of the day.

Until her face appeared.

Instead of her normal shy, welcoming smile, she wore an anxious frown. Obviously something about this evening's plans didn't thrill her.

"We don't have to go." Trent rushed forward to meet her at the bottom of the steps, taking her hands in his.

She clasped his fingers tightly enough to cause wrinkles in her white gloves. "Your mother—"

"Isn't here." Trent lifted a hand to Adelaide's cheek. Whatever had caused the apprehensive look in her eyes, Trent wanted to vanquish it. If the world beyond the front door was causing her grief, he was more than happy to turn her around and escort her back up the stairs until it no longer bothered her. Anything to bring back the happy woman who'd gone to Gunter's with him that afternoon.

How could he care this much about someone he hardly knew, someone he hadn't bonded with, couldn't tell what she was thinking with a single look? Every married couple he knew that was also in love had that. Georgina once said she heard her husband, Colin, in her head even when he wasn't there. His relationship with Adelaide didn't look anything like what Trent knew love to be, so why did it bother him so much that she wasn't happy? "Please tell me what's wrong."

"We should go." She tilted her head into his hand with a soft, sad smile. "Everyone is expecting us."

Trent bent his knees and ducked his head to look Adelaide in the eyes. They were still large, still a pure, clear blue, still framed by thick black lashes, but something was wrong. "Where are your spectacles?"

She held up her oversized reticule. "In here. Mother's going to be there tonight, and she fusses when I wear them to balls."

Trent frowned and wanted to hit something. All the work he'd done over the past few weeks—getting her to smile and talk and laugh with his friends and family—and her mother had broken it with the mere promise of her presence. He kept his touch gentle as he pulled the reticule from her wrist.

His mother would swat him with her fan if she saw him opening a woman's reticule, but this was his wife, and these were extenuating circumstances.

The slim novel tucked in the bag made him smile as he dug around for her spectacles. He found them wrapped in a soft cloth and tucked into her spare pair of slippers. Georgina must have taught her that trick when she'd been here two days ago. After unwrapping the frames, he slid them carefully onto Adelaide's face. He shifted his hands until his palms cupped her cheeks, his thumbs grazing right below the spectacle frames. As her eyes drifted shut he leaned down and brushed a light kiss across her lips. "Mother or no mother, I want you to be able to see when I dance with you."

As she blinked up at him, her eyes adjusting to the lenses once more, he vowed that no matter what her life had been before, he was going to make her future one better. Starting tonight.

Chapter 24

As had become his habit when they entered a venue where dancing was available, Trent pulled Adelaide to the dance floor immediately. He always seemed to time it so that they walked into a waltz. Whether or not he was that knowledgeable of song order at balls or he actually arranged it with the different hostesses and orchestras, Adelaide didn't know. And she didn't care. She simply enjoyed starting the evening wrapped in her husband's arms.

He smiled down at her, almost making her forget that she had another night of uncomfortable interactions ahead of her. One day, God willing, these social functions wouldn't make her want to run screaming into the night. The number of people crowding the ballroom meant that the *ton* had arrived in London full force, and there was sure to be someone more interesting than her for the masses to focus on very soon.

Unless her mother did something to change that.

The pressure of Trent's arm at her back pulled her back to the present. The warmth of his hand through her glove reassured her. She enjoyed dancing with Trent.

She knew he was a superb athlete, spending a great deal of his time at athletic clubs, boxing, fencing, or even playing cricket. He'd mentioned once that he liked rowing, as well, but hadn't had much chance to do it since school. The Thames was a bit too crowded for a rowing team in London. All of those athletic pursuits made him strong and graceful and he led her around the floor with confidence.

Secure that he would lead her the way she needed to go, she let her mind drift. They'd had fun the past few days. Their outings had seemed less like obligations and more like excursions. They'd had such fun eating their ices that they'd been unable to contain their laughter, and more than one person crossed the square to chat with them. Well, him, mostly. Everyone had been very polite to her, but it was becoming obvious that nearly the entire aristocracy loved Trent.

Did she love him too? What did that mean? Love. Years ago, an aunt assured Adelaide her mother loved her, but if that was love, what was this she felt with Trent? Was it love that she hoped one day very soon he'd stop leaving her at the foot of the stairs in the evening? Was it love that she looked forward to seeing him smile and scoured the obscure texts in the library looking for strange facts to make him laugh, that she was spending each morning with Mrs. Harris learning to cook a perfect rasher of bacon? Was it love that she couldn't move forward with the drawing room because she so desperately wanted him to like it?

Did he like the green that was currently in the room? Did he want it designed for large gatherings or merely intimate visits? Those things seemed like something someone in love would know. Wouldn't they? Could it be love if she didn't know his preferences?

All too soon the song was ending and Trent was bowing. Adelaide dropped into a hasty curtsy before laying her hand on his arm to be escorted from the floor.

As soon as they cleared the dance floor, her mother appeared from seemingly nowhere. "You two simply look divine together. Fate is certainly kind, isn't she?"

Adelaide's tongue felt thick and swollen. What was the proper response to something like that? Stating that fate was considerably kinder than her own mother didn't seem like the correct response. If for no other reason that Trent was unaware of the fact that fate had next to nothing to do with their marriage, and they could have been rescued.

"You look lovely tonight, Mother." When in doubt, compliment—at least when it came to her mother. Acknowledging her superior taste in fashion always put the countess in a good mood.

"Have you met Mrs. Seyton yet, darling?" Mother fluttered her fan lightly as she sidled up to Adelaide's free arm and looped her own through it.

"I'm afraid I haven't had the pleasure," Adelaide mumbled. How ridiculous she must look with her husband on one arm and her mother on the other. As if they were about to begin a strange country reel.

Mother tugged lightly at Adelaide's arm. "You simply must meet her. She has the most splendid little house in Brighton. They don't use it much, so she's always willing to let me stay there when I need to visit the coast. Sea-bathing is very beneficial for the constitution, you know."

"I would love to meet Mrs. Seyton, Mother." To be honest, she was just grateful that her mother wished to introduce her to another woman instead of making more suggestions about which men she could use to make her husband jealous. She pulled her arm from Trent's. If meeting Mrs. Seyton would placate her mother, she'd be more than happy to get it over with.

"Yes. Well, perhaps I can introduce you later."

Adelaide's mouth dropped open a bit as her mother faded into the surrounding crowd.

"I see you made it," a male voice sounded from behind her. "We had to take a very circuitous route to avoid the mess on Bruton Street. It was a wagon full of lumber, so there's fortunately no loss, but it's taking them a dreadfully long time to clean it up."

Adelaide turned to find Lord and Lady Raebourne smiling at

them. Was that why her mother had left? "You're my new favorite people."

The stunned silence was the first indication that the words had actually come out of her mouth instead of staying safely locked in her head.

Trent looked from her to Lady Raebourne and then out over the crowd before he tilted his head and smiled at the marchioness. "You might be mine as well. Anthony, we'd be more than happy to visit with your wife for a while if you have anyone you need to speak with. Or punch you need to fetch."

The other couple looked from Trent to Adelaide with equally confused expressions.

Lord Raebourne scratched behind his ear. "I was going to speak to—"

"Wonderful!" Trent rocked back on his heels. "You take care of that while we stay with your wife."

Lady Raebourne hooked her arm securely into her husband's. "I'm not sure that's a good idea."

Trent laughed. "Nothing nefarious, I assure you. Simply trying to help Adelaide become more comfortable with a few people in Town. She had to leave all her friends behind in the country, you know."

Lady Raebourne's expression turned more than a little skeptical. Adelaide was fairly certain hers had as well. Trent hadn't shown the least interest in her personal friendships since they'd gotten married and now he wanted to encourage her friendship with the one person they'd come across that her mother was afraid of? It wasn't very subtle of him. Sweet, but not subtle.

After staring at Trent for a few tense moments, Lady Raebourne released her husband's arm. "If you wish."

"Oh, I wish." Trent's actions didn't match his words as he was once more looking around the room. Finally he found what he was looking for, but they didn't set off across the room again. Instead he simply smiled.

With another questioning look in Trent's direction, Lord Rae-bourne slipped off to take care of his business, leaving the three remaining people to stand around staring at each other. As much as Adelaide enjoyed the fact that Lady Raebourne's presence kept the countess away, they couldn't stand like this all evening.

Trent apparently had other plans. "How is the redecorating going?"

"Hmm. Slowly. I'm having trouble selecting the right fabric." Lady Raebourne cut her eyes in Adelaide's direction, making her want to squirm. "Anthony won't tell me what he wants."

Trent tried to hold back a laugh, but it sputtered out anyway. "Anthony doesn't care what your parlor looks like."

Lady Raebourne sighed. "I know. But I still want him to like it."

"Then put furniture he's not afraid to sit on in there. As long as it's comfortable and you're happy he won't care what it looks like."

Adelaide blinked, looking from Lady Raebourne to Trent and back again. How was it that all of these women were more clever with words than she would ever be? She struggled just to say what she meant, never mind layering it into a conversation in such a way that it either portrayed an unsaid second meaning or unearthed answers no one was willing to ask for. With a silent thank-you to Lady Raebourne, Adelaide began thinking through the furniture she'd seen in some of the galleries, mentally discarding anything with spindle legs or delicately carved backs.

"Might I have the next dance?"

Adelaide blinked out of her contemplation to find Mr. Given-dale standing in front of her, and Trent gritting his teeth. Adelaide had enjoyed dancing with the man before—as much as she could enjoy dancing with anyone other than her husband, anyway—and would have accepted without much thought if it hadn't been for Trent's apparent dislike of the idea. Yes, the man had feigned a scheduled meeting with Trent, but she'd heard her father complain of men doing the same thing in an attempt to gain an audience, so was that really such an awful thing? Even with the card he'd been stopped at the door by Fenton. Was there more going on here than Adelaide realized?

"I'm afraid I was planning to dance the next two with Lady Adelaide."

Beneath Adelaide's fingers, Trent's arm relaxed as they both turned to Griffith, who had come up behind them as Mr. Givendale spoke. It was obvious Mr. Givendale wanted to object, but there was nothing he could do except acquiesce. Having a duke in the family did have certain advantages.

She let go of Trent's arm a bit reluctantly but was happy to be going back to the dance floor, where she had at least some idea of what she was doing and could avoid a great deal of conversation if she wished to. Griffith's wide chest expanded and released on a sigh as the music began, his expression almost grim as he took the first steps in the dance.

"Thank you for dancing with me." Adelaide knew singling her out to dance had gone a long way toward getting her accepted by people she still didn't feel like she fit in with. She'd been in London mere weeks and already missed the freedom of the country. She supposed she should get used to it though. Trent lived year round in the city, only taking short trips to his country estates.

"Has he been coming around?" Griffith whispered in her ear as they passed each other in the dance.

Adelaide looked back to where she'd come from. Mr. Givendale was in a low conversation with Trent. With similar coloring and height, the two men made a handsome picture. Mr. Givendale's hair was a touch darker, and his high cheekbones gave his face a bit more starkness, but there was no denying his good looks. The appealing picture stopped, however, when one looked closer at the men's faces. Mr. Givendale looked almost smug, while Trent's face remained as devoid of expression as she'd ever seen it. She came to Griffith's side as they circled. "He's been by to see Trent, though he obviously missed him."

Griffith nodded, a thoughtful look on his face. "Does Trent know?"

"I believe Mr. Givendale left a message with Fenton yesterday afternoon, but I don't know if Trent has received it yet."

Silence fell as they went through the next formation of the dance. They approached the end of the line of dancers before Griffith spoke again. "Trent has a tendency to assume the best of people. He's never had a need to do otherwise."

Where was Griffith going with this? Adelaide didn't for one moment believe that Griffith would share information like this without a reason. "I've noticed."

They stopped at the end of the line, facing each other while the next formation was executed. "Do you? Assume the best, I mean?"

Did she? It wasn't something she'd ever thought about. She never assumed the best of her mother—experience had taught her otherwise—but her father often got a bit more lenience from her. "I think it depends upon the person."

He nodded before letting all expression fall from his face as he saw something over her shoulder.

The ballroom was crowded, and the line of dancers pushed up against the people milling around beside the dance floor, leaving them very accessible to anyone who wished to speak to them. For instance, someone like her mother.

"You are such a dear, Duke," she said from the edge of the dance floor. "I'm so thankful you've accepted our girl like a sister. We must have you to dinner next week in gratitude."

Adelaide counted the music, praying it would speed up so they could leave the edge of the group and move their way across the floor once more. How could her mother try to finagle her way into the duke's inner circles like this? Very well, she knew how, but it was still a bit tiresome that Mother was trying to use her this way.

Had Helena had this problem? Probably not. Helena had likely been just as bad.

Griffith nodded. "The whole family has accepted her. She is one of our own."

Mother tittered. She actually tittered. "Of course, we'd love to have all of you, including the Duke of Marshington."

Griffith nodded again. Adelaide couldn't believe he was actually agreeing to this. He was a duke. Politeness only had to go so far. "I'm sure he would be delighted, along with Lord and Lady Raebourne. Even though she's married now, after her time as my ward, I still consider her family."

Adelaide looked to the side in time to see her mother turn pale. "Of . . . of course. I shouldn't have disrupted your dance. We'll discuss a date at a later time."

Griffith gave her one more nod before taking Adelaide's arm and rejoining the dance.

"She's never going to have you to dinner now," Adelaide whispered. "She simply cannot abide Lady Raebourne."

The grin Griffith sent her way made him look so much like Trent her heart turned over a bit. "I know."

~

Trent's heart pounded in his chest, and his fingers relaxed their fists as he saw Lady Crampton slink away from the dance floor without taking Adelaide's smile with her. Whatever Griffith was saying had actually drawn a laugh from his wife, something he'd thought impossible given her sullen mood in the carriage on the way to the ball.

Though he'd never cared for Lady Crampton, the more he saw her interact with her daughter, the more baffled he became. It made him want to find his own mother and write sonnets to what a wonderful parent she'd been. Part of him wished there was a way to eradicate the countess from Adelaide's life, but the woman

228

was her mother. A certain amount of respect had to be granted to her because of that.

Respect, yes, but not free access. He could respectfully limit their interaction if he was clever. There hadn't been much cause for him to be deliberately clever in his life. Charming, yes, but never clever. He could only hope he was up to the challenge.

As the dance ended, Lady Crampton found the couple again, all but dragging Adelaide off with her, disappearing into the crush. Trent worked his way around the ballroom until he found them again, only to wish he hadn't. The two women were talking to Mr. Givendale. What was the man up to?

There was nothing he could do about it in the middle of a ballroom, though. Neither his wife nor his mother would thank him for making a scene. Especially simply on the basis of not liking the way the man smiled at Trent's wife.

He tore himself away from the torture of watching Adelaide speak to Mr. Givendale. Amelia was still standing near him though her husband had rejoined their little group. "I don't suppose you'd like to move into my house for a while?" he asked.

Anthony frowned. "You mean the one you aren't even living in at the moment?"

The marquis jerked as his wife nudged him with her elbow without a thought to being gentle about it. "Keep your voice down. And I don't think he was talking to you."

"Well, you're certainly not living anywhere without me."

Trent wished he could go back and change things so that he'd never asked the question in the first place. It was rather ridiculous. He needed other options. "Who other than your wife does Lady Crampton avoid?"

Anthony frowned. "You're asking the wrong man. I make a point of not noticing anything Lady Crampton does. Lord Crampton too, if I can manage it." Anthony took Amelia's arm, preparing to escort her to the floor for the next dance. "Georgina's on the floor now, which means Colin is around here somewhere. If anyone would know, it would be him."

Trent glanced over the dancers, and sure enough there was Georgina. Despite being married, she still dressed in white, though it was broken by a wide emerald-green sash and covered with so many embroidered flowers the white was more of a suggestion than an actual color on the dress. But Georgina never attended an event like this without her husband. Trent and Colin had met at the club for billiards earlier this week but hadn't really talked about how Trent had ended up married. Still, the man knew everything about everyone in London. If anyone could suggest who Trent needed to use to make this plan work, it would be Colin.

Once the dance was over, he followed Georgina to a nearby window where he not only found the Scotsman, but Lady Blackstone as well. He greeted his mother before turning to Colin. "I need information."

Colin took a sip of lemonade and leaned one shoulder against the window casing. "The price of corn has gone down now that the war is over. You're better off investing in oats."

"You handle my investments, so I trust that's already been taken care of." Trent shifted to lean against the wall next to Colin, trying to keep the conversation looking casual. "Who does Lady Crampton avoid?"

"Why would I know that?" Colin coughed on the lemonade he'd sucked in on his surprised gasp.

"Because you always know who doesn't like each other."

"Only as it applies to business, and Lady Crampton's inclinations don't have all that much to do with Lord Crampton's." Colin looked toward the ceiling as he thought. "Now, he tends to avoid Anthony and Amelia and never seems to have much to do with Mr. Burges. Oh, and he refuses to have anything to do with Spindlewood."

Georgina shook her head in surprise. "As in the Duke of?"

Colin nodded.

Trent's mother flicked her fan open. "That is hardly surprising."

Trent, Colin, and Georgina all looked at her with wide eyes. Mother never indulged in malicious gossip, but it sounded as if she was about to jump right into something London would think was rather significant.

When she didn't say anything else, Georgina finally let out an exasperated "Why?"

Mother looked at them as if she simply expected them to know, but Trent couldn't think of a thing he'd ever heard about Spindlewood. Other than the fact that the man's mustache was most unfortunately shaped, the old man didn't do much of anything interesting.

"The Duke of Spindlewood has a son."

"Three, if we're being particular," Colin murmured.

Mother waved her fan in Colin's direction as if brushing off his words. "Only one who will one day be the duke. And Isabel very much wanted to one day be his duchess."

Trent felt himself pulled into the drama of the short tale. Lady Crampton was a countess, so it was sometimes difficult to remember that she'd started off aiming higher than that. "What happened? Obviously she's not waiting to become a duchess right now."

"The Duke accused her of being after the money and the title and threatened to cut his son off from anything that wasn't entailed unless he married someone other than Isabel. Embarrassed her thoroughly by bringing forward one of her friends, who verified all the times the woman had plotted and planned to encounter Spindlewood's heir. She then tried to trap the son in a compromising position so they would be forced to marry—only she ended up snaring the old duke instead of the son. She couldn't show her face in a ballroom for the rest of the year."

Trent gave a low whistle. Was that why Adelaide requested an introduction to him at the Ferrington ball? That scandal would certainly be enough to make a woman such as Lady Crampton avoid a man for the rest of his life. It was rather amazing that she'd been able to land an earl after the scandal that had probably ensued from seemingly propositioning a married duke.

After thanking his family profusely, Trent went off in search of his wife, hoping against hope that he wouldn't find her in Givendale's arms on the dance floor. As he went he kept an eye out for the Duke of Spindlewood.

With any luck, the old man was feeling chatty this evening and Trent and Adelaide could spend the next half hour at his side.

Chapter 25

Adelaide climbed into the carriage with a small sigh of relief. Had an evening ever been so exhausting? She'd done her best to make everyone happy, but what was she supposed to do when they wanted different things from her? Her mother obviously wanted Adelaide to be vivacious and personable, and she had truly tried to be those things. While she had absolutely no intention of following through on her mother's less-than-veiled suggestions that, with just the slightest bit of effort and coercion, Adelaide could use her new status as a member of the Hawthorne family to improve her mother's and sister's social positions, there didn't seem to be a reason not to at least try to be nice to the people Mother introduced her to.

That was until she saw Trent waiting for her to come off the dance floor after sharing a quadrille with Mr. Givendale. Her husband hadn't frowned or even looked unhappy, but he'd been stiff as he took her arm. Adelaide let her head fall back on the carriage seat and roll to the side so she could watch Trent adjust his coat and situate himself on the seat beside her. Had a man ever spent so much effort on a woman?

After collecting her from Mr. Givendale, Trent had spent the rest of the evening at her side, engaging them in conversation with the Duke of Spindlewood and his grandson and sharing dance formations with Lord and Lady Raebourne. He was obviously trying to keep her away from her mother and having a great deal of success in doing so.

Which meant no matter what she did, one of them was going to be disappointed. Never before had Adelaide been faced with such a decision. Her parents rarely had strong opinions about the same thing, so it was easy enough to please both of them. And Helena was happy as long as everything in the room revolved around her. But now there was a battle going on for Adelaide's attention and someone was going to have to lose.

As Trent's laugh rolled softly across her ears, Adelaide was afraid that the loser was going to have to be her mother. And she was more than a little afraid of what the repercussions would be when that happened.

If Trent's objective with this courtship had been to make her feel like someone worth winning, he was succeeding. What she'd thought would be a dreadful evening had turned into one of the most delightful nights she'd ever had in her life. And it was all due to the man beside her.

What did that leave her with? Gratitude? Certainly. He was an answer to a prayer she hadn't known how to phrase. Love? Maybe. She still wasn't certain she knew what love was, but if it meant wanting to spend the rest of her life making someone else's life better, then yes, she loved him.

The horses broke free from the crush in front of the house and trotted easily though Mayfair, leaving the two of them snug in the darkness of the carriage. It had become a habit to take the long way home, knowing their time would be limited once they got there.

Trent reached through the darkness and took her hand. "Did you enjoy this evening?"

It was his standard question, and she'd never thought to wonder why before. Was he concerned? Did he feel responsible for her?

Was it possible he was coming to view her happiness as essential as she was coming to view his? Or was it a safe inquiry, relying on the commonality of a shared event to start a conversation? Rather like his discussions on food. The questions and uncertainty swam through her head and made her dizzy. "It was a very pleasant evening. Did you win your fencing match today?"

He settled closer to her until their shoulders brushed and began talking to her about the fencing club. He had won his match, but he found plenty else to tell her about as well. The other people he'd talked to, a funny story about the lady's dog that had run into the club leaving his mistress shrieking on the pavement outside.

Adelaide listened, but she also wondered why she felt so unsettled. They'd spent several evenings this way now, and it was always nice, but it bothered her too. They were married, yet they weren't, courting but not. She didn't know wifely things such as household budgets and where they got their tea, or even what he liked for breakfast, but she knew what his kiss tasted like. Their courtship lacked the restraints a normal relationship would have, allowing them to do things such as ride through Mayfair in a darkened carriage to spend half an hour alone in a dimly lit hall. But their marriage lacked the security that normally came with the institution. She didn't know where he spent his days or even his nights. There was a constant need to look her best whenever he saw her, despite the fact that she'd somehow managed to end this evening without her fan.

She had so many questions about him but no answers. If he enjoyed physical activity so much, why wasn't he taking a more particular interest in his estates? Why was he sketching plans for pineapples and then stuffing them into a drawer? Why did he treat her like the most precious thing in the world when they went out together and then drop her at their doorstep? Which Trent was she really married to?

A public marriage in name only wasn't going to be enough for her much longer. The better she got to know Trent the more she wanted to make this marriage work, only she didn't know what to do next.

"Have you ever had a dog?" Trent asked as the carriage pulled up in front of their house.

"Once. One of the foxhounds had puppies, and the smallest one wasn't doing well. So I cared for it, and soon it was following me all over the house." Adelaide gathered up her skirts.

"What happened to him?"

"He got older and stronger. And one day we were out for a walk and he saw the other dogs training. I didn't have the heart to keep him with me all the time after that. I still visited him every now and then. He turned into a decent hunting dog."

She took his hand and let him help her out of the carriage. She hadn't thought about Milkweed in years. It had been a ridiculous name for a dog, but she'd been a lonely six-year-old girl, and sometimes six-years-olds were ridiculous. The truth hadn't gone quite like Adelaide had told Trent and the look of near pity on his face told her he guessed at the truth.

The truth was they'd been out walking and he'd naturally snuffed out a bevy of quail and sent them soaring into the heavens. Her father had asked her if she thought Milkweed would like to come with him on his next hunt. From then on she'd only seen him when she snuck down past the barn to the kennel where they kept the dogs. Eventually she stopped even doing that.

As usual, Fenton was waiting at the door. After letting them in, he locked the front door and left them in the hall, a single lantern burning on a side table to hold away the blanket of darkness.

"Where did you learn to dance?" Trent asked.

Adelaide flushed, knowing the question was born of the other things she'd shared about her time growing up—how her mother had continued to treat her like a child even as she reached the age when other girls were thinking of who and when they would marry. It had always been Helena's turn first, as if Mother only had enough energy for one child at a time. "Dancing lessons are easier with additional couples. I was partnered with my brother, Bernard. He didn't like it much, but he suffered through it because father said he had to. I sometimes wonder if Father made him do it for my benefit as much as Helena's."

"Adelaide, I . . ." Trent's voice trailed off, not as if he didn't know what he wanted to say but as if he didn't have the words to say it. She knew how he felt. She felt like that almost all the time these days. Like life was throwing so much at her and she knew how she wanted to respond but didn't know how to express it or motivate herself to actually do it.

But she knew what she wanted now. She didn't want his gentle platitudes about how he was going to take care of her—he'd proven that with more than words tonight. She didn't want him to say that she should have had more as a child—there was no gaining it back, and after seeing how Helena turned out she wasn't sure she wanted to have gotten it anyway. Right now Adelaide wanted the unvarnished truth that came when he kissed her, when he couldn't hide the harshened breathing and the unsteady hands, when he didn't rely on his charming words or winning smile. She wanted what only she received.

As if he could read her mind, he slid his hands up her arms. His gloves had been discarded in the carriage. One of the few wifely things she knew about him. He couldn't stand the feeling of evening gloves and shed them as soon as he was out of public.

Small calluses covered his hands from years spent rowing and fencing, and she felt every one of them as his hands slid off her gloves and onto her upper arms, pausing below the cut sleeves of her ball gown. He held her steady as he stepped closer and lowered his head. She loved this moment each night, lived for it when the evening grew tedious.

One hand released her arm and slid along the back of her neck, dislodging the pins that had already worked loose at the bottom of her coiffure.

And then his lips were on hers. There was no fumbling hesitancy now, as she felt the familiar warmth of his lips brush gently against hers before returning again with more pressure. She felt his teeth, his tongue, things she never would have thought a woman would enjoy, but she did.

She took her own step forward, pressing into the kiss in a way she hadn't done before. More than his hands bore evidence of his athletic pursuits and she rested her hands on his shoulders, wishing she dared to wrap them around him, to hold him to her the way she wanted to.

A small cry escaped her lips as he pulled away, and he returned immediately, giving her the second kiss he'd always denied her before.

But the kiss was brief, and before she was ready he was pulling back once more, farther this time until her fingertips fell from his shoulders.

"Don't go."

She didn't realize she'd said the words out loud until he sucked a harsh breath in through his teeth, but she wasn't upset that she'd said it. Thank goodness her subconscious had more courage than she did. But she didn't want it to be her subconscious that kept him here. She wanted to have the nerve to say it deliberately, to ask him to stay and mean it.

A deep breath filled her lungs and pushed her shoulders straight. She licked her lips and said it again.

"Don't go."

Curls he'd knocked from their moorings draped over her shoulder, emphasizing the fast rise and fall of her chest. The form he'd so admired as it came down the stairs draped in utter perfection was even more enticing in its altered state. The ensemble, naturally mussed and broken by simple virtue of Adelaide being in it, drew him in the way perfection could not. Because it was her. No one else lived in their clothes like she did, without guile or concern for appearance.

She blinked at him, her spectacles magnifying what little moonlight made it into the room and highlighting her clear blue eyes until he wanted to drown in them. That wasn't possible, so he did the next best thing.

He decided to drown in her.

She'd asked for so little since they'd married, had gone along with everything he'd declared. And when she finally asked for something, all she seemed to want was him.

Could anything be more humbling?

There was also a part of him that wanted to stake his claim, to prove to her and all of the men like Givendale that he was her husband and no one else. He hadn't liked watching her smile at another man. Perhaps if he did this, if he took that last step in making their marriage real, her most special of smiles would be only for him.

He stepped forward again, throwing caution to the wind and wrapping his arms around her. She pressed against him, already lifting her head for his kiss, wanting it as much as he wanted to give it.

For weeks now, he'd been wrestling with how to love her, how to get her to love him. Maybe it wasn't so important that he figure it out. Maybe it was more important that he be with her. It wasn't as if he was going to get to change his mind at the end of this courtship. The awkwardness they'd brought home with them was gone, and maybe that was enough. Maybe it would have to be.

The kiss was different this time, tinged with nerves and excitement as he realized this time he didn't have to pull back. This time he wasn't going to slip out the back door to meet the carriage in the alley. This time he could enjoy everything about his wife. Not just could, but should.

Her arms crept around his sides, pressing into his back as she went up on her toes in an effort to get closer.

He broke the kiss, grinning like a fool. He hoped she could sense it in the dark, knew how happy he was to be staying tonight. One arm was already tucked around her shoulders, holding her close. He bent and slid the other hand behind her knees, lifting her high against his chest as she squealed and wrapped her arms around his neck.

The motion pressed his face into the place where her neck and shoulder met. He kissed her there before lowering her enough that she could snag the lantern with one hand while keeping the other wrapped over his shoulder. He climbed the stairs, holding her tighter with each step. He'd never been so glad for the relatively small house that allowed him to reach the bedchamber without hiking down long corridors.

They didn't call for her maid, and his valet was across town, so they fumbled with each other's fastenings, falling into fits of giggles when her dress confounded Trent to the point that he threatened to fetch a knife. She was fascinated by the unfolding of his cravat, even taking a moment to try to re-create the folds herself. He'd thought that once they finally got to this point there'd be a rush, driven by the same sense of urgency that had nibbled at his nerves when he kissed her each night. But now that they were here, steps away from the bed he hadn't been able to sleep in since he married this woman, a calm sense of rightness took away the need to hurry.

She looked right in this room, the room that was more his than anywhere else in the house. It was one of the few rooms he'd taken the time to refurbish when he moved in. Much to the dismay of Mrs. Harris, the rest of the house hadn't been necessary to him. But this room was his private sanctuary, the place where only he went, and now his wife would be there as well.

The soft light from the lantern flickered over the bed, creating its own sense of magic as he pulled back the covers before taking her hand and guiding her the last few steps across the floor. He didn't know what Adelaide knew about tonight, and what he knew was limited at best, but that didn't matter. They would take it slow and discover it together. It had taken them nearly a month to get there, but tonight would finally be their wedding night. It was a natural act, designed by God to bring a man and woman into perfect union.

Trent kept that in mind as his heart raced and his lungs filled with the intoxicating combination of heat and roses. He gathered her in his arms and kissed her, savoring the freedom to enjoy his wife, even if there were moments of awkwardness where he could only guess at what he was doing. If her smiles and sighs were any indication, she didn't mind his fumbling. The way her hands brushed his shoulders and back proved that she reveled in the new freedom as well.

Trent pulled her close, wondering what he'd been so afraid of, but knowing that they'd been right to wait. This moment should be the most easy, natural thing in the world. All of the reservations he'd had about this marriage were about to disappear. He grazed his fingers over her cheek, knowing the morning light would bring them a whole and splendid new marriage.

Chapter 26

A few hours ago Trent had been sure he was done with sitting in chairs, waiting for the sun to rise. He'd thought his nights of sleepless contemplation were over.

He was afraid they were just beginning.

If anything, this night, this moment was worse than all the sleepless nights that had come before. This time he wasn't waiting for the first rays of sunlight to bring him new opportunities and fresh hope. No, on this morning, on which he wasn't going to be able to bring himself to even attempt to eat breakfast, he was waiting for daybreak to give him permission to flee the scene of his atrocity and seek advice from the only person he could.

His Bible sat forgotten on his leg. The answers were probably in there somewhere, but in his agitated state he hadn't been able to find anything but genealogies, proof that what men had been accomplishing for centuries either came at a great cost to their wives or Trent was a dismal failure.

On the other side of the connecting door, Adelaide slept. He knew she slept because he'd gone to check on her every half hour since he'd carried her to her own room. He was glad she slept, but he couldn't. Couldn't even bring himself to return to the bed. He'd hurt his wife. He hadn't meant to, hadn't even known that he could, but somehow the moment had gone from blissful and beautiful to tragic in a single instant. Her squeal of pain still echoed in his ears, refusing to give him peace.

So he sat in his father's chair and waited for the sun.

How often had his father sat in that very chair, contemplating the questions of life? While Trent was fairly certain his father had never had to come to terms with this particular question, he knew the man had struggled with more than one life decision in this chair. He was a duke, after all. Making life-changing decisions seemed to be all they ever did. But his father had been lucky enough to know and love his wife before their marriage. The story of how his father had pursued his mother was almost famous among the *ton*. Courting her for over a year. Buying an estate next to her father's so he could continue courting after the Season was over.

Was that what Trent had wanted? Was it the reason he'd been so hesitant to focus on one woman before now? Or had it been that he'd instinctively known there was something wrong with him? That any woman who married him would be getting a bitter life sentence of pain. Since he had obviously done something wrong, did that mean there couldn't even be children?

He left his curtains open, watching the building across the street so he could know the moment the sun's rays hit it. He could have gone to the breakfast room, where the sun would shine through the glass, but he had no idea what time she rose. What if he ran into her? He wasn't sure he'd ever be able to look her in the face again. Not after he'd turned her sweet request into such an abomination.

The sun streaked the sky, lighting on the rooftops across the street. He waited until the attic windows of the house across the street glinted in the sun before he rose from the chair to dress. The muscles in his legs protested, stiff after their prolonged time in one position. He didn't ring for Fenton, choosing instead to dress himself. He didn't even know if the butler knew Trent had spent the night at the house.

His tying of the cravat wasn't anything to speak of, but otherwise he looked like any other aristocratic gentleman going for a morning ride. He hoped his household thought so, anyway. They had no need to know he was riding but one street over and not to Regent's Park or even Hyde Park.

Mrs. Harris was coming out of the breakfast room as Trent made his way toward the small stable at the back of the property. "May I say how nice it is to see you this morning, my lord?"

The twinkle in the housekeeper's eyes nearly choked Trent. He had to get out of there. "Yes, well, let's not mention it, shall we? We don't want to embarrass anyone."

For once he hoped his staff would act like staff and not make any comments like that to Adelaide. While she'd initially seemed to accept the marriage more easily than he had, she was probably regretting it now. There was no need to constantly remind her of the regret they couldn't change.

Knowing he didn't have far to go, Trent made himself think of his horse and walked him the short distance to Anthony's house. The butler threatened to throw him out, but since Trent had charmed his way through the kitchens and was already at Anthony's study door before the butler saw him, Trent was able to convince him not to. He'd already asked one of the footmen downstairs to tell Anthony he was here because he didn't trust the stiff-necked butler to do it.

Trent tried to settle into a chair in Anthony's study, but he couldn't do it. Lots of men had books in their study, but Anthony's walls were lined with floor-to-ceiling bookshelves. So many books made him think of how much Adelaide would enjoy looking through the shelves for unusual titles. She probably wouldn't hunt down obscure facts for him anymore. She probably wouldn't even speak to him.

He paced. From window to door and bookshelf to bookshelf, but he didn't have long to wait before Anthony came busting in still tying his dressing gown. "What's wrong?"

"I need . . . I don't . . . I can't . . ." Trent fell into a chair, elbows on his knees and head in his hands, as words, the one thing that had always saved him before, failed him. "I've botched everything."

Anthony stopped in the middle of the floor. "And you came to me?"

Trent looked up, wondering if his despair was evident. "I didn't know where else to go."

Shock drifted across Anthony's face, but he contained it quickly. Trent didn't blame him. While he and Anthony had always gotten on well enough, often fencing or going riding together, Anthony had always been more Griffith's friend than Trent's. But Trent was counting on that friendship being extended to him now.

"Is anyone hurt?" Anthony asked slowly as he lowered himself onto the edge of the chair next to Trent's.

"No." Trent fell back to slump into his own chair. "At least she said she isn't. Well, not anymore, anyway."

"Ah." Confusion and even worry dropped from Anthony's face to be replaced by a ghost of a smile as he sat deeper into the chair.

"I shouldn't have come here." Trent wanted to stomp out of the room, but the truth was he really didn't have anywhere else he could go.

"I'm sorry, I'm sorry." Anthony wiped a hand over his face and did his best to erase the smile. "What happened?"

"I stayed the night."

"I gathered as much."

Trent popped back up to resume pacing. "She asked me to stay. I wanted to stay."

Anthony leaned back, watching Trent go back and forth across the room as if he were watching a tennis match. "That's a good start."

Once more words failed him as he didn't begin to know how to tell Anthony what had happened next.

"I'm assuming there was kissing at that point." Anthony couldn't quite hide the humor in his voice, even though he managed to keep from smiling. He was intently studying his fingernails in order to keep from laughing.

"Yes," Trent growled. "There was kissing."

More silence. Finally Anthony looked up. "Was it good?"

Trent groaned at the memory. "The best."

"So it was everything else that was the problem, then?" Anthony wasn't even trying to keep the smile off his face anymore, and Trent couldn't bring himself to care.

He braced his hands on the desk and leaned forward, hunching his shoulders and dropping his head. "It didn't work."

Anthony barked in laughter before taking huge breaths to try to contain it. "I'm sorry, I'm sorry. What didn't work? Er, was it you?"

Finally the other man seemed to realize the awkwardness of their conversation as two high spots of red formed along his cheekbones.

Trent glared at the marquis. "No. I worked just fine. It was the . . . Well, the process didn't work. I bungled it, Anthony. I thought I knew what to do. I've certainly heard about it plenty of times, but then it didn't . . . go right. And then I hurt her. I hurt my wife, and I don't know how to fix it."

He rubbed his hands over his face hard, as if he could wipe away the events of a few hours prior, surprised when they came away wet. When was the last time he'd cried? His father's funeral? Maybe the first day he'd gone off to school and his father hadn't been there? But if ever there was anything to cry over as an adult, failing at one of the prime responsibilities as a man was certainly a good one.

Anthony rose and crossed the room. He took Trent's shoulders in his hands. "Trent, it happens. There are plenty of men who bungle their wedding night. Though most of them do it on their actual wedding night."

"I'm sure you didn't bungle your wedding night," Trent muttered before breaking away from Anthony and throwing himself back into the chair. The tufted club chair rocked back on its legs with the force of his weight.

Anthony's good humor disappeared as he slowly sat in the other chair, looking every inch the powerful marquis that he was. "I think Amelia would have happily accepted some bungling on my part if it meant I came with a purer past, but that's not of consequence here. Is my experience the reason you came to me, Trent?"

"No." Trent hated himself this morning. First he'd hurt his wife, and now he'd hurt his friend by unintentionally bringing up his dark past. "Griffith isn't married, so what does he know about it? Colin and Ryland are married to my sisters, so I'd really rather not have this conversation with them."

Anthony relaxed and held his hand out, palm up. "Point taken. The thing is, Trent, if you got your information about how last night should have gone from the boys at school, it's not a wonder that it didn't go as planned. As for hurting your wife, I'm afraid the first time is difficult for a woman no matter what—a man too, for that matter. How was she this morning?"

Trent didn't answer, couldn't answer. He avoided Anthony's gaze but couldn't bring himself to actually get up out of the chair, as that would be too obvious an avoidance of the question.

"You didn't see her this morning?"

"I saw her." He had. He'd slipped in to make sure she was still sleeping peacefully before he left.

"Did you talk to her? Kiss her? I can already tell you didn't try again."

"Try again? Are you crazy? I broke my wife last night. She cried out in pain, and I caused it."

Anthony sighed. "Didn't your father ever . . ."

"No. I was so young when Father died. I don't know if he ever even talked to Griffith. It's not a subject that comes up on a regular basis with us."

"No, it wouldn't." Anthony scrubbed his hands over his face.

"Awkward though it will be, I promise you I will talk to Griffith before he marries."

"He won't have this problem." Trent grunted.

Anthony lifted that annoying single brow. "He won't?"

"Do you think Griffith would be foolish enough to be trapped into a marriage? No, he'll know and love his wife before it ever becomes an issue. I have to think if I'd known Adelaide better, if we'd fallen in love like we were supposed to, last night would have gone better."

"Maybe." Anthony shrugged. "But probably not. You aren't the first man to fudge his wedding night and somehow the human race continues. Which means people get past it. You just have to take your time and learn together. Next time will be easier."

"Not if she hates me. I should have waited. What if what we've built isn't strong enough to withstand this?"

Anthony sighed. "Do you love her?"

Trent stared at the other man, feeling like the life had drained out of him. "I don't know."

Chapter 27

There's a moment of bliss when the morning arrives, when sleep still clings to the brain and all of the bad memories have yet to awaken.

Then there's the moment when everything crashes into reality with a heartrending wrench and sleeping until sometime next week sounds like a fabulous prospect.

Adelaide rode through both of those moments before daring to open her eyes. A quick glance revealed she'd somehow gotten back to her room, even though she'd fallen asleep in Trent's bed the night before. *Fallen asleep* was probably not the correct term. Cried herself into unconsciousness while he held her and stroked her hair would be a much more accurate description. She wiggled and twisted, verifying for herself that the pain indeed had been momentary and didn't return with the cold light of morning. The pain had in fact been gone before she'd fallen asleep, but part of her feared it would return.

A frown touched her face as she pushed back the covers and fought her way into a seated position. She had told him there was no more pain before she fell asleep, hadn't she? It had been uncomfortable and scary, but not as painful as she feared Trent thought. She'd been startled more than anything. And rather disappointed in the whole event, or rather the end of it. Trent had obviously not enjoyed it, and she knew she hadn't, so the only reason to do it would be in order to gain children. Unless, of course, it wasn't always like it was last night.

She dressed and then took fifteen minutes to decide if she wanted to have breakfast downstairs or in her room. On the one hand, she was hoping to catch Trent—if he had not already left the house. On the other, she would rather avoid the knowing looks the staff was probably giving each other this morning. As much as she wished she had someone to talk to, this wasn't the kind of thing she could discuss with her housekeeper. All of her new friends, if they could even be considered as such, were related to Trent, and she didn't want them to know that she had failed at being a proper wife.

Her mother was out of the question, as she would probably say it was the perfect time for Adelaide to make some sort of outlandish request of her husband. As if Adelaide would use his sense of guilt as shop credit. No wonder her father rarely spoke to her mother.

She could try her sister. Helena had been out from under their mother's thumb for well over a year now. And they were sisters. That would count for something, wouldn't it? Adelaide knew it was a foolish hope even as she thought it, but desperate people had been known to cling to slimmer hopes. Unfortunately even an absurdly early call to visit family would have to wait a couple of hours.

She had Rebecca fetch a breakfast tray, but after that her room felt stifling. If she wanted to preserve her sanity, she was going to have to find something to do.

Books had always been a source of solace for her, and the small library Trent had created from the old music room had become her favorite retreat.

She stumbled through the door, making the unpleasant discovery that the library was being cleaned by Lydia. A pregnant Lydia.

Proof that the maid and the valet had managed to muddle through what Adelaide and Trent had not.

Of all the servants to receive that knowing smile from, Lydia was probably the worst.

"Good morning, my lady." Lydia smiled, but any veiled suggestion behind it could only be put there by Adelaide's imagination. She hadn't expected the young woman to be that discreet. Surely everyone knew Trent had stayed the night last night.

Assuming he had stayed the night. What if he'd retreated back to Hawthorne House after taking her back to her room?

"I can finish later, if you'd like." Lydia packed up her dustcloth and cleaning supplies in a small bucket. "No one normally uses the room this early."

"No, no. Now is fine. I'm simply getting a book." Adelaide grabbed for the closest shelf and pulled off the first volume her fingers could find. "This book."

Now came the smile that said Lydia knew too much. And given her current situation, she probably did know too much. She certainly knew more than Adelaide. If things didn't go well with Helena, would Adelaide possibly be desperate enough to seek advice from the parlormaid?

"That's an interesting choice, my lady."

Adelaide glanced down to discover herself holding a book on animal husbandry. She slammed it back onto the shelf as if it were made of burning coals. Why was such a book even in a library in Town? That sort of thing belonged in the country.

"There's several novels over there." Lydia pointed to the larger bookcase on the other side of the room from Adelaide.

That would certainly be better than a manual on mating animals. Adelaide tried to hurry across the room without looking like she was hurrying. She was tempted to simply grab a book and run but that hadn't worked well for her a few moments ago, so she made herself look long enough to at least be sure she wasn't picking up a volume of love poems or the latest romantic gothic novel.

Out of the corner of her eye she saw Lydia squatting down to dust the bottom shelf.

"When is the baby coming?" Adelaide really didn't want to know, but at the same time she did. It was rather fascinating, having a servant with child who was not trying to hide it, as she'd heard of other servants doing. Besides, asking after the baby seemed to be one more way to immerse herself in this household where everyone else seemed to know each other's business.

Lydia stood and stretched her back. "This summer." She ran a hand over her belly. "We're hoping to be settled in Hertfordshire before then. We were going to go next month, but Lord Trent asked if we could stay a bit longer. I think he wants to be a bit more settled before finding a new valet."

A wash of pink touched the maid's cheeks, as if she realized she might have said a bit too much. Did all the servants talk about them like that? Had Lydia simply forgotten she was talking to Adelaide and not Mabel or Eve?

Adelaide snatched an innocent-looking book from the shelf. "I'll take this one."

Lydia said nothing but gave a tight smile as Adelaide scurried out the door.

The morning crawled by until Adelaide couldn't take it anymore. Even though most of London's inhabitants were probably still in their dressing gowns, she dressed for the afternoon, gathered Rebecca, and departed from the house within the hour. The ride to Marylebone didn't take long, though they had to take more than one detour to avoid some of the areas under heavy construction. Soon Adelaide was marching to her sister's door, new calling card in hand. She ran her thumb over the name.

Lady Trent Hawthorne.

It was strange to think of the aversion she'd felt when first seeing these cards. Nothing could be further removed from her current sense of pride.

The butler took her card and admitted her to the hall but had her wait there while he went to see if Lady Edgewick was home.

Adelaide prayed Helena was home. They'd never been particularly close, but who else could Adelaide turn to?

The butler returned, showing her into a drawing room and showing Rebecca to the kitchen, but it was another fifteen minutes before Helena arrived.

"Sister!" She entered the room with her deep red skirt billowing around her, arms extended as if she were greeting a long-lost friend. In a way she was. Adelaide and Helena hadn't really spoken since Helena's wedding. Nothing beyond a handful of increasingly brief letters.

Adelaide stepped into the hug with some confusion and not a little bit of relief. She'd been afraid her sister wouldn't want anything to do with her. Was it possible that marriage to a viscount had settled her?

Helena led them over to a sofa and sat, still clasping Adelaide's hands in hers. "Have you come to extend an invitation to the Duchess of Marshington's ball?"

Adelaide blinked. "Miranda is throwing a ball? I had no idea."

The sour turn of Helena's mouth killed Adelaide's budding hope that her sister was going to be of any comfort. "The paper this morning said she was undergoing preparations for such. Some even assumed it was in honor of you."

Adelaide sighed. She didn't think Trent's sister would be honoring her anytime soon. Not if he had anything to do with it. "I haven't heard anything."

Helena's shoulders slumped a bit. "Do remember us if she asks you about the guest list. Oh, and Mother told me she asked you to give a hint or two about sponsoring Lord Edgewick for your husband's fencing club. He's simply dying to get in there."

"I don't think I have any say in who Trent sponsors."

A frown marred Helena's smooth, pale face. "Why did you come, then?"

Sudden anger flashed through Adelaide. Her chest actually warmed with the emotion, her fingers curled in to her palms, nearly cramping as they threatened to poke a hole in her gloves. She had done everything ever asked of her growing up. She'd worn Helena's castoffs. She'd been Helena's dance partner, even learning the male steps for a dance or two. She'd waited quietly while every other girl her age took their bows and started finding husbands. But never, not once, had Helena thanked her for it or considered that maybe it hadn't been what Adelaide wanted to do. The bitterness of it all felt thick on her tongue as it coated her words with sarcasm. "I don't know. Perhaps I thought I'd come see my sister since we were in the same county for the first time in a year."

Helena waved a hand in the air. "We barely saw each other when we lived in the same house. Sentiment is for fools, Adelaide. Though I must congratulate you on having the nerve to trap the duke's brother. Such a shame you weren't able to land the duke himself."

The smirk on Helena's face indicated she didn't think it was a shame at all. Adelaide guessed that if it had been the duke who tumbled through the old wooden floor, Helena would have been beside herself with anger that her younger sister now outranked her. The truth was Adelaide still outranked her, but not by a significant amount.

Now, however, the only question that remained was how soon Adelaide could leave without being rude. Any notion of confiding in Helena had been obliterated by the unshakable feeling that her older sister would gladly trade the personal gossip for a voucher to Almack's.

The conversation fell flat then, though they did each manage to say a few things about the weather and the traffic. Even that topic brought another sour turn to Helena's lips because it only served to remind her that Adelaide was living in Mayfair while Helena was in the very respectable but not as exclusive Marylebone.

Helena plucked a stray thread from Adelaide's skirt. "You are going to get me an invitation to that ball, aren't you? We are family, after all."

And with that Adelaide didn't care about being rude anymore. She stood to her feet. "Sentiment is for fools, Helena." Nothing was going to mend the rift between the sisters, at least not anytime soon. Helena's mouth dropped open as Adelaide pushed past her and left the drawing room.

Her grand exit was spoiled a bit by having to wait in the front hall for her maid to be collected from the kitchen, and her sister did nothing but glare as she left the drawing room and stomped off.

Despite the indignation, which Adelaide decided she had every right to wallow in, sadness threatened to overwhelm her as she watched her sister's bold red skirts disappear. The difference between her relationship with Helena and Georgina's relationship with Miranda was stark and revealing. And it made Adelaide feel too many things at once, particularly on top of the confusing tumult of emotions from the night before.

Restless and tense, she didn't want to return to the house on Mount Street. When she was in the country, she'd taken long walks to sort things out in her mind. There weren't any rolling hills or rambling forests in London so she went for the next best thing.

She went to Hyde Park.

Chapter 28

Despite Anthony's assurances, Trent retreated to Hawthorne House instead of returning to his own lodgings.

Griffith looked up from his desk and grinned before looking back at the ledger in front of him. "Someone didn't come home last night. Or should I say someone finally went home last night."

Trent grunted and walked to the dart board to pick up the handful of darts. Griffith had installed the board several years ago, after he and Anthony became friends. No matter how much Griffith practiced, though, Anthony could still beat him soundly. Trent wouldn't admit to any aspirations of beating the marquis—at least not until he was considerably more proficient than he was now—but it was nice to have something to do when he came round to bother his older brother.

Juggling the darts in his hands, Trent walked across the room until he was even with Griffith's desk. The heavy fragrance of Griffith's preferred morning tea still hung in the air, letting Trent know he really was disturbing the normal way of things with these morning visits.

He couldn't bring himself to care.

He let the first dart fly, frowning when it embedded in the outermost ring of the board. "I saw Anthony this morning."

Griffith glanced at the clock. "You've been busy. Rough night?"

Only a brother would dare to give a duke the look Trent gave Griffith. Even then it probably wasn't as scathing at Trent wanted it to be. His experience at giving strong, harsh looks to people was rather limited. "You could say that. Anthony's decided you're probably as woefully uneducated as I was so he intends to have a talk with you before you marry."

"Sounds delightful. Why are you here, then?" Griffith ran a finger down a column of numbers in the ledger before dipping his quill in the inkpot and jotting the sum at the bottom of the page.

One more reason Trent would make a terrible duke. Numbers took him forever to deal with. Though they might not if he spent as much time with them as Griffith did. He wasn't willing to find out.

He threw another dart, pleased when this one landed a bit closer to center. "I'm here because I think he's wrong."

"And you're basing this on . . . ?"

Trent threw two more darts in quick succession, one of them pinging off the metal hanger and the other one smacking into the wooden wall below the dart board. "He thinks I love my wife."

Slowly, ever so slowly, Griffith set the quill down on the desk. "And you don't?"

The remaining two darts clattered across Griffith's desk as Trent dropped them so he could pace. Considering the frequency with which he had been indulging in the habit lately, he was going to need new boots by the end of the week. "I don't know. How can I? I'm not even sure I knew she existed two months ago. And now she's here and she reads and hates carrots and would rather be living in the country. And I can't believe I'm saying this but I've actually considered taking her there. I don't know if that's love or a sense of obligation because I've muddled the only marriage either of us will ever have."

Griffith sat back in his chair, folded his hands over his middle, and stared at his thumbs.

Trent stopped pacing and braced his hands on his brother's desk, leaning over until he could skewer the larger man to the chair with his gaze. "Why haven't you married yet?"

That one infuriating eyebrow winged upward. "Why do you think?"

"Because you're an exacting perfectionist and there isn't a woman alive who would put up with having to keep her teacup three inches from the edge of the table at all times?" Trent pushed off the desk and resumed pacing.

Griffith tried to frown, but the edges of a grin crept through. "I don't make anyone else place their cup that way."

"Ah, yes, but we aren't married to you. We can ignore all your little personal rules. She'll have to live with them." It was well known in the family that Griffith liked things a certain way. He thought through everything, even the order in which he ate his meal. Trent had made the mistake of asking him about that once and had to sit through a bewildering discussion on how the flavors of different foods interacted and how some tastes lingered on the tongue, altering the experience of future bites.

"In a way, that's true." Griffith picked up the quill and ran his finger along the edge of the feather. "I have a plan for selecting a wife. It will happen soon enough, but I've already decided that when I marry her, I'll love her."

Trent scoffed. "It's not as easy as it sounds. Believe me, I'd be eternally grateful if I could just point to Adelaide and say 'I love her' and have everything fall into place. But I don't know how she thinks or what makes her happy. We're not connected like Ryland and Miranda or Colin and Georgina. Even Mother and Lord Blackstone have that certain thing about them when you look at them. That look that tells you they know each other inside and out. Isn't that what love is? It's what I always imagined I'd have. I remember Father quoting bad poetry to Mother and making her laugh all day long as she remembered it. I wanted that. I was going to take my time like Father did and have the next epic love story."

He collapsed against the wall, his voice growing small as he acknowledged out loud for the first time the death of the only dream he'd ever allowed himself to have. "That was the plan."

Griffith sighed and set his arms on the edge of the desk, one thumb rubbing along his forefinger. "Trent, you didn't give your life to Jesus to follow your own plan. You have to follow His plan, and for whatever reason He gave you Adelaide and you accepted her. Now what are you going to do about it?"

"How do you make yourself love someone, Griffith? And I'm not talking about the good Christian kind of love, where we extend charity and grace and forgiveness. That's the kind of love that keeps us from using our social clout to shun people like Lady Crampton." Trent placed his hands on Griffith's desk and leaned forward, this time pleading for help instead of glaring him into submission. "Griffith, how do I love my wife?"

Adelaide had enjoyed Hyde Park from the seat of Trent's curricle, but she adored it on foot. The Serpentine sparkled like a sea of jewels, and this far from Rotten Row she could hear the birds instead of the clatter of carriage wheels and snorts of horses. She lifted her face so the sun could reach past the rim of her bonnet, enjoying the heat on her skin when she felt chilled to the bone. It wasn't the kind of cold that came from the wind or wearing a dress that was too thin. The chill seemed to actually be coming from her bones, making her numb to everything.

She stepped on a rock, the sharp point digging through the thin sole of her slipper and proving at least one part of her could still feel something. With a yelp she danced sideways off the rock, stepping on her hem and nearly tossing herself nose first into the water she'd recently been admiring.

"My lady!" Her maid rushed forward, but Adelaide righted herself first, though not without smudging the bottom of her dress in the dirt and grass.

She frowned at the stain, knowing it wasn't the first dress she accidentally marked. As she walked away from the Serpentine she watched the smudged fabric dance above the toe of her slipper. A slipper she suddenly realized had lost its decorative bow somewhere along the way.

"Rebecca?"

"Yes, my lady?" The maid scurried from three paces back to Adelaide's side. Trent's unorthodox staff must be rubbing off on Adelaide since it even crossed her mind to suggest her maid stop walking so far behind her.

"How many dresses have I ruined since we came to London?"

"Completely ruined? Only two, my lady. I was able to fashion repairs on all the others." The maid sounded almost proud of Adelaide for ruining only two dresses. There was something rather ridiculous in that, considering Rebecca likely didn't have more than four or five dresses in her entire wardrobe.

Adelaide restrained the urge to sigh. "And how many shoes?"

Rebecca beamed at her. "Oh, I've been able to fix all but one of those. I remembered to request extra ribbons from the cobbler this time."

Adelaide reached the top of a small rise and stopped to look around the park at all the people who seemed to have their life under control. "Hats?"

"I rearrange the feathers and ribbons sometimes, but we haven't lost a hat yet." The maid bit her lip. "Please don't ask about the gloves."

Adelaide knew better than to ask about the gloves. Her mother had started buying gloves in mass quantities almost as soon as Adelaide had gotten old enough to wear them.

No wonder things had gone so badly last night. Adelaide was

a klutz. She'd never really had to admit it before, though she was fairly certain everyone knew it. They'd been wealthy enough and her mother had liked to shop enough that her wardrobe destructions were never that noticeable. There was always another dress, another pair of shoes, another hat, fifteen more pairs of gloves.

But there wasn't another Trent. She couldn't shove her husband into the ragbag and get another because she'd messed this one up.

It was time for Adelaide to grow up and stop blaming her upbringing for everything.

Perhaps it was even time to stop trying to make everyone happy. Her mother wanted her to be socially ambitious and popular. And to be honest, the skills she'd acquired growing up—of doing whatever was expected of her and disappearing whenever she wished—would probably stand in her in good stead if she wanted to pursue such a life. But she had only to look at her parents to see the cost of living life that way, a cost she wasn't willing to pay.

But what did Trent need her to be? Despite his claim to the contrary, he enjoyed being social. He spent time at the clubs, taking her out for rides and meals and ice treats. He needed someone poised, capable, and polished who could attend the horse race with him one day and the opera the next with a sophisticated soiree in between. She knew now that she could handle herself in all of those situations, could interact with numerous people as long as she didn't have to start the conversation. The only problem was that she did so while looking like an oafish simpleton.

Trent hadn't asked for this marriage. The least she could do was give him a wife who was a real lady. A wife who rose to the expectations created by the women who'd already filled his life.

She strolled along, trying to figure out what ladies did that she needed to learn. Elegance and poise such as Georgina possessed was a necessity. It was doubtful that young lady ever returned to the house less presentable than when she left it. Wit, such as Miranda and Lady Raebourne utilized, would certainly be an asset. The way both of them and even Griffith were able to turn conversations and politely handle people with a turn of phrase was a skill she desperately wanted to learn. Could such a thing be learned? Could any of them teach her?

With renewed purpose, Adelaide trod across the park and hailed a hack to take her and Rebecca back across Mayfair. There was only one thing, one person, all of those women had in common. And the very thought scared her until her mouth turned dry.

At least three times she raised her fist to stop the driver and have him turn around. Each time she took a deep breath and whispered a pleading prayer for strength before letting the driver continue. Rebecca sat in the other seat in wide-eyed silence, occasionally glancing out the window as if to discern where they were going.

Finally the carriage stopped at another town house, and Adelaide was presenting her card to another butler. Her entrance this time was immediate and welcoming.

Adelaide waited in the drawing room, determined not to run. Less than five minutes passed before she heard someone enter behind her. She whirled around, pasting a smile on her face that she hoped looked confident and friendly instead of reflecting the ill feeling that was growing in her midsection. "Good afternoon, Lady Blackstone. I need your help."

Chapter 29

Trent should have known better than to ask his brother a question. Griffith didn't do things like a normal man, speculating and pulling from his prior knowledge to answer a question. No, when Griffith needed answers, he researched.

"Can I leave now?" Trent tilted his head back over the edge of the club chair he'd sprawled in. It had been an hour since Trent asked his question, and Griffith had responded by summoning a footman and sending out three letters. Then he'd gone back to work and told Trent to make himself comfortable.

"No."

That was it. No explanation, no reassurances. And yet, Trent waited. It wasn't as if Griffith was going to come after him and bodily restrain him if he tried to leave. At least he didn't think Griffith would do such a thing. But he'd asked a question, and Griffith seemed to think the answer was coming, so Trent waited. His older brother had never let him down before.

A loud *thunk* drew Trent's attention, and he rose, waiting for Griffith to stop him from leaving the room. When no objection came, Trent wandered out of the study and toward the front hall. Finch stood next to Trent's traveling trunk, discussing with Griffith's butler how to transport the trunk back to Mount Street.

"Finch?"

"Yes, my lord?"

Trent cleared his throat. "What are you doing?"

Finch looked at the trunk and then back at Trent, a hint of worry creeping across his face. "Packing us to return home, sir? His Grace informed me that you had decided to move back."

Trent stared at the trunk. Part of Trent wanted to resist, to send the trunk back upstairs and return things to the way they'd been yesterday.

But things weren't the same as they'd been yesterday. And while Trent didn't regret his courtship plan, it was time to move on. There was no reason to stay in Hawthorne House any longer.

"Should I take it back upstairs, my lord?" Finch shifted his weight from foot to foot, casting anxious looks at the trunk, the butler, and the corridor that led to Griffith's open study door.

"No." Trent swallowed. "No, Griffith is correct. It's time for us to go home."

And it really was. Was this what Griffith had been keeping him here for? Had he been giving Trent the time needed to come to his own conclusions and understand that it was time to move on?

A forceful knock echoed through the front hall and Gibson, the butler, strode calmly to the door to answer it.

"I had a feeling such a summons would be forthcoming," Anthony said as he patted Gibson on the shoulder and strolled into the house, looking exceptionally more put together than he had when Trent invaded his home early that morning.

Trent's mouth dropped open a bit as Anthony turned him toward the back of the house and gave him a light shove in the direction of Griffith's study.

Trent stomped into the room and glared at his brother. "You called in the cavalry?"

Griffith shrugged. "I don't know the answer, and you've already established that what you've learned from books and rumor is wrong, so the obvious choice is to ask someone trustworthy with firsthand experience."

"Griffith, I'm touched." Anthony placed a hand over his heart and pretended to swoon into the club chair across from the one Trent had been occupying.

"Don't be." Griffith grunted and began stacking his ledgers and clearing his desk. "I hear there's going to be a lecture before I marry."

Trapped in what was sure to be life's most awkward conversation ever, Trent fell back into his chair and draped his arms over the sides before sticking his legs out to cross them at the ankles.

Anthony's grin was unrepentant. "Would you rather get it from Trent? I'm assuming he'll have time to figure everything out by then, unless you've got something in the works you're not telling us."

"He has a plan," Trent muttered, happy to see someone else under scrutiny, if only for a little while.

Griffith didn't even blink or bother raising his arrogant eyebrow. He also didn't hesitate as he continued putting his things in order. "I always have a plan."

The next knock interrupted the conversation, and Colin entered with Ryland on his heels. Trent's brief reprieve was over. The assembling crowd would give him helpful, godly advice, but he had no doubt that they were going to humiliate him first.

"Gentlemen," Griffith said, rising from his position behind his desk once everyone had claimed seats around the room. "The question I'd like to put to you today—more for Trent's benefit than my own, though I do find myself curious as well—is what you mean when you say you love your wife. And how one is supposed to go about attaining that emotion."

Three powerful men stared. Not a word was spoken, leaving the tick of the mantel clock the only noise in the room. Griffith waited them out. Trent tried to do the same but found himself fidgeting under the weight of silence.

"Well, that was not what I expected," Anthony said at last.

Colin ran a hand behind his neck and cast a look over at Ryland before addressing Griffith once more. "You realize that's a bit of a tricky question, don't you?"

That drew forth the arrogant eyebrow. Trent was really going to have to discover an exercise of some kind to learn how to do that. "If the question were simple I wouldn't need to assemble all of you, would I?"

"I think what he means," Ryland said dryly, "is that he and I are married to your sisters, and this discussion has the potential to get more personal than you might like."

Griffith nodded in understanding before leaning back against his desk and crossing his arms over his wide chest. "Trent informed me that Anthony has already covered a discussion of the more physical aspect."

Trent groaned and closed his eyes, praying for the Lord's return. Any moment now would be nice and then he wouldn't have to deal with the problem or this conversation.

Ryland's smirk was evident in his voice. "That must have been interesting."

"You have no idea." Anthony kicked Trent's extended legs. "Pay attention, pup. We're only assembling for this conversation once, so take notes."

"First, know you aren't going to change her." Colin held up a single finger. "You love her as she is, flaws and all, because you've got flaws of your own that she's going to have to embrace."

A laugh burst from Griffith before he could attempt to contain it to a series of snorts and coughs. "Please tell me you've mentioned that part to Georgina."

That mental image took the edge off of Trent's anxiety. Georgina was exceptionally good at presenting a picture of perfection to the world.

Anthony nodded. "But at the same time, you are going to change each other. The closer you get to her, the more you'll adapt to each other. It's hard to explain, but it happens. One day you're making yourself wade through acres of flowers because she likes them, and before you know it, instead you're just having to accept a ridiculous number of vases filled with fresh flowers all over your house."

"Sounds fragrant," Griffith muttered.

Anthony grimaced and shrugged.

Ryland sat forward and stretched one long arm toward Griffith's desk, where a Bible sat on the corner. "You really want to love your wife? Let's talk Isaac and Rebekah."

"I'd think Ephesians would be a better place to start." Colin leaned an elbow on the arm of his chair in order to better see the Bible in Ryland's lap.

Anthony crossed the room to lean over Ryland's shoulder. "What about First Peter?"

Griffith remained leaning against his desk with his arms over his chest, but he turned his head and caught Trent's eye with a self-satisfied smile on his face. Trent had to concede to his older brother once more. As much as he hated to admit it, calling these men in had been the right thing to do. One could never go wrong with advice from the Bible.

⌒

"I need you to teach me how to be a lady." Adelaide sat in her mother-in-law's drawing room wishing there was another way to describe what she wanted. Also wishing that she'd decided to go to Miranda, Georgina, or even Lady Raebourne first. But this new idea of taking charge of things hadn't had much time to grow a logical side yet, so she'd gone straight to the person who'd taught her daughters the skills she wanted to know.

"Nonsense." Caroline waved a hand through the air. "All you lack is a bit of grace. You've the tact of an angel and there's absolutely nothing wrong with that, though perhaps a bit more gumption is in order."

Adelaide blinked at the matter-of-fact compliment. "Oh."

"Now. Let's start with how to sit." Caroline led Adelaide over to a grouping of chairs.

Sitting seemed like a strange thing to teach. Adelaide had been successfully getting in and out of chairs for as long as she could remember. Had she been doing it wrong? How could there be a wrong way to do it? Adelaide lowered herself into the chair. Once seated she tried to fold her hands gently into her lap, but the dress pulled at her shoulder. Her skirt was folded underneath her in a way that severely limited how much she could move without wriggling her clothing into a better position.

She turned wide eyes to Caroline in time to see her nearly float into her own chair, skirts delicately spread on the seat to allow adequate movement in all directions.

Adelaide couldn't even sit in a chair correctly. This was going to take considerably more than a single afternoon.

~

She was late. Caroline had made her rise and sit so many times that her legs were burning by the time she'd gotten home. Dressing for the night had taken twice as long as normal, and now she stood at the top of the stairs, terrified to take the first step.

There were no polished black evening shoes visible in the hall at the bottom of the stairs. Was it possible he wasn't here yet? Could she still await him in the drawing room so that she wouldn't have to notice if he'd lost that look of wonder he always wore when she came down the stairs?

"You're lovely."

The deep, quiet voice at her side made her jump and clutch for the top of the stair railing.

With a firm hand gripping her elbow, she knew she was in no

danger of tumbling headfirst down the stairs, but it still took her a moment to pull her gaze from the treacherous stairs.

To her right, in the corner of her vision were the shoes she'd been expecting down below, the polished leather catching the light of the stairway candelabra. Her gaze climbed up, across buff-colored trousers and then the blue stripes of his waistcoat before giving way to the deeper blue of his cutaway coat. One hand clasped her elbow while the other rested at the small of his back, emphasizing his broad shoulders and making her middle jump in a way she'd thought it never would again.

But it was his face that truly robbed her breath. The wonder was still there, thank God. But it was veiled now, with some other undefinable emotion. Fear? Worry? Was he as nervous to see her again as she was to see him?

"You're home."

"Yes."

She didn't know what to say to that. She'd wondered if, even dared to hope, he would be returning. Was it possible they could move forward and she could stop worrying if he ever meant them to be more than only a public couple?

"Shall we?" He let go of her elbow and offered his arm. For the first time in their wedded life they walked down the stairs together. It was an important moment, Adelaide knew, and she did her best to follow Caroline's hasty instructions so she didn't muss the elegant picture they surely made.

They didn't say anything as they crossed the hall, but he pulled her to a stop before they reached the door.

"Adelaide." He cleared his throat and turned her to take both of her hands in his own. "I need you to know I'm going to be a good husband."

Thick emotions she couldn't begin to name choked her throat.

His gloved hand lifted and smoothed his bent knuckles across her cheek. "You don't have to say anything, but I do. I want to

269

make things right with you, and I think, from here on, we move forward without a plan or a scheme. Could we do that? Can you give me one more clean slate, Adelaide?"

"My mother knew." The words tumbled out of her mouth, as if her tongue were racing to get her own confession out of the way so they could claim a new start together.

Trent opened his mouth and then shut it with a click of teeth. He blinked at her. "Knew what?"

"That we were there. In the ruins. She was the one we heard drive by."

"And she left you there to force our marriage?"

Adelaide winced, knowing she needed to come completely clean but not wanting to. "She thought you were Griffith."

Silence pressed in for a moment, and then Trent threw his head back and laughed. "No one can accuse us of being normal, Adelaide, that is for certain."

An answering smile stretched across her face, and giddy freedom bubbled into her own laughter.

He leaned over and skimmed a gentle kiss along her lips. "No more secrets, no more schemes. I promise not to hurt you again, Adelaide. I will be a good husband."

The little memory of her snooping through his study drawers ran through her mind, but she pushed it away. That wasn't a secret, not really. It was the type of thing people learned when they lived together. As long as she never brought it up it would never be an issue.

The tightness around his green eyes lessened as his laughter faded into a brilliant smile complete with a deep dimple in his left cheek. As he escorted her out the door, Adelaide thought about her feet, made sure her head was held steady so she wouldn't dislodge her feathers or her curls, and maintained a respectable distance between her body and Trent's so as not to accidentally trod on his foot the way she had a few nights ago on their way in to a musicale.

The ache that hit her legs as she tried to climb into the carriage almost made her turn back and decide the opera wasn't worth going to after all. Only the knowledge that she'd still have to climb stairs to get back into the house propelled her forward. After meticulously adjusting her skirts so that she wouldn't pull off any ribbons or stress any seams, she folded her hands in her lap, keeping her average-sized reticule secure so it wouldn't lose any of the fringe circling the base. Without a book inside, the bag felt light, and she worried that she would swing it around indiscriminately because of that.

Trent climbed in after her, easing into the seat with the same unconscious care that he always did. He wasn't pretending to be a consummate gentleman. It had been bred into him while he was still in short pants.

"Did you know," she said as the carriage began rolling, "that one of the first operas in the United Kingdom was performed on a covered tennis court?"

Laughter immediately filled the carriage. Trent reached over and took Adelaide's hand, pressing it between his own. That alone made her mad dash through the library at Lady Blackstone's house worth it. She'd wanted something to break the potential tension of the evening, and the book on the history of the theater had provided exactly what she needed.

He didn't say anything as the laughter faded away but he wrapped his hand around hers and stared at it, running one finger along the seam of her glove, following it from finger to finger, sending shivers from her hand, along her spine, to the tips of her toes curling in her slippers. "There's one more thing I need to say, Adelaide. I want to apologize. Last night I—"

"Please don't." Adelaide lifted her free hand and pressed her fingers over his lips, causing surprise to break through whatever thoughts had been focused on setting things right. "We're starting over, remember? Clean slate. I'm well. Honestly, I am. So I think the best thing we could do now is enjoy the opera."

He looked at her for a moment, long enough that she began to wonder if they were going to discuss it after all. But then his smile returned, his even, white teeth barely visible through the curved lips. "Agreed. We'll enjoy our evening. Have you ever been to the opera?"

She shook her head. "No, but once Father took me to Birmingham with him, and we went to the theater."

"How old were you?"

How old had she been? It had been several years. Before Helena had started coming to London. "I think I was twelve. Perhaps thirteen."

"And that was the last time you went to a theater?" His voice was quiet as London rolled by the carriage window.

"I always caught the traveling shows when they came through Riverton." She knew that wasn't what he meant but she didn't want his pity tonight. She wanted to be a lady, worthy of respect and perhaps even a little bit of love. If they were going to start anew, that seemed like as good a goal to work for as anything.

They climbed out of the carriage, and Adelaide was so distracted she almost snagged her trim on the carriage door. She sucked her breath in between her teeth as she carefully leaned back to dislodge the trim from the door hinge. Perhaps tomorrow she could make it an hour without mussing up her outfit. She at least needed to make it for the hour she was going to spend at Caroline's house practicing how to sit and learning how to walk. Perhaps they could adjust the lesson to include climbing into carriages properly.

She curled her fingers around Trent's offered arm, giving it a light squeeze that drew another one of his dimple-inducing, heart-stopping smiles, making her remember his passionate kisses before everything had gone wrong. She smiled to herself as they entered the opera house. Maybe she didn't want to forget everything about the past twenty-four hours after all.

Chapter 30

Trent was supposed to be responding to something Colin was saying—that was a person's normal role in a conversation, after all—but instead he was staring at his wife on the other side of the conversation circle in Griffith's opera box. Something was different, and Trent had no idea what it was. He couldn't say for sure what it was about his wife, but she was not the same young woman he'd become accustomed to taking about town.

They'd arrived at the opera with barely enough time to greet the other occupants of the box before settling in for the first act of the performance, which meant intermission was the first opportunity they'd actually had to converse with Colin and Georgina, who had decided to join them tonight. The current conversation was mostly between Georgina and Adelaide, though Colin threw in an observation or two along the way. They stood in a circle behind the chairs, stretching their legs and avoiding some of the curious eyes that always watched the aristocratic boxes for interesting gossip.

Not that there was much of interest to be seen with two married couples as the only occupants of the box, but Trent was starting to crave his privacy in ways he never had before. It could possibly have something to do with having had his life dissected earlier that day by a group of men he highly respected.

They were discussing the costumes of the first act now, something Trent really didn't have an opinion on because he hadn't paid much attention. He'd been too busy making sure Adelaide was enjoying her evening. If they hadn't had their vague but cleansing conversation in the carriage, he would have counted the change as awkwardness or even worry, but he truly felt they'd moved on. Moved on to what he wasn't sure, but they'd moved beyond whatever limbo he'd put them in with his courtship idea. Still there was something more, something missing. His eyes ran the length of her, wondering if she needed to stretch her legs more than they were already doing. He'd brave the crowds in the outer corridors if she needed to walk.

But she wasn't fidgeting. She was hardly moving at all, which was very unlike the Adelaide he'd come to know. Normally she exuded a quiet but bubbly sort of life, which was probably how she always ended up with her ensemble in disarray. Trent's lips quirked up as he took in his wife once more, this time searching for some adorable flaw in her appearance.

"Don't you agree, Trent?" Colin smirked as he aimed the question Trent's way.

He wasn't about to admit that he hadn't been listening, so he took the risk of agreeing. "Of course."

"There, you see, Adelaide? Trent agrees that it would be ridiculous to stay in London during the summer heat. Now you've only to decide which of the estates you want to go to."

Trent wanted to glare at Colin—he really did—but there was such hope in Adelaide's face that he couldn't look away from it. He didn't know when or how the topic had veered away from the bizarre costumes of the opera, but did it matter?

Scripture from his afternoon at Hawthorne House drifted through his mind.

"*. . . she became his wife, and he loved her . . .*"

"*Husbands, love your wives, even as Christ also loved the church, and gave himself for it.*"

". . . giving honour unto the wife . . ."

Trent looked at the joy on Adelaide's face at the mere thought of returning to the country, and his decision was made. What was keeping him in the city year-round, anyway? Just because he stayed on one of his estates for a while didn't mean he had to get involved in the day-to-day running of things. His estate managers could carry on as if he weren't there, and he'd be taking care of his wife, giving of himself for her. It wasn't easy and it didn't feel like love yet, but it felt right and that was a start.

"Why don't we go to Suffolk?" Trent asked, unable to resist running one knuckle down her cheek when it was lit by such a wide smile. "I've yet to see it. You spent time there as a child, didn't you?"

Adelaide nodded. "Father always stayed there when he went to the races. He usually took me with him. We stopped going about five years ago."

When Helena had come to London. Had life stopped for her with her sister's societal debut? Trent gave serious consideration to calling her parents on the carpet for their favoritism and negligence, but that would require spending time in their presence, and he was becoming more and more determined to avoid that unless absolutely necessary—and to keep Adelaide as far away from them as possible as well.

"It's settled, then. We summer in Suffolk. Maybe Colin and Georgina will even come visit."

Now he was volunteering to host country house parties? Was there anything he wasn't willing to do if it meant making Adelaide happy?

Colin rubbed his chin in thought. "I've never really looked into horses. They're a rather unpredictable investment, but it could be fun."

Georgina sighed. "You don't need another project." Her nose wrinkled. "And horses smell."

Colin frowned. "But I've already stepped away from the shipping, and now I'm putting less in corn. I need something to do."

"Be glad you didn't marry a businessman, Adelaide. I spend half my life competing with profit shares and stock exchanges." Georgina tempered the complaint with a small smile.

No one had been more surprised than Trent when Georgina had declared herself in love with Colin. Perhaps because he'd seen them at the beginning of their acquaintance when the mere sight of the man made Georgina flush with irritation.

That volatile emotion had transformed over time, making them one of the most devoted couples Trent had ever known. The way they helped and supported each other was a thing of beauty.

Servants began dousing some of the candles, signaling an end to the intermission. Colin wound an arm around his wife's waist as he led her back to her chair. "You know, if you want me to put down the newspapers, all you have to do is ask."

His sister's cheeks pinked slightly, and Trent hurriedly escorted Adelaide to their seats at the front of the box.

Sometimes Trent really hated being such good friends with his sisters' husbands.

⌒

She wouldn't have thought one small change could cause such a disturbance in her morning routine, but the knowledge that Trent would be in the house seemed to change every pattern she'd formed over the last few weeks. Adelaide had gotten in the habit of dressing herself in the mornings and only requiring Rebecca's services when she dressed for the afternoon.

But now Trent was home. Would he expect her to come down properly dressed and coiffed? She stared at the ceiling, wondering if she should ring for Rebecca or simply keep to her normal routine. Whatever she chose couldn't be as awkward as their return from the opera.

He'd escorted her in, but it seemed strange somehow for him to lean in for a kiss as had been their custom before . . . well, before. Especially since he hadn't stopped at the bottom of the stairs but had escorted her all the way up to their shared parlor. The enjoyment from the evening made the unusual end feel all the stranger. He'd darted in and given her a quick kiss before exchanging a stilted good-night and retreating to his room.

Now knowing he was on the other side of that door, that she'd be seeing him at breakfast, that she was going to have to watch every move she made for the entire day and not just the evening, all of those things made her terrified to get out of bed.

The soft knock at her door made her jump. At first she thought it came from Trent's room but then the door from the parlor opened and Rebecca came in. "Good morning, my lady."

Adelaide sat up in bed. "How did you know to come this morning?"

Her maid pulled back the curtains, letting in the morning light before bustling to the dressing room. "Lord Trent will be at breakfast this morning." She paused at the door and tossed Adelaide a smile that could almost be termed cheeky. "I'm starting to learn how this house functions, my lady. It takes a bit of getting used to."

"I know what you mean." Adelaide threw the covers back and submitted herself to Rebecca's ministrations, already missing the comfort of her old morning dresses and braided hair. Lady Blackstone's rules had been firm, though, that she was never to let her appearance put her at a disadvantage. Adelaide assumed that included when she was dealing with her husband.

The sacrifice was worth it though, when Trent's eyes followed her across the breakfast room to the sideboard. She fixed her plate, carrying it to the table carefully. Rebecca had stared openly when Adelaide returned from the opera last night looking nearly as put together as when she'd left. It had been a difficult thing and she had nearly broken her fan, but overall she'd been impressed with herself, if a bit uncomfortable. There was candle wax on her glove and she'd apparently bumped her toe against a soot-stained wall at some point, but the dress was intact, her hair still perfect—or as perfect as it could be with hair that now occasionally got trapped in her eyelashes—and her reticule unblemished.

She intended to continue her appearance-maintaining habits this morning, even if they took more thought than she liked to give her clothing. So much thought that last night she often had trouble following the conversation and giving adequate attention to her gloves at the same time. Eventually she hoped the careful movements would become second nature and she wouldn't have to think about them all the time. Being a proper lady was exhausting.

Her plate made it to the table without incident, but it unnerved her to try to sit correctly with Trent's eyes glued to her. He waited until she was situated to resume his seat.

"I'll be out for a while, but I'll be back in time for our ride this afternoon." He cleared his throat and ran his napkin through his fingers. "Assuming you still wish to go for a ride."

She nodded. "That would be nice. I don't have any other particular plans."

And so their morning went.

And every morning after for the next two weeks.

From what little Adelaide knew of marriages, the Hawthorne ones notwithstanding, theirs was a better than average existence. They talked. She continued to look up interesting facts to share on their afternoon rides. Cooking was turning out to be something she enjoyed and was actually good at. After Adelaide mastered the cooking of bacon, Mrs. Harris had moved her on to more complicated dishes.

It wasn't the most ladylike of pursuits, but even Caroline had been forced to admit that Adelaide would never be a normal lady. Though she still gave Adelaide suggestions on how not to ruin slippers and hemlines, she'd given up on the gloves and simply suggested Adelaide keep an extra pair in her reticule now that a book no longer took up most of the space.

Mr. Givendale came by to visit Trent twice more, always when he wasn't home and always when another visitor had just left, leaving Adelaide stuck in the front hall when he tried to gain entrance. She never invited him in for tea again, but they always seemed to stand in the front hall chatting for a few moments without her ever intending to enter into a conversation. Fenton would clear his throat and Adelaide would wish the man a good afternoon. It had been odd but never concerning.

They went to his mother's card party and let everyone in the family believe that everything had worked out between them, and in a way she supposed it had. It hadn't become the marriage she'd been hoping for when he first proposed his courtship idea, but it was better than she'd actually thought she'd have.

She did want children though, and she didn't know how to broach the topic.

Now sitting at the breakfast table two weeks after Trent had moved back in, her fork poking holes in her ham, she admonished herself to keep giving it time.

"Mr. Lowick is coming by today. I don't know if you know him. He manages the Suffolk estate."

Adelaide nodded as she carefully chewed and swallowed her toast, taking care that not a single crumb escaped. Caroline's lessons had gotten easier to apply but she still had to be very conscious of everything she did. "Oh, yes, I remember him. Would it be a terrible imposition of me to greet him while he's here? He used to sneak me candies when I was a child."

"Of course. I'll have someone let you know when he's been shown to my study, and you may come in at your leisure. I haven't met him yet, though we've exchanged letters a few times." Trent's plate was empty, but he didn't leave the table. "Have you any other plans for the day?"

Adelaide sighed. Was this what they were to become, then? Polite strangers sharing a house? Little more than housemates? A rather lonely existence stretched out before her and the pressing need to establish a connection—any connection—made her heart race. "Your mother is coming by this afternoon."

Trent choked on his tea. "My mother?"

Adelaide nodded. She hadn't told Trent of her lessons because she didn't know what he'd think about them. Despite his declaration that they were to have no more secrets between them, the intimacy of that moment before the opera had disappeared, and she felt compelled to maintain the idea that everything was perfect. That she was perfect. "She's going to show me how to address invitations."

"How to address . . . I see. Good. I'm glad." He took another sip of tea and adjusted the fork he'd put down on his empty plate moments before. "Are we having a gathering?"

Panic tightened Adelaide's grip on her own fork. Should she have cleared her plans with Trent beforehand? It had been a spur-of-the-moment decision at Lady Blackstone's the day before, an act of near desperation in her attempt to be a better wife. "I thought we might have your family over for dinner, a sort of trial gathering, if you will. The house isn't really ready for much entertaining. Your mother and I thought about three weeks from now would be good timing."

Trent smiled, easing Adelaide's unease. "That's a splendid idea. Be sure to include Anthony and Amelia." His smiled dropped a bit at the corners. "Is it . . . ? Are we only inviting *my* family?"

The thought of having her mother and Helena in the same room as two dukes and a marquis made Adelaide want to push the rest of her breakfast aside. "Yes. I think my family might wait for another time."

Or never, given that she couldn't remember the last time her mother and father had attended an intimate gathering at the same time. They rarely even sat down to dinner together at home in the country.

She was beginning to have an idea as to why.

"I think that might be wise." Trent fiddled with his fork a bit more, seeming about to say something else before changing his mind. Instead he stood and started to lean over her chair as if he were going to give her a kiss before starting his day. She rather hoped he would follow through on the motion, but he righted himself instead. "I'll be in my study if you need anything. Mr. Lowick should be here in a couple of hours."

"All right." She watched him walk from the room before turning back to her plate.

They were making progress, weren't they? He'd stayed after finishing his food and had almost kissed her good morning. There was no need to wallow in self-pity simply because things weren't moving as fast as she'd like.

She stabbed at her breakfast until it turned cold and then abandoned the unappetizing mess to retreat to her small study to take care of what little correspondence she had before Lady Blackstone arrived. At the top of the pile was a note from her mother inviting her to tea that afternoon. Who invited someone for tea? Did her mother think she'd be so rude as to not return the exceedingly brief visit she'd made earlier that week? While it was true Adelaide had contemplated doing such a thing, she didn't think she'd have had the nerve to follow through on the notion.

The three other items on her desk were easily taken care of, and then she had nothing to do but wait and stare at the peeling wall coverings and compare their sad state to that of her own life until Lady Blackstone was announced.

Chapter 31

There were fewer than ten people in Trent's family. Invitations to a simple dinner should not have taken very long—at least Adelaide hadn't expected them to. She hadn't counted on Lady Blackstone's exacting measures on proper penmanship and address. By the time the countess was satisfied, Adelaide had done four complete sets of invitations. They had then pulled Mrs. Harris in to discuss the menu, which took another half an hour but thankfully didn't leave Adelaide with a cramp in her wrist.

By the time Lady Blackstone took her leave, Mr. Lowick had been in Trent's office for two hours, and Adelaide was afraid she'd missed him. Not that it would be that devastating. Trent had promised they would go to Suffolk this summer, so she would see the man then. It wasn't even that she'd been all that close to him. He'd been employed by her father, after all. Adelaide thought maybe it was a desire to establish the connection between her past and her present, to remind herself and Trent that something good had come of their union.

She knocked softly at Trent's study door.

"Enter."

With a proper ladylike smile that even Lady Blackstone would approve of, Adelaide pushed her way into the room. "Pardon the interruption—a little later than expected, but I'm afraid my morning went a little differently than planned."

Trent grinned without restraint. "My mother made you write everything six times, didn't she."

"Well, four, but the invitations look stunning."

Surprise and something that might have been pride flickered across her husband's face. "Four? Your penmanship must be exquisite. I dare you to send out the first set and see if she notices."

Such a thing had never crossed her mind—would never cross her mind, as she'd never been brave enough to step outside of expectations before. Marrying Trent had been enough out of the normal way of things to make her the subject of speculation for another three years, at least. Still, the invitations were only going to family members, and the playful gleam in his eyes was so tempting that she found herself drawn in. "Perhaps the second set. I spelled your sister Georgina's name incorrectly on the first set."

The approval in his smile made her want to send the first set out even with the incorrectly spelled name.

Trent stood and came around his desk, sweeping an arm toward the country gentleman standing in front of one of the chairs in the study. "You remember Mr. Lowick, don't you, Lady Adelaide?"

Adelaide had completely forgotten the man was in the room, but she tried to cover it with a gracious smile and a tilted head, berating herself for having forgotten her manners and determined to be perfection for the rest of the meeting. "Of course. I'm glad I was able to see you before you left. I remember walking the estate with you and my father as a child."

"Oh, yes," the older man said. "I used to sneak you pieces of peppermint as we walked." He pulled a small tin from his pocket. "I still carry some everywhere. Would you care for a piece?"

As she smiled and took a piece, it was nice to be reminded that not all of her growing-up moments were dark and dismal. The sweet flavor of the peppermint brought back images of sunrises on dew-dampened fields and horse rides across flowery meadows. Summer couldn't come soon enough for her country sensibilities.

"Your timing is perfect, Adelaide. Mr. Lowick and I were just finishing up." Trent crossed the floor to stand next to her, as if they were a single unit sending off one of their guests. Would they stand like this when they greeted his family at their dinner party? Stand together as the couples filed out? She was suddenly looking forward to an evening that had seemed more of a chore or a rite of passage a few hours earlier. Of course, once everyone was gone they would probably coldly part ways and go to their separate rooms unless she could take the time between now and then to convince him that she was a perfect wife despite their earlier stumbles.

Mr. Lowick slid a stack of papers into his leather satchel. "I'll take the mail coach Monday morning and start implementing these crop plans as soon as possible. It's still early enough in the spring that the changes should be easy enough to make."

"Oh, wonderful. Are we going to do the pineapples, then?"

Silence met Adelaide's question. Tense silence. Adelaide bit her lip. She wasn't supposed to know about the pineapples, had only come across the plans because she'd been going through Trent's drawers, but she'd still been dreaming of them as a unified, sharing couple, and she'd been unable to let the opportunity to prove she knew something about him slide by.

The stunned curiosity on Mr. Lowick's face proved that pineapples had not been discussed in that meeting. She was almost afraid to look at Trent, but she told herself that being a coward would only make it worse to deal with later.

His easy smile was gone, replaced with a dark frown. Irritation narrowed his green eyes, devoid of any trace of laughter. All the softness she'd grown accustomed to seeing in his face disappeared. She'd never seen him mad, wasn't sure many people had, but there was no doubting that he was feeling the emotion now.

"What do you know of pineapples?"

A glance away from Trent's angry scowl revealed that Mr. Lowick really wanted to leave. Only Adelaide and Trent were blocking the door, and she didn't think Trent would take kindly to a suggestion that they move out of the way. "I was looking for the invitations Fenton set aside for me. Lady Raebourne said sometimes you stuff them in a drawer. I saw the drawing and was curious. I'm so sorry. I shouldn't have looked, I know, but it was fascinating. And I thought maybe, since Suffolk had so many horse farms you would be able to get the . . . well . . . the necessary elements for your plan. I never meant . . ." Adelaide swallowed, her mouth dry after her rushed explanation. "I never meant any harm."

Trent rubbed his hands over his face and pushed his fingers into his blond hair, sending it flopping around his head in a tangled mess that only made him look more fashionable and handsome. It really wasn't fair that the man wore dishevelment so well.

"Begging your pardon, sir, but I've heard about pineapples. They're very precious, but I don't know that they can be grown in England." Mr. Lowick held his satchel in one hand and scratched his head with the other.

The sigh that drug its way out of Trent's chest sounded painful. As if he knew he were about to say something he would later regret.

"The Dutch." Trent stopped and cleared his throat. "The Dutch have come up with a method for growing them in greenhouses. I sketched out a few modifications to make it more efficient, but I hadn't planned on doing anything with it."

"And it involves horse, er, byproduct?"

"Yes." Trent nodded, his lips pressed tight and his eyes sad as he fought some inner battle. Adelaide couldn't believe she'd done this to him. After all of her intentions, all her plans to be the best wife she could possibly be, she'd gone and done this. Exposed something he'd never meant to show anyone. Though her limited knowledge recognized the plans were well thought out and rather remarkable, he obviously thought they weren't and had meant them to remain private.

When nothing more was said, Mr. Lowick finally cleared his throat. "Well, I'll be off, then. I'm staying at the Clarendon if you need me, my lord."

"Of course, Mr. Lowick." Trent nodded and pulled Adelaide away from the door with a gentle hand on her arm. Even in his anger he still treated her gently. Adelaide's admiration for the man grew.

If only she hadn't wrecked whatever remained of his admiration for her.

They stood there, waiting in silence until they could no longer hear the manager's footsteps.

Then they waited a few moments more. Adelaide wasn't about to be the one to break the silence. She didn't know what Trent was thinking or what she should do, so she fell back on the habits of childhood and waited.

When Adelaide was twelve she'd worked for months to learn how to scoop an uprooted shrub from the ground as she rode by, the way she saw them do in one of the trick-rider shows that had come through the village. Of course, that rider had picked up a handkerchief, but he'd been male, considerably taller than Adelaide, and able to ride astride. She decided picking up a tangle of branches was enough of a feat for her to master.

She'd shown no one, though, afraid they would laugh at the amount of time she'd spent on such a ridiculous feat. Her brother had seen her practicing one day and brought her father out to see the spectacle. He'd beamed at her and shown all his friends who came to the house until she turned thirteen. After that he deemed it unseemly to show off such tricks to his friends, but Adelaide never forgot how much he'd encouraged her for those few months.

"You've known about the pineapples for a while, I gather."

Trent's voice was quiet, and he looked tired, as if all the righteous anger had slid through him, leaving him drained and exhausted.

Adelaide blinked, trying to reconcile the man in front of her with the vibrant, athletic man she normally saw, but she couldn't do it. Everyone had secrets, and it seemed she'd somehow stumbled onto Trent's, but she didn't know what it meant or why. Why would such a confident man be unwilling to share such innovative ideas? Was it possible that when it came to things of the mind he doubted his abilities in ways he didn't when it involved physical exertion? "Yes. Since, well, a long while."

He took a deep breath and blew it out slowly between pressed lips. "I'm going for a walk." His gaze found hers, and her heart broke over the torturous look in his eyes. "I need to walk when I'm upset. It isn't you. I want you to know that. We'll talk later."

"Are we still going to the Bellingham ball tonight?" Adelaide wanted to go to him, wrap her arms around him, and offer comfort for a wound she still couldn't identify. But she knew that it hurt, and that knowledge was enough for her to want to make it better.

"Yes. I . . . Yes. We're still going. If you want to."

Adelaide nodded, not sure what to do but trying to trust him when he said they would talk later.

Trent looked at her, and already she could see him pushing the sadness down to wherever he normally stored it. The light was coming back to his eyes and the anger was nowhere to be seen. But it wasn't enough to erase her memory of his earlier emotion.

"It's just a walk to clear my head. I'll be back." He came forward and tipped one knuckle under her chin, forcing her to look into the green eyes she found herself avoiding. "We're going to make this work, you and I. In time, we'll learn how to rub along well." He brushed a light kiss over her lips and walked out the door.

Leaving her alone in his study. After what he'd just learned, how could he trust her?

Her eyes drifted to the bottom drawer of the desk, where the pineapple papers probably still resided. It would be so easy. She could get them now, send them to Mr. Lowick at the Clarendon. She could play the role her brother had played for her all those years ago.

Indecision glued her feet to the wool rug. While the revelation of her horse riding escapades had ended well, the initial feeling of betrayal had driven a wedge between her and her brother for a while. She'd forgiven him, of course, and until now she never thought of the bad part of the story when she looked back and remembered.

Her familial relationship had weathered the betrayal without any lasting damage.

But would her marriage? Trent had promised they'd talk later, that they'd learn how to rub along well together, which was all she'd ever thought she'd get in a marriage. So why was she suffering disappointment that she was going to get what she'd expected?

The walls of the house seemed to press in until she couldn't stand them anymore. So she did the one thing she'd planned on putting off for as long as possible.

She went to visit her mother.

Chapter 32

Trent walked all the way to his fencing club and spent half an hour stabbing a straw-filled dummy with his sword because he didn't trust himself to spar with an actual person. The long walk home still didn't free him from the agitation crawling under his skin, so he took his horse to the less crowded Regent's Park, but at that time of the afternoon the bridal paths were still too crowded for him to lose his frustrations in the wind of a hard gallop.

Which was how he ended up back at Hawthorne House, throwing darts in Griffith's study.

"It occurs to me," Griffith murmured as he sliced open the seal on a letter, "that I've seen more of you since you married than I did when we lived under the same roof."

"Nothing works, Griffith." Trent threw another dart into the dead center of the board. At least his irritation was improving his aim this time. "I've done everything a man does to court a woman."

Griffith didn't say anything but rose to take three of the darts from Trent's hand. He tossed them toward the board with an easy grace that still sent the tips sinking deep into the cork—proof that while his older brother lacked most of Trent's athleticism, it wasn't due to lack of strength.

Trent leaned his hip against Griffith's desk and watched the darts fly. "I know it's only been a matter of weeks, but things should be accelerated for us, shouldn't they? There are couples who met at the Season's first ball who are now announcing their betrothals. I thought it was working, but today all those soft feelings disappeared in a single moment. I didn't want her anywhere near me. I failed, Griffith. I failed at courting my wife."

Griffith crossed the room to collect the darts from the board. "I've been thinking about this, and I have a question. Have you tried being married?"

The pressures of the dukedom had finally addled Griffith's brain. Didn't he realize that being married is what had gotten Trent into this situation in the first place? "I am."

"No, you're not." Griffith tossed a dart and then handed one to Trent. "You're trying to conduct a courtship that has no rules or order to it."

"It seemed like a good idea at the time." Trent's dart landed three inches right of center. He'd be off the board again by the time Griffith finished imparting his wisdom.

Griffith considered the dart in his hand, weighing it like he appeared to be weighing his words. Trent wasn't going to like whatever came next because it usually made too much sense to refute.

"Obviously," Griffith said, "something happened this morning. You don't want to talk about it, and I respect that, but the fact is you've run from it. You're here. Again. Leaving your marriage to be picked up and pieced back together by one person, which as we learned in here not too long ago, is never what God intended marriage to be."

Trent crossed his arms over his chest, trying his best to look imposing so Griffith wouldn't continue. It was hard to scare a mountain. "I didn't ask for this marriage, Griffith."

"And yet it's the one that God gave you. If you don't protect it, who will?"

He'd never thought of it that way. Oh, he'd told Griffith he trusted God's plan and that this must have happened for a reason, but he wasn't sure he'd actually believed any of it. At what point had he stopped trying to do things to fix the situation and let God handle it for him? Never. In fact he'd run from being in the one place God needed him to be in order to make what Trent had promised he would make: a God-honoring marriage. One couldn't be married from across town or even across the room if he didn't accept that the woman involved was well and truly forevermore the woman he had to protect and cherish above all others.

Including himself.

"I haven't married," Griffith said quietly.

Trent pulled himself from his thoughts to find that Griffith had finished throwing the darts and was now simply watching him. "So I've seen."

"I've seen a lot of marriages though, and there's one thing I've noticed. They have good days and they have bad days. But at the end of the day they're still married and that makes them deal with the situation."

Trent frowned. He'd been mad at Adelaide, but she was still his wife. He couldn't walk away from her like a man in a normal courtship could. Tonight he was going to walk back into that house and take her out for the evening. And at the end of the evening he would take her back home. To his house. Their house.

And there was nothing he could do about it.

Which made him even more angry than he'd been about Adelaide snooping through his papers.

Griffith pried the last dart from Trent's hand and tossed it at the board, giving a small smile as it landed in the center ring. "God gave you this marriage, Trent. Now what are you going to do about it?"

⁓

Adelaide gave a bemused smile as she looked around her mother's large drawing room. The invitation to tea had not been the close family gathering Adelaide had assumed it would be. The gathering of people sitting on sofas or talking in corners could almost be considered a midafternoon party.

The mix of people was strange. About half of them were married, the ages ranging from hers to possibly a little older than her mother. Most of them were ladies, but a handful of gentlemen were scattered about the room as well. She'd met all of them at one time or another at her mother's urging, but hadn't realized that they were actually all friends of a sort. Including Mr. Givendale. It probably shouldn't surprise her that the man who made Adelaide the most wary she'd ever been was apparently good friends with her mother.

He sat beside Adelaide on the rose-colored sofa, his leg pressed scandalously close to hers while they sipped their tea and talked to the other people seated in the cozy circle. Mrs. Seyton sat on his other side, meaning no one looking would think twice about Mr. Givendale's nearness, but Adelaide knew there was no need for his knee to bump against hers.

"May I take a moment to compliment your appearance this afternoon, Lady Adelaide? That dress is very becoming on you."

"Oh yes, it is." Lady Ferrington leaned forward in her chair to more closely inspect Adelaide's skirt. "Is that muslin? Wherever did you find it in such a lovely blue? And the cut is divine."

"A beautiful dress is meaningless if it doesn't grace a most becoming woman." Mr. Givendale saluted her with his teacup, drawing giggles from the rest of the people in the circle.

Adelaide buried her face in her teacup. Did none of these people think it odd that the man was complimenting a married woman?

"There is something different about you today, though, Lady Adelaide." Mrs. Seyton narrowed her gaze. "Have you always worn spectacles?"

There was still tea in her mouth when Adelaide gave a slight gasp, drawing forth a short set of coughs. "Ah, yes. I've always worn spectacles."

"It's the hair." Mr. Givendale leaned toward Mrs. Seyton, effectively pressing his leg more tightly against Adelaide's. "She's pinned it back."

Not even Trent had noticed that her hair had finally grown long enough to be pinned back in a fashion that more closely resembled the current style. But no matter how easy and charming Mr. Givendale's conversation was, she couldn't seem to quell the notion that he wasn't simply being friendly. His leg bumped hers once more, and she set her cup on the nearby tea table. "Please excuse me. I need to speak to my mother for a moment."

She rose, tugging the edge of her skirt from underneath Mr. Givendale's leg, and crossed the room to where her mother stood, near a corner, alone for the first time all afternoon. "Quite the gathering you have here, Mother."

Wide blue eyes blinked slowly in Adelaide's direction. It was obvious now where Adelaide had picked up the affectation, but she dearly hoped she didn't look like that when she did it. "Of course it is. People get bored during the afternoon, Adelaide. Especially if they don't have unmarried daughters to take about. I discovered that last year."

Last year. While Adelaide had been home in the country with an outgrown governess acting as companion.

"And Father doesn't mind?"

"Your father doesn't know, and I expect you to keep it that way. He only allows me to plan one social event a month, but he's never limited my use of tea and biscuits." Mother looked across her casual gathering. "You are being careful with Givendale, aren't you?"

Adelaide's eyebrows shot up, and she looked from her mother to the man who'd been plaguing her since she arrived. "Careful?"

"Yes, darling." Mother finished her tea and set the cup on the table. "A flirtation is all well and good, but things get rather uncomfortable if you take it any farther than that. He's quite amusing, though, so I keep him around."

Adelaide didn't know what to say, so she stood there, gaping like a landed fish.

"He'll marry one day, though I don't see his behavior changing much. Marriage vows have never been sacred to him. Still, he has his uses. If you're going to continue flirting with him, you might see if he would be willing to sponsor Edgewick, since you haven't seen fit to ask your husband."

"Why not simply have Helena do it?"

Mother's mouth screwed up in a frown. "Edgewick is the wrong coloring. Givendale only pursues women with fair-colored husbands. In case there's a baby."

"In case there's a . . . Mother!" How had Adelaide reached the age of one-and-twenty and never truly known her mother? She should have seen it. All the signs had been there but she'd always thought that somehow, at the end of the day, her mother would do what was right.

"Well, you haven't a title to worry about. And no one is saying you have to do anything with Givendale, but if your marriage isn't making you happy, you'll have to make your own happiness elsewhere." Mother shrugged. "It's a fact of life. I found my happiness in doing what I could to raise Helena's stake in life."

Adelaide thought she might be sick.

Especially when a green-wool-covered masculine arm reached into her field of vision holding a plate with three small sandwiches on it. "Did you try one of these yet?"

"Those are wonderful, aren't they?" Mother reached out a hand, her long, tapered fingers lifting a sandwich from the plate.

"I think I need to get out of here," Adelaide whispered through a throat tight with she didn't even know what. Amazement? Revulsion? Horror?

"It is a bit crowded." Mr. Givendale set the plate down. "Would you like to walk through the conservatory? I've never been there, but I hear the roses are already starting to bloom."

Adelaide blinked at him, his blue eyes much closer to her than they should be, and a dozen realizations occurred to her.

She couldn't walk with him in the conservatory, even if she'd wanted to, because she didn't know where it was. She'd never been in her family's London home because she didn't belong in this world. She didn't want this world, her mother's world. God had saved her from her mother's attentions and from being raised to accept this as normal, and she wasn't going to waste that gift to earn the approval of someone who hadn't affirmed her in twenty-one years.

And whatever mess she and Trent had made of their marriage, they'd still been honest with each other. She knew he was trying, and she dearly hoped he knew she was as well. Even if she never had a happy marriage like she saw in the rest of the Hawthorne family, she could at least have an honorable one. She owed Trent, owed God, that much. She owed herself that much.

Mr. Givendale took her hand in his own. "Are you feeling well? There's a smaller drawing room across the way if you need to sit for a while."

Adelaide was definitely going to be ill.

"Good-bye," she muttered before pushing her way past him and all but running from the madness of the drawing room. She found her pelisse by the door but didn't see her bonnet, and she wasn't going to wait around for it to be fetched. It went against her new efforts of ladylike appearance, but the *ton* was just going to have to forgive her for an afternoon of wind-ravaged hair because she wasn't staying in this house a moment longer.

Chapter 33

He'd never hated balls before. Well, that wasn't true. He'd always thought he hated balls. Nowhere was the courtship dance of the *ton* more evident than inside a ballroom. Even those who were in London to simply enjoy the camaraderie and festivities of the Season could turn obnoxious in a ballroom. If they didn't have anyone of marriageable age in their own family, they took delight in gossiping about those who did.

But tonight he came to the realization that until now he had only found balls annoying.

Because he truly hated this one, and they'd barely stepped foot in the door.

Had his mother not brought the entire family out in a show of support he'd have skipped the evening entirely, but he respected her efforts and what she was trying to do. She didn't know that what Trent really needed was to be home with his wife, having a long discussion about what had happened this afternoon. Since he'd returned home too late for them to talk, he'd gotten dressed and hurried down to the drawing room. She'd seemed a bit confused at first, coming down the stairs with a bit of hesitation in each step, but as her face came into view he knew it had been the right thing. There was something exciting about waiting for his wife, watching her come down the stairs, getting the chance to admire her in a way he didn't get to for the rest of the evening.

This moment of grandeur was the least he could give her. He'd known better than to dabble in things best left to his brother, but he'd thought no one would ever know. As long as he didn't show his thoughts to anyone, didn't put anything into action, nothing would ever come of it and he would go through life as the carefree pugilist without anyone the wiser.

His illusion of protection had shattered today with one innocent question.

And in return he'd shattered her.

He swept her into their customary waltz, but she felt stiff tonight, stiffer than their current strained emotions would have justified. At least in his opinion. He was quickly learning that he had to remember his view of things wasn't the only one that mattered anymore.

"Are you well?" he asked softly in her ear.

She blinked up at him. "Of course. Why do you ask?"

Why had he started this conversation on the dance floor? He cleared his throat. "You seem . . . different tonight."

Her eyes widened and then narrowed. "Different?"

He tried to smile through the looming panic. "Different. You don't look quite like yourself. And it isn't only the pinned-back hair."

"You noticed?" A small smile touched her lips and her shoulders relaxed a fraction. "I didn't think anyone besides Mr. Givendale was going to notice."

The muscles in Trent's shoulders seized and he pulled her closer. "When did Givendale notice?"

She winced, and he immediately relaxed his hold. "At Mother's. I stopped over there for tea this afternoon."

"Did he . . ." Trent swallowed and guided her around the end of the circle of dancers. "Are you all right?"

Her eyes widened as she realized what he was really asking. "I left. I mean, I didn't do anything. Not that he wouldn't have or didn't . . . I'm not really sure, because I don't really know about such things, but even my mother warned me to be careful."

They stumbled through the rest of the dance, and Trent couldn't help but see all the places he'd mishandled their situation. His worry that he would hold her hand but not her heart was proving more than valid. And all because he hadn't been willing to risk his own heart. As Griffith said, he hadn't been willing to be truly married.

He escorted her to the side of the dance floor, but her grip on the inside of his elbow lacked its usual strength.

He couldn't feel his feet. They were numb, as if his custom boots had suddenly shrunk to the size of a child's foot. The sensation was also threatening to overtake his hands. The only thing he was sure he could feel was his heart, and it wasn't beating in any kind of steady rhythm. Was he dying? He'd never heard of someone's heart giving out at the age of twenty-four, but stranger things had happened. Maybe if he died Adelaide would go on to find happiness.

Perhaps even with Mr. Givendale.

Trent scowled into the crowd in general since he didn't know where the wife-stealer was at that particular moment. She'd link her future to that man over his dead body.

"I should probably greet my mother at some point this evening."

The blood drained into his too-small boots. She would rather be with her mother than him?

"Of course. Would you like me to help you find her?"

Her eyes looked somewhere in the vicinity of his left elbow. He'd thought they'd moved past her talking to various parts of his person instead of his face. "No, I think I see her."

He feared she was lying, but there was nothing he could do about it, so he nodded and let her disappear into the crowd of people around them.

A wall of windows looked over Piccadilly Street, and he positioned himself between two of them so he could watch her. It took him a while to find her, but once he did he didn't let the crowd take her from his gaze again. She did find her mother, or rather her mother found her. He couldn't resist the small smile that formed as he then watched her seek solace at the side of Amelia or Anthony or, once, in a discussion with the Duke of Spindlewood.

Trent stayed in his spot. Watching her. Wishing he were somewhere else. Anywhere else. Somewhere totally devoid of people. Well, not all people. He needed to talk to Adelaide. The emotion boiling in his gut was unfamiliar, and he didn't know what to call it, but it was fast taking over every part of his mind and body.

Thirty more minutes of torture and they would have stayed long enough to satisfy his mother's sensibilities and avoid a lecture from an annoyed Ryland that he'd drug himself out in society for nothing. Thirty minutes should be plenty of time for him to find some control over himself and think of the right words to say that would convince Adelaide she wanted to leave. Thirty more minutes and he could be on his way home, where he could rip off his cravat and jacket and be comfortable.

The crowd shifted, and he lost Adelaide for a few moments. He told himself not to worry. She was managing herself with aplomb even though he knew she didn't like being the focus of so much attention—and she was probably feeling a bit torn up inside as well. At least he hoped she was, though at the same time he didn't want her to be suffering the agony he was at the moment.

People shifted once more, and Adelaide's profile came back into view. Her smile was stiff now, as if she didn't want to talk to whomever she was talking to but couldn't find a polite way out of the conversation. Trent couldn't see who she was conversing with, even when he stood to his full height. What he wouldn't have given for Griffith's height at that moment.

A look around the ballroom revealed the rest of his family

was engaged in other conversations or pursuits, leaving no one to rescue his wife but him. Which was as it should be, really. It was cowardly of him to park himself on the side of the ballroom and leave her to fend for herself, but pleasant inane conversation was beyond him tonight. Even his closest friends had deserted him after a brief conversation.

Trent cut his way through the crowd, twisting and turning as if he were in the ring instead of the ballroom.

He broke around a tight knot of gossiping mothers to see Adelaide's own mother at her side. Lady Crampton was smiling and Adelaide was frowning. A dark, intense frown he'd never seen on her face before. Whatever was happening she didn't like it, and the fire in Trent's gut finally found a focus. Whatever was causing his wife distress was about to be vanquished by sheer determination if nothing else.

Especially when he identified the third person in the conversation.

Mr. Givendale was ignoring Adelaide's frown, using the charm that had gotten him into more than one party without an invitation.

"You really should check with Lord Trent for when an acceptable time would be to meet with him." Adelaide's voice finally reached Trent as he veered around one last grouping of people. "You've wasted two afternoons this week alone coming by when he wasn't there."

Trent stumbled to a halt. Givendale had been coming by the house? On the pretense of having business with Trent? The only time Trent ever saw the man was in one of his sporting clubs. Trent would never trust him enough to have anything to do with him elsewhere. Didn't really trust him at the clubs since the time he'd tried to hide weights on his opponent's fencing foil.

Lady Crampton tittered as if there were something funny about the encounter. "You'll have to excuse Adelaide, Mr. Givendale. She's only been in London a short while. Have you met my son-in-

300

law, Lord Edgewick? He's quite the fencer and would be a welcome addition to your club."

"I can hardly recommend a man I've never fenced with before, Lady Crampton. Perhaps Lord and Lady Edgewick could meet me at your house one afternoon. Lady Adelaide, you should come as well and visit with your sister while the match is taking place."

While Adelaide might not have been sure of Givendale's intentions, Trent certainly was. Everything about him reflected a man on a mission. Heat surged through him, bringing feeling back to his fingers and toes as he shouldered his way to his wife's side. "That won't be necessary."

While his very skin seemed to burn with heightened emotion, his heart calmed into a steady beat as Adelaide's shoulders relaxed and her gloved fingers wound tightly around his hand.

Mr. Givendale smiled. "Oh, you intend to be home this week, do you?"

Trent's eyes narrowed. "I do. I've found my home quite pleasant to be at for several weeks now."

The other man nodded. "Perhaps, Lady Crampton, we can schedule this meet-up in a few weeks?"

This was going to end right now. Trent might have an almost insurmountable obstacle between him and his wife, but he was going to take care of it. Somehow. And this man wasn't going to get in his way. "Perhaps you can," Trent said, "but rest assured that Adelaide will never be a part of it."

"Strong words." Givendale lifted Adelaide's other hand and kissed the knuckles before she had the presence of mind to yank her hand back to her side. "Until we meet again, Lady Adelaide. Perhaps over tea?"

Lady Crampton tried to laugh, but it came out a nervous squeak. Trent had never had such a desire to punch a woman in his life. "Stay away from my wife, Givendale."

"Oh, she's your wife now, is she? A couple of months ago she was the woman who ran you out of your own home. I'll just wait until you take up residence at Hawthorne House again. How long will that be? One week? Two?"

He couldn't hit Lady Crampton, but Givendale was another matter entirely.

The screams that echoed off the ballroom walls brought the first conscious realization that he had followed through on his desires. He shook the haze from his eyes to see Givendale rising from the chalked dance floor, touching his nose to see if Trent's punch had drawn blood. Adelaide's hand was still clenched in Trent's left, and he pried his fingers free so he could step fully in front of her.

Givendale stepped forward, clenching and releasing his fists. "That was unwise."

Trent grinned, feeling in control and like himself again, even if that strong emotion still rolled through him. "But satisfying."

A few giggles scattered through the crowd that was growing around them.

"You think you're better than me, *Lord* Trent? I may not have the honorific yet, but at least I'll come into a title one day. You're simply going to fade away."

"God willing." Trent rolled his own shoulders, trying to ease the tension and make it look like a careless shrug. "The Lord knows I'd make a horrible duke."

"You don't make a much better pugilist."

Trent's grin was true and wide. There wasn't much Trent knew in this life, but he knew he could box and fence with the best of them. If it came down to it, he could have Givendale carried out of here in need of a surgeon and not even break a sweat. Trent boxed for the enjoyment of it though, and this wasn't a war that could be won with fists anyway. He'd started it too publicly. The winner of this battle wouldn't be the one who hit the other hardest, but the one who won the crowd over to his side. He'd seen too many public confrontations to think it would go any other way.

Fortunately Trent was almost as good with words as he was with his fists.

"How about we find you someone else to fight, if you don't feel I'm up to your standards. Perhaps one of the other men you've pretended to visit under the guise of business? I have a feeling I'm not the only man whose house you've watched to know when he's in residence."

It was a shot in the dark but one Trent felt was likely to land somewhere. Givendale's method was too polished, his expectations too clear, for it not to be something he'd done many times before.

Gasps rolled through the crowd at Trent's accusation.

The other man sneered. "You've no proof."

Trent crossed his arms and settled into the most arrogant stance he could muster. He thought he might have even managed to lift his right eyebrow a little. "I've no need of any. You just gave it by not denying the accusation outright."

The appearance of arrogance clearly riled Givendale, so Trent took it one step further, turning to address the crowd and taking his eyes off his opponent. He kept himself between Givendale and Adelaide but tried to look unconcerned. "If you care about your wives, men, take care in doing business with this man. Not only is he without principles, but he is also without discretion."

"You dare?" Givendale spit out. "I could see you at dawn for that."

Trent narrowed his gaze at Givendale. "Did you or did you not tell at least three people at Gentleman Jack's that you knew more about my private business than you should?"

Murmurs ran through the crowd as men worked their way to the edges with anger in their clenched jaws. He didn't see his brother or his friends among them, but he was counting on them to have moved in to flank Adelaide, offering her protection should this crowd get unruly.

"Frankly, Givendale, I don't care what you do. There will always be those who turn a blind eye to the life you like to lead. I, however, am not one of them. So I say it again. Stay away from my wife."

"While you're staying away from my daughter, you can avoid *my* wife as well." Lord Crampton stepped up and crossed his arms at the edge of the circle. If the venom in his glare was anything to go by, he wouldn't be one of the ones carrying Givendale out if things turned ugly. He'd likely help in the beating.

Trent felt his neck heat up, knowing Adelaide's father was witnessing this. At the same time he was glad that at least one of her parents seemed to care about her.

Givendale spit at Trent's feet. "You've humiliated me."

Trent crossed his arms over his chest and gave his head a sad shake. "No, you've humiliated yourself."

Then Givendale attacked.

Chapter 34

If there'd been anyone in London who hadn't heard about his marriage before, there wasn't one now. Nor would there by any more rumors that the marriage had been anything other than a love match. Starting a fight in the middle of a ballroom tended to quell that sort of thing.

As Givendale slammed into Trent, sending him down to the floor where his shoulder drilled into the wooden surface with the force of both men's weight, it was almost enough to convince himself.

The strength of Givendale's hit sent the pair sliding across the floor, making finely dressed men and women scatter and squeal. A fist barreled into Trent's ribs as he scrambled to his feet. Fists flew as Trent adjusted to Givendale's movements. He took two more punches before taking control of the fight and making sure the weasel wouldn't be stealing kisses from anyone anytime soon. In return Givendale connected his knee to Trent's side. Evening clothes with seams, buttons, and other accoutrements weren't as forgiving as the linen shirt and breeches he normally boxed in. He wasn't sure if it was the seam of his waistcoat or his flesh tearing, but the pain that lashed through him gave him a pretty good guess.

Trent's rebuttal was a swift punch to the breadbasket that sent

Givendale doubling over, making it simple work to send him to the floor with a less than gentle nudge of Trent's knee.

A few men came forward to assist Givendale from the premises with less than helpful intentions. Trent winced as more than one foot trod on Givendale's toes and a couple of fists connected with ribs Trent had already bruised. There would probably be a few butlers getting new instructions when it came to Mr. Givendale. It was well known that at least half the *ton* marriages were little more than a sham, but woe be to the person who actually got publicly caught, particularly if he was caught by the very man he was making a fool of. Givendale wouldn't be doing much of anything in the near future, which was a good thing, since that meant he couldn't call for pistols at dawn.

The fight would be old news before Givendale could call for retribution. Oh, it wouldn't soon be forgotten, and Trent was sure to be infamous for a long time to come, but Givendale's suffering would probably be short-lived.

Unless he tried something with Trent's wife again.

Noise exploded through the ballroom as Givendale and his escorts cleared the door. Trent's chest heaved with breaths so harsh he thought he might actually be breathing in the noise along with the smell of sweat and blood. He looked down at his still-clenched fist to find a smear of red across his hand. The burning emotional monster still rode him, and he knew he needed to leave.

He looked back at Adelaide for the first time since the confrontation began. She was still where he'd left her, supported on either side by Miranda and Amelia. The fight had moved him halfway across the ballroom, and people were quickly filling in the gap, but he could still make out the stunned face and pale features that hit him harder than anything Givendale had managed to land. What would she think of his forceful answer to the problem of Givendale? If she actually cared for the man, he'd probably just given her the final push that would send her to his side.

She might even go to him tonight to nurse his wounds. It wouldn't change the fact that she was married to Trent, but it could change everything else.

And to think he'd wanted a courtship. What would he have done if Adelaide had been free to walk away? He could hardly have punched every man who tried to win her heart.

Her horrified blue gaze met his tortured green one through the glare of her spectacles.

He didn't know what to do. He couldn't go to her, covered in sweat and the blood of the man she might care for more than him.

So he did the only thing he felt he could do.

He looked for Griffith.

He didn't have to look far. His mountain of a brother was cutting through the crowd to Trent's side, Ryland immediately behind him. "Get her home for me. Or wherever else she wants to go if she doesn't want to be there. Just get her out of here safely."

Ryland placed a hand on Trent's shoulder. "Consider it done."

The Duke of Marshington looked across the crowd to his wife and jerked his head toward the side door opposite of where Givendale had been taken out. After a brief nod, Miranda began ushering Adelaide through the crowd, slipping quietly along the edge so as not to draw attention to their departure.

Ryland looked at Griffith. "You've got him?"

"As long as he can walk."

Trent scowled at the pair of them, but as long as Adelaide was taken care of, he didn't care what they did with him. Someone bumped into his back, and fire shot across his shoulder, nearly sending him to his knees.

"Off we go, then." Griffith wrapped a hand around Trent's arm and guided him outside with more speed than skill. "My carriage is around the corner."

Breathing harshly through his teeth, Trent nodded and turned the way Griffith had pointed, his forceful stride eating up the pavement at a pace that actually exceeded that of Griffith's normal long stride.

The footman saw them coming and jumped to open the door. It wasn't until Trent was faced with climbing into the vehicle that every hit Givendale had managed to land made itself known. A groan vibrated through his gritted teeth as he climbed in and threw himself onto one of the seats.

Griffith unhurriedly climbed in after him, carrying one of the carriage lanterns. As the conveyance began to roll, he set the lantern on the floor. "How bad is it?"

Trent undid the buttons on his waistcoat and pulled the linen shirt from the waist of his trousers. Every move was agony, and he was soon breathing harder from the effort to move sore muscles than he had been after the exertion of the actual fight. His side had a definite, distinct pain.

Air hissed through Griffith's teeth as Trent pulled the shirt up. "You need a surgeon."

Trent looked at his side. In the light of the lantern it did look bad. The blood wasn't running freely though, so he guessed it was more of a scrape than anything else. "I'll clean it up at home."

He looked up at his brother's stern expression. "I promise if it's worse than a scratch I'll send for the surgeon myself."

Griffith crossed his arms over his chest.

Trent flopped onto the seat, leaving his ruined clothes in their state of disarray. "Honestly, Griffith, do you think Mrs. Harris would let me do anything less?"

His brother grunted but said nothing else on the fifteen-minute ride to Trent's house. He started to get out and help Trent inside, but Trent held up a hand to stop him. "I can make it inside on my own. I won the fight, remember?"

"Did you?" Griffith lifted an eyebrow as he let the question sink in.

Yes, he had won the physical fight with Givendale, but whether or not he'd won the prize remained to be seen. "I'll see you tomorrow."

Trent didn't wait for a response as he walked into the house with as much grace as possible. His legs weren't damaged or even very sore, so it was mostly his back and side causing him to walk like an overworked laundress. His hands also hurt, but that didn't affect his walk any.

When Fenton opened the door, Trent simply held up a hand in a bid for silence as he walked past and stumbled up to his room, shucking his cravat, jacket, and waistcoat as he went.

Trent rolled his shoulder, trying to ease the discomfort as he achieved the sanctuary of his bedchamber. He pulled his shirt over his head and turned to look at his back in the mirror. The light from the lamp played over his skin, picking up the darker colors that were starting to discolor along his ribs.

He washed the blood off, revealing that the wound on his side was indeed a long scrape with a shallow cut near the front that had caused most of the smeared blood. Considering his own stiff movements, he was fairly certain that Givendale wasn't cleaning himself up tonight.

Trent couldn't find a lot of sympathy for his opponent. He'd probably be begging God's forgiveness for that in the morning, but tonight he was caught in the mire of his human fallibility and couldn't help but be glad he'd gotten the best of the man who seemed intent on ruining his chances for a happy marriage. Not that Trent hadn't done at least as much damage himself. He clearly didn't need outside help in that effort.

He stretched his arm once more, wincing at the pain but knowing that he couldn't let the muscle tense up—that would make the pain much worse.

Despite the energy still flowing through his veins, he tried to convince himself to go to bed. Wandering the room wasn't helping his sore body, and any moment the pulsing frenzy would leave his system and his energy would fade into nothingness.

He leaned toward the mirror to check his face one more time

to make sure the small cut along his cheekbone wasn't bleeding again.

A soft sound jerked his gaze from his face to the reflected area beyond his right shoulder. He spun around, desperate to see it with his own eyes, but the truth was there in a white cotton gown with a bright blue wrapper.

She hadn't gone to Givendale.

She had come to him.

⁓

She'd told herself not to come, that the day had been too full of emotions and it would be best to save any conversations for the light of a new day. But as she'd lain in bed, waiting for sleep that refused to come, all she could think about was how slowly he'd been moving when he left the ballroom. How stiffly he'd held his body when he met her gaze across the heads of circling bystanders.

Once Miranda had gotten her clear of the ballroom she'd tried to rush around the side of the house to find him, but the crush of curious people had been more than she could stand. Everywhere she went people pressed in, trying to get her to tell them why Trent had felt the need for such a public altercation with Givendale. As if she wanted to talk about something so personal with people who were still near strangers. Ryland put an end to the questions with a glare and ushered her into his carriage, offering to take her wherever she wanted to go for the night.

The offer had broken her heart because she knew that the order had come from Trent. After everything that happened, he was giving her a choice, as much of a choice as he could. Somehow she knew that no matter what she did he would always choose their marriage. He'd proven as much tonight.

So she'd come home and gotten in bed, trying not to listen for the sounds of his groans in the next room, racking her brain for anything she could do that would ease his suffering. Suffering he'd picked up on her behalf.

One of the medical texts she'd glanced through when looking for interesting facts to share with Trent explained that smoothing and manipulating the muscles could ease soreness from the body. She hadn't read the whole text and so had no idea what methods the book actually called for, but if she could help him, she wanted to try. No one had ever stood up for her, implicitly believed in her like he did. As much as she was coming to crave a deeper affection from him, she would be satisfied if his protection and confidence were all she ever had.

Afraid she'd lose her nerve if she waited for him to answer a knock, and knowing that it was possible he was already asleep, she'd eased the connecting door open.

She expected him to be collapsed into his faded wingback or sprawled across the bed. She wasn't expecting to see lantern light playing across his muscled and bruised torso. Suddenly offering to rub the soreness from his muscles didn't seem like such a good idea. Or perhaps it was the most inspired idea she ever had.

"Adelaide?" He crossed the room in three long strides and took her shoulders in his hands. "Adelaide, are you well?"

He'd been knocked so hard that he slid at least six feet across a ballroom floor and he was concerned about her well-being?

"I thought I might . . . That is, I wanted to see if I could help you. I've read that massage can ease the pain after, em, after physical altercations."

Trent's eyebrows shot up as he smoothed his hands up and down her arms. The silk wrapper and cotton nightgown were no match for the warmth of his hands, and she wanted to sink in to it, suddenly feeling chilled at all the ups and downs she'd experienced today.

His voice was rough, and he had to clear his throat before the words came out clearly. "It can. There's a surgeon that comes by the fencing club sometimes. He sees to the occasional sore muscle in exchange for free membership."

"Oh." Adelaide's eyes widened, and she blinked. If it was normally performed by a doctor, could she do it wrong and actually end up hurting him more? "Should I call for a surgeon, then?"

"No, no, that's not what I meant." He ran his gaze over her, brows pulled in as if he couldn't decide what he wanted to do next. He glanced over his shoulder at the bed before closing his eyes and whispering something she couldn't quite understand. When he opened them again she caught her breath at the intensity she saw in his emerald eyes. It had to be a trick of the lantern light, but for a few moments all of the sentiments of the day seemed to be swirling in his gaze. "If you want to help, I won't turn you away. But know you don't have to do this."

She was surprised to find herself smiling. Even her bones seemed to be shaking inside her from a combination of nerves and the memory of the last time she'd been in this room. Yet somehow, she still wanted to smile. "I want to help."

He nodded before going to the bed to lie down on his stomach. "Most of the tension seems to be in the left shoulder."

"Okay. Do I just . . . push on it?" Adelaide moved the lantern to the table beside the bed and found herself wishing she hadn't. Even scraped and discolored his back was a thing of beauty. And she had volunteered to touch it.

He turned his head to grin at her. "I'm not sure. I've never been on that side of it to see what he does. Just try something. I'll let you know if it hurts."

"All right, then." Adelaide rubbed her hands together, her fingers so cold she didn't dare place them against his skin. She blew on them to warm them up, contemplating his back and trying to decide the best place to start.

"You don't have to do this, Adelaide. I've been punched before. My body will recover."

"No," Adelaide said softly, then repeated the word with more conviction. She decided to start at the top and work her way down. Her first touches were so light they barely made an impression in the skin, but as the heat from his body melted the ice in her fingers she began to press harder, running her hands along his shoulders and down his spine.

His first groan had her snatching her hands back as if she'd been burned. She knew she should have called a physician. It was foolish to practice medicine with only a few paragraphs of a medical text for guidance.

"Noooo," he groaned. "Feels good."

That was a good groan, then? Pleased, she set her hands to the task once more, almost forgetting that the beneficiary of the exercise was supposed to be him. She was getting such enjoyment out of running her hands along his skin that she stopped thinking and trusted her instincts on where to go next.

After a while his groans were replaced by a soft snore.

She smoothed her hands over his skin one more time, enjoying the texture and avoiding the long scrape. Then she took the lantern back to her room with a smile.

Chapter 35

Adelaide was certain that one day she would walk down this church aisle and not be the subject of everyone's speculative stares. It didn't help much that she knew the stares were more for Trent than for herself—she was still in the line of everyone's vision, still part of the story on everyone's lips, and still uncomfortable with the whole thing.

But if that was the price she had to pay for walking the aisle on Trent's arm, she'd accept it. She'd sat up most of the night thinking about her life and come to the very difficult conclusion that if she had to choose between pleasing her mother and pleasing Trent, her mother was going to lose. She was fairly certain that decision was even biblical.

Griffith was already in the family pew when Trent and Adelaide slid into the box.

The duke looked his brother over before lifting one side of his lips. "You're looking well. Considering."

Trent straightened the sleeves of his coat. "He barely touched me."

Since Adelaide knew how much he'd moaned while climbing into the curricle that morning, she was impressed by his façade of painless movement. She was also honored that he had allowed her to see his suffering and trusted her to keep it secret now. She smiled. Perhaps he would need another massage later.

Heat immediately flushed her cheeks. She shouldn't be having thoughts like that. Especially not in church. She yanked her fan from her wrist and waved it rapidly in a furious bid to cool her cheeks.

"I'd love to know what you're thinking right now," Trent whispered in her ear.

She blushed harder. At this rate God wouldn't need to strike her with lightning. She was going to catch fire all on her own.

"Thank you for the massage last night."

Really. If the man did not stop whispering in her ear, she would not be held responsible for the spontaneous combustion of the church.

"Last time I felt that sore I couldn't get out of bed the next morning. I felt almost normal this morning."

She turned her face to find his less than an inch away. Anyone looking at them would think they were about to kiss. For a moment even she thought they were about to kiss. "I am glad to hear that. Truly I am."

"Perhaps I could return the favor."

His gaze bore into hers, making her think of all the things he wasn't saying. Was it possible that they could still enjoy some of the other things like kissing even though the rest of it hadn't worked for them? She'd certainly enjoyed those other things, and she'd enjoyed giving him a massage last night. And she really couldn't handle this conversation and expect the skin not to burn off her face. "Trent, we're in church!"

"Adelaide, we're married!"

She screwed up her face in confusion. "What has that to do with anything?"

Griffith leaned toward them. "You do know it's considered rude to whisper."

Trent grinned back at his brother. "We're in church. One should always speak in reverent tones in church."

"One should also speak of reverent subjects," Adelaide murmured.

The deep, low laugh that reached her ears shivered down her spine to land in her middle with a tightening thud. "What could be more holy than the union of two people in the eyes of God?"

Adelaide lifted a brow, almost giddy to learn she had the skill when Trent had once confessed how much it bothered him that he couldn't do it. "Perhaps the union of a man's soul with the risen Savior."

"Touché." Trent didn't seem overly concerned that he'd conceded her the conversational point, and why should he? Her cheeks still flamed at the implications of his earlier conversation. It would be a miracle if she heard a thing the rector said this morning.

<hr />

They dined at home that night. Throughout the quiet dinner and when they'd later retired to the upstairs parlor, Trent found himself searching his brain for topics that would make her laugh, make her smile. He couldn't get their banter at church out of his mind. It fed the craving he had for more talks like that one. Adelaide didn't often rise to his baiting statements, but when she did, he sat in awe of her quick wit. When he thought back to their wedding day, when she'd been unwilling to even look him in the eye, he never would have guessed that she would blossom into the woman sitting across the parlor from him.

Well, sort of the woman across from him. For those few moments when her blush had threatened to overtake her senses, she'd seemed like the Adelaide he married instead of the one that had been so distant for the past few weeks. But even though their relationship had turned some invisible corner last night, she still seemed different. So what was causing it?

The parlor was quiet and comfortable, the perfect place to relax on a quiet Sunday evening. She read while he pretended to. The book he'd brought up was boring, but he kept turning the pages, counting to ten each time she turned one so he wouldn't give away his inattention to his book.

"You've got it upside down," she said quietly.

Trent knew that trick, so he ignored her and turned another page, gathering his wits before he looked down at his book . . . and discovered that it was, indeed, upside down. He snapped it shut and threw it onto the seat of the chair across from him. "No wonder it was boring."

She grinned at him over the top of her own book, and he looked at her, really looked at her. Her hair was neat, looking almost normal with the hair pulled out of her face. That wasn't all it was though. Her dress was in perfect fashion—just as the rest of her new clothes were—the feathers on her slippers nothing out of the ordinary. Everything looked just as it should.

Everything looked just as it should.

That was it. She'd looked perfect for weeks now. What had happened to his Adelaide?

With a frown he reached out and pulled a pin from her hair, sending two curls cascading over her shoulder. Then he bent down and snagged her slipper off her foot, tossing it in the direction of her bedchamber.

He sat back, satisfied with the changes. "Much better."

"Was that really necessary?" Her exasperated sigh delighted him.

"Yes. You looked too perfect."

She blinked at him—perfect, adorable blinks. "Too perfect?"

"Hmm, yes. It's taken me a while to place it, but yes, you looked too perfect."

She set her book to the side, confusion stamped across her face. "Are you saying you'd rather I walk around with mismatched gloves, smudged slippers, and ripped hems?"

"Not all at once." He shrugged. "You never did all of those at once. I just rather liked that I was the only person who ever saw you when everything was perfect."

She tucked one leg underneath her and leaned over the arm of her chair to look him in the face, eager curiosity molding all of her features into a blend of wide-eyed inquisition. "But your mother gave me very specific instructions on how to keep everything in order. I must admit it's difficult to think about every move I make all the time, and I take a full inventory every time I visit the retiring room. It's very frustrating to find that even with all the care I find little things wrong."

"While I fully respect my mother, I didn't ask to marry her." Trent stopped and shook his head. "That came out entirely wrong."

Adelaide stared at him for a moment. "You didn't ask to marry me, either."

"Actually, if you'll recall, I did." Trent smiled as Adelaide blinked at him once more.

He leaned across the gap between their chairs and captured her lips in a kiss.

What he'd meant to be a sweet meeting of the lips soon grew as he cupped her face in his hands and drove his fingers into her curls, setting more pins free and sending more tendrils dancing around her shoulders.

"Adelaide." Trent swallowed as the word came out too rough to be understood. "Adelaide, do you think we could try again?"

She glanced at the door to his room and then back to his eyes before leaning forward and capturing his lips in a kiss of her own.

Their days fell into a pattern once more, and while it wasn't all that different than what they'd done before, it felt like everything had changed. They would breakfast together in the morning. She would then curl up in the chair in his study and read while he worked for an hour. Then he would go off to one of his clubs while she met with Mrs. Harris or went to see Lady Blackstone. Unless she was in the presence of the countess, she stopped worrying so much about her appearance. It was incredibly freeing to finally relax again.

Sometimes she even deliberately set part of her ensemble wrong just so Trent could find it. He had started gently and quietly correcting the mishap. If they were alone when he did it he followed it with a kiss.

Trent would return home in the late afternoon and take her for a ride before bringing her back home to dress for dinner. They'd only gone out once in the past three days and that was to a small gathering a friend of Trent's from school was having. Otherwise they dined in and then retired to the parlor.

Trent taught her how to play chess. She read to him from some of her Minerva Press novels, using funny voices for the different characters, like she would if reading to a child. Once they even played a silly game of jacks, though they spent more time chasing the errantly bouncing ball than scooping up knucklebones.

Then they retired to his bedchamber, and sometime in the night she would come half awake while he carried her to her own bed.

On the surface everything looked wonderful. Anyone looking in would think they'd finally embraced their marriage and were as in love as any young couple who'd gone about it in a more conventional way would be.

But Adelaide knew differently.

She knew the balance they had was incredibly delicate. The unspoken-of incident with the pineapple papers stood between them, an ignored barrier to finally moving forward. She wasn't careful of her shoes anymore, but she feared taking another wrong step with Trent, and it kept their conversations superficial.

And she didn't like it.

Darkness pressed around them, as comfortable as the heavy

blankets on top of her and the warm, hard shoulder she was using as a pillow. She loved this part of the day, when she was warm and happy and as close to her husband as any person could be to another. Sometimes they exchanged whispered stories about their childhood, other times they lay in silence.

She snuggled closer to his side and traced a looping design across his chest. "It's so warm here. The cold always wakes me up when you take me back to bed. Maybe I'll just stay here tonight."

Trent laughed, causing her head to shake on his vibrating shoulder. "And send Rebecca and Finch into scandalous despair?"

"Finch is married," Adelaide muttered. "I think he could handle it."

He brushed her hair away from her face. "You know I could come to your bed instead. Then you wouldn't have to get cold when I move you."

She pouted. She felt ridiculous doing it, but she didn't want to be deprived of his bed. "But I like your bed. It's the most beautiful piece of furniture I've ever seen."

He kissed her gently on the lips. "Then we'll have one made for you just like it. Though I can think of several things you would rather have carved into the headboard than a hunt."

"A bed like this is too expensive, Trent. I'll redecorate my room eventually, and I'll find a lovely bed, but I'll always love yours more."

One finger tipped her chin up, and she could see Trent searching for her eyes in the pale moonlight that crept around the edges of the curtains. "You really don't know how much money I have, do you?"

"Trent, stop it. You're a younger son. I know we'll always be comfortable, but I can't expect you to be able to live like your brother."

Trent tilted his head back. "No, not like my brother. But probably similarly to your father."

Adelaide sat upright and twisted in the bed to stare at him.

There was no way that he was as rich as her titled father. He was a younger son whose brother had already inherited. "It's not necessary to go into debt to impress me, you know."

Trent laughed and pulled her back into his arms. "My father left me a generous sum, and Colin's been managing that for years, even before I knew he was managing it. Interfering brothers are sometimes beneficial."

"Oh." Adelaide went back to tracing designs across Trent's chest, wondering if she dared ask what had been bothering her all day. For several days really. She knew their delicate idyll couldn't last forever, but did she really want to be the one to break it?

"Trent?"

"Yes, my dear?"

"Will you please tell me about the pineapples?"

Chapter 36

He tensed, and it actually pulled her closer to his chest until he was hugging her to him. That more than anything convinced him it was time. It was time to let down his guard, time to let her in.

Time to be married.

"I don't know if I can explain it." He took a deep breath. "But I'll try."

She smoothed his hair back with soft fingers but didn't say anything, patience lacing her content expression. A part of him wanted to lash out, though, tell her it wasn't her business, tell her that, if she hadn't looked into his private papers, she'd never have known about the pineapples and they could have gone happily on in their current bliss.

"It's foolish," he whispered.

She propped her head up on her hand and gave him an encouraging smile. "I thought the plans looked quite brilliant, actually. A remarkably efficient use of space."

Trent laughed, surprised that he could, given what he was about to tell her. She was going to think he was touched in the head. "Not the plans themselves. The reason they've stayed in that drawer."

"Oh."

He sat up and ran his hands through his hair. It helped that he couldn't see her face now. "Planning crops and making changes to the way things run is something a duke does."

She frowned. He couldn't see it, but he could feel it. Adelaide expressed herself with her whole body. "No, that's what estate owners do."

He shrugged. "And when I was growing up, the estate owner was a duke. And I learned about estates because I sat in on lessons with my brother, the future duke. So those things . . . Those are ducal things. And I don't want to be good at them."

The blankets rustled as she sat up and then shifted to her knees in front of him. "Trent, just because you weren't born to the title and don't make plans for half the country doesn't make your abilities any less than Griffith's."

"No, you misunderstood me. It's not that I don't think I'm any good at it—it's that I don't want to be. I don't want God to look down and think that I might be a better duke than Griffith."

Trent swallowed hard, knowing what he was about to say was absurd, was not logical, that it was a bit of nonsense implanted in the mind of a young boy. And yet he couldn't get past it. "That's how I lost my father."

Adelaide crawled into his lap and wound her arms around his neck, laying her head on his chest. He could feel her breath, thought maybe he could feel her heart, unless that was his own pounding hard enough for two. It made it easier, holding her but not having to see her face. He could accept her comfort without worrying about her censure. "God saw that Griffith would be an amazing duke, and He made it so. Father even said it was going to happen. I just don't think he thought it would happen so soon."

There was quiet for a long time. Trent wanted to fill it but he didn't know what else to say.

Eventually she broke the silence for him. "Trent, growing pine-apples won't make you any more fit to be a duke."

"It's not the actual growing of the pineapples. It's the act of getting involved in things like that."

Adelaide sat up and took his face in her hands. "May I be blunt, Trent?"

Trent froze at the sternness of her words. He'd been expecting gentle understanding, maybe even some platitudes and comforts. "Of course."

"You would make a terrible duke."

The tension eased out of Trent, and he laughed. "I would, would I?"

"Yes. There is so much more to having a title than seeing that your estates are profitable. You also have to manage people. And you, my dear husband, would be terrible at that."

Trent looped his arms around her waist. "I beg your pardon. People love me."

"Exactly. People love you. You set them at ease. Before your altercation with Mr. Givendale, when have you ever seen the bad in someone? Trent, you are a fabulous person, and the world is better off because you're in it, but I'm afraid you would have a very difficult time foreseeing potential problems if you were a duke."

Adelaide's observation didn't cure his irrational fear right away, but it did help put it in perspective. It gave him a tool to combat the insecurities and fears. It gave him the courage to consider doing some things without constantly looking over his shoulder to make sure Griffith was all right.

He pulled Adelaide into his arms and kissed her. He wasn't sure what he was putting into this kiss, but it was something more, something different than he'd given her before, and she kissed him back as if she realized it.

Then he held her and kissed her on top of the head. "Have you ever eaten a pineapple?"

Adelaide's happiness rose with the sun. All was right with her world . . . until Fenton announced that her mother and sister had arrived for a visit. Then the happy bubble burst into a dozen pieces, still recognizable and probably even fixable, but broken nonetheless. How did her mother always seem to know when Adelaide was finally feeling happy? Did Adelaide's happiness somehow siphon off some of her mother's own joy? Did the world really shift that much just because Adelaide smiled? It had been over a week since the altercation in the ballroom, and Mother had been doing a very good job of avoiding her or keeping their public encounters polite and brief.

Apparently it was too much to ask that they settle into that routine for the foreseeable future.

She had Fenton take them to the drawing room, even though it was a bit sparse. Workers were coming tomorrow to re-cover the walls and hang new curtains. Adelaide hadn't decided the furniture she wanted yet, unable to find something both sturdy and feminine to fill the space, but she didn't see that as a reason to continue looking at shabby walls. Particularly since one of the windows was already bare.

With a glance in the mirror to ensure that she wasn't too disheveled, Adelaide went downstairs to greet her guests, reminding herself they were, indeed, her guests and this was her home. She asked Mabel to have tea sent to the drawing room. There was no reason to dawdle over things and prolong the visit unnecessarily.

She felt a bit guilty, wishing her family hadn't come for a visit while at the same time busily planning for an extended visit with Trent's. But the truth was, her family wasn't as nice as his. And while she truly wanted to honor her mother the way the Bible told her to, she was having a hard time reconciling it with the verses that told her to stay away from fools.

If she took a little longer going down the stairs than normal, no one would know but her. And if she made a face at the drawing room door before pushing it open with a smile, that too remained her little secret.

"Darling." Mother rushed forward with her hands extended in a show of affection Adelaide hadn't even seen her bestow on Helena. "I've been so worried about you. I haven't really been able to speak with you since The Incident."

Adelaide hadn't known someone could actually talk in capital letters, but her mother had managed to do so. An awkward pat from Adelaide brought an end to the uncomfortable hug.

"I don't think it's as dramatic as you're making it out to be, Mother. Certainly not an occurrence that needs to be referred to with its own name." Adelaide perched on one of the faded chairs just as Lady Blackstone had taught her. She could easily rise if need be but didn't look as if she were trying to rush her guests out the door.

"Even I heard about it." Helena's eyes were wide as she gave her head a solemn nod.

Adelaide's eyes narrowed at her sister. "You subscribe to every gossip rag in London, Helena. Of course you heard about it."

Helena dropped the false innocence. "And your husband's altercation was written up in every single one of them."

"So was your exchange with Lady Raebourne two years ago, but we didn't give that occurrence its own name and speak of it in hushed tones." Adelaide couldn't believe she was calling forth the biggest scandal her family had ever had—or ever been caught in, as Adelaide was beginning to believe was the case. She felt a twinge of guilt at bringing up the past, but if Helena was going to attack Adelaide's husband, everything was fair game. "If I recall, you wrote me that the entire thing was being exaggerated and shouldn't have been worth more than a few drawing room giggles."

Adelaide paused while Fenton brought in the tea service. Once he departed, she looked back at her sister. "Do you still wish to use the number of articles as a gauge for an event's level of scandal?"

"Really, Adelaide, the two events hardly compare." Mother folded her hands in her lap and pursed her lips.

Adelaide didn't know why they'd come, but it seemed she'd somehow managed to put a crack in their intentions.

Her moment of satisfaction died when her mother took the teapot and began pouring Helena's cup. This was Adelaide's home. She should be serving the tea. For her mother to take up the pot was an establishment of power that went beyond rude to insulting. As Adelaide debated whether or not to wrestle it from her just to prove a point, the drawing room door opened.

Expecting a servant but hoping for one of her new sisters-in-law, Adelaide turned to see who was entering. She was very glad she wasn't holding the teapot when Trent walked in. Shock would have probably had her dropping the thing.

"Sorry I'm late, darling." Trent crossed the room and sat on the settee with her as if it were perfectly normal for a husband to take visitors with his wife. It was amazing how different the word *darling* sounded on his lips than her mother's. "Oh good, I'm glad I didn't miss tea. Five sugars and a splash of cream, if you will."

Mother frowned as she prepared the cup, but the tight compression of her lips she passed off as a smile was back by the time she handed the cup to his waiting hands. She then proceed to make Adelaide a tea nearly white with cream before making one for herself.

Adelaide took a closer look at Trent. She thought he'd said he was going to be fencing with Anthony today. As he leaned forward to accept his tea she noticed his pulse jumping in his neck. His hair, tousled in the current fashion, looked damp at the temples and a little more rumpled than it had when he left the house that morning. Had the man run from Anthony's house to be here with her so she wouldn't face her mother alone? Fenton would have had to send Oswyn even before he'd come upstairs to talk to her.

What man made those kind of arrangements if he didn't care

about his wife? No one. They hadn't gotten there through any conventional means, but no one would be able to convince her there wasn't at least a little love in their relationship.

She took a sip of her tea and found Trent frowning at her cup. She gave a tiny shrug, trying to tell him that she didn't care overmuch that her mother had poured. Whether the message was conveyed or not, Trent decided to move on.

"I trust I'm not interrupting anything." Trent settled deeper into the settee and sipped his tea. It was more than obvious that he didn't care if he was interrupting or not—he wasn't going anywhere.

"Of course not, my lord," Mother said behind her teacup.

Adelaide bit her lip to keep from grinning. Trent, being a younger son set to inherit nothing beyond some money and family connections, was all but worthless in Mother's eyes. As a countess she outranked Trent in her own opinion, and it must rankle to have to appease him, even a little bit.

Helena, however, had no such problems.

"Were you part of the horse race last week, my lord?" She fluttered her eyelashes in Trent's direction. His eyes widened and he made a hasty swallow of tea before coughing lightly.

"I don't believe I was. I do sometimes gallop through the park in the mornings, though, so I may have inadvertently joined a pursuit in action."

Adelaide gave him a little grin. "Do you often join races accidentally?"

"It's been known to happen." Trent grinned back at her, ignoring the other two women in the room.

"And do you win?"

"Of course." Trent saluted her with his teacup. "Why play if you've no intention of winning?"

"Even when you had no intention of playing."

He winked at her. "Sometimes those wins are the most satisfactory."

Adelaide ducked her head in a blush, having a sudden feeling they weren't talking about horse races anymore.

Mother set her cup down with a rattle. "I hear your sister is giving a ball next week."

And thus the true purpose of the visit was revealed. They still hadn't received invitations to the ball. Knowing how Miranda felt about Adelaide's family, that slight had probably been intentional. And brazen in a way that only a famously eccentric duchess could get away with.

"Is she? I wouldn't know. I don't handle the invitations. Particularly not hers." Trent sipped his tea again.

Adelaide tried not to smirk. She really did.

Helena smiled and fanned the room with her lashes once more. "I'd be happy to help you learn how to organize your social calendar, Adelaide. You've never really had to do such a thing before."

"Yes, I know. Such skills are certainly easier to practice when one comes to London for a Season." Only the fact that she held a cup of hot tea kept Adelaide from clamping her hands over her mouth. Where had such an impertinent statement come from?

She glanced at her husband, expecting stunned censure in his face—instead he looked almost proud.

The silence that fell over the drawing room was thick enough to swim in. The only person who looked comfortable was Trent. He drank his tea and smiled at everyone as if he had no idea of the undercurrents that had been stirred up.

"I've heard that Montgomery House has a lovely ballroom." Helena ran a finger along the edge of the saucer. "I've heard the floor is inlaid with the image of a peacock."

"Is it?" Trent lifted his brows in Adelaide's direction. "Won't that be exciting to see? Of course, I don't know that we'll be able to see it with the crush of people Miranda's invited. We'll have to go by another day to look at it properly."

"That sounds lovely," Adelaide murmured, wondering how

long it would be before her mother and sister asked outright for an invitation or gave up hope. She was almost embarrassed for her family and desperate to change the subject to something they wouldn't feel humiliated by. "How is Father doing?"

Mother waved a hand in dismissal. "He's doing acceptably well. Bernard is down from school for a while, and your father's been taking him around to some of the clubs and such. Not that he can join yet, of course, but it's so important to teach young men the proper social interactions early. I was able to do much the same with Helena."

Adelaide saw her cup shaking in her hand, heard the rattle of china. Part of her knew she'd eventually drop the thing if she didn't put it down, but that part of her didn't seem to be in control of any of her motions. Her mouth worked, however, though without her normal discretion. "Bernard is in London?"

"Of course. What else would we do—leave him in Hertfordshire with the nanny?"

"That's what you did with me."

Gentle fingers pried the rattling cup from her hands before wrapping her icy fingers in warmth.

Mother looked stunned, as if she suddenly realized her faux pas. "Your father has only Bernard to deal with. I couldn't very well teach you and Helena the same things at the same time. You were too young back then. Besides, things are different for gentlemen."

"Yes, they are." Trent squeezed Adelaide's hands and then stood. "For instance, a gentleman is perfectly within his rights to remove people from his home when they upset his wife."

"My lord—"

Trent crossed his arms over his chest and glared at the countess. Mother turned her attention to Adelaide. "Adelaide, I—"

"Before you say anything, you should know I have no intention of asking Miranda to adjust her invitation list." Adelaide was still shaking, the quakes coming from somewhere deep inside her and causing her voice to tremble slightly. There was no misunderstanding her words though.

Helena shifted to the edge of her seat. "I can't tell you how upset it always made me when Mother insisted we leave you behind. I tried, Adelaide. Truly I did. Perhaps now that we're both on our own we can finally be sisters."

Adelaide frowned, still focused on her mother. "Nor will I ask Trent to stand up for Helena's husband. He owes you no such thing."

Mother looked as if her head were about to explode, making Adelaide very glad the workers hadn't come by to replace the wall coverings yet.

Adelaide stood and wound her arm around Trent's, clinging to him to keep herself upright. "This has been a lovely visit. But I'm sure you'll understand that I have a pressing engagement to prepare for. I'll have Fenton see you out."

Trent smiled at her. A full-blown smile, complete with dimples and teeth and a light dancing in his eyes. "Shall we, my dear? I believe we're scheduled for dinner with the Duke of Spindlewood."

They left the room, but Trent pulled her to the side after they left the room, tilting his head to listen. Angry whispers lashed from the room, too indistinct to hear clearly, but it was easy enough to grasp that they were arguing.

Trent patted Adelaide's hand and led her away. She kept glancing at the drawing room door as they started up the stairs. "Aren't you worried they'll destroy something? They sound very angry."

"Aren't we gutting the room tomorrow?" Trent looked at the door and then glanced around the hall. "Fenton!"

"Yes, my lord?"

"When our guests decide to take their leave, make sure they go straight to the door without any detours. Have Oswyn help you, if need be."

"Of course, sir." The bald butler bowed before pulling the bell-pull to summon Oswyn. Then he stood in the hall like a sentinel.

331

Trent sent Adelaide a questioning glance. "Satisfied?"

Traces of dried sweat were still visible at his temples, proof that he cared more than he'd put into words. "Yes, I believe I am."

"Good." They continued up the stairs to the parlor. Before they parted ways to dress for the evening, he took her hands. "It's possible that honoring your mother is sometimes accomplished simply by not telling the world what a heartless person she can be."

Adelaide thought about how broken she felt after every encounter with her mother and how long it took to put herself back together afterward. She hadn't noticed the pattern when she lived at home, but now that the instances were farther apart, it was obvious. "I think you might be right. Are we really dining with Spindlewood tonight?"

Trent squinted and tilted his head. "Well, I did hear he was dining at Vauxhall Gardens tonight, and we're meeting Georgina and Colin there, so in a very broad sense of the word, yes. Yes, we are."

Delight bubbled up and burst forth as laughter from her lips. "Oh, Trent Hawthorne, I love you."

He looked like she'd hit him with a fire screen. She didn't want to wait to hear him spout gentle platitudes. "Vauxhall Gardens, you said? I'd best go see what Rebecca has laid out for me to wear."

Then she fled into her room, her pounding heart leading the way.

Chapter 37

Sleep was a blissful escape where questions and confusion took a holiday, allowing a person momentary peace, even if they weren't awake to enjoy it. It was an escape denied to Trent that evening. He sat in his chair, watching the light from his candle flicker to the corners of the room. Shadows played over the figure huddled beneath the covers in the center of his bed. He didn't know what to do, but he knew he had to do something. They couldn't avoid it forever. He just had to find the courage to ask her about what she'd said, the same way she'd mustered up the courage to ask him about the pineapples.

He didn't know how long he'd stood in the parlor after she left. Finch found him there, staring at a wooden door as if it could answer all the deepest questions in life. But it couldn't. She probably couldn't even answer them. Not that he would ask. How could he ask the questions that had swirled through his mind without hurting her with his lack of ability to say the words back?

What did "I love you" mean anyway?

They'd certainly sorted out the physical issues of their marriage relationship, but that couldn't have been more than a small part of loving his wife as God had called him to do. Caring for her, putting her needs above his. He was trying to do all these things, committing himself to her well-being.

Did that mean he loved her?

He slid the Bible from the drum he used as a table next to his father's old chair, flipping to the verses in First Corinthians that Anthony had mentioned all those weeks ago. A lifetime seemed to have passed since then, leaving him feeling older and wiser and befuddled all at the same time.

When he'd looked at them before, the verses had seemed like a condemning mass of things he lacked. They also hadn't said anything specific about husbands and wives so he'd used that as an excuse to ignore them. Now they looked more like a checklist, a map to what it took to love a person.

Suffereth long.

Kind.

Envieth not.

Is not puffed up.

He wasn't perfect—no man was—but he could see all those things when he looked at his life with Adelaide. It had never occurred to him that she was flattered by Givendale's attentions or encouraged them in any way. What was that but kindness and lack of envy? Not to mention trust.

Doth not behave itself unseemly.

Well, he had punched a man in the middle of a ballroom, but he didn't think that was what God meant.

Rejoiceth in the truth.

Like confrontations over pineapple plans and interfering mothers?

Beareth all things.

Believeth all things.

Hopeth all things.

Endureth all things.

That was a lot to ask of someone. The candle sent licks of light across the page, highlighting the truth of God. If this was love, this was what he needed to do. Because God had commanded him to love his wife as Christ loved the church. Which meant he had to love her above himself, with everything in him, even unto death. *Beareth, believeth, hopeth, endureth.* What did that look like in a marriage?

He considered her problems his own. To the extent that he'd told Fenton to send word if Lady Crampton ever came calling. Then he'd run the entire way from Anthony's house. A short distance to be sure, but he'd still run.

He had every confidence that she would rise above her upbringing. That the glimmers of strength he saw would only grow if he nurtured them properly.

And above all else he knew that she was the only woman for him. Not because of some fanciful poetic look but because God had given her to him and he trusted the Lord's judgment.

But did all of that mean he'd learned to love his wife? If there was one thing the passage in front of him made clear, it was that love was considerably more than the emotion that drove men to write poetry and subject themselves to societal events they would otherwise avoid. In fact nowhere in the passage did it say anything about knowing what the other person was thinking or feeling as if you couldn't live without them. Love seemed to be more about what you did and gave for the other person than about what they brought to you.

He slid the Bible back onto the large Army drum and blew out the candle before making his way across the room. It might shock Finch, but tonight Trent was going to hold his wife. And tomorrow he was going to start examining his life, looking for anything that was keeping him from fulfilling this most sacred of jobs: loving his wife.

⁓

Adelaide stood in the corridor outside the parlor, trying to decide if she really wanted to go in. Trent had asked her to have tea with him this afternoon. She'd accepted before thinking it through, but now she wondered if it would be best to limit their interaction until they'd both had a chance to move past her instinctive statement the night before.

Breakfast had been more strained than it had been since the first morning after they'd married. Every time he took a breath she expected him to say something about what she'd said. To either ask her about it or give her some watered-down platitudes in return.

He did neither. Instead he acted just as he'd been doing for the past several days. He asked after her plans, shared funny stories about something that had happened at the club the day before. And then invited her to take tea with him.

They'd gone their separate ways after she'd agreed, but now the time was here and she wished she'd been able to come up with an excuse.

"I beg your pardon, my lady." Fenton appeared behind her with the laden tea tray, effectively forcing her to walk into the room.

Fenton set the tray on the low tea table and then sent a significant look toward Trent. He nodded, and Fenton left the room quietly.

What had that been about?

"Would you pour?" Trent asked.

"Of course." Adelaide sat, trying to remember how he took his tea.

"Cream and five lumps of sugar."

"Oh, yes." Adelaide poured a bit of cream into his cup and then dropped sugar in it before giving hers the same treatment. She lifted it to her lips and sipped, hating the taste as it hit her tongue but ignoring it as she'd trained herself to do.

"How do you take your tea, Adelaide?"

She blinked. "Same as you."

"Hmm. And the same as Miranda? The same as your mother?"

She opened her mouth to answer but snapped it shut with a

click of teeth. With a calm she didn't really feel, she slid her cup onto the table.

Trent's cup joined hers as he leaned forward to look her in the face. "How do you like your tea?"

"I don't."

He jerked back with a stunned expression on his face. "I beg your pardon."

Adelaide swallowed and rubbed her hands over her legs. "I don't like tea."

Fenton entered again with another tray. This one filled with teacups. He set in on the table and left.

"You don't like it at all?"

She shrugged. "Not really. It's just simpler to fix it the same way I fix someone else's. I've yet to find a combination I like."

Trent plucked a cup from the tray. "Then let's find out, shall we?"

An hour and two more pots of tea later, Adelaide sat back and folded her hands in her lap. "I think we could put an official seal on this declaration now. I don't care for tea. Although it is more palatable with a significant amount of milk and the slightest bit of sugar."

Trent leaned back in his chair, enjoying his own cup of tea. "We'll have to keep it our secret. They might kick you out of England if it becomes public knowledge. What do you like, then?"

"Coffee. Mrs. Harris brews wonderful coffee. I always have two or three cups at breakfast."

His face showed surprise. "That's coffee? I thought it was chocolate. My sisters insist the day can't begin without a hot mug of chocolate."

She shook her head. "Chocolate is good but coffee is wonderful."

He settled back in his chair and crossed his booted feet at the ankles. "Tell me something else about you that no one else knows."

Adelaide looked over the scattered cups, the dregs of tea long forgotten in a quest to discover what she liked. She didn't need the words. This was proof enough for any woman.

She leaned back in her chair and copied his pose. "I've been stuffing a strip of linen into my dancing slippers in case I have to partner your uncle Charles again. He steps on my toes."

Trent roared with laughter and drank another sip of tea.

Neither left the room for another hour.

⌒

Trent paced the study wondering why on earth he thought this would be a good idea. It was a terrible idea, he was going to bungle it horribly, and he'd spend the rest of his life making it up to Adelaide.

"Your brother has arrived, my lord."

Trent nodded at Fenton. "Thank you."

It was time to go downstairs. He should have already been downstairs. This was Adelaide's first time as hostess, and he should be there to support her. Instead he was upstairs fretting like a girl before her first ball. Why had he done this to himself? Two weeks ago Adelaide had told him she loved him. She'd said it again four days later as she drifted off to sleep. Each day he saw it in the way she spoke to him, looked at him.

After examining himself for a week he'd come to one conclusion. Somewhere along the way he'd learned to love his wife. And he'd learned to embrace her belief in him. He'd sent copies of the pineapple plans to Mr. Lowick two days ago. He'd thought of telling Adelaide everything last night, but then he'd had this idea. At the time he'd thought it brilliant. Now he knew he was insane.

He ran down the stairs and into the newly decorated drawing room. She'd insisted it be done in time for her dinner, scouring London to find the appropriate furniture. She'd done a fabulous job. Upholstered in red and gold, the sofa reminded him a bit of the wingback chair in his room, with elaborate curves along the top of the back. It still had the thin curving legs that were so popular, but it had eight of them, joined together with a grid of wooden bars underneath, providing a strong appearance, so he wasn't afraid to sit on it.

Griffith was taking in the room, kicking lightly at the legs on the sofa. He looked up at Trent. "You'll have to tell me where she found this. I'm going to get one for the white drawing room."

Trent walked to the new walnut cabinet and poured Griffith a glass of water from the decanter he'd had Mrs. Harris prepare in preparation for this evening. He poured himself a sherry before taking the water to his brother. "Are you going to get one in white?"

"Not a chance. I'm leaning toward a peacock-colored cut velvet."

Trent nearly choked on his sherry while Griffith calmly drank his water.

The rest of the family arrived, and Adelaide bustled about, eyes wide with nerves and excitement as she greeted everyone, making sure they had drinks and running out of the room every ten minutes to check on Mrs. Harris.

It was a relief when Fenton finally called them to dinner.

As was always the case when the family got together, everyone stood for a moment looking around and doing mental calculations of rank to see who was supposed to go first. Two dukes, a marquis, and an earl tended to have that effect on a social situation.

"Would everyone simply go to the dining room," Trent grumbled. "And sit wherever you please? It's family."

Adelaide gasped next to him and paled a bit. "But the place cards," she whispered. "I've been studying days on the proper position of the place cards."

"Wait!" Trent sighed and gestured the group back into the drawing room. "Mother, if you please?"

In short order, Mother had everyone properly lined up for the short walk to the dining room, where she beamed at Adelaide after a glance at the place cards.

It felt strange to sit at the head of the table when every man in the room save one outranked him. But it filled him with happiness to look down the table and see Adelaide beaming in success as everyone began to eat. Especially since she'd had a part in creating several of the dishes on the table, including the platter of bacon set directly in front of him.

Before the dessert could be brought out, Trent rose to his feet. "If I may have your attention. As you all know, this year did not start out as expected for me. I had no plans to marry and certainly no plans to marry so quickly. Yet our God is a God who knows more than we do, though we frequently act otherwise. And in His infinite wisdom, He brought me a wife who suits me more than anyone else ever could."

He walked around the table and knelt beside Adelaide's chair. He thought he heard Georgina sigh but didn't look her way. His eyes were only for Adelaide, locked to the light blue eyes that brought her face to life, even though it was a trifle pale at that moment.

"Adelaide, you read some of the strangest things I've ever heard of, your taste in food is somewhat questionable, and you can't keep an ensemble together for more than half an hour."

Griffith coughed. "Ahem, brother, I know I'm the only unmarried man in the room, but I don't think this is the kind of thing a woman wants you to tell her in front of other people."

Trent ignored Griffith, pushing on. He was trusting that he knew Adelaide, that this public declaration would give her confidence in his love. Dear God, he prayed he was right.

"But, Adelaide, all of those things only make you, you. And I wouldn't change one single thing about you. If I had it to do all over again, I'd happily crash through that floor and sit in the ruins with you all night. And I'd ask you to marry me all over again, but this time it wouldn't be because I had no choice."

Trent swallowed, hoping he could get through the next part without having his tense throat steal his voice. "Adelaide, I know it's not normal, but we threw normal out the window a long time ago. I'd like to take this opportunity to ask you to marry me all over again, because I love you. And I can't wait to grow pineapples with you."

More than one person sniffled behind him as the sentimentality of the moment washed over everyone. But he also heard a few murmurs about pineapples, letting him know a bit of confusion had leaked into the moment as well. And he wouldn't have had it any other way.

Adelaide, looking not at all confused, sniffed and let the tears course down her cheeks to get lost in her wide smile. "I love you too," she whispered, "and I'd love to marry you again and grow lots of pineapples."

Epilogue

"You could have warned me that it took two years to grow these things," Adelaide grumbled as she waddled into her husband's specially constructed greenhouse. Layers of carefully made shelves filled with dirt and whatever else it took to grow the tropical fruit lined the room, and at the far end, where the first plants had been planted two years ago, were lovely green-and-brown spike-covered lumps.

Adelaide poked at them, having to fully extend her arm since her belly kept her from getting too close to the shelf. "They're rather ugly, aren't they?"

Trent laughed, as she'd intended him to. He'd been beside himself for months, as it became apparent that it was a toss-up which would come first—the harvesting of his first pineapple or the birth of his first child. Adelaide was rather glad it was the pineapple so she could be here for the moment. She would have hated to be confined to her room, recovering from childbirth when he pulled the first plant.

"Shall we?" He held a wicked-looking long knife in one hand, and a gleam of anticipation lit his face. His cheeks were going to hurt later from all the smiling he was doing, but it would be worth it.

343

"Yes, please." As much as she wanted to be here for this moment, she also really wanted to sit down. Her back was aching like never before, and her feet were so swollen she'd had to wear her dancing slippers with the extra padding removed.

Trent hacked the first pineapple free from its plant and took it to the worktable at the end of the greenhouse. They'd brought a large platter out with them so they wouldn't have to wait to taste it.

He cut off a section and held a dripping chunk of yellow fruit out to her. She took it between her fingers and waited while he cut his own. Years of work came down to this moment. Soon after he'd begun his plans in earnest, Trent had offered to buy her a pineapple so she could taste one, but she'd told him she'd wait and let his pineapples be the first she ever tasted. At the time she didn't know how long they took to grow. Now she just hoped she liked it and didn't cast up her accounts the moment it hit her tongue.

"Shall we?"

Trent tapped his piece of pineapple against hers, and they both took a large bite.

Adelaide didn't know what she'd expected, but that wasn't it. The tart-and-sweet flavor hit her tongue and then seemed to swell through her whole head. "That's fabulous," she cried before popping the rest of the chunk into her mouth.

Trent laughed and cut the rest of the fruit up to share with the staff who had gathered for the occasion. It was the first taste of the exotic fruit for more than one person, and it was fun to watch the looks that ran across their faces.

Before long though, she really needed that chair.

And perhaps the midwife.

"Trent."

"Yes, my love?"

"I think I need to go to the house. And for the last time, we are not naming this child Pineapple."

Acknowledgments

Dear Reader, you have no idea the small but intense village required to put this book into your hands. It would absolutely never have happened without the blessing of the Lord and the support of my husband and kids. The shout-outs to them may get repetitive, but they fall short of the acknowledgments my family deserves. Seriously. I could write this entire section on that small group of people, but then you wouldn't read it and all the other important people wouldn't get thanked.

Another constant in my writing is my amazing beta readers, who really worked for their thanks on this book. Your honest feedback made all the difference, even when it made me grumble. Your willingness to read the second draft after the train wreck of the first draft continues to humble and amaze me.

To my Aunt Delana, who feeds and shares my obsession with Rolos, thank you for providing fuel for the editing process.

To Trent's fan club, I hope his story lived up to your expectations. If not, well, they were a little daunting to begin with. I love you all, though, and you are the reason I get up every day and write. You are also the reason I don't go to bed so that I can meet my deadlines.

Take a moment to marvel over the artistic talents of the Bethany House cover art team. Thank you all so much for bringing Adelaide and Trent to life in a way I never thought possible, right down to Adelaide's unfashionable bangs. I'm convinced you all are truly magicians. Hugs to the rest of the Bethany House team as well, for believing in me and this book and walking through the process with me.

Finally, I'd like to thank HP, for making a laptop sturdy enough to handle everything I've thrown at it. This book was written in about fifteen different locations and would never have gotten finished without the ability to write anywhere with a laptop that has held up to dance class, car lines, and being stepped on by a five-year-old.

Kristi Ann Hunter graduated from Georgia Tech with a degree in computer science but always knew she wanted to write. Kristi is an RWA Rita® Award winning author and a finalist for the Christy Award and the Georgia Romance Writers Maggie Award for Excellence. She lives with her husband and three children in Georgia. Find her online at www.KristiAnnHunter.com.

Sign Up for Kristi's Newsletter!

Keep up to date with Kristi's news on book releases, signings, and other events by signing up for her email list at kristiannhunter.com.

Don't Miss the First HAWTHORNE HOUSE Novel!

Lady Miranda Hawthorne secretly longs to be bold. But she is mortified when her brother's new valet mistakenly mails her private thoughts to a duke she's never met—until he responds. As she sorts out her feelings for two men, she uncovers secrets that will put more than her heart at risk.

A Noble Masquerade
HAWTHORNE HOUSE